Maryland Brides

SECRETS JEOPARDIZE THREE
HISTORICAL ROMANCES

TAMELA HANCOCK MURRAY

D1021433

BARBOUR
PUBLISHING

Dear Reader,

Thank you for reading *Maryland Brides*. Many of my friends and relatives live in the beautiful state of Maryland. The stories in this book are set in bustling Baltimore and also in the lovely, bucolic countryside. Maryland has so much to offer: beaches, peaceful country life, and vibrant city scenes. I love them all! I hope you will love this trio of stories, too. Each offers romance and intrigue, finally ending with Vera Howard finding love at last with a most surprising hero!

Though I live in nearby Virginia with my husband and two daughters, I visit Maryland often. I am privileged to write to God's glory and for you!

I always enjoy hearing from readers. Please contact me through Barbour Publishing, and make sure to visit my Web site at www. tamelahancockmurray.com

May God bless you and yours!

Sincerely in Christ,
Tamela

LOVE'S DENIAL

Dedication

To Michelle Kreiss Keating—a woman of God and my lifelong friend.

Chapter 1

W
here is Aunt Daphne? Why isn't she here to meet me? This is the height of rudeness—me traveling all this way to see her—and my aunt off to who knows where.

Eleanor Kerr stood by the vacant fireplace in her aunt's parlor and waved her white silk fan, painted with depictions of exotic birds, in front of her nose. Stirring a small portion of nearby hot air did little to allay the discomfort of Baltimore in the summer. Having just arrived at her aunt's house, she was still dressed in her stiff traveling suit, a condition she was eager to amend.

She lifted a tendril of deep auburn hair that had come loose from her chignon and tucked it back into place. Papa had sent her to Maryland so she could escape the tropical climate in Louisiana—the state they called home. Malaria had killed her mother more than a year ago, a fate that he didn't want for his only daughter. Yet the summer heat felt no less intense in the formal parlor of Aunt Daphne's row house than it had back in her home in Louisiana.

In her heart, Eleanor knew that Papa had other reasons for sending her to Baltimore. As Mama's illness had progressed, Papa had let business matters slide while he spent nearly every penny on doctors who, in the end, could do nothing. Mama's death had left him so lethargic that he had lost all interest in life. Eleanor wished she could have stayed with Papa to lend support as he revitalized his business. But he would not permit her to remain with him. Her new life in Baltimore promised to be quite different from that of a pampered only child. Here, she would be expected to become self-sufficient by learning her aunt's trade—that of a seamstress.

Eleanor fingered the collar of the suit that she had sewn herself. A pleasant and productive pastime would now be the way she would earn her keep, though not the life of her dreams. Thankfully, she possessed both the talent and patience for sewing while she waited to see what the Lord really had in mind.

She increased the motion of her fan, which offered some relief. At least Eleanor's initial period of mourning had passed, so she was no longer required to swelter in a black frock. Not that she minded bearing a little heat and observing the restrictions of mourning. Wearing black had been the least she could do to show the world how much she missed her mother. She was finally becoming accustomed to the muted hues she was now permitted to wear. The dull colors served as a badge for Eleanor to honor her mother. Feeling her eyes mist, Eleanor blinked back tears and forced herself to remember that her dear mama was at home with her heavenly Father.

But for now, earthly matters awaited. Eleanor speculated about reuniting with a relative she hadn't seen in years. They had enjoyed a vigorous correspondence, so Eleanor knew she could expect a certain amount of comfort with her aunt.

Although the youngest of Papa's ten siblings, Daphne was well past her prime to marry and had set up a fine house for herself. The parlor strove mightily to replicate Queen Victoria's palace. A gilded mirror that Eleanor recognized as having once been in Grandmama's house hung from ceiling to floor. It was situated between two front windows of equal height that were dressed in white lace curtains. Eleanor knew without being told that her aunt's choice for winter draperies would be heavy velvet, most likely in a deep blue to reflect the colors in the busy botanical wallpaper that covered all four walls. Along the edges of the walls, hardwood floors gleamed. She could smell the pleasant odor of freshly applied beeswax. The center of the room was protected from the dirt and grime of shoes by a rug light in both hue and weight as was the fashion for Southern homes in the summer. No doubt the covering would be replaced by a lush, dark Oriental rug once the temperatures dipped.

With a gloved hand, she leaned over and ran her left forefinger along the edge of a table carved from mahogany. She lifted it to her face and recognized that not a speck of dirt sullied the white cotton. No surprise there. Each piece of furniture was polished, and she eyed no visible dust. Out of curiosity, she peered into the top of a table and discovered that she could see her reflection almost as well as if she were looking into a mirror. The house clearly reflected the fussiness of the dreary spinster seamstress who was the lady of the house. Eleanor's disposition lent itself to tidiness, but she decided that meeting her aunt's expectations for order would be a challenge.

Lord, I pray that my fears will be unfounded and that Aunt Daphne and I will prove to be kindred spirits. Let my presence here not be a burden upon her. Lead me in Thy will, heavenly Father. In the name of Thy Son, I pray. Amen.

A sense of peace enveloped her. The trip had tired Eleanor. Cutting her glance to a sofa slipcovered in white, she contemplated taking a seat but thought better of it.

"There you are!"

With a twist of her lace-covered neck, Eleanor turned her face toward the door that led to the entry hall. A redhead who could only be Aunt Daphne breezed into the parlor. She wore a large hat with a brim that seemed to be as wide as the span of Eleanor's arms when outstretched. Earlier that day, Eleanor had donned her traveling dress, a linen affair that was the color of rich coffee flavored with half a cup of thick cream. At the time, she had felt stylish even though her current stage of mourning demanded that she wear subdued shades. But now, amid such a flourish of color, she felt downright drab.

"Welcome!" Aunt Daphne glided to her, reached out, and pulled Eleanor to her with a gusto that caught Eleanor by surprise and nearly resulted in her loss of balance.

Eleanor touched the brim of her beige hat to straighten it. She surveyed the floor without moving her head much, hoping that none of the artificial white magnolia flowers on the hat's beige ribbon had become detached and fallen off.

"Thank you." Eleanor trusted that her voice and expression seemed sweet.

Aunt Daphne held her at arm's length. Her green eyes looked Eleanor over and seemed to register approval. "Did you have a good trip?"

"Yes. I found my train compartment agreeable and shared most of the trip with two sisters traveling to New York. They were pleasant enough."

"I'm sorry I'm late in returning. I had planned to be here to greet you upon your arrival. Were you waiting long?" Her charming manner made Eleanor see why her papa said that her aunt had been quite the belle in her younger years. Not that she seemed all that old. Born a decade and a half after Papa, Aunt Daphne seemed younger than her thirty-nine years.

"No, only a few minutes."

"I trust that my driver took good care of you."

"Indeed. Henry was most pleasant."

Aunt Daphne released her grip so she could gesture with her hands. "Mrs. Alden took longer than I expected to choose her lace, and then I had to settle the bill with her son. Honestly, Raleigh Alden is such a vexation. I pity the woman who falls for his handsome face because she will have quite a wretched life with such a miser!"

"If Mr. Alden didn't want to pay the bill, then you can simply say that you won't provide your services for his mother anymore," Eleanor suggested.

"What? And lose my best patron? Never!"

Eleanor wasn't sure how Mrs. Alden could be Aunt Daphne's best patron if her son didn't want to pay the bill.

"He thought the lace his mother chose was too expensive," Aunt Daphne said in response to her unspoken question. "I had to convince him otherwise. You'd think he couldn't rub two nickels together, when in reality, his is one of the wealthier families in the Baltimore area."

"You certainly have had a difficult afternoon." Eleanor wondered if the events were typical for her aunt.

"Lest you think you've moved into bedlam, let me assure you that every afternoon is not like this one!" When Aunt Daphne removed her hat, Eleanor noticed that it was most astonishing. The hat was burdened with quite a chore in holding up artificial lemons, limes, oranges, and bananas tied together with a bright yellow bow. Eleanor knew she could never carry off such a concoction, but Daphne wore it well.

Her aunt placed the bright yellow creation on the mahogany stand. "Have you eaten?" Without the hat for a distraction, Eleanor noticed that her aunt's face still held the beauty of her youth.

"Yes," Eleanor answered. "I took a meal on the train, thank you."

"Good. Cook gets awfully grumpy when I ask her to prepare an extra meal. You might as well know that now as later," Aunt Daphne informed her.

"How dare a servant be grumpy with her mistress. Papa never would allow such a thing in his house," Eleanor pointed out. "Why don't you fire her?"

"Fire her? Oh, my dear, do you have any notion of how difficult it is to find a good cook? As it is, I have to let her off on Sundays and Thursdays."

"She must have it easy, cooking for one. I'd conjecture that she has the better end of the bargain."

Her aunt flinched. "So you say. But you see, with the advent of your arrival, her duties have doubled."

"True. And speaking of my arrival, I am ready to retire to my quarters, by your leave." Realizing that she still enjoyed the status of a guest, Eleanor tried to keep her voice from sounding too demanding.

"What was I thinking? Of course you're tired." Aunt Daphne turned slightly and swept her arm toward the foyer. "Your room is upstairs. It's the second door on the right, beside my room."

"Thank you." Eleanor didn't move right away, expecting her aunt to escort her. Instead, Aunt Daphne peered into the gilded wall mirror and brushed her hands over her chignon. Eleanor watched her for a moment until she turned back to face her.

"Well?" Aunt Daphne asked. "Is there a question?"

"No, Aunt Daphne."

"Then unless you didn't learn how to tell right from left at that fancy finishing school that graduated you, I suggest you get situated. For future reference, breakfast is served at six on the dot, luncheon is served at the stroke of noon, and dinner is served at six thirty every night. No exceptions." She nodded once toward the grandfather clock that could be seen from the parlor although it dominated the front hall. "It's already five thirty. I'd best prepare now."

"My, but you are organized." Eleanor wasn't accustomed to such a strict schedule and wondered how she would cope. Unsure of what to do next, she stared at her aunt and discovered she couldn't move one foot in front of the other.

A flash of realization swept over Daphne's face. "You aren't used to doing anything for yourself, are you? I know your father. He spoiled you rotten, I'm sure." Her kind tone belied her biting words. "As you can plainly see, there is no man in this house to see to it that your pretty little slippers never touch a drop of mud on the street. Here, you will find yourself comfortable, but you will also discover that the Kerr women fend for themselves."

"Yes, ma'am." Spurred by her aunt's words, Eleanor finally found the will to travel up the stairs to her room. She would be fending for herself, indeed. She prayed she was up to the challenge.

———

The following morning, Eleanor watched as Aunt Daphne quickly ate her breakfast. She sat at the head of the dining room table. After a brief blessing, she tapped the top of her eggshell off and proceeded to dip fingers of toast into the egg, drawing out the runny yolk. Now she was holding the ceramic eggcup with two fingers and spooning out the solid egg white in a ladylike but determined fashion. After sopping up the last of her runny egg with a piece of toast, she still managed to be dainty as she set the tidbit in her mouth.

"This breakfast is delightful." Since she relished runny eggs, Eleanor planned to savor each bite. "And according to our discussions with Cook about the week's menu, there are more good things to come." She allowed herself a tiny smile. Cook's ample figure attested to her skill in the kitchen.

"I'm glad you are finding it agreeable here so far." Aunt Daphne tapped her napkin and quickly set it aside.

"My, what is your hurry, Aunt Daphne?" Eleanor asked.

"Didn't I tell you? We have an appointment today."

"We. . .have. . .an appointment?"

"Of course. With Mrs. Alden."

"Your best patron." Eleanor rose from her seat.

"You remember. Good. In this business, one learns to be accomplished at remembering names. And trust me: Mrs. June Alden is one name you'll want to remember."

"I would think you would be hesitant to return today after yesterday's dispute."

"Oh, that was with Mr. Alden." Aunt Daphne waved her hand in the air as though Mr. Alden were no more than an imaginary bug. "I wouldn't call it a dispute, just part of doing business with them."

Dispute or not, Eleanor felt reluctant. "Why don't you handle it? You don't need me."

"Of course I need you. You've got to learn the seamstress trade sometime. And there's no time like the present, as they say. Now come along." Aunt Daphne headed toward the foyer. Her heels clicked on the hardwood floors, then were silent when her feet made contact with a rug, then clicked on hardwood once again.

Eleanor knew she was compelled to follow a woman with such a determined pace. By the time she reached the front door, Aunt Daphne had already donned her hat. This time, she wore a crisp white affair with red roses and plumes all around, which matched her white dress embroidered to perfection with red roses.

"My hat!" Eleanor looked down at her morning dress. The beige frock was one of her more sprightly looks, with white lace on the bodice as bold as she dared while in her second stage of mourning. "I'm afraid this won't do."

"Nonsense. Of course it will do. The color suits you so well." Aunt Daphne sighed. "Sometimes I wish my hair wasn't quite so red. You auburn-haired beauties can wear just about any color you wish and look wonderful."

Eleanor wasn't sure if her aunt was flattering her so she would hurry along or if her words were sincere. She suspected her words sprouted from a combination of both. "If you insist, I'll wear this."

Aunt Daphne studied her. "You sewed it yourself, didn't you?"

Eleanor nodded. "Of course."

Aunt Daphne fingered the lace on the bodice of Eleanor's dress near her shoulder, then checked the hem of her skirt. Her inspection earned Eleanor a nod. "Very good. This is a fine example of your work. Soon we will double our business."

"Obviously, if we visit our best patrons every day." She couldn't resist a little sardonic smile.

Aunt Daphne laughed. "Mrs. Alden must look at muslin samples today, as she took too long with her lace yesterday. Doing business with her takes longer than with most of my other clients. She tends to delay each process. She does have a companion, a rather dreary girl named Vera Howard, though she is from a good family. Otherwise, Mrs. Alden is a lonely old soul."

Eleanor nodded with understanding.

"Don't forget your sewing basket," her aunt called to Eleanor, who rushed up the stairs.

"I won't," she called back, even though she hadn't thought about it despite the fact they had discussed nothing but sewing for the past few minutes. The idea of being a businesswoman had just begun to take hold of her, and carrying sewing notions with her at all times was merely a beginning.

Father in heaven, I beseech Thee to be with me!

Moments later, Eleanor hurried to the waiting carriage. As she situated herself, Eleanor straightened her hat, a simple mauve invention with a ribbon of lace that matched her dress. She secured her hat with a long stickpin made of ivory.

"I must say, the materials of which your hat is comprised outweigh in quality the imagination of your milliner," Aunt Daphne noted.

"Truly?" Eleanor patted the brim. "I rather like this hat."

Aunt Daphne shrugged. "It's well enough, I suppose. But we must take you to Eva's to have more hats made for you."

Eleanor self-consciously touched the brim of her understated hat. She liked her own style and wondered if she could feel comfortable dressing as outrageously as her aunt. "I assume she is your milliner?"

"Yes, and she makes me a hat in exchange for a dress. It's a sweet scheme that lets us both cut a fine figure everywhere we go."

"Eva, Vera, Raleigh Alden, Mrs. Alden—my head is swimming as I try to remember all these names."

"Don't worry. You sound as though you will do just fine. I must admit, remembering Raleigh Alden is easy enough. Every eligible lady in town sees him and swoons on the spot." She sighed. "If only I were a decade younger."

"Aunt Daphne!" Eleanor leaned toward her. "I thought he was a miser."

"He is. And so I shall let him pass by. Not that he has ever made any overtures toward me, really." She looked over her niece. "He's a little older than you are. Just about to see his thirtieth birthday, I'd say."

"My, how you talk." Eager to discourage any potential for matchmaking on her aunt's part, Eleanor deflected the conversation from herself as quickly as she could. "With all this calculation and speculation, am I to assume you are ready for another suitor after all these years?"

"Your father told you." Aunt Daphne's pretty features tightened, and her body stiffened.

Her stricken look sent a shot of discomfort through Eleanor. Yet if the two women hoped to live together in peace, she realized she might as well tell her aunt what she knew. She leaned her back against the seat to convey a casual attitude. "Oh, someone mentioned once that you had many suitors, but one in particular stood out among the rest."

Aunt Daphne nodded. "Long ago, when I was young. We courted fifteen years, in fact. Then he met someone else and, and. . ." Her lips drew together to form a tense contour.

"I know." She took Aunt Daphne's hands in hers. Her aunt's thumb bore a callus from years of working as a seamstress, but otherwise her hands were softer than Eleanor had anticipated. "Obviously, he suffered from a severe lack of judgment."

Aunt Daphne's eyes misted, a sure indication that she had never recovered fully from her heartbreak. Looking down at her hands in Eleanor's, she nodded several times in a rapid motion. "That's what all my friends say."

Eleanor gave her aunt's hands a firm squeeze, then released them. She hadn't imagined she could befriend her spinster aunt, but already she felt a bond with Daphne.

"I do enjoy my freedom," Aunt Daphne observed. "And if I were to marry, most likely my husband would insist that I give up my career."

"You might give up fashioning dresses for wages, but I doubt you would be forced to abandon sewing forever," Eleanor couldn't resist noting. "On the contrary, you might be busier than ever making frocks and bloomers for a brood of little ones."

"At my age?" Aunt Daphne's laughter tinkled throughout the carriage. "I would barely have time for a husband, and the arrival of a baby would be a minor miracle at best."

Eleanor studied her aunt's face. "Maybe you could consider a widower with children."

"Oh, I've had my share of those to come knocking, but who can travel and see the world when one is responsible for someone else's children?"

"Travel?"

"Oh yes. I would love to travel. That is my dream. To save up enough money to travel the world." Excitement caused her voice to rise in pitch and speed. "Wouldn't you like to take a steamship to Europe someday? Or maybe even see the pyramids in Egypt?" She set her gaze toward the window, staring out it as though she could see the sphinx just on the horizon rather than the lawn of a fine house they passed.

Eleanor hesitated. "Well, I just did travel across the country." She didn't add that the experience had cured her of any desire to journey anywhere else for the next few months—or years.

Aunt Daphne turned her attention to Eleanor. "Exactly. Wouldn't it be a wonderful idea for the two of us to travel together?" She clasped her hands at the thought.

Eleanor felt the muscles in her chest tighten. "Travel together?"

"Yes. I was hoping that perhaps you'd be keen on the idea of being my traveling companion—and the daughter I always wanted."

Eleanor clenched her hands and rubbed her fingers together. Looking down, she felt her eyes moisten. How could she not be flattered by her aunt's emotions? Then again, how could she tell her aunt that she had no desire to see the world? "I—I haven't thought much about traveling, really. In fact, I've barely had enough interest to observe the sights on this very trip."

"Oh, you'll learn Baltimore soon enough." Aunt Daphne dispatched a pitiable look her way. "I know why your dreams have been so small. You've been so burdened with responsibilities and occupied with tending to your sick mother. *Tragic* is the only way to describe her death. But let's not speak of it now. We must put on a happy demeanor if we are to please Mrs. Alden. Remember, we are there to provide our patrons with happiness, not to trouble them with our concerns."

Eleanor remained silent. Spending long amounts of time in a confined space, whether in a luxurious carriage, a train, or a steamship, held no appeal for her.

She couldn't imagine a scenario where she would desire to globe-trot. Rather than embracing the world after being confined to her time of mourning, Eleanor had made up her mind to live as a religious solitary. What better way to escape heartbreak and pain in the world? She remembered her mother and wished she could have died in her place. Eleanor knew in her heart that her grief was as strong a reason for Papa's insistence that she relocate as his concern for her physical health. He had seen her rebellion when he insisted she head to the safety of a cooler climate so she, his only child, could remain well and start life anew. But a religious life was not his plan for her and certainly no idea of her aunt's.

No one but Eleanor knew how many nights she had spent in anguished prayer, seeking guidance from her heavenly Father. Despite her pleas to let her live a life alone, she felt no leading in that direction.

"Child," Aunt Daphne said, interrupting her thoughts. "Why are you so pensive?"

Eleanor didn't rush to answer. Clearly, Aunt Daphne had big plans for her. Should she tell all and risk her wrath? Or perhaps if she were honest, Daphne could help her find her calling. She took in a breath and spoke. "I know that Papa has asked you to teach me to be a seamstress, but that is not my wish. Ever since Mama's death, I have been praying for guidance on how I might live life as a religious solitary," she confessed. "I was in hopes that you might have suggestions as to how I might pursue that course here in Baltimore."

"A religious solitary?" Aunt Daphne's laughter echoed throughout the carriage. "Don't be silly, Eleanor. You are much too beautiful to cloister yourself. Your father knows that, and he knows your disposition. We'd better follow his instructions."

"I know that Papa has my best interests at heart, but it is inner beauty I seek."

"And I am sure you possess that in abundance." Aunt Daphne studied her. "I know you do. You radiate beauty. And our local bachelors will see that soon enough."

Eleanor felt her face flush hot. "I am not interested in a courtship, Aunt Daphne."

"We shall see," Aunt Daphne said as the carriage came to a stop in front of a brick Georgian-style house with a spacious lawn. "Here we are. The Alden residence. Your first test will be your meeting with Raleigh Alden, Esquire. Are you ready?"

"More than ready." She lifted her nose in the air, practicing her most snobbish look. She was determined to take on her aunt's challenge and pass her first test.

She would steel herself against any and all winsome bachelors. And that included Raleigh Alden, Esquire.

Chapter 2

With fear and trepidation, Eleanor stepped out of the carriage. What would Mrs. Alden be like? An image of an aged dowager formed in her mind. She pictured a stout woman dressed in an elaborate silk frock sewn by Aunt Daphne, looking through spectacles down her nose at Eleanor. She shuddered, then walked behind her aunt, assuming her role as apprentice. On the one hand, she wanted nothing more than to hide behind her aunt's skirts. On the other, she hoped she wouldn't prove to be too outspoken once she overcame her initial shyness—an unfortunate trait she longed to master.

At the end of the walk stood a sign posted on a wooden stake, painted in a stodgy black script. RALEIGH ALDEN, ATTORNEY AT LAW. The very existence of the sign lent importance to Raleigh's station.

"His clients have to come a ways to see him, don't they?" Eleanor suggested.

"He always talks about leasing an office in the city, but so far, he hasn't." Aunt Daphne shrugged. "I suppose he has plenty of business as it is. He's quite good, you know. Now come along."

The two women headed up the curved brick walk toward the front door.

Eleanor hissed, "Shouldn't we go to the back door?"

Daphne slowed her pace but didn't stop. "We may be seamstresses, but we are not ordinary. Mrs. Alden considers me almost as a friend. We go to the front door."

Eleanor noticed that her aunt lifted her head with a confident air and strode along as though she were equal to the occupants of the streamlined, brick mansion. The arms of two massive oak trees surrounding the house looked as though they were cradling the building. She could imagine surveying such oaks when Caecilius Calvert, second Baron Baltimore, became Maryland's first governor in the seventeenth century. Shaking such silly thoughts out of her mind, she admired the flowers by the stoop and along the front of the house. A sizable group of healthy gladiolas was in full bloom, obviously tended by an expert gardener.

Aunt Daphne lifted the large brass door knocker and waited. A butler promptly answered. "Good morning, Miss Kerr." He nodded to Eleanor.

"Good morning, Monroe."

"Mrs. Alden is expecting you. You may go up now."

Up? Eleanor wondered what location the butler meant. Why wouldn't they be meeting Mrs. Alden in one of the formal rooms on the first floor?

Aunt Daphne nodded and stepped into a foyer much grander than Eleanor had seen in recent memory. Then again, she had stayed to herself and had had few occasions to visit the truly wealthy back in Louisiana. Without a moment's hesitation, Aunt Daphne glided toward an oversized mahogany staircase. The deeply colored wood contrasted well with the white wallpaper with a gold damask pattern.

"Come along, Eleanor," Aunt Daphne prompted.

Feeling like a small child upon being issued a command, Eleanor flinched but obeyed. She followed her aunt up a curved staircase that five people could have ascended side by side in comfort. When she reached the top, she looked down and noticed that the height was almost dizzying, but somehow the foyer appeared even more imposing from such a vantage point.

The clacking of her aunt's heels warned her not to dawdle. Aunt Daphne led her down an expansive hallway. They passed occasional tables decorated with flowers that were most likely plucked from the formal gardens. Eleanor looked up and noticed that portraits of people from other eras in history flanked the hallway. She presumed the finely attired lords and ladies were Alden ancestors.

She watched her aunt turn into the fourth door on the left.

"You're late," a shrill feminine voice chastised her aunt before her second foot had stepped over the threshold.

Late! Eleanor didn't think so and wondered how her aunt would defend herself.

Eleanor hovered in the hallway, wary of entering the room. As though she could read Eleanor's thoughts, Aunt Daphne sent her a look that commanded her to enter behind her. Eleanor tiptoed over the threshold, hoping she could stay close enough to her aunt so as not to draw attention to herself.

"I beg your indulgence," Aunt Daphne said, displaying a surprising humility that Eleanor hadn't seen from her previously. "There has been some excitement at my house upon the arrival of my niece."

Oh no! Aunt Daphne wasn't going to let her fade into the wallpaper!

To Eleanor's horror, Daphne stepped aside so Eleanor would come into full view of their patron. "Mrs. Alden, I would like to present my niece, Eleanor Kerr."

The elderly lady was propped up in a bed that was big enough to sleep four in comfort. The headboard was fashioned from a rich brown mahogany embellished with elaborate carving. Eleanor fought the impulse to run her fingers over the smooth wooden dogwood flowers. Despite the heat, Mrs. Alden chose to remain under a thick coverlet of white eyelet lace. Since the woman wore a bed jacket and a high-necked gown of white, Eleanor had trouble discerning where Mrs. Alden ended and the bedsheets began.

Pillows covered in white cotton reminded Eleanor of fluffy clouds. If Mrs.

Alden had held a harp and had wings—and if she hadn't been wearing a white nightcap with gray tendrils of hair peeking out strategically—Eleanor imagined she might have looked like an angel in a Renaissance painting. Eleanor wasn't sure whether to approach Mrs. Alden and shake her hand or curtsy as though the woman were royalty. Remembering Mrs. Alden's importance to her aunt, Eleanor decided to make a motion that would not require her to speak. She curtsied.

"A curtsy!" Mrs. Alden clapped. "How delightful, my dear. It is not often that one of the younger generation is quite so charming."

"She's a Kerr through and through." Pride rang through Aunt Daphne's voice. The reward made Eleanor feel a little less squeamish about her unfamiliar gesture. "I know you won't mind Eleanor's presence here, Mrs. Alden. I'm thinking about allowing her to work with me on a regular basis."

Allowing her to work? Eleanor thought the matter was settled. Maybe she could pursue other dreams after all.

"What a grand idea. I think she will make a charming addition to your business." Mrs. Alden eyed the far corner of the room. "Perhaps your apprentice could fashion a frock for Vera."

Eleanor snapped her head in the direction where a young woman sat. Apparently she had been observing without making her presence known. Considering that her chignon was of a bland color and her dress a mint green similar to the color of the wall, the feat of blending in was easily accomplished.

"Of course, she would be pleased to fashion a frock for Vera," Aunt Daphne answered for Eleanor. "As you can see, my niece sews a fine seam. She, herself, made the dress she is wearing."

Mrs. Alden crooked her finger toward Eleanor. "Come closer and let me see your handiwork, young lady."

Nervous that she might say or do something that would lower Mrs. Alden's opinion of her—and consequently Aunt Daphne—Eleanor resolved to keep her answers polite but as brief as possible. She obeyed despite suddenly becoming aware of her beating heart. Mrs. Alden wasn't unkind, but she somehow managed to frighten Eleanor all the same.

The old woman leaned closer and stretched out an aged, bony hand sprinkled with brown liver spots. Eleanor tried not to cringe as the old woman fingered the black lace on her dress much as Aunt Daphne had earlier. After such thorough examinations, Eleanor feared the poor little piece of delicate crochet work would soon become ragged with wear.

"Very fine. Very fine, indeed," Mrs. Alden clucked. "Vera?"

Vera rose and approached the bed. "Yes, ma'am?"

"How would you like for Eleanor here to make you a dress?"

"Thank you. But I—I don't have much need for a dress, Mrs. Alden." Vera's voice was as refined as it was shy.

"Stuff and nonsense! Of course you have need for a dress. How about a new church dress in a nice shade of green to go with your eyes?"

Since Mrs. Alden pointed out the color of Vera's eyes, Eleanor noticed that they were indeed a startling shade of green. Vera nodded. "Yes, ma'am. That would be very nice."

"I'm sure Eleanor will have some marvelous ideas for Vera," Aunt Daphne assured Mrs. Alden.

"Good. Perhaps Eleanor can stop by at ten in the morning on Friday for Vera's initial fitting."

"Yes, she can," Aunt Daphne affirmed.

Eleanor wondered how Vera felt about Mrs. Alden speaking for her, determining the time of the fitting and the color and occasion for the dress. Then she realized that she had been permitting her aunt to speak for her as though she were a mute. Eleanor couldn't resist throwing a sympathetic look Vera's way. Vera cast her eyes downward in return. Eleanor made a mental note not to suggest any shade of hue that was too vibrant, lest the thought overpower such a reticent soul.

"Now, Eleanor," Mrs. Alden said, "Miss Vera Howard is more than a companion to me. She is descended from one of Maryland's finest families. I expect you to take the utmost care with her dress."

"I will, indeed, ma'am."

"Very well."

Eleanor cast her gaze toward the young woman, who sent her a shy smile before returning to her place in the corner.

Since Vera obviously wasn't prepared to talk, Eleanor watched as her aunt showed several muslin and lace samples to her client. Mrs. Alden lingered over each decision as though the garments she was ordering would be her last. To Eleanor's eyes, the nightwear set that Mrs. Alden wore looked elegant. Why she was ordering more was beyond Eleanor's capacity to reason. But who was she to object to any business for her aunt?

Eleanor marveled at how Aunt Daphne skillfully increased Mrs. Alden's initial order from one nightgown to add a bed jacket and nightcap. As she chose one fine sample after another, Eleanor could see that Aunt Daphne was pleased.

"Well, that should serve you quite nicely, Mrs. Alden," Aunt Daphne proclaimed upon the culmination of the order.

"Good. Raleigh is in his office downstairs. He should be finished meeting with his client by now," Mrs. Alden said. "He'll be glad to settle the bill from my last order."

"Yes, ma'am." If Aunt Daphne wanted to throw Eleanor a doubtful look, she resisted the urge. After quickly putting away her samples, she snapped her brown leather bag shut and left the room, motioning with her head for Eleanor to follow her.

Eleanor was starting to feel more and more like a lackey instead of a woman in charge of her own destiny. She prayed for the strength to remain humble.

She followed Aunt Daphne down the stairs toward the first floor, then to a spacious room in the front of the house. Eleanor wished that Vera hadn't become her first client. Then she wouldn't have to worry about settling any bills with the dreadful Raleigh Alden.

"Maybe I should wait in the carriage," Eleanor whispered.

"No. You'll be making clothes for Vera, so Mr. Alden needs to meet you." Aunt Daphne stopped in front of the door and fumbled through her bag. "I can't find my account ledger. Will you go to the carriage and fetch it for me?"

"Of course." Eleanor was more than happy to delay her meeting with Mr. Alden.

"Don't tarry, and come right into the office."

"I will," Eleanor promised as she heard Aunt Daphne knock on the office door.

"Come in." The masculine Southern drawl didn't sound nearly as threatening as Eleanor had imagined it would. In fact, the voice sounded rather melodious and pleasant. Maybe its owner wouldn't be such an ogre after all.

She hurried to the carriage, discovered the book where it had fallen onto the floor, and rushed back to the house as she had promised.

"I just paid you more than ten dollars. What is the meaning of such a large order for today?" The Southern drawl had become clipped.

Eleanor stopped near the door, afraid to enter.

"Your mother expressed a need for new clothing, and I intend to fulfill it." Aunt Daphne's voice indicated that she had no notion of relinquishing her order.

"A need! Pshaw!" he objected. "Mother already owns fifteen nightgowns, seven hats, three robes, and five bed jackets."

"How conscientious of you to keep such a close count."

"Mother is getting on in years, and her health is failing. It is my duty as her son to see to it that she is not taken advantage of."

Taken advantage of! Why, how dare he accuse her aunt of trying to take advantage of anyone!

Though she had all but cowered before Mrs. Alden in deference to her age and status, Eleanor felt differently toward this arrogant man. Certainly he was important, but he had no right to treat her aunt in such a way.

She listened for her aunt to defend herself but heard no retort. Eleanor couldn't tolerate the suspense. She had to interrupt and set affairs straight then and there.

Eleanor stepped into the room. Though she shut the door behind her, she kept her hand on the glass doorknob. In her fury, she clutched it as though she were a war ship and the knob her only anchor against a rising tide. Then she noticed Raleigh Alden. She strained to keep from gasping. Aunt Daphne had been right about his handsome features and dashing demeanor. No wonder the women swooned!

Remembering her ire, she composed herself. "Mr. Alden, I'll have you to know that my aunt would never take advantage of anyone! On the contrary, it is you who are robbing your dear mother if you deny her the small pleasure of a few nice garments in which to spend her waning years!" As her anger grew, she felt her body flush.

Only after she finished her speech did she notice a pair of blue eyes that twinkled like stars in the midnight sky. A straight nose led to even straighter teeth.

"Eleanor!" Aunt Daphne cried.

"Well, it's true." She straightened her shoulders. "You would never sell any woman a garment she didn't truly want to wear." She looked squarely at her aunt. "And any woman would be happy to wear clothes fashioned by you, Aunt Daphne. They are among the most exquisite I have ever seen!"

Her rage spent, Eleanor looked at Raleigh. Instead of the anger she expected, his expression seemed open, as though he could burst into laughter if his funny bone were tickled with the lightest touch of a feather.

He glanced at her and seemed to sit a bit straighter, and his face lit with fascination. Eleanor knew she wasn't being vain. Clearly, in spite of her outburst, or perhaps because of it, she had piqued his interest. Suddenly shy, she took a newfound interest in examining the pattern of the red floor runner.

"You speak with great boldness for one who has not been introduced." Raleigh looked at Aunt Daphne as he rose from his seat situated behind a large mahogany desk that had been polished to a mirrorlike finish. "I'm assuming this is the apprentice of whom you spoke?"

Since Raleigh's attention was now on her aunt, Eleanor summoned the courage to observe him. Funny, he didn't look like the cheapskate that her aunt had described. His dark hair was polished to a sheen, the current popular style. His blue seersucker suit was tailored in the latest fashion, and Eleanor could see even from across the room that his tailor had sewn an expert seam. How could a man who dressed himself in such a fine manner object to a bit of lace for his mother?

"Yes. Mr. Raleigh Alden, may I present my niece, Miss Eleanor Kerr. Miss Eleanor Kerr, this is Mr. Raleigh Alden."

"How do you do, Mr. Alden?"

"How do you do?" He nodded, the twinkle still lighting his eyes. "I understand you have an issue to discuss with me?"

"Never mind my niece," Aunt Daphne apologized. "She has been a bit excitable since she's had such a long trip."

"A long trip? From where?"

"Louisiana," Aunt Daphne answered. "The New Orleans area."

"Ah, the land of hanging moss and spicy food." Raleigh folded his arms but looked at her with an expression of renewed interest. "So how do you like Baltimore?"

"I'm afraid I haven't been here long enough to ascertain how I like it. I do know that the weather isn't as cool as I thought it might be."

"Cool in the summer? You would have to move much farther north for that." His voice softened so much that the drawl returned. "Might I offer you a glass of iced tea?"

She didn't want to take a glass of tea from Raleigh, but since he had brought up the subject, she was feeling a bit thirsty. "That might be nice."

"Have a seat." He motioned to the two chairs in front of his desk. "And you, too, of course, Miss Kerr," he said to Aunt Daphne.

Aunt Daphne's eyebrows shot up. "I suppose you might wish to call us Miss Daphne and Miss Eleanor to avoid confusion."

"With your permission." Raleigh picked up a silver bell on his desk and rang for the butler, who promptly appeared at the door.

"Yes, sir?"

"Monroe, deliver us three tall glasses of iced tea."

"Yes, sir." Monroe disappeared.

"Now," Raleigh drawled, "perhaps we might all come to our senses as we drink our tea." He sent a direct look to the elder of the two women. "Miss Daphne, you have been my mother's seamstress for a number of years. Perhaps you are not trying to take advantage of her good nature."

"Of course not." Aunt Daphne sniffed.

"But certainly you can understand why I would question this extravagance."

"The extravagance is hers, not mine, Mr. Alden," Aunt Daphne said. "She chose the finest Irish linen and lace embroidered in Italy for her latest lingerie set."

"With your encouragement, no doubt."

Her encouragement? Was he trying to insinuate that Aunt Daphne insisted that her customers overbuy? Eleanor tightened her lips.

Aunt Daphne didn't hesitate to answer. "I simply showed her all of my samples. She chose the finest because she has a good eye for quality." Aunt Daphne set her hands in her lap.

"And you do as well, sir," Eleanor interrupted, "judging from the tailoring of your fine suit."

"Thank you, but I am a businessman and must dress accordingly."

Eleanor took a moment to observe the office, which appeared much as she had expected. Obviously a legal office would be open to public scrutiny at a moment's notice, and the opulent furnishings and spotless appearance of the room reflected its occupant's esteemed stature. "I can see that you are serious about your business. Shouldn't your mother enjoy some of the fruits of your labor?"

"Of course. . ."

Eleanor felt ire rise inside her with an intensity she hadn't remembered in quite some time. For her aunt's sake, she didn't mind cowering before the lawyer's mother. Although Mrs. Alden seemed high and mighty, she was a worthy client. But the arrogance of her son! It was just too much. Entirely too much.

"I see a Bible on your shelf." Eleanor nodded to a spot behind Raleigh's right shoulder. "The heavenly Father commands us to honor our mothers and our fathers."

"Yes," Raleigh accepted her point.

Monroe entered and placed the tea before them without a sound.

"I honor my mother by making sure that her interests are protected," Raleigh pointed out. "I haven't been here in Baltimore long, having just returned home after living in Tallahassee, Florida, the past ten years. I only returned to care for my ailing mother."

"And if I might say so, I do admire your sacrifice," Eleanor said. "Are you an only child as I am?" She took several swallows of the refreshing liquid.

He guffawed. "Hardly. I have six brothers. All of them have families of their own, however. So I, the youngest by far and a bachelor, took the duty with cheer, for I am fulfilling the Lord's commandment."

"And part of your duty is to see that your mother is well dressed," Aunt Daphne pointed out.

"Not at the prices you're charging."

As if Aunt Daphne could control the cost of fine imported goods!

"I apologize for the increase, but my costs have risen; you must consider that I have no choice but to pay dearly to import your mother's fabrics." Aunt Daphne took a sip of her tea, a gesture that Eleanor suspected she was using to control her indignation.

"I wish you would not tempt her with the finest textiles. As you know, she is a professional invalid and receives very few visitors. She hardly needs the finery you propose even though she can well afford it."

Despite the cooling effects of the iced tea, Eleanor felt hotter than the July sun. She had no intention of sitting there any longer and listening to this man criticize her aunt, no matter how attractive and well dressed he might be. Against her better judgment, she rose from her seat.

"Mr. Alden, with all due respect, I will not tolerate your insults toward my aunt. Consider our order canceled."

Chapter 3

Raleigh tried to compose himself when he heard Eleanor's unexpected proclamation. He stood in deference to the fact that Eleanor had risen from her seat. "Canceled? You're canceling my mother's order—just like that?" Raleigh snapped his fingers.

"Yes. Just like that."

Raleigh was taken aback. Surely a cancellation would save him money, but now that the threat was at hand, he wasn't sure he wanted the order to be terminated. His mother was certain to be unhappy now that she had selected material, only to find that she wouldn't be receiving her new cap, bed jacket, and gown after all. She always looked forward to receiving her new outfits with great anticipation.

Raleigh didn't know how to respond to the irate young woman standing before him. He knew he should be upset by her behavior, but he enjoyed hearing her educated phrasing executed with a Louisiana drawl. Even though Daphne claimed her niece was overwrought from her recent trip, he had a sneaking suspicion that she was one to speak her mind regardless of the circumstances.

Daphne jumped from her seat with such haste that she nearly spilled the glass of tea she was holding. "Don't listen to her. She hasn't been herself since she lost her dear mother."

For the first time, Raleigh realized that Eleanor's plain dress was edged with the black lace of a woman in the second stages of mourning. A sense of shame overwhelmed him. "Allow me to express my deepest sympathies, Miss Eleanor."

"Thank you." Her voice softened only somewhat.

"She only has another month left before she can return to her normal life," Daphne informed him.

"I know that must be pleasant news for you," Raleigh told Eleanor.

"Yes, although I shall always mourn for my dear mama deep within my heart."

"Of course." He observed that she couldn't have yet seen her twenty-fifth birthday. If so, she would be at least six years younger than he. A successful lawyer well versed in dealing with people who didn't always want to reveal the truth, the whole truth, and nothing but the truth, Raleigh prided himself on his ability to read faces for signs of intrigue or deception. He searched Eleanor's face for a hint that she referred to her grief in order to make him squirm. He found nothing in her features but sincere emotion. Indeed, he felt like a heel for quarreling over his mother's clothing expenses when Eleanor had no mother at all.

He felt the ladies' eyes upon him as they waited for him to settle the account. He pursed his lips together. After his arrival in Baltimore, Raleigh had not been pleased to discover the untidy state of his mother's financial affairs. Though most of the merchants had treated her with honesty, Raleigh's sharp eyes had spotted several irregular charges to various accounts, and he had spent no small amount of time securing refunds for his aging parent. June Alden had never worried about money and as a result had proven too trusting, leaving her vulnerable to being overcharged for goods she did use or billed for goods she never bought. Surely the Kerrs were too smart to begin such a practice now that he had taken charge of his mother's affairs. But for her sake, he had to question them.

"I realize that taking on the employ of your niece has resulted in an increase in your expenses," he told Daphne. "I do hope my mother will find her services of enough value to justify this propagation in price."

"Wait," Eleanor protested. "I am an expert seamstress in my own right, and I plan to be an asset to my aunt's business. As for the increase, I had no idea that her price was going up until she told you herself."

"While I do not approve of my niece's outburst, she does speak the truth," Daphne assured him.

"Very well," he said. "But do not think for a moment that my mother's orders alone can support your business."

"We never would think such a thing." Insult colored Daphne's voice. "I have plenty of clients to keep me busy."

"But not all of them are as wealthy as my mother," Raleigh pointed out.

"Perhaps not, but they do pay their bills without a fuss." Daphne's mouth straightened itself into a firm line, and her steady gaze met his without flinching.

Her meaning wasn't lost on Raleigh. Perhaps he wasn't showing his best manners in being so difficult about settling his mother's bill, however extravagant.

Raleigh looked at Eleanor with a more discerning eye. She was a beauty, for certain. Eleanor was far more pleasing to the eye than her aunt, and Daphne Kerr had been a known beauty in her day. Though he guessed she had passed her fortieth birthday, remnants of her former glory were evident on her still-youthful face. He studied the younger Kerr woman for a second time. How could he not admire Eleanor, a woman of such courage and conviction—a woman who was willing to risk losing a client to defend her aunt?

He opened his lips. "You're right."

Eleanor's brown eyes lit, and her mouth dropped open. "I am?" Just as quickly, she shut her lips. "I mean, I know I'm right. Of course, I'm right."

Raleigh suppressed an amused look. So she didn't think she would win the battle she had so bravely waged. Had her emotions overcome her common sense? Or was she merely courageous to a fault? Either idea intrigued him.

Eleanor straightened her narrow shoulders. "I'm glad you see the sensibleness of my position, Mr. Alden."

"Indeed, I do." Raleigh turned his face to Daphne. "I wouldn't like for my clients to argue over my fees, and I should show you—and your niece—the same courtesy. Forgive me."

"I—I, of course."

"I will settle my mother's bill in a timely manner." He returned to his desk, sat down in the brown leather armchair, and reached for his fountain pen and book of blank bank drafts. "How much do you need today, Miss Kerr?"

For the first time, Daphne appeared flustered. "Fifty percent, as always." He watched as she searched her papers. She found an itemized statement written on lined paper and handed it to him. "With the rest payable upon delivery of the garments. If that is agreeable to you."

He looked over the charges. A deposit of twenty dollars seemed a bit extravagant for a night set, but Raleigh nodded and proceeded to make out the draft. Perhaps the amount was in reality not unreasonable at all. Raleigh knew that his mother was purchasing more than a nightgown. She was buying a bit of companionship and interaction with her seamstress. Why else would she permit Daphne to saunter up the front walk as though she owned the place?

He supposed that even though they paid Vera Howard handsomely the young woman was barely beyond her teen years and could only provide so much conversation, cooped up as she was with his mother.

Raleigh handed Daphne the bank draft. "There you are. I give you this deposit in good faith." He looked over at Eleanor. "I expect you to sew the fine seam you promised."

"Oh, but I will be sewing your mother's gown, Mr. Alden," Daphne said. "Eleanor will be fashioning one for Miss Howard."

"Pity." Pity? Had he spoken aloud? Raleigh kept his eyes on the bank draft book as he returned it to the top drawer of his desk.

"Pity?" Daphne's voice betrayed her surprise.

He searched for a rapid recovery and composed himself enough to look at her without wavering. "As you are no doubt aware, my mother is a kind but strict taskmistress. She would teach your niece well how to please even the most discerning patron."

"True." A shadow of a smile kindled itself upon Daphne's face.

Raleigh pictured Vera, his mother's unobtrusive blond companion. Fine frocks would be wasted upon her slight frame. "Who ordered the dress for Miss Howard?"

"Your mother," Daphne responded without missing a beat as she completed her entries in her account ledger.

"Oh." He wondered why but simply smiled at the women and rose from his seat. "Thank you, ladies. I bid you both a good day."

After the required pleasant responses, he watched the two women retreat. Both of them held their heads up, but Eleanor's footfalls were heavy with defiance.

Since her back was to him, Raleigh allowed a grin to impress itself upon his lips. Despite his protests, he couldn't help but anticipate the occasion when he might once again see the beautiful Miss Eleanor Kerr.

"Well," Aunt Daphne noted moments later as they got into their waiting carriage, "I do believe that was the easiest time I've had collecting from Raleigh Alden since he arrived here from Florida."

Eleanor positioned herself in the space beside her aunt. "The easiest time? Then you must have needed a bullwhip to collect in the past! The nerve of that man. He is as awful as you said. Even worse!"

Daphne positioned herself in her seat, the overpowering, sweet scent of lily of the valley toilette water escaping from the folds of her dress as she adjusted the fabric. "So you believe me now?"

Eleanor felt herself flush. "I never said I didn't believe you."

Aunt Daphne harrumphed and withdrew her fan, swishing it back and forth to cool her face.

Though the carriage had already begun to move, the motion resulted in no relief from the heat. Wilting in the hot air, Eleanor followed her aunt's example and began fanning herself. Less nervous now that the encounter with the Aldens had concluded, she could relax enough to observe the sights they passed. Grand houses stood on large green lawns, houses she could only hope to enter as a seamstress, never as a guest.

A twinge of envy shot through her. Her conscience offered a quick retort.

"For what is a man profited, if he shall gain the whole world, and lose his own soul?" The words from the book of Matthew rang through her head.

A thought occurred to her. "Aunt Daphne? Do you know the people who live in these grand houses?"

Her aunt peered at the particular house they were passing on Dumbarton Road. "That's the Marshall place. Mrs. Alden said that the original owner built it right after the War Between the States." She tilted her head toward a Federal-style home surrounded by tall oaks. "The Harrisons live there."

"And you know all of them personally?"

"Not all of them. But I suppose at least half the people who live along this road are my patrons." Aunt Daphne sat back in her seat and gave a little smile.

"Do you think they know the Lord?"

"Do they know the Lord? Whatever makes you ask such a thing?" Arched eyebrows and an increased speed in waving her fan told Eleanor that her question puzzled her aunt.

"I just wondered. That's all." Her voice was soft.

"Well, I do know they go to church. Isn't that enough?"

"Not according to scripture. I suppose almost every respectable person goes to church at least some of the time. You have to want to know and love the Lord. To have a relationship with Him."

"That's all well and good, but we can't take on new clients based on how they feel about the Lord," Aunt Daphne advised. "We're in the business of sewing fine dresses for elegant people, not mending their souls."

"I suppose."

"When you work with the public, as we do, you can't be judgmental and stay in business for long."

Eleanor stared at her boots.

"If it makes you feel better, I'll have you know that I've sewn a few church dresses in my time."

Eleanor let out a forced laugh. "I'm sure you have."

"Now, I don't want you conflicting my clients with religious questions." She leaned toward Eleanor. "Do you understand me?"

"But the harvest is rich, and there are so few harvesters."

"You're not going to use Baltimore as a mission field and especially not through my business."

"I'll try to be careful."

"I hope you do a better job of that than you did today. Your papa wrote me and described you as a shy and retiring girl. Clearly, he misinformed me."

"He didn't misinform you, at least not intentionally. I am not quite as outspoken in his company. He is my father, and the Lord commands that I honor him. And he has earned my respect so that even if he weren't my father I would hold him in the highest regard."

"I'm not surprised to learn of your feelings. I think highly of him as my brother." Aunt Daphne tapped her gloved fingers on the top of her fabric sample case. "So tell me, why did you stand up to him?"

"To Mr. Alden?"

"Yes."

Eleanor stalled. "I—I didn't like the way he was treating you." Just outside of the window were sturdy row houses, a sign they were nearing their part of the city.

Aunt Daphne patted her on the knee. "I've been in business for years and have dealt with all kinds of people. I assure you, I can take care of myself."

"I know, but—"

"But nothing. Don't you realize that you almost lost a large order? And not just any order, but a significant request from an important client. I only hope that you won't make such a grand and foolish gesture again by trying to terminate a sale."

"But you said yourself that you have plenty of clients."

"Yes, but not so many that I can terminate one a day and still hope to maintain my business. I don't think you realize the cost of keeping a house on one's own."

"No, I'm sure I don't."

"Well, you had better acclimate yourself to the idea. You're not in Louisiana anymore. Your papa isn't here to bail you out of trouble."

"Maybe I should go back, then."

Aunt Daphne sighed. "Really, Eleanor, you must learn to make your way in this world. The first item on the agenda is to discard this dangerous habit of making rash proclamations. You must think before you speak. This is a business, not a social or religious endeavor."

"If I could be a religious solitary, I wouldn't have to speak at all. I could just pray all day."

Aunt Daphne let out a hearty laugh that filled the coach. "Where did you get such an idea?"

"From a book," Eleanor admitted. "It was about a woman who lost the love of her life—a sailor who was killed in a shipwreck. She cloistered herself and spent the rest of her days in sweet solitude and prayed for all the ships at sea whenever there was a storm." She sighed. "So romantic."

"Romantic, indeed." Aunt Daphne sniffed. "I'll see to it that you're far too busy here to waste your time with those awful dime novels." She lifted her hands with a motion that showed her disgust and let them fall back on her lap. "A young woman like you in the real world needs to be much more resourceful than a silly little fictional character like that."

"She wasn't silly. She was daring for taking such a vow."

"Perhaps she was, but I can judge by your behavior today that you, my dear niece, wouldn't last a minute. Why, I'd venture a guess that you couldn't even pray in silence for more than half an hour at best."

Eleanor fiddled with the tip of her parasol and wished that she could prove her aunt wrong. But alas, she knew she couldn't.

In fact, judging from her outburst that day, she couldn't hold a civil tongue in her head for long, at least not when the time arose to defend family members. She remembered Raleigh's expression—a combination of surprise and amusement—when she spoke out of turn. Surely her outburst had lowered his opinion of her. Not only must he think her to be an opportunist, but also her tantrum was hardly becoming of a lady—and certainly not a Christian woman.

How could she prove him wrong on both counts?

Even worse, why did she care? The realization struck her that she hadn't bothered about what any man thought of her—not in quite a long while. Perhaps not ever. Her time of courtship had hardly blossomed before her mother took ill, and Eleanor had wanted nothing more than to be near her. Then her period of mourning precluded any opportunity to pique the interest of the local eligible bachelors. Not that she would have been in any frame of mind to entertain suitors, even if society hadn't frowned upon such a practice for a woman grieving over the loss of her mother.

Eleanor cut her glance to her aunt. Dressed in such a flamboyant style and color, Daphne was nothing like Eleanor's mother had been. A grand lady in style, though not in position, Mother had spurned embellishments on her clothes and had favored fabrics dyed in hues of cream or a whisper of pink. Her soft-spoken ways reflected her deep and spiritual personality. Admiring her mother, Eleanor had imitated her manners as much as her own fiery personality permitted, obviously with limited success.

Lord, she prayed silently, *I have only been here a half day, and already I have shown myself to be a failure. A dismal failure. Help me!*

Raleigh skimmed a legal brief and laid it aside. The case was routine, a fact that didn't help him concentrate on his work. Images of Eleanor, the beautiful new seamstress with big brown eyes, popped into his head with relentless regularity.

Raleigh had become all too aware since his return to Baltimore that any number of eligible ladies considered him a desirable suitor. Ladies who lived in fine homes, who were born into Baltimore's best families. Why, then, had none of them interested him enough to begin a courtship in earnest? Why was his longing for love piqued only by the auburn-haired seamstress from out of state?

He chuckled as he recalled Eleanor's fine defense of her aunt. He admired her command of language and her passion in its use. His admiration stemmed not just from his professional experiences, but also from his position in society.

Dressed as she had been in the muted hues of the second stage of mourning, Eleanor Kerr hadn't appeared to be one to show such spirit. He wondered what she would be like once she returned fully to life.

Though Baltimore was the town of his boyhood, the city felt alien after he had been so long among the tropical climate and more relaxed attitude of Florida's capital, a place he had grown to love. He had been to Louisiana once to visit an uncle who had made good in New Orleans. The hanging moss on the trees, the warm waters of the Gulf of Mexico, the ebb and flow of the mighty Mississippi River—he could understand why she would miss such a place.

He and Eleanor were both the proverbial fishes out of water. Yes, that was it. That was all that explained his odd attraction to her. A bonding of sorts, the type of emotion that two passengers might share as they trekked across the country together on a train or across the ocean on a transatlantic steamship voyage.

Yes. That was it. That was all. The initial fluttering of his heart would soon still, just as surely as a train would arrive at the next station and as surely as a ship would dock at the next port.

The sound of a tinkling bell interrupted his musings. He sighed and waited.

"Raleigh!"

Mother. Ever so predictable. Within the first few days of his homecoming, he had become acquainted with her routine. Each day flowed into the next with barely a ripple of change.

"Yes, Mother." He rose from his seat and hurried up the stairs. Soon he entered her room and positioned himself a few paces from the foot of the massive bed where she spent most of her time. "What can I do for you, Mother?"

"I understand there was some disagreement over my bill."

"Who told you that?"

She lifted her nose ever so slightly. "Never mind who told me."

Raleigh tightened his lips but remained silent. No doubt one of Mother's loyal servants, most likely Monroe, had rushed to inform her of the afternoon's argument.

She peered down her nose at him. The gesture reminded him of when he was a little boy and she wanted him to confess that he was the ringleader of his group of friends who broke into the abandoned Nash place to explore for hidden treasure. Experiencing the extent of her ire hadn't been worth the expedition's findings—nothing but accumulated filth and the occasional nonhuman resident.

"Did you give Daphne her deposit?" she asked.

"Yes, ma'am."

"Good. I don't want you to dispute her charges anymore. I won't have it said about town that the Aldens are worried about money."

He weighed his next words, careful to maintain the tone of proper respect she deserved. "And I don't want it said about town that you are an innocent and generous lady waiting to be swindled."

"I've known Daphne ever since she opened up shop. She would never swindle me."

"Not intentionally, I'm sure. But her rates have gone up with the arrival of her new apprentice."

"What is your opinion of her new apprentice, Raleigh?" Vera asked.

He snapped his head in the direction of the corner where Vera had set up permanent residence. His opinion? How could he respond?

"I'm interested in the answer to that question, as well," Mother prompted. "Did you find her disagreeable? Is that why you quarreled about the bill?"

"No, no," he assured them. What could he say about Eleanor? That he already found her intriguing? No, he couldn't admit that. Never.

"Well?" Mother asked.

"Uh, well. I haven't had time to form an opinion about the niece. I can only assume that if she is a family and business relation of a person you trust she is respectable enough."

He let his gaze bore into Vera since she had first posed the query. What possessed her to ask such a question? Why would she care one way or the other about his opinion of the new seamstress?

Vera nodded and looked down at her lap, where her delicate hands were clasped.

"Why do you ask?" he couldn't resist inquiring. "Is there some concern about her that you need to express?"

"Oh no. No. Not really. I just wondered what your opinion was. After all, she will be sewing my dresses."

"Is that so?" Raleigh turned his attention to his mother. "I understand that was your idea."

"Yes. She would never ask."

"No, not at all," Vera chirped.

"She hasn't ordered a dress sewn since the cotillion, and I think the time has come for her to have a new frock. You know how careful our Vera is with a dollar," Mother pointed out. "She would never be as extravagant as you accuse me of being."

His mother's unspoken messages were evident to Raleigh. More than once, she had hinted that she wouldn't be opposed to his making a match with Vera, an impoverished yet highborn young woman. Even though he felt not the least bit of attraction to Vera, who tended to disappear into the wallpaper, he saw no reason to be unkind. "Yes, I do admire Vera's fortitude."

"You do?" Vera's plain face lit up.

"Uh, yes." He kept his voice even. It was one thing to be kind, but quite another to offer false encouragement. He supposed that if he were to be entirely truthful he could point out that Vera was being paid more than enough money to purchase her own dresses, but since his mother wanted to offer her companion a gift, so be it. But why?

"Vera needs a fine dress for the party we'll soon be hosting," Mother said, answering his unspoken question as though she had read his mind.

"Party? I see no reason for a party."

"For your homecoming, of course. Certainly, it is a cause for celebration. I was thinking we could invite a hundred of our close friends."

Raleigh calculated the cost of food and entertainment for such an extravaganza. "There really is no need for all that."

"Oh, certainly there is." She paused. "Or at least a small dinner party."

Raleigh had already learned his mother's tactic of introducing one ridiculous idea before telling him her real intent. "Perhaps that can be arranged."

"I can start helping Mrs. Alden make plans right away," Vera offered.

"Yes, you do that," Raleigh answered, knowing his voice held no enthusiasm. "But Vera, I want you to know that if you don't wish for Eleanor Kerr to be your seamstress you don't have to feel obligated to her."

"Really?"

"Of course not. I'm sure Daphne would be glad to sew your garment."

"Oh, that's quite all right. I think I can get along with Eleanor well enough. Thank you for your consideration." She blushed and looked back down at her hands.

As Raleigh exited the room, a sense of nervousness overcame him. He wasn't sure what the women were planning for the party, but he had a feeling those plans involved him—and a future he had no intention of living.

Chapter 4

A few days later, Raleigh had just returned home from a grueling morning in Judge Ross's court when he spied Eleanor walking toward his house. Suddenly feeling chipper despite the fact that the Lord had chosen that day to water the flowers with a light rain, Raleigh hurried his step to meet her—although not too quickly, he hoped.

"Good afternoon, Miss Eleanor," Raleigh greeted her as soon as she was within comfortable earshot. He tipped his hat but not enough to lose the protection it offered from the rain.

She peered at him from underneath her open umbrella. "Good afternoon, Mr. Alden."

He watched the weeping sky. "A lovely day, is it not?"

She looked upward, and when she laughed, the sound reminded him of a tuneful flute. "A lovely day, indeed, if you like gray."

"Gray can be a fine color in its place." He chuckled. "So, what brings you here today?"

"I have an appointment to discuss dress patterns and fabrics with Miss Vera," Eleanor answered as she ascended the veranda steps.

He took her by the elbow, a gesture she didn't seem to mind in the least. For the first time, he felt pleased that his mother had ordered a dress for Vera.

They both stepped onto the veranda. Eleanor shook her wet umbrella with firm but delicate motions. Raleigh opened the door for her. "I trust your aunt is well?"

Eleanor's features became as dark as the day. "Regrettably, she is indisposed with a cold."

"Yes, this is a season for such ailments." As he removed his hat and placed it on the mahogany stand in the entrance, Raleigh noted how the house had developed a dank odor as the wood absorbed dampness but couldn't release it back into the heavy atmosphere. He wondered if there was an end in sight to the wet weather.

Monroe, alert as always, had placed a portion of yesterday's newspaper underneath the stand in anticipation of Mr. Alden's dripping hat. "I am so sorry to hear that your aunt has succumbed to illness," Raleigh said. "Please send her my good wishes for her recovery."

"I will." Eleanor deposited her folded umbrella into a brass stand beside the door. "She will be grateful for your good wishes, I'm sure. She is trying to bring solace to herself by reading."

Raleigh looked around for Monroe, who had not made himself available. He extended his hands in silent offer to take Eleanor's wrap.

After setting down her seamstress's box, she swept herself out of her ivory-colored cloak and handed it to him. "Thank you."

Raleigh nodded. "I'm glad to hear she is reading. Immersion in a good book is one of my favorite pastimes. And I have an extensive library to prove it."

"You seem quite proud of that."

"I suppose I am," he admitted as he shed his overcoat. "Are you a reader?"

"Yes." She looked at the floor. He wondered if her sudden unwillingness to meet his eyes was borne out of modesty or fear of his judgment of her tastes.

"Perhaps you would like to expand your horizons. I could lend you a book," he suggested.

She looked up into his eyes. "You would do that? For me?"

"If it pleases you." He smiled and hoped his expression didn't reveal that he had an ulterior motive. If he loaned her an expensive volume, she would feel obliged to return it. The transaction would offer him an excuse to see her again and to enter into a lively discussion about what she enjoyed reading. "What subjects interest you?"

She averted her eyes once more. "Oh, I read stories. But my aunt doesn't care for the stories I select."

"To each his own, I say. Why should she criticize you?"

Her face flushed from a creamy buff to a most flattering shade of pink. "I always read scripture to Mama while she was suffering so. The words comforted her. But when she was asleep, I took my mind off my troubles by reading dime novels."

"Oh." No wonder Daphne didn't care for Eleanor's stories. Dime novels hardly offered a young woman the type of intellectual stimulation she needed. Despite siding with her aunt, he decided to encourage her rather than alienate her. "Tell me about your favorite story."

To his surprise, she didn't pause to consider. "My favorite inspired me to pursue the life of a religious solitary."

"A religious solitary?" Experienced in concealing emotions from years of pleading legal cases, he summoned all his expertise to keep from laughing aloud.

"Yes. No one seems to think I would be much of a success at it. Not Papa. Not Aunt Daphne. And I can see by your expression, not even you."

So his act of concealment hadn't been successful! He pursed his lips, then spoke. "I thought Mother mentioned that your aunt attends Lovely Lane Church. Don't you worship with her?"

"Indeed I do."

"Well." He chuckled. "According to my reading, your spiritual tradition encourages going out among the poor and reaching out to society rather than confining yourself to solitude."

Her eyes studied the fresh arrangement of pink roses that sat upon an occasional table, yet he could tell by her intense expression that she saw not the flowers but was peering into the doubts in her mind.

"Perhaps," she finally agreed. "But I do believe there is room for different types of religious expression within the confines of the Christian faith, as long as they are scriptural."

Her thoughtful answer impressed him. "You have a good point, indeed. Nevertheless, I have difficulty picturing you wasting away in a dark hole, praying all day and night."

"That's what everyone says, although for the Christian, prayer is never a waste."

He was increasingly impressed by her quick wit. "Yet another point well taken."

She sighed. "I suppose I tend to blurt out what I feel and believe before considering the consequences."

"There, there. Don't become discouraged. The Lord can use any personality to serve Him."

"Do you really think so?" Her eyes lit with hope.

"Indeed I do." He made a mental search of the books on his library shelves with the intent of making a recommendation. "Perhaps I can suggest a book written in the Middle Ages that may give you some insight. *The Imitation of Christ.* Would you care to borrow it?"

"The Middle Ages?" She hesitated. "I don't know. Is the book terribly long and hard to read?"

This time, he held his amusement to himself. "Not terribly on either count. And the chapters are all very short. Like devotional reading. You can peruse a chapter a day in addition to your current spiritual readings without finding it a burden."

"Well, I suppose if you suggest that I should read such a book I would find the time spent to my benefit. If you wish to loan me your copy, I accept with gratitude. And I promise to take care of, with my best efforts, any book you entrust to me and to return it as soon as I have completed it."

"I'm sure you will. Otherwise, I would not have offered to entrust you with a book from my personal collection." He noticed that Monroe was approaching from the back hallway.

"Good afternoon, Mr. Raleigh." Monroe kept his eyes on Raleigh.

"Afternoon, Monroe."

"I beg your forgiveness for my delay. There was a problem in the kitchen.

But all is well now, let me hasten to assure you."

"Of course," Raleigh agreed.

Monroe shot a mean look toward Eleanor. "Is this seamstress disrupting you, sir?" Raleigh noted his disdain as he lingered on the word seamstress.

"Not at all, Monroe. We have been partaking in a rather lively discussion," Raleigh said. "Rather, I am more likely to be disrupting her day."

"Not at all, Mr. Alden," she assured him.

Raleigh flashed Eleanor a smile before returning his attention to Monroe. "Will you escort Miss Kerr to Mother's room?"

"Of course, sir." While Monroe was obsequious toward Raleigh, his glance sent in Eleanor's direction chilled the foyer. Raleigh thought he knew why. More than likely, Monroe questioned the station that Mrs. Alden ascribed to the Kerrs as more than ordinary seamstresses. Daphne and Mrs. Alden had a special bond that no doubt would soon extend to Eleanor.

"If you can abide the interruption to your work, Miss Kerr," Raleigh said, "I can bring the book up to you as soon as I retrieve it from the library."

She paused in midstep. "Are you sure that wouldn't be too much of a bother, Mr. Alden?"

"Please. Call me Raleigh." As soon as the words left his lips, he felt Monroe's gaze boring into him. "And no, it wouldn't be a bother at all."

Her face lit as brightly as the sun illuminating the morning sky. "Thank you."

Raleigh concentrated on her face, deliberately ignoring Monroe. "I'll retrieve the copy for you as soon as possible."

"Thank you."

Her uplifted lips turned into an unhappy straight line. He could see that she felt a twinge of disappointment in that he hadn't invited her to join him. He could understand why. An avid reader, Raleigh enjoyed the mere sensation of being in a library, private or public. The musky odor of leather-bound volumes comprised of fine paper, the room dimly lit to protect valuable tomes, oversized chairs that invited one to sit and linger, stillness that encouraged study—he forced himself to suppress a sigh at the thought. Her unexpressed disappointment pleased him. Surely she was proving herself to be a kindred spirit.

One day, he would feel free to invite her to while away as much time as she liked amid his book collection. But for now, he wanted to conduct himself as a gentleman. No need to fuel the fires of gossip among nosy servants. Private moments between unmarried men and women were not appropriate, even though the new century had dawned. Sometimes he wished convention wasn't quite such a strict taskmistress.

"If you will follow me, Miss Kerr," Monroe offered as soon as Raleigh left them.

Eleanor nodded and climbed the stairs, following Monroe's lead. If only she could have asked Raleigh Alden to let her peek into his library. Obviously he was proud of his collection of books. Why shouldn't he be able to show them off, even if only to his mother's seamstress?

She straightened herself as she approached Mrs. Alden's door. The pungent smell of liniment would have led her to the right entrance even if Monroe had not.

"Miss Eleanor Kerr to see Miss Howard," Monroe informed the ladies.

Mrs. Alden's voice floated into the hallway. "Oh, good. Do send her in."

Monroe stepped back, never allowing the stern look to leave his features.

Eleanor did her best to ignore him as she stepped over the threshold with warm greetings for the ladies.

"Monroe," Mrs. Alden called before he left her earshot, "please bring us a spot of tea."

"Yes, I shall bring you and Miss Vera tea," he agreed.

"And a cup for Eleanor, too."

Eleanor protested, "Oh, I couldn't—"

"Nonsense. If I am feeling a chill, then you must be, too. Of course you'll have tea with us."

"Yes, ma'am. It would be an honor." Eleanor didn't dare look at Monroe. She could only imagine how displeased he was with this new development.

She noticed that, as usual, Vera sat in her white satin vanity chair. Eleanor wondered if she ever ventured out of her place. Mrs. Alden was wrapped in white, looking like an aged cherub with smooth skin and hair, which she insisted was prematurely gray. Both women had expressions of anticipation on their faces. Their gazes followed Eleanor's every move.

She searched the room for a spare seat and eyed a wooden chair that matched an oak vanity table. She nodded toward it. "May I?"

"Certainly," Mrs. Alden said.

Eleanor set her box of sewing notions upon the chair, opened it, and withdrew a few swatches of fabric and a measuring tape. "I hope you like the fabric samples I selected. Aunt Daphne made several excellent suggestions."

"Then I'm sure we'll be delighted," Mrs. Alden said. "We want something quite fancy, something that will make our Vera shine at the dinner party."

Eleanor looked to Vera for further input, but the young woman just stared at the swatches as though the colors mesmerized her. "All right, then," Eleanor said. "How about green to match your eyes? I also brought a swatch of a particularly nice blue. Or perhaps red?"

"Red?" Vera fanned herself. "Red would never do for a lady."

Eleanor flushed, imagining her face must have looked as red as the silk she held in her hand. "I beg your pardon. I was thinking it was cheerful, that's all."

"She meant no harm, surely," Mrs. Alden said. "I favor the blue."

"Before you decide, I have more selections." Eleanor held two swatches of fabric—one yellow and one blue—to Vera's cheeks. "Both of these are nice, but I do believe yellow brings out the golden highlights in your hair. Very flattering."

"Yellow? That is oh so bright!" Vera squirmed. "Oh, do you really think I should be so daring? I don't want the gentlemen there to think I'm making too extraordinary of an effort to attract their attention."

"No one will think that," Eleanor assured her. From the corner of her eye, she saw Monroe arrive with the tea. "They will just think you're beautiful, that's all."

She put away the swatches. "We'll measure after tea, perhaps?"

"A grand idea," Mrs. Alden agreed.

Vera kept her gaze on her lap, a gesture Eleanor took as shyness.

"You have a fine figure," Eleanor assured her. "I'll find it easy to sew for you."

Vera looked up. "Really? You truly think so?"

"Of course I do." Eleanor wondered why a young woman from such a good family would care what she thought of her. Yet Eleanor found Vera's questions endearing.

"I can't wait to see the dress when it's finished." Vera's enthusiasm reminded Eleanor of a little girl awaiting a birthday celebration.

"I promise to do my best work for you," Eleanor assured her.

"I'm sure any dress you sew will be beautiful, since you are Daphne's niece."

"I'd like to think my sewing is superb, but I confess that I never imagined I would make a living as a seamstress."

"Really? What did you think you would do?"

"I—" She almost said, "become a religious solitary," but since she had arrived in Baltimore, she had been told time and again not to nurse such a notion. "I don't know, really. I suppose before Mama died I thought I would marry and live happily ever after. But she fell ill, and—and. . ." Tears threatened.

"There, there." Vera patted her hand. "God has a plan for everyone. You'll find out what He has in mind for you soon enough."

"I do hope so," Eleanor said, taking a sip of tea.

"In the meanwhile, you'd best bloom where you're planted," Mrs. Alden advised.

"Bloom where I'm planted?"

She nodded. "That means, sew the finest line of stitching you can while you're a seamstress. The job may not seem like His bidding now, but you never know where it might lead." Mrs. Alden tilted her head toward Vera. "Just like my girl, here. One never knows what might occur at this dinner party. Once she's dressed in finery, as she should be, she might get noticed by someone special."

Vera blushed crimson once again. "Oh, Mrs. Alden, how you do talk."

"Do you have anyone in particular in mind?" Eleanor couldn't help but ask.

"No. No one." Vera's adamant shaking of her head told Eleanor otherwise.

Her curiosity was piqued, but she knew better than to ask.

"We shall have many fine gentlemen present." Mrs. Alden clasped her hands in obvious rapt anticipation. "Perhaps even Flint Jarvis."

"Flint Jarvis?" Vera gasped.

Eleanor stopped stirring her tea long enough to observe the exchange. The name meant nothing to her, but apparently he was of some repute about town. Aunt Daphne had told her that as a new businesswoman Eleanor would need to keep her eyes and ears open. Perhaps this bit of gossip was her first test.

"Oh, you can't possibly invite him!" Vera continued.

"Indeed, I can and I will! He is certain to add interest and mystery to any event he attends," Mrs. Alden said. "And no one can deny that he would certainly be a handsome addition to my dinner table."

"Handsome, yes. But with all due respect, do you really think Mr. Alden will get along with someone rumored to be a man about town?" Vera asked.

"Oh, Flint and Raleigh are great friends. And of course, he is my friend Jessica's nephew. Raleigh won't mind at all."

"But what lady shall we invite for Mr. Jarvis?"

Mrs. Alden crossed her arms. "I haven't thought that far ahead yet. But I shall think of someone, I'm sure. We still have time."

"Indeed." Vera shut her mouth and fanned herself as though a burst of heat had entered the room. Since silence penetrated, Eleanor decided that if she was to find out more about the mysterious Mr. Jarvis the time would be later rather than at the present moment.

"Shall we select a dress pattern?" Eleanor asked.

Vera clapped her hands. "Oh yes, let's!"

Eleanor couldn't suppress a smile. She didn't remember ever seeing Vera so animated. Certainly the poor girl hadn't had a new dress sewn in ages—or was the prospect of romance more to her liking?

"How about this?" Eleanor showed Vera a picture of a lace-embellished ball gown that was modest yet formfitting.

"Oh, that's much too bold," Vera said.

Mrs. Alden took the picture out of Eleanor's hand and examined the picture for herself. "Bold? No, I think this is just right."

Vera thumbed through the other patterns that Eleanor had brought. "I was thinking something more along these lines." She showed Mrs. Alden a high-necked dress with full proportions.

"Where will he find you amid all that fabric?"

"I could amend the pattern to suit," Eleanor hastened to offer.

Mrs. Alden studied the picture. "Well, I suppose a nip here and a tuck there." She paused. "As long as Vera's fine figure is evident."

"An easily accomplished feat," Eleanor assured them both.

As the afternoon progressed, Eleanor found that Mrs. Alden agreed with her ideas. She drank her tea as Vera expressed her concern that the dress not be too revealing. Assuring her that it wouldn't, Eleanor packed her box after completing her tea, then took her leave.

She let out a tuneful whistle as she went down the stairs, then remembered that such a feat was hardly ladylike. Yet apparently her tune had caught the attention of Raleigh Alden, since he was standing at the bottom of the stairs. She had been so wrapped up in helping Vera choose her fabric and pattern that she had almost forgotten his promise to bring her a book. Was he waiting to meet her? Eleanor's heart skipped a beat.

"Leaving already, Miss Eleanor?"

"Yes, my appointment went well."

His smile lit the room. "I hope Mother wasn't too difficult."

"Oh no. Not at all," Eleanor hastened to assure him.

"I beg your pardon for not bringing the book up to you as I promised. I was interrupted by a client," he explained. "So if you have a moment now, would you like to see my library?"

"Yes, I would." She glanced at the grandfather clock in the parlor and noted the time. "My livery isn't due to arrive for another quarter hour."

"Next time, allow me to send my coach," he suggested as they walked side by side through the hallway.

"Oh, I couldn't bother you—"

"Of course. It's no bother. I insist."

Eleanor hadn't expected Raleigh to be so friendly. She had been warned that men who were too sociable too soon might be looking for favors beyond what would be advisable for her to grant. Yet nothing in Raleigh's demeanor was leering or suspicious. Inexplicably, she felt comfortable, as if she was right where she belonged.

"This is it." He unlocked a heavy door at the end of the hallway and let her step into the room first. He stepped in behind her, keeping the door open.

The room was larger than she expected, but she wasn't surprised to find it dark and lined with books from top to bottom on all four walls. Overstuffed chairs sat across from each other in front of a table, inviting one to read.

"No wonder you wanted to loan me a volume," she noted. "If you add even one more slim book to your collection, where will you find room for it?"

His pleasant laugh filled the room. "I can always find room for another book, I assure you." Immediately he strode to a shelf and retrieved a volume. "Here it is. The book I promised."

"How did you manage to find it so quickly?"

"The Dewey Decimal Classification system. I have implemented it here with great success."

"I don't think I know that system."

"I can explain it to you, if you like." Without pausing, he launched into a detailed and enthusiastic explanation of the ten main categories, followed by how they were further divided into call numbers based on the metric system. Eleanor grasped little of what Raleigh told her, but she had the distinct feeling that she would find more opportunities to learn all about the brilliant Melvil Dewey.

Monroe's voice interrupted. "Miss Kerr, your carriage awaits."

"Oh! Where has the time gone? I'm so sorry. I must depart, Raleigh." She tapped the volume. "I do thank you for loaning me this book. I shall begin reading it tonight."

"I eagerly await your insights." His eyes sparkled. Eleanor wondered if he were simply happy to find a new student or if his interest was based on more.

Chapter 5

Two weeks later, Eleanor stood in the small entryway of Aunt Daphne's house and thumbed through several letters and bills that had just arrived by post. She stopped when she saw a cream-colored envelope addressed in elaborate script. The return address was familiar.

She gasped. "The Aldens!"

Eleanor shut the front door and hurried down the hall, her boot heels clacking against the hardwood. Upon reaching the entrance to her aunt's small study, she peered inside. "Aunt Daphne!"

"My dear child," she answered from her seat at the desk. Cook was standing in front of Daphne, no doubt receiving instructions about the week's menu or asking for yet another raise in the food budget. "Why are you in such a hurry? I could hear you running down the hall practically from the front door."

"I'm sorry." Eleanor held up the invitation. "But look! There is an invitation addressed to us."

Aunt Daphne chuckled. "Yes, we do receive invitations upon occasion. It's not as though I know no one in town. Most likely it is for the Strang wedding. I'll reply later."

Eleanor shook her head. "No. It's from the Aldens."

"The Aldens?"

"The Aldens?" The whites of Cook's eyes grew wide against her broad face. "Ain't they some fancy people you sew for, Miss Daphne?"

"Yes, they are an important family," Aunt Daphne agreed.

Eleanor nearly jumped up and down with excitement. "Might we open it now?"

"Dear, dear. You are like a small child in your anticipation." Aunt Daphne's smile gave away her bemusement. "Since you're so eager to see what it is, why don't you open it?"

Eleanor picked up a letter opener from Aunt Daphne's desk and slit open the envelope at the fold. She drew out the invitation. "They're asking us to come to the dinner party."

Aunt Daphne nearly dropped her fountain pen. "The dinner party? The one we've been making dresses for all this time?"

"I know of no other."

Aunt Daphne's eyebrows arched as she set her pen down, but her expression didn't reveal the surprise that Eleanor had anticipated it would. "When I

43

delivered her nightgown, Mrs. Alden mentioned something about including us, but I thought it was just idle talk. I never expected her to follow through."

"But she did!" Eleanor didn't bother to contain her zeal. "Oh, how wonderful of her to think of us! Or maybe it was Vera's idea. I do think she considers me rather a friend, you know."

Aunt Daphne contemplated Eleanor's statement. "Yes, I think she might. Still, I am a bit surprised."

Eleanor clutched the missive to her chest. "Might we accept?"

"Indeed, we must," her aunt answered. "I think not accepting would be unforgivable. Leave the invitation with me, and I will write a formal response as soon as I'm finished here."

Eleanor strode across the room and handed the invitation to her aunt. "Oh, thank you!"

Aunt Daphne wagged her finger at her niece. "But don't mention the invitation to them when you go over there today. That wouldn't be polite until I've had a chance to respond."

"Oh." She wasn't sure how she could conceal her excitement, but Eleanor understood her aunt. "Oh, but of course I won't."

Eleanor practically danced out of the room. Imagine! She would be going to the dinner party at the Aldens! She felt like Cinderella. Humming to herself, she made her way to the sewing room adjacent to the kitchen and gathered her supplies to make the trip to the Aldens'.

She wondered what type of dress she should wear. Aunt Daphne had a good number of the latest patterns in stock, so she would easily be able to find a fashionable style. Perhaps a dress with a sash to emphasize her tiny waist. She wondered if she should sew herself large sleeves or something closer to her arms. Which way should she go? She tapped her chin with her forefinger. Overblown sleeves were likely to make her look top-heavy, especially since she wasn't too tall. Something in the middle. Yes, that was the answer. Sleeves that weren't too large or too small, but just right. Like Goldilocks. She imagined the little fairy-tale heroine eating three bowls of porridge and sitting in three chairs. Despite being many years older than the little girl in the story, Eleanor giggled.

What about the neckline? She knew many ladies seized the opportunity of an evening event to flaunt ample cleavage. Eleanor wondered what it would be like to enjoy the attention an immodest neckline would bring to her person. She quickly shook the thought out of her head. As a servant of Christ, she knew she had to suppress her vanity and remain reserved before a party of mixed company. The man she would one day marry would be sure to appreciate the fact that she valued herself enough to keep herself only for him. The thought sent a wave of heat to her cheeks. How could she—a maiden—let her mind wander to such imprudent thoughts!

She deliberately turned her mind to lace. Aunt Daphne had just received an order of lace from Ireland. Eleanor took in a breath when she recalled one particular pattern of delicate flowers crocheted with remarkable skill. Yes, she would add a bit of lace to the neckline, sleeves, and perhaps the hem. But the expense! She grimaced. Aunt Daphne would dock her pay to cover the cost, but to her mind, the sacrifice would be worth the result.

To ensure her aunt wouldn't promise the lace to someone else, Eleanor scurried into the sewing room to set it aside for herself. The box from Ireland still sat on the floor by the south wall—not a surprise since the sewing room remained in a perpetual state of organized chaos. Quickly she retrieved the intended lace from the box and was about to take it up to her room when several bolts of fabric caught her eye. Which one would she choose? She twisted her mouth. In order not to appear in the same fabric as someone else, she and her aunt would have to find out what other guests would be present and make sure to fashion their dresses out of something different. Eleanor's official time of mourning had finally passed, so she would be allowed to wear a color more daring than lavender. Yet the bright reds and yellows didn't speak to her. Her glance fell upon a bolt of rose-colored silk. Yes. That was it! Rose. Not too daring, but not too meek. Just right. She giggled once more.

The grandfather clock chimed the hour. She gasped when she remembered her appointment with Vera. She had to prepare to go to the Aldens'. Her thoughts taking a different turn, Eleanor hoped her new client would be pleased with her progress.

Smiling to herself, she folded the yellow gown with care so as not to wrinkle it too much. Vera was her favorite client out of the customers she had gained since arriving in Baltimore a few weeks ago. Some of the older matrons were fussy, and others wanted her to perform a magical feat with her sewing—as if her dresses would somehow take off decades and make them once again the center of attention. Still others bickered over the price even though they had chosen expensive fabrics, making Raleigh's protests seem mild in comparison. And some customers insisted on selecting styles that wouldn't flatter their figures, then blamed Eleanor when the dresses turned out exactly as she had predicted: unappealing. If she hadn't known better, she would have thought Aunt Daphne directed Eleanor to her most difficult clients, so she wouldn't need to please them anymore.

Her time in Baltimore had already proven trying, but she made sure not to complain to Papa. He had enough problems trying to reestablish himself in business back in New Orleans. Eleanor's gift to him was to give him no reason to worry about her.

In the letter she had written to Papa just that morning, Eleanor had focused on Vera. She was different from the rest of the ladies whom Eleanor had met.

Shy, but not too shy to express an opinion, she seemed genuinely pleased with Eleanor's suggestions on color and style. Predictably, Vera looked beautiful in the frock Eleanor was in the process of fashioning for her—and she made sure to tell her so. Even Mrs. Alden's eyes lit with pleasure when she eyed her companion wearing the new dress. Surely Eleanor had pleased everyone who counted in the Alden house.

Eleanor sighed. She wished Vera could enjoy a life beyond that of being Mrs. Alden's companion. With her pleasing demeanor and gentle spirit, Vera could make a fine wife and mother. But when she hinted to Vera about her interests, Vera was reticent to say anything. She merely cast her gaze at the polished hardwood floors and let a shadow of a smile touch her lips. Eleanor fancied that Vera had some secret love. Maybe some mysterious man would come and sweep her off her feet one day. Eleanor hoped so.

"Maybe Vera's Mr. Right will be at the dinner party," she muttered to herself. "I remember they said something about Flint Jarvis. Hmm. I wonder about this Mr. Jarvis. Whoever could he be?"

She had little time to contemplate further since the hands on the clock were moving rapidly. Gathering her things, Eleanor made a lively step into the hall and prepared herself to call out to her aunt that she was ready to depart. What a shock to discover Aunt Daphne waiting for her at the front door. Eleanor stopped in her tracks.

"I'll be going with you today to fit Vera's dress."

"Oh?" Eleanor knew disappointment showed in her voice. Over the past week, she had rather enjoyed going to the mansion alone, uninhibited by Aunt Daphne's watchful eye.

"Didn't I tell you?" Aunt Daphne asked as she slipped on her gloves. "I have an errand with the Aldens, too. In addition to the bedclothes she ordered from me, Mrs. Alden has decided to have a dress sewn for herself."

"A dress? So she'll be going to the dinner?"

"I don't think she would miss it for anything." Aunt Daphne looked out of the window on the side of the front door as if she were surveying the world itself and looking for Mrs. Alden on the horizon.

"I'm so glad to hear she wants to attend," Eleanor said. "It will do her good to get out of her bed for once."

"She very much enjoys the consideration that people give to the bedridden, I do believe," Aunt Daphne noted, returning her attention to Eleanor. "But the prospect of a party is even more pleasing. I'm glad her son is amenable to the idea. At first, I thought he might forbid it."

"Oh, he isn't as bad as all that." Eleanor twirled her white parasol, digging its end into the floor.

"You don't think so?" Aunt Daphne's tone of voice told Eleanor that her question was rhetorical. "I confess I'm a bit worried about your unbridled enthusiasm about this invitation from them. I don't want you getting grand ideas."

"I don't have any grand ideas." The parasol moved faster until Aunt Daphne shot her a warning look. Eleanor stopped twirling it abruptly.

"Oh? I understand from Mrs. Alden herself that you have made a point of talking to Mr. Alden upon each visit."

Eleanor squirmed. Had Raleigh's mother been listening to every word they spoke while pretending indifference to their chatter? Or had Monroe tipped her off to their conversations? She performed a mental rundown of their exchanges and was grateful to realize she had never said a word to Raleigh that she believed to be contrary to her faith or social etiquette.

"I haven't made a point of talking to him," Eleanor said. "He's made a point of talking to me."

"Oh, is that the way it is? I wouldn't have pictured you as being quite so supercilious."

"Me?" Eleanor clutched her throat. She had never been described in such a way before, at least not to her face and not by one whose opinion mattered to her. "I don't mean to be so vain. It's just that. . .he always is present whenever I visit."

"And that pleases you?"

Eleanor didn't know how to respond. Ever since she had laid eyes on him and he had been so kind in light of her outburst and then even begun loaning her valuable books from his library, she had formed a fondness for him. So, of course, his presence delighted her, but she had the distinct feeling that her feelings weren't mirrored by Aunt Daphne. "The last time we conversed, he invited me to join the revival services at his church beginning next week. And I accepted."

"Without my leave?" Aunt Daphne sniffed and tugged at the waistline of her bright yellow dress.

"I didn't think I needed your leave to attend church. And of course," Eleanor added, making sure to soften her voice, "you are more than welcome to join us."

"I just might do that."

"You'd enjoy the services, I'm sure. Raleigh said the guest minister is quite energetic and gives a wondrous message whenever he preaches."

"Indubitably." Aunt Daphne's tone indicated she wasn't so certain. She peered out of the window again.

"Raleigh has taken it upon himself to loan me some books from his library," Eleanor added. "Surely such attention is a privilege."

"Yes, he does seem to appreciate your intellect, which I admit, judging from our conversations on current affairs and the like, demonstrates your good schooling," Aunt Daphne conceded. "But are you sure that your mind is all he appreciates?"

"I hope he finds my appearance pleasing, although he has never mentioned anything." Eleanor self-consciously smoothed her beige skirt.

"I had hoped for a less ambiguous answer from you. I'm afraid you have disappointed me."

"Disappointed you? Why, I thought you would welcome any friendly overture from him since you yourself said he was quite difficult. Hasn't he been more pleasant since I started sewing for Vera?" Eleanor ventured, hoping the answer would be in the affirmative.

"Yes," her aunt conceded. "But in spite of the invitation we received, you must remember that you are only a seamstress. Any attentions from someone such as Raleigh Alden will only lead to trouble."

"Trouble?" Eleanor quivered.

Aunt Daphne glanced out the window once more before leaning closer to Eleanor. "Don't repeat this, but just last spring, one of the Blackston maids was sent away after she became too familiar with the elder son of the house."

Eleanor gasped. Mrs. Blackston was one of their best clients. She had just ordered two dresses for the fall season, and they expected her to place an order for at least two ball gowns for the winter holidays. "I don't believe it."

"She is a fine woman, and she did the best she could with her children. I don't fault her, even though her sons have quite the reputation."

"Of course, she is not to blame. A devout parent does not guarantee religious children," Eleanor said. "God has no grandchildren."

"True. Nevertheless, you don't want any part of such scandal."

"Aunt Daphne! You know me better than that!" Eleanor protested. "Besides, I think we are more than servants to the Aldens. Why, even though I've only known her a short time, I consider Vera a friend. And Raleigh certainly has an excellent reputation."

"True," Aunt Daphne admitted. "I just hope he lives up to it."

"He does. He has always been nothing but a consummate gentleman in my presence. I'm sure his interest in me is only intellectual and spiritual. That's all." She lifted her forefinger for emphasis.

"Indeed? And he cannot find someone in his own set to share conversation with? Someone like Miss Vera Howard, perhaps?"

"Vera?" The young woman had never confided or even hinted at any interest in Raleigh other than as her employer. "I would imagine he could converse with her anytime he pleases. And I'm sure he does."

"Unless he is talking with you, instead."

"Don't be silly, Aunt Daphne. I am not standing in anyone's way."

"I hope not." She gathered her supplies and lavender parasol, which matched the lavender accents on her dress. "In any event, I was so in hopes that you wouldn't set your cap for anyone at all, at least for a few years."

"Oh, I'm sure I can stay in business with you as long as you need me."

"Not only that, but we should take this opportunity to travel together. I've saved up a little money, and as soon as you gather a little nest egg, we can take a fine tour abroad. Perhaps even sail on a steamship to worlds unknown to us." Aunt Daphne stared ahead, her look vacant as though she were concentrating on a picture in her mind instead of the copper-colored walls.

Eleanor tried not to cringe. This wasn't the first time her aunt had broached the subject of world travel. Over time, she had developed the distinct feeling that her aunt only agreed to her extended presence in her home so she could cultivate another woman to share her dream of travel. But alas, even with all the hints and talk, Eleanor still had not developed the desire to see the world. The most adventure she craved was reading about Old Testament battles. How could she tell her aunt she had chosen the wrong person to be a traveling companion?

Eleanor sent up a silent prayer when the carriage pulled up, meaning she didn't have to decide to reveal her feelings at present.

"Finally! I thought Henry would never get here. Let us be on our way." Without further ado, Aunt Daphne strode out the door, and Eleanor followed her.

The ride to the Aldens' was silent except for the *clip-clop* of the horses' hooves and the sounds of the city streets teeming with people, horses, carriages, carts, and streetcars. Eleanor thought about Aunt Daphne's admonitions. Surely Raleigh didn't have his eye on Vera. But if he did, how could she interfere? Indeed, how could she be so bold as to think she would have the power to stand between them, even if she tried? She shook her head, tossing the very thought out of her mind.

Perhaps her fears would be allayed once she saw Raleigh that day. After all, wasn't he the one who was responsible for her being invited to the dinner? Surely he was. Who else?

But despite Eleanor's hopes, she was disappointed to find that Raleigh didn't greet her as usual. Perhaps he didn't realize she had an appointment at that hour. Then again, she hadn't finished with the latest book she had borrowed, so Raleigh had no reason to greet her. Perhaps she had told Aunt Daphne more of the truth than she originally hoped. Perhaps Raleigh's interest in her really was only spiritual and intellectual.

Moments later, Eleanor set only half her mind to the appointment as she watched Mrs. Alden inspect Aunt Daphne's work.

"Yes, I do believe this color is quite appropriate for me. I do so like mint green. So fresh and lively for late summer," Mrs. Alden said.

"It will bring out the green in your eyes."

"As if anyone will be paying any attention to my old eyes." Mrs. Alden let out a laugh.

"Oh, I'm sure you will be the belle of the ball," Aunt Daphne said.

"No, I imagine one of our young girls will be," Mrs. Alden said.

"I quite imagine that Vera will be the belle of the ball," Eleanor speculated.

"Oh, pshaw. You are too kind," Vera said.

Eleanor studied her client. Her blush indicated that despite her protests, she hoped something would develop. Eleanor prayed it would.

"I do hope you're planning to accept our invitation to the dinner," Mrs. Alden said. "I trust it arrived."

"Yes, ma'am," Aunt Daphne answered. "And, of course, I do plan to respond in the affirmative. We are so pleased to be included."

"Included in what?" a male voice interrupted.

Eleanor instantly recognized the tenor. Her heart betrayed her with a lurch. Before turning in the direction of the voice, she made sure to set her expression in a neutral fashion so as not to make obvious her feelings. As usual, Vera shyly cast her eyes downward. Aunt Daphne's face adopted an icy refrain.

"Raleigh!" Mrs. Alden addressed her son. "Don't you believe in knocking first?"

"I would have, but as you can see, my hands are occupied." He hovered in the doorway and tilted his head toward the tray of tea and biscuits he held. "Besides, I surmised that if you ladies weren't decent, the door would have been shut."

"Where is Monroe?" Mrs. Alden asked.

"I was on my way upstairs, so I offered to bring tea myself. I hope you ladies don't mind." He nodded to each one as he entered and set the tray down on the proper table. "Besides, if I don't offer to take on Monroe's duties now and again, I lose out on all the gossip. You ladies were saying?" His eyes twinkled, reminding Eleanor of how Saint Nicholas looked in pictures so popular around Christmastide.

Mrs. Alden didn't seem to mind answering. "I was just saying to Daphne and Eleanor that I do hope they'll accept my invitation to the dinner."

"Oh?" Raleigh's dark eyebrows arched; then he smiled as if forcing himself. "My, but we have expanded our guest list greatly, have we not?"

Eleanor hoped she managed to hide her upset. So he was shocked that they were included? And after she had all but insisted that he had been the one who was responsible for their inclusion. Why did he act as though he didn't want them there at all? She felt tears threaten.

Heavenly Father, help me! Have I really developed such strong feelings already? What is wrong with me? What was I thinking?

"This dinner party isn't for the society pages. We can always put on a ball for them later. I just want everyone who means anything to our family to be there," Mrs. Alden proclaimed. "A small affair, really."

"But, of course, I would be delighted for both Miss Kerrs to be present." He smiled at each of them. "I do hope you will be in attendance."

"But, of course," Aunt Daphne assured.

Eleanor contented herself with a slight nod. So Raleigh Alden wanted them there as long as the event wasn't meant for the society pages. As long as he could keep them under wraps, he could pretend not to know them but as seamstresses. As much as she hated to admit it, maybe her aunt was right. Maybe Raleigh Alden was nothing but a snob.

She thought about her earlier silliness when she had run into Aunt Daphne's room and found the Irish lace. She wished she hadn't bothered. One of her old dresses would have to do.

No, even better, she didn't have to go to the party at all.

Chapter 6

Aunt Daphne, I feel a bit puny." Eleanor leaned against the door frame of her aunt's bedroom. She clutched her stomach and groaned.

"You've been feeling a bit puny for a while now." Aunt Daphne placed the palm of her hand on Eleanor's forehead. "You don't seem feverish."

"No. I'll be all right."

"First you bowed out of going to the revival, and now this." She crossed her arms in obvious displeasure. "Don't tell me you don't want to see Raleigh."

Eleanor swallowed. How had her aunt learned so much about her in such a short time?

Aunt Daphne adjusted the sleeve on her emerald green evening dress, which looked well against the light green paint and white cotton curtains decorating her generous room, then turned from her vanity mirror to inspect her niece. Her mouth straightened itself into a tight line. "Don't be ridiculous, child. Raleigh Alden is just a man. And you'll be meeting many more at the party."

"I don't want to meet more men. And my stomach really does hurt." She spoke the truth. Eleanor's stomach pained her and had been protesting off and on for several days, regardless of how much or how little she ate. Even restricting herself to chicken soup hadn't helped. Eleanor entered the room and reclined on the bed, a large affair covered with a blanket crocheted from cream-colored tobacco twine.

"You finished your dress, didn't you?"

"Yes, ma'am."

She had deliberately dawdled over sewing her own dress. But even though she had tried to beg off with the excuse that she was too swamped with orders from clients, Aunt Daphne wouldn't budge. Once she saw Eleanor's outdated gowns, she insisted that Eleanor make herself a new one. "I sewed the last bit of lace on the sleeves this morning."

"Good." She shot Eleanor a look through narrowed eyelids. "Judging by the look of things, you won't get into your dress in time to go. But that's your plan, isn't it?"

Eleanor swallowed before setting the dress on her lap. "I don't understand, Aunt Daphne. Why the sudden change of heart? I thought you didn't want me to go to the dinner. Now you seem as though you want nothing more."

Aunt Daphne cleared her throat. "I just didn't want you getting grand ideas, that's all. I can only be thankful that my best client saw fit to include us in her plans. Of course, we cannot insult her by sending regrets at the last moment."

"I suppose not." Still, Eleanor had the feeling that her aunt wasn't being totally honest.

"Now look here, child," Aunt Daphne remonstrated. "We accepted the invitation, and we're going to go whether we want to or not. I want you to go to your room and get dressed now. And do something with that hair. I'll call Ginny to help you."

Seeing that even sickness wouldn't excuse her from their social obligation, Eleanor sat up, then rose to her feet. "That's all right. I can dress myself."

"What about the buttons in the back?"

Eleanor had forgotten about those. In an effort to add interest to her gown, she had sewn a row of silk-covered buttons a half inch apart from the tip of the neck to the point of the waist. Even with a buttonhook, Ginny would most likely struggle to secure her in the dress.

Aunt Daphne seemed to read her mind. "Yes, vanity is expensive, isn't it?"

Eleanor remembered the cost of the Irish lace. "Yes, it is. Expensive, indeed."

"You'd best get going. The carriage is due to arrive in less than an hour," her aunt advised. "Did Ginny bring you the soup and bread as I asked?"

"Yes, but I'm not hungry. Besides, we'll be eating dinner at the Aldens'. At least, that's what I thought."

"Of course, we'll be eating dinner at the Aldens'. But you certainly don't want to go there on an empty stomach. You'll be too hungry."

"I don't understand."

Aunt Daphne clucked her tongue. "Poor girl. Your mother wasn't able to teach you, was she? And of course, your father wouldn't be expected to teach you proper etiquette regarding a dinner party. Men aren't supposed to know our little secrets."

"Secrets?"

"Yes. Always go to a dinner party—or any other type of social event—on a full stomach. Then you will be able to resist the urge to overeat while you're there."

"You think I overeat?" Eleanor inspected her waist, which didn't show any evidence of a large appetite.

"Of course not. But you don't want to eat as you normally would, because if you do, you may appear to be unladylike. Men watch for those signs."

Eleanor thought back to her earlier years when she enjoyed the camaraderie of social gatherings and partook of delicious food without worrying about criticism. "Aunt Daphne, I don't intend any disrespect, but isn't what you suggest just a bit deceptive?"

"Many a happy marriage is based upon a little bit of deception."

Eleanor wasn't sure how her aunt's cynical statement could be accurate. And since Aunt Daphne had never married, Eleanor questioned her wisdom. Still, she decided to keep her thoughts to herself. "I suppose I'd better be getting dressed."

"Good. Meet me at the front door when you're ready."

An hour and a half later, the carriage pulled in front of the Aldens' home and the driver assisted the ladies in disembarking. No other carriages were positioned in the driveway.

"Apparently we are the last guests to arrive," Aunt Daphne noted.

"I'm certain we're not so very late," Eleanor said, in spite of the fact that she wasn't so sure. She could only hope that her declaration would spare her a speech from her aunt on her tardiness in preparing for the party.

Aunt Daphne contented herself by glancing at her with steely eyes, using her sharp peripheral vision. Eleanor concluded that the coach driver's presence prompted her aunt's effort to refrain from dispensing a lecture.

Eleanor had followed her aunt's advice and eaten a half bowl of Cook's delicious soup and the hot roll provided. As much as she longed for the freedom of childhood that allowed one to eat as one pleased, perhaps her aunt was right. At least her stomach wouldn't embarrass her by growling before dinner, although pains reminded her of its presence now and again.

Monroe answered the front door and directed them to the parlor. The floor and furniture had been waxed to a high gloss for the occasion. Not a knickknack was turned in an odd direction. The candlesticks were filled with new beeswax tapers at least a foot in height.

Instantly, Eleanor felt Raleigh's gaze upon her. She sensed that he had been anticipating her arrival. When she sent him a shy look, interest lit his eyes. Then she remembered his surprise that she and her aunt had been invited to this event. Perhaps he merely noticed her because she was his guest?

He strode over to them and exchanged a brief greeting with her aunt before turning toward her. "Good evening, Eleanor."

"Good evening." Knowing that to do less would be impolite, she extended her hand in greeting. Not hesitating to take the opportunity, he surprised her by brushing his lips briefly against the back of her hand above the knuckles. She became conscious of her rapidly beating heart.

"I trust by your presence here that you are feeling well?"

"Yes, better, thank you." Indeed, her stomach pains had subsided, though they had been replaced by regret that she hadn't gone to the revival with Raleigh. Perhaps her stomach's protests had been spurred by anxiety rather than by a physical malady.

"If I may say so, you look exceptionally lovely tonight."

His words made her every doubt disintegrate. "I am quite pleased that you do say so. And your observation has made me feel more beautiful than I have since. . .since. . ."

Before my mother died.

She couldn't express herself. Instead, her gaze landed on the floor, where she got a good look at Raleigh's black leather wing-tipped shoes.

"I'm as tongue-tied as a schoolgirl. I must look like such a ninny," she murmured.

"Not at all," Raleigh answered.

Although she hadn't intended on his hearing her, Raleigh's response gave her the courage to look into his face.

"I know you have just come out of mourning," he added. "Don't worry. Before you know it, you'll feel at ease at a little soiree such as this—just as if you were drinking tea in your own parlor."

She looked about the room, where the small number of partygoers dressed in finery mingled. "I don't know."

"How about if we find out?" He extended his elbow so she could take his arm. "If I may?" He looked at Eleanor, then Aunt Daphne.

"I hope you don't plan to monopolize her all evening," Aunt Daphne warned. "After all, this is her first time out since my dear sister-in-law passed on."

"Aunt Daphne!" Eleanor admonished. How could her aunt say such a bold thing to their host?

"I'll try not to impose too much," he assured her with a chuckle. "I never force my attentions upon any lady."

"Indeed." Aunt Daphne sent him a sly smile and, with a wave of her fan, strode to another part of the room.

"And you would never need to do so," Eleanor hastened to assure him. "I'm so glad you greeted us, in any event. I need to return the book I borrowed." She handed him the small volume that she had been holding since her arrival.

"Already? My, but you are a fast reader." He set the book on a nearby occasional table, next to a small mixed bouquet of summer wildflowers in a cut-crystal vase.

"Indeed? I thought myself rather a slow one. I've been sewing many dresses and gowns as of late and have had very little time to delve into reading, aside from my morning and evening devotions."

Mrs. Alden's voice rang through the room. "Raleigh!"

Raleigh looked over at the corner where his mother sat, with Aunt Daphne hovering by her hostess seated in a blue velvet and mahogany chair. She crooked her finger, motioning for him to join her. Raleigh nodded and moved his elbow forward. "Why don't we start with my mother?"

"Are you sure?"

"Of course, I'm sure. You don't think you'll get away with not speaking to your hostess, do you?" His tone was teasing.

"And I have no desire to avoid her. She has always been delightful to me." She sent him a smile and followed him to his mother's perch.

Mrs. Alden was, as expected, dressed in the mint green dress that Aunt Daphne had sewn for her. Elaborate embellishments had taken Aunt Daphne a week of almost constant work to sew, but the effort had been worthwhile as far as demonstrating her aunt's sewing expertise. Had Mrs. Alden been her client, Eleanor would have advised her to appear in a dress with fewer adornments, so she could look more dignified as would have been appropriate for a woman of advancing years. But Aunt Daphne had said she didn't care if Mrs. Alden wanted to dress like a schoolgirl—her job was to make her happy. Funny, she didn't look too happy at the moment.

"Raleigh," Mrs. Alden said as soon as proper greetings were exchanged, "have you seen to it that Eleanor is introduced to Mr. Jarvis?"

"She only just arrived." Oddly, Raleigh seemed to be trying to hold back an irritation that had been missing earlier. "Of course, I'll introduce them, Mother. I had no indication there was any special hurry."

Mrs. Alden cleared her throat. "I want all of our guests to become acquainted, of course."

Eleanor surveyed the room. Vera was standing by the fireplace. Unable to control her emotions, she swallowed with pride when she noticed how well Vera's dress looked on her. They had worked together to choose a flattering style and pleasing embellishments, and the result appeared to be a great success. For a moment, Eleanor wished more people were present to appreciate her handiwork. Gaining new admirers would only increase her sewing business.

A proverb from scripture popped into her head. *"He that is greedy of gain troubleth his own house."*

She sighed. "Yes, Lord, I know I have enough."

"What was that?" Raleigh asked.

She flinched. "Oh, nothing. I'm sorry. I was just admiring. . .uh. . .everything."

"Why, thank you, Eleanor." Mrs. Alden's smile looked self-congratulatory. "Now run along, Raleigh, and introduce Eleanor to our other guests."

Eleanor realized that Mrs. Alden didn't mention any need for Aunt Daphne to meet the guests. She looked to her aunt. "Don't you want to meet everyone else, too?"

"Oh, I'll have plenty of time to talk to everyone. You know me. I'm a regular social butterfly. You two go right ahead."

Eleanor nodded, hoping the gesture disguised her wonder. Her aunt didn't seem to be the least bit vexed by what Eleanor would have perceived as a slight. Furthermore, she had cautioned Raleigh not to keep her all evening, yet she had moments later encouraged her to stay by Raleigh's side to be introduced to the other guests. Sometimes Eleanor just couldn't discern what her aunt was thinking.

She glanced at Raleigh. He had pursed his lips. Perhaps he didn't like being told to run along. Eleanor suppressed a chuckle as he led her to where Vera conversed with a man whom Eleanor could only assume was the fabled Flint Jarvis. Dressed in fine style, he appeared in a black evening suit that flattered a trim physique. Eleanor didn't find his aquiline nose or slightly protruding lips appealing, but when he laughed, apparently at some witty comment that Eleanor couldn't hear, his countenance seemed pleasant enough. Eleanor sent a conspiratorial smile Vera's way. Apparently when she was with an attractive man, Vera could display formidable wit and charm.

Eleanor eyed two other men not far away who seemed to be engaged in their own conversation. The first was short and stocky, and while his appearance wasn't displeasing, she saw nothing memorable about him. The second seemed close to Mrs. Alden's age. His black hair was streaked with gray, but his eyes were lively. Eleanor guessed the two had been invited to round out her dinner table. No doubt, since invitations from the Aldens were desirable and they were known for employing the best cook in town, the bachelors were more than happy to oblige.

Dinner. Now there was a thought. Pleasant odors wafted in from the back of the house. Surely the bell to summon them would be ringing soon. Funny, her stomach no longer ailed her at all. Why did being near Raleigh make her feel so much better? Now that she was close to him, she realized that she didn't mind the fact she was being led toward a strange man she had never met.

Raleigh made the introductions with practiced skill.

Flint Jarvis gave Eleanor a passing glance but didn't seem to register much fascination with her. Instead, he spoke to Raleigh. "Have I seen you since I returned from my trip to the Orient?"

"No, I don't believe we have conversed since I moved back to Baltimore."

"The Orient?" Eleanor couldn't help but note. "A journey there sounds quite exotic—and dangerous, Mr. Jarvis."

"Oh, please. *Mr. Jarvis* is my father. Do call me Flint."

Eleanor cut her glance to Raleigh, who sent her a small nod. She wasn't sure why she sought his approval. Still, she was glad he didn't seem to think she would be too bold by accepting Flint's invitation to call him by his Christian name.

"Speaking of names," Raleigh said, smiling at Eleanor. "Flint prides himself on his middle name."

"Oh, what is that?"

"Danger, my girl," Flint answered.

"Danger? Your mother named you *Danger?*"

As the two men burst into laughter, she soon realized why her remark seemed so amusing to them. Flint had been speaking metaphorically, but she had jumped to the conclusion that he had been speaking in the literal sense. Eleanor felt a warm blush rise to her cheeks. *They both must think me a ninny!*

"Oh, I see the joke now," she managed.

"I did catch you off guard, which is understandable," Raleigh said. "I beg your forgiveness."

"None needed," she responded. "I may be the source of amusement one moment, but the joke will be on someone else next time."

"How admirable," Raleigh said.

"I agree," Flint noted. "My real middle name is not that imaginative, though I never run away from a challenge. I know all there is to know about my friend Raleigh, so Miss Kerr, why don't you tell me about your travels?"

"My travels?" Eleanor squirmed. "I'm afraid there is not much to tell."

"Oh? It was my understanding that you aren't from around here."

"Oh, I'm not. But my train trip from Louisiana to Baltimore is the extent of my adventures. And I'm afraid I didn't enjoy the journey enough to be eager to travel more in the future."

"Then maybe you should have taken a luxury train car."

"Perhaps that would have helped." As soon as she realized her confession was an admission that she couldn't afford such expensive train accommodations, again a flush of embarrassment filled her. Truly she was among a class of people where she was out of place.

"Eleanor is a fine businesswoman," Raleigh said. "She is wise not to waste her money on frivolities that only offer temporary pleasure."

Eleanor sent him a grateful look.

"Like the dresses the ladies are wearing tonight?" Flint joked. "I should say a pretty penny was spent on them all."

"And rightfully so," Raleigh hastened to defend her. "Besides, I'm sure they can wear their dresses to many events."

Flint raised his eyebrows. "Then you don't know women, my boy."

"Excuse me," Eleanor said. "It's been lovely meeting you, but I must speak to my aunt."

"I hope we will be seated near one another this evening," Flint said. "I would enjoy hearing about your aspirations of seeing the world. Surely you have some, despite your protests to the contrary."

"No, indeed. I'm afraid I have no aspirations to see the world. Even if I could travel in luxury, I don't think I would take the opportunity. Reading about Old Testament battles is adventure enough for me."

"Well, that is disappointing to hear."

"I'm sorry," she apologized, even though she didn't know why she should have to express regret over her basic personality. She was the way God made her, and she knew He had made no mistake. Then she remembered someone else God made—someone who was more like the type of woman Flint sought. "My aunt wishes to travel. Isn't that right, Raleigh?"

He paused, then nodded quickly. "We've never discussed it, but Eleanor certainly knows her aunt better than I. Together they operate a business sewing fine and frivolous dresses for the local ladies."

"Oh." Flint's eyes took on a glint of embarrassment. Eleanor guessed he wouldn't have made such disparaging comments about the ladies' dresses had he known. "Oh, indeed. And a fine business, I'm sure it is. Anyone who helps our local ladies to appear happier and more beautiful is only doing our fine city proud."

"Thank you."

"So." He looked around the room. "Am I to assume your aunt is the redhead talking to Mrs. Alden?"

"Yes, she is."

Flint put his hands on his hips and inspected Aunt Daphne. Eleanor wasn't sure she felt so comfortable with how he seemed to take in every detail of her appearance. Seeming to notice she was being observed, Aunt Daphne shot her gaze toward him. To Eleanor's shock, she could almost see bolts of lightning flash back and forth between their eyes.

Raleigh appeared to sense the immediate attraction, as well. "I'm assuming you won't object, Flint, if I introduce you properly."

"Not at all." Flint's voice didn't hide his eagerness.

"If you will pardon me," Eleanor said, "I should like to speak to Vera."

The men nodded, and she was excused.

As Eleanor stepped over to her friend and client, who had just broken away from a conversation, she thought about Raleigh. He had not been the least bit miffed at her for bowing out of going to revival services at his church and had defended her to the limit when Flint made tactless remarks. How could she stay upset with him? She couldn't.

Reaching Vera, Eleanor touched her shoulder. "Vera! You look gorgeous."

"Thank you. You did a fine job on my dress." Vera's lips barely moved as she spoke. While she was never one to be overly expressive and ebullient, her manner seemed stilted, even for one so prim.

"Thank you, but it's not just the dress," Eleanor assured her, touching her sleeve. "Your beauty always shines."

"You do exaggerate."

"Not in the least."

Vera didn't seem eager to continue their conversation. Surely she wasn't suddenly taking on an air of snobbery simply because they were among a few of the

Aldens' intimates. Eleanor decided to wait and see what Vera would do next.

Vera looked around the room as though searching for another person to approach. Her gaze rested a little longer on Raleigh than it should have. Eleanor considered commenting on how dashing their host appeared on this particular evening but thought better of it.

"Are you having a good time?" Vera asked, apparently deciding that escape from Eleanor was impossible at the moment.

A sense of sadness filled Eleanor at the thought. Perhaps she had misjudged the extent of Vera's warm feelings toward her, after all. In the meantime, Eleanor wasn't sure how best to respond to Vera's query.

Grateful even to be included in the evening, she searched for a truthful statement. "I haven't been out in so long. This is truly a blessing for me. I'm so appreciative of being included." As soon as she made mention of the last sentiment, Eleanor regretted how much she sounded like the grateful servant rather than a woman who could hold her own amid the other guests. She could only conclude that Flint and his thoughtless comments had unnerved her more than she realized.

"I see you've met Flint Jarvis," Vera noted, looking over toward the bachelors as they conversed with Eleanor's aunt. "Isn't he debonair?"

"Uh, yes. Yes, he is. He seems to have many excellent stories about his travels."

Vera sighed. "I haven't had the privilege of speaking to him at length, but he did share an anecdote with me earlier this evening." Her glance roved toward Flint, and she let out another sigh.

Eleanor let out a little gasp. "Vera! I do believe you're becoming smitten!"

Vera stared at her hands, clasped at her waist, as though they had become an extreme source of interest.

Eleanor placed her hand on Vera's. "Oh, you must take every chance you can to converse with him."

Fear lit Vera's eyes. "No. Never!"

"Never? But why not?"

Vera shook her head. "Never. That's all I have to say."

Chapter 7

Vera and Eleanor had moved to a group of chairs off to the side, hoping to mute the noise from some of the louder partygoers. Raleigh chose to break away from his conversation across the room and join them. Nevertheless, Eleanor was determined to get to the bottom of Vera's strange behavior. At the same time, she didn't want to embarrass the young woman in front of Raleigh or make an issue out of the fact that Vera seemed especially interested in a conversation her aunt and Flint Jarvis were having near the punch table.

She kept her voice low. "Vera, why wouldn't you want to speak to Mr. Jarvis? This is a party, after all. Aren't you supposed to converse with all the guests?" Eleanor knew her friend was shy, but she hadn't expected her to react so violently at the idea of talking to a man. "And certainly he would be flattered by your attentions."

Vera crossed her arms and stared at Flint, who was holding court by the unlit gray stone fireplace as he spoke to enraptured guests. "I won't debate that point. Isn't any man flattered by the attentions of any woman?"

"Vera!" Raleigh intervened. "Do you really hold us men in such low esteem?"

"Aren't you flattered by the attentions of all women?" Her lips tightened as her chin tilted upward.

"Only the pretty ones." The mischievous look in his eyes showed that he spoke in jest. Yet when he offered a glimpse to Eleanor, she knew he meant to say she was one of the pretty ones.

Eleanor fanned herself in the vain hope that she might discourage a blush. "I'm sure he'd be delighted to have you listen to his accounts of travel to the Orient. I'm afraid I was quite a disappointment to him as an audience."

"You? I can't imagine that you would be a disappointment to anyone," Vera's voice was devoid of sarcasm.

"Hear, hear," Raleigh agreed.

Eleanor's feelings toward Raleigh were growing more tender by the moment. "I appreciate your vote of confidence, however misplaced it may be. Aunt Daphne wants me to be a traveling companion for her, but alas, I have no interest in world travel."

"I see no fault in that," Raleigh assured her.

"Neither do I," Vera agreed, "but I do believe it would be quite glamorous to take a steamship cruise."

"In first class, of course. I fancy that steerage isn't quite what you have in mind," Raleigh noted.

"I can't even afford steerage." As though she suddenly realized the implication of what she said, Vera turned an apologetic face to Raleigh. "Not that you aren't quite generous to me, Raleigh. I sometimes feel as though I hardly do enough to earn my keep."

"I assure you, though I love my mother dearly, I have no doubt that you earn more than your keep. I would be at a loss to keep her in the good humor that she stays in because of your devoted companionship to her."

"Thank you."

"If only she were in robust health, then I could contemplate the possibility of sending you both off on a cruise together." He folded his arms and peered at the corner of the ceiling. Eleanor could almost see the cogs turning in his head. "Perhaps with her doctor's permission. . ."

"Again, I thank you, but that is quite all right. I'm not sure such a situation is what I had in mind." Vera's posture slumped, a sign Eleanor took as a gesture of defeat. She wondered why Vera acted so.

Eleanor decided to change the subject. "I must say, Mr. Jarvis seems to have a lot of leisure time to make complicated journeys. I wonder what his business is." She took a sudden interest in a bouquet of summer flowers atop an occasional table, so she could avoid eye contact with either Raleigh or Vera. Asking about a person's source of income bordered on discourtesy, but she had to wonder.

"I don't know all the details, but he has told me he keeps an office near the harbor," Raleigh told her.

Eleanor nodded, even though she still wasn't sure what he meant. Did Mr. Jarvis hold an ordinary job? If so, he would never have the time or the financial resources to enjoy such an extravagant lifestyle. But if he was an heir or was independently wealthy through some other means, why would he need an office near the wharf? She wanted to ask more but knew that to probe would be the height of rudeness. She had been bold enough to show any interest in his employment.

She watched as Vera looked over at Flint and his rapt audience. "Mr. Jarvis doesn't seem the least bit disappointed in your aunt."

Eleanor inspected the twosome. "Indeed." She raised her eyebrows despite her best attempts not to appear shocked. She had never seen her aunt look so ebullient and alive. Considering her proclivity for attention-getting bright colors and her lack of reticence in any situation, that feat was quite an accomplishment.

"Yes, I'd say the two of them don't need me. They seem to be getting along splendidly," Raleigh said. "Why, they are so engrossed in their own conversation that I don't believe they even noticed earlier when I excused myself."

Eleanor held back an expression of surprise. Who would have thought that her aunt would become so animated with the evening's mystery man? Setting the puzzlement out of her mind, she decided to address Raleigh. "I can't imagine anyone being so obtuse as not to notice your absence."

"So you would miss me should I go away?" An expectant light haunted his eyes.

Surprised by his response, Eleanor realized that her statement had been too bold. She searched for the proper quip. "Oh, you are such a jokester." She resisted the urge to touch his arm, choosing instead to fan herself.

"Do you really think I am joking?"

Vera rescued her. "Raleigh, really, must you be so probing?"

Eleanor sent her an appreciative look. To her surprise, she caught something strange in Vera's expression—almost as though she were peeved. But over what? Surely Raleigh's silly question hadn't provoked her so.

"I beg your pardon," Raleigh apologized. "I suppose I'm caught up in the romance of the evening." He looked at Eleanor but not long enough for her to return his gaze.

"It's so lovely to watch two people become enamored with one another." Vera's voice held a hint of wistfulness. "Don't you agree, Raleigh?"

"Indeed." Raleigh looked into Eleanor's eyes.

His repeated gestures sent her stomach into a pleasant lurch. She wanted to look into his eyes in a daring way but discovered she couldn't overcome her sudden feeling of shyness.

"Indeed," Vera said.

Eleanor turned her attention to her friend. Vera's voice seemed clipped, almost as though she were vexed. Why would Vera have any reason to be vexed? Unless she was jealous of Aunt Daphne. Yes, she reasoned. She was jealous of Aunt Daphne. That had to be the reason for her sudden foul mood.

"Vera," Eleanor said, "why don't you join Aunt Daphne and Mr. Jarvis?"

"Me?" Vera cut her gaze to the pair. "But they look as though they are conversing quite well without any distraction."

"Oh, I'm sure they won't mind."

"But your aunt Daphne. . ."

"Don't vex yourself about her."

"But Mr. Jarvis seems so enamored with her," Vera objected.

"Perhaps, but she has no intention of following up on any prospective suitors. Marriage is the farthest thing from her mind," Eleanor assured her, and she meant it.

"Eleanor's right," Raleigh agreed. "Are you not aware that—if you'll pardon me—but isn't Miss Kerr at least ten years older than Mr. Jarvis?" He looked to Eleanor with a searching expression.

"Far be it from me to tell her age."

Raleigh chuckled. "Of course. What was I thinking? But to look at them, well, let's just say that an odd match they would make, certainly."

"Certainly," Eleanor didn't hesitate to concur.

"So, Vera, do go on and join them," Raleigh encouraged her.

"Well, all right." Vera excused herself and headed toward the gregarious twosome.

Eleanor watched her aunt's expression go from enchanted to irked. A guilty pang shot through her. Had she been wrong to let Raleigh encourage Vera?

"Now, my dear," Raleigh said, "will you not join me in a fresh glass of lemonade?"

My dear? Had he just called her *my dear*? A shiver of happiness traveled up and down her spine. "Oh yes. But of course."

⸻

Later over dinner, Raleigh watched as Flint kept his attentions directed at Daphne. Poor Vera tried her mightiest to attract his interest, but no matter how often she attempted to divert attention to herself, Flint found some way to turn the conversation back to the elder seamstress.

Raleigh wouldn't have believed the turn of events if he hadn't been there to witness them himself. He felt pity for Vera. The girl was shy and easily blended in with the beige wallpaper patterned with blue roses in their dining room. He wished Vera and Eleanor had remembered the hue of paper before dressing Vera. He suppressed a sigh as he watched her do her best to put on a show of confidence, batting her long lashes at Flint, touching her coiffure with her fingertips to attract attention to her hair and face, talking just a notch too loudly. He had never seen the girl act in such a manner.

Eleanor, on the other hand, was her usual composed self. No matter what the circumstance, she always seemed to know what to say, the proper inflection of voice to employ, and when to comment. Though she was a mere seamstress, Eleanor conducted herself with the poise of a woman trained for much larger expectations in life. He had a feeling that moving to Baltimore had been a comedown for her.

He had concluded that seeming out of place was a factor that attracted them to each another. Beginning a new life in a different location was never easy, as he had learned from his recent relocation. Everyone—even people one may have known before—was but a stranger. He could only hope that this little dinner made Eleanor feel just a bit less alone.

Not that she would be alone for long. Her smooth skin was touched by pink in her cheeks. Stunning eyes glimmered in the candlelight. Why hadn't he taken closer notice before? He suppressed a sigh. She was the image of modern loveliness, reminding him of a ladies' periodical advertisement for the latest beauty cream. Surely Flint would have been attentive to her the entire evening had she not rebuffed his only interest—traveling the world.

Flint. What an unlikely match for Eleanor, in any event. At least he thought as much. He eyed his mother, who beamed as she relished her long-forgotten role as belle of the ball. Years had melted from her face. If he hadn't known better, he would have thought that she fancied herself a teenager again, holding court among all her guests, including a number of prospective suitors. Yet her eyes kept darting back and forth from Flint, to Eleanor, then back again. Why did he sense that this evening's mission was more than just to reunite friends and acquaintances to celebrate his return? Could matchmaking have been a secret agenda? And if so, for whom?

He couldn't help but wonder. If Mother had hoped that Vera would find a suitor, judging from the girl's interest in Flint, she could count the evening a success. Yet he couldn't imagine that Mother would want her companion, a young woman of whom she thought highly, to marry and hence leave her employment. Then why? What intrigue was happening before his eyes that he was witnessing but could not decipher?

Not wishing Vera to make a fool of herself, Raleigh resolved to engage her in conversation from time to time, hoping to lure her away from her obvious grabs at Flint's attention. He wondered what topic of conversation might interest his mother's companion.

"So, Vera," he ventured, "how do you think Mother's new liniment is working for her?"

"She seems to be doing better with it, thank you." Question answered, Vera smiled, then turned her face back toward Flint, who was outlining his plans to explore the Caribbean.

As soon as was polite, Raleigh tried again. "Vera, what book are you reading now?"

When she turned back toward him this time, the look on her face conveyed no interest or pleasure. "Dickens."

He waited for her to name the Charles Dickens title, but she didn't comply. "A fine author, indeed." He opened his mouth to elaborate, but she cut him off.

"Yes. Quite intriguing." With that, she lifted her spoon to partake of the lobster bisque and tilted her head toward Flint, who still held his audience, which included his mother and Daphne, bewitched.

"Dickens certainly makes Old England come alive," Eleanor, sitting on his other side, suggested.

Miffed by Vera's multiple rebukes, he felt no guilt in taking notice of Eleanor. Let Vera make a fool of herself, for all he cared. He had tried enough times to rescue her. Let her wallow in her own folly.

Raleigh sent Eleanor what he knew to be his most devastating smile. "Yes, Dickens certainly does make Old England come alive. It's almost as though he lived through it himself."

"You are too witty." Eleanor's chest shook with laughter.

He could see by her unabashed response that her amusement was sincere, not an act to convince him that he was oh so charming. Her sincerity endeared her to him even more than she already was. In fact, he hadn't planned on becoming her defender that evening. What did he care if Flint wanted to make a remark or two about women's frivolities? Yet when Eleanor's face showed that she didn't take kindly to his observations, Raleigh found himself stepping in. And then later with Vera, he boosted Eleanor with more compliments—sentiments he suddenly realized he meant in all seriousness. What was happening to him?

As they talked about nothing and everything, reluctantly allowing themselves to be interrupted by other dinner guests when they cared to join the discussion, Raleigh studied Eleanor. Her beautiful brown eyes sparkled in the candlelight. He hadn't noticed before how random strands of red shone amid her auburn tresses. Her voice sounded to him like a pleasant melody, expressing high-minded ideas. No matter what plans his mother may or may not have had for the evening, he knew one thing: The threat of Flint, weak as it turned out to be, had left him with no uncertain feelings.

He was falling in love with the beautiful seamstress.

—◆—

"Oh, Eleanor, I can't believe what a night I had." Aunt Daphne's voice filled the foyer.

"Shh, Aunt Daphne," Eleanor cautioned. "You'll wake the servants."

"Let them wake up. Let them share in my happiness." Aunt Daphne clasped her hands and stared at the ceiling, although Eleanor could see from her vacant expression that her mind wasn't focused on the wainscoting.

"Oh, Aunt Daphne, it was only a dinner party. Surely you couldn't have fallen madly in love with a strange man over the course of one evening."

"But oh, what courses they were!" Aunt Daphne noted. "Escargot, fruit and cheese, lobster bisque, salmon, vegetable salad, crown rack of lamb and potatoes, then a fine dessert of fresh berries and cream." She sighed.

Eleanor recalled the feast with no small amount of delight herself. "Yes, they were. I do believe that was the most splendid meal I have ever experienced. And the company and conversation were even more delightful." A picture of Raleigh popped into her head. She didn't urge it to leave.

"Ah, yes," Aunt Daphne agreed. "Mr. Flint Jarvis is an extraordinary man!"

Flint Jarvis? Oh, yes. Reality brought Eleanor's mind home. "I could see you thought so. And so could everyone else."

"Is that so?" Aunt Daphne turned her nose skyward. "Let them see."

"Let them see, eh?" Eleanor tilted her nose at her aunt. "And let them talk, too?"

"And let them talk." Aunt Daphne's voice didn't seem as strong, and her head returned to its normal position.

"What about Vera?"

"Vera, indeed. I saw how she flirted with Flint." Aunt Daphne shrugged. "But all's fair in love and war."

"But what about her feelings? She's so shy and sheltered."

"Can you say that ten times very quickly?"

"Joke all you like, but—"

"She's not my client," Aunt Daphne snapped.

"Speaking of clients, does Mr. Jarvis know you're a seamstress?"

"Of course. Why do you ask?"

Eleanor shrugged. "He made a disparaging remark about women's frivolous dresses, a remark that Raleigh rebuffed."

"Oh, you know Flint and his dry wit."

Eleanor tried again. "Dry wit to you, but I do believe Vera's interest in him is serious."

Aunt Daphne's lips twisted, showing that Eleanor's chastisement had not fallen on deaf ears. "I'm not worried about Vera. I've known her ever since she became Mrs. Alden's companion five years ago. She has no other ambition."

Eleanor crossed her arms over her chest. "Is that what you really think? Or what you only hope?"

"Why. . .why," she stammered, "Vera and I can't be compared. We're so. . .so different."

"Yes. She is much younger than you are, I'm afraid. Much closer to Mr. Jarvis's age, perhaps?"

Aunt Daphne sniffed. "I'll have you to know that I am very well preserved for my age."

"That is even worse—if you are, indeed, older than you appear."

"How can you even think of speaking to me with such insolence?"

"I beg your deepest indulgence," Eleanor hastened to apologize. "It's just that. . .well. . .people like to talk when gentlemen pay court to ladies a bit older themselves."

"And you think that's what happened here?"

"I confess, I do." Eleanor decided not to be more specific and mention the others' observations.

Aunt Daphne shot her a mean look.

"Forgive me. But if I am not honest with you, who will be?"

"Dear, dear girl. I suppose you are right." A light of worry fell upon her face. "Did I really behave as badly as all that?"

"Oh no, Aunt Daphne. I would never say that you behaved badly."

"Really?"

"Really."

Aunt Daphne let out a large sigh. "I suppose a confession is in order. I thought you were the one I would have offended tonight, if I offended anyone."

"Me? Don't be ridiculous."

"Then Mrs. Alden's plan must not have been as obvious as I told her I thought it would be." Aunt Daphne paused.

Plan? Eleanor remained silent, knowing that her aunt wouldn't be able to resist filling the stillness with the sound of her voice.

"Mrs. Alden thought that Mr. Jarvis would be quite taken with you."

Eleanor didn't know how to respond. "I suppose I should be flattered. Mr. Jarvis is obviously a popular man." A popular bon vivant, indeed. But he had impressed her not in the least. Raleigh, the man she had seen time and time again in circumstances nothing short of ordinary, was the one who had captured her heart.

"Yes, Flint is quite popular," her aunt agreed, bringing Eleanor back to the present.

"But why would Mrs. Alden care about my romantic prospects?" Eleanor asked.

Aunt Daphne opened her mouth, then shut it just as quickly. A moment passed before she decided to respond. "Never mind. As I said, all's fair in love and war. I wasn't in favor of meddling before, and I'm certainly not in favor of trying my hand at matchmaking again. But I do want your assurance: You are not interested in Mr. Jarvis in the least, are you?"

"Certainly not. I have no interest in him. I gather from your query that you plan to encourage him?"

"Indeed I do." Aunt Daphne patted Eleanor's hand. "But don't you worry a bit. Knowing you, I'm sure you can content yourself with your Bible as a companion until the Lord sends someone else."

So she hadn't noticed Raleigh's attention toward her. Eleanor had a feeling that Aunt Daphne's lack of observation was for the best. "Let us retire, shall we? The time to awaken tomorrow morning to prepare for church will be here all too soon," Eleanor pointed out. "Good night, Aunt Daphne."

"Good night."

Eleanor headed up the stairs, eager to be alone, so she could contemplate the evening's events. Funny, the mysterious Flint Jarvis had turned out not to be so fascinating after all. Rather dull, in her eyes. Yet he enthralled all the others. Eleanor wondered how he could be so gallant and dress in such fine clothing if, indeed, he held an insignificant job. Slim evidence that something was amiss, but Eleanor didn't like where her instincts were taking her. She had to find out more about the mysterious Flint Jarvis before her aunt could be hurt. And she knew just where to begin.

Chapter 8

Eleanor felt a twinge of nervousness on her way to the Alden house. Was she being silly in telling Raleigh about her aunt's unmitigated attraction to Flint Jarvis?

She suppressed a sigh of exasperation. Ever since they had returned from the party, Aunt Daphne had spoken of nothing but Mr. Jarvis. Eleanor could distract her briefly by commenting on the dresses everyone wore, but the conversation would soon turn back to the world traveler.

Eleanor wished nothing more than for her aunt to be happy—even to see the world and leave Eleanor behind to hold down the business—if, and only if, the man she chose as a companion was worthy of her. And Eleanor was not at all sure that Mr. Jarvis fit the bill.

She remembered Mr. Jarvis and shuddered. He kept his audience of men and women alike enraptured with tales of exotic journeys, assuring them from time to time of his reluctance to boast. Eleanor grimaced. Reluctant? He hadn't stopped bragging the entire evening. The only time he seemed reticent was when one of the men asked how he managed to tear himself away from his occupation for months at a time so he could take long vacations. Then his mouth clamped shut more tightly than a house shuttered in anticipation of a hurricane.

As she disembarked from the carriage, she realized she wouldn't have to knock on the door. She spied Raleigh sitting on a lawn chair near a magnolia tree, looking over some papers. Her heart pounded. An unbidden image of what life with Raleigh would be like popped into her head. She could see herself walking across the freshly manicured lawn under a cloudless sky of blue, bringing him lemonade and cookies—lemonade that she had squeezed with her own hands and cookies that smelled of fresh cinnamon and had been baked with her love.

A second image of him entering the house after a hard day at court came into focus. He would breeze through the front doorway and head without hesitation to the drawing room, where Eleanor would be awaiting his arrival. She would be ready with coffee that had just been brewed, its bracing odor filling the room with a hospitable air. The evening paper would be folded so that his favorite section was immediately readable. His slippers would be ready for his tired feet. She had never seen his slippers, but she imagined them to be fashioned of black kid leather. Once he was settled, they would exchange accounts of their day, relishing one another's company.

Her daydreaming led to her steps slowing their pace. Perhaps dawdling was for the best, since she didn't want to appear too eager to see him.

He looked up from his papers and eyed her, pleasure evident in his expression. He rose from his seat and ambled toward her. "Eleanor!" he cried as soon as he was within earshot. "What brings you here on this fine day?"

The sound of his voice reminded her of a delightful symphony. And if she could judge by his rapt expression, he seemed glad to see her, too.

She swallowed and wished she had thought to drape a piece of cloth or two in the crook of her arm so she could appear to be on business. As it was, surely she appeared rather bold to be visiting as though she were an intimate of the family. Then again, she wished she could talk to Vera to gain knowledge of her account of the party. Perhaps she could at that. Yes, that would be an excellent excuse.

For now, she had been pressed to answer a query from Raleigh. She would never admit she was glad to see him, despite the fact that she was. "I thought I might see Vera."

He grinned. "You want a full accounting of her version of the dinner party, eh?"

"And they say men don't understand women in the least," she teased.

"I claim no special understanding of the minds of ladies," he said, "but I can make an educated guess from time to time."

"Speaking of the party, my aunt certainly considers it the social event of the season."

He chuckled. "I'm not so sure anyone else would give our little soiree such a grand title, but I'm glad to hear she enjoyed herself. I trust you did, as well?" His voice held a question of hope.

"Yes, yes, indeed. The food was outstanding, and the conversation even more so, present company included." Realizing she had been too forward, she cast her gaze downward. At that moment, she noticed that the Aldens' lawn looked exceptionally green, much greener than the others nearby. Or was she imagining the degree of its emerald sparkle?

"I agree."

The soft tone of his voice encouraged her to look into his face. He was just as handsome under the unforgiving glare of sunshine as he had appeared amid flickering flames of beeswax candles, a condition that tended to flatter even the craggiest skin. But he looked just as vigorous, his complexion as healthy, his hair as shiny in broad daylight. Perhaps even more so.

"You do?" she blurted.

"Yes, I enjoyed the company and conversation immensely." His blue eyes took on a gentle light, and his voice remained low in volume. He moved just a bit closer to her.

Unable to form an intelligent response, she inwardly blamed her sudden awkwardness on the spicy bay rum scent he wore. She resisted the desire to clear her throat—an action that would make a grating, unladylike sound that was sure to prove unappealing.

"Oh, yes. Our conversation," he said. "I remember now. I promised to loan you my copy of *Romeo and Juliet*."

"Oh, yes. Yes, you did. I look forward to reading that. I do hope to see it performed someday."

"Baltimore is a big and important city that attracts people of high culture. I'm sure a traveling company will soon visit, and we can see it then. Or even a local production may be staged at some point."

Was he inviting her to see the play with him? She hid her anticipation under a bland mask. Surely issuing an invitation to an indefinite event at an unspecified date in the far future was simple—and noncommittal—enough that he could take the leap with little risk.

"Perhaps," she agreed. "But in the meantime, I assure you I have plenty of entertainment with my aunt at present."

"Oh?"

She swallowed. "Ever since she got back from the dinner party, all she can talk about is Mr. Flint Jarvis."

"Really?" He glanced at the empty, wrought iron lawn chairs and gestured toward them. "Please, won't you sit with me for a moment? Unless Vera is expecting you at a certain time, that is."

"No. No, she isn't," Eleanor had to admit. She decided to take him up on his offer to seat herself, in spite of the fact that the wrought iron chairs weren't especially inviting. Since they were situated under an oak, she glanced at the portion where her dress would touch, to be sure the fabric wouldn't encounter any outdoor debris. Only after she was satisfied that her garment would remain pristine did she sit.

"Do tell me about your aunt. You can trust me to keep anything you say in confidence."

Eleanor had visited with all intent of unabashedly sharing her concerns with Raleigh, but now that she was with him, the reality that she could be construed as betraying her aunt weighed on her mind. She hesitated.

"Come now, my dear. Aren't we the greatest of friends by now?"

My dear. There was that name again—a sweet nothing that nevertheless sent a pleasant shiver through her. She knew she had to speak with caution, lest she reveal too much. "Yes, I do feel we have a wonderful friendship. I am quite honored by that fact."

"On the contrary, I am the one who enjoys the honor."

She had watched carefully for any hint of deception in his voice or face but found none. She couldn't help but marvel at the fact that the man whom her aunt had found so distastefully cheap was now her friend—possibly her best friend here in Baltimore. She watched Raleigh settle back into his chair as much as a body is able to settle on unyielding wrought iron. She could see that he wasn't about to pressure her into voicing any observation against her will.

Eleanor took a moment to collect her thoughts. She inhaled, the gesture bringing to her attention the fresh scent of the evenly clipped grass. Noticing that the azalea bushes underneath the front windows of the house had lost their blooms, she wondered what color they would produce come next spring. In the meantime, floppy white petunias had made their appearance along the sides of the walkway. She peered at the white fence that blocked from view a generous vegetable garden, which consumed much of the side and backyards. Oh, to enjoy such space, with enough room to sow such a variety of plant life!

She glanced at Raleigh and noticed he wasn't even looking at her. Instead, he seemed to be making similar observations. She wondered how much he could really appreciate the yard when he had grown up in this house.

The realization that she couldn't linger all day struck her. *Lord, let me speak to Raleigh, whom I know to be Thy fellow servant, with wisdom. Let the purity of my motives be apparent. May Raleigh's response be led by Thy wisdom, as well. I submit my petition to Thee humbly and in the name of Thy Son, Jesus Christ. Amen.*

She spoke, the sound of her voice breaking into the stillness. "Raleigh."

He looked upon her, his comely features filled with kindness. "Yes?"

"I hope you realize that I do not mean to gossip, and certainly I do not intend to make any but the most flattering observation about my own aunt. I only mention her infatuation because I worry so about her."

He leaned toward her. "You worry? I must say, I find your concern rather charming. She took care of herself for many years before your arrival. I have the impression that she can continue to take care of herself now."

"Perhaps, but I have a feeling she has never encountered anyone like Mr. Jarvis in the past. She has spoken of nothing but him ever since the party, and her ramblings have become quite tiresome, I hate to say."

He chuckled. "I'm not at all sure that a little flirtation at a social function is anything to fret about."

"I think she considers it more than a flirtation," Eleanor confided. "I'm afraid she is in love after just one evening, and I suspect she is not being over-confident. I suspect her feelings are returned."

"And what if they are? I'm sure your aunt will see to it that you are always well taken care of. And you told me yourself that your father in Louisiana is concerned about your welfare above anything else." He allowed his gaze to catch hers. "Although if I may be so bold, your absence would cause the city of Baltimore to lose much of its sparkle."

"How you do talk, Raleigh." She clutched her fingers around her lace fan until she became conscious of each rib. Considerable restraint was needed to keep her from employing it to good use. "Please understand that I am not concerned about myself."

"I believe you. In fact, your involvement with others is one of your most endearing qualities."

Eleanor wasn't used to such flattery. This time, she decided a good whiff of fresh air was what she needed. She extended her fan and waved it as casually as she could, considering how her heart fluttered. "I do have some reservations about Mr. Jarvis." She hesitated. "I never should have mentioned this to you. You are my friend, but you are also his friend, after all. I am putting you in a most unfair position even to express the least bit of concern. Forget I ever said anything. I beg your deepest indulgence. If you'll excuse me, I'll be on my way." She rose from her seat.

He followed suit. "No, no. Please. I'm the one who should be asking your deepest pardon, and indeed, I do. Please, feel free to speak with the utmost frankness. What is your worry, and how might I be of assistance in easing your mind?"

Eleanor took in a breath and looked into his eyes to search for his real feelings. His expression was kind, and he really did seem to be concerned along with her. "All right, then. I saw the look of interest in Mr. Jarvis's eyes as he held court with my aunt. There was no denying it."

"Surely that doesn't surprise you. Anyone can see that your aunt is still a beautiful woman."

"Agreed. But to my way of thinking, Mr. Jarvis puts on far too many airs. And he seems far too wealthy for a man who claims to hold an insignificant position in the wharf district."

"Is that what he claims? That his position is not one of significance? I would find that hard to believe, myself."

"So you don't know exactly what he does for a living?"

"He mentioned in passing that he's in shipping. I must explain."

"Oh. I see." So he didn't know as much as Eleanor had thought. Still, now that she had broached the topic, she had to press on or abandon the subject forever. "But can't the term *shipping* mean almost anything here in Baltimore? Why, what if he's a smuggler?" She clenched her fists at the thought.

"A smuggler?" Raleigh's laugh echoed against the tree trunks, and back. "What an imagination you have. What type of books did you say you used to read back in Louisiana?"

Eleanor bristled. "You know only too well." Recovering her composure, she continued. "I know that not every man is honorable."

"But Eleanor, if we accused every man who works at the wharf of being a smuggler, then half of Baltimore would be thrown in jail tonight."

"True," she conceded. "But you can't tell me exactly what he does. Have you ever handled any of his financial affairs as his lawyer so you would know for certain?"

"No, I can't say that I have."

"And you have never witnessed him at his office."

"No, but why would I? I have no concerns in the shipping business."

"So, then, he could be doing anything and you wouldn't know about it. Why, he could even be a thief—or worse—and you would be completely in the dark."

Raleigh didn't answer for a moment. He tightened his lips and stared forward, his eyes adopting a blank light as though they looked but didn't observe what they were seeing. "I suppose."

"I have grown fond of Aunt Daphne since my arrival, and I would be loath to see her begin to keep company with a man of ill repute."

"As would I. But what do you recommend that I do about it?"

"Could you find it in your heart to investigate further? Just to ease my mind and to protect my aunt. After all, she is more than just a seamstress to your dear mother. Anyone can see that Mrs. Alden is quite fond of Aunt Daphne."

"I won't deny that. But to poke my nose into another man's affairs, where it doesn't belong. . ." His lips twisted into an uncertain line. "You're asking me to take an awfully big risk."

"You have many important clients. I'm sure you know how to poke and prod without being observed."

He didn't answer right away but peered into her eyes. Sensing that to do anything else would make her seem less than determined, she returned his stare. Not for the first time, she noticed the purity of the color in his irises. They caught the light like jewels.

"You have such a pretty face," he observed.

I do? The fact that he was willing to express himself in such a way made her wish she could dance without seeming foolish.

He cleared his throat. "And with such beauty, you need not worry about business."

Her feet, which had felt so light an instant ago, now seemed to be immersed in concrete. Did Raleigh, seemingly such an astute and modern man, think she was dumb just because she was a woman? "How dare you!"

"I beg your pardon. I didn't mean—"

"Don't try to wriggle out of this one," she insisted. "I know exactly what you mean. You don't need to patronize me, Raleigh Alden! I am more than a pretty face. I'm as smart as any man. Maybe even smarter than some." Another thought occurred to her. "I can't help but wonder why you are so unwilling to help me, considering all that my aunt means to your mother."

And how much I had once hoped I meant to you.

Digging her heel into the ground in hopes of gaining enough confidence not to wither, she added, "Perhaps you're so reticent to make a few casual inquiries about your friend Flint Jarvis because you are the one with something to hide."

"Something to hide? Me? Never!" he exclaimed. "How can you even suggest such a foolish thing?"

Deciding that she would be better off if she let Raleigh's newly awakened ire work in her favor, Eleanor didn't answer.

"I'll show you I have nothing to hide. And neither does Flint. I'm sure of it."

"Good. Then you can truly relish the sweet victory of proving me wrong."

"Sweet victory, indeed," he said. "Yes, it will be sweet. I have no need to tolerate such an insult. I will investigate Flint, if for no other reason than to show you just how mistaken you are."

———

Raleigh was so peeved by the time Eleanor departed that he hardly noticed she had not ventured in to visit Vera as she had professed was her purpose. So she had come to see only him after all, to send him out to investigate Flint.

He remembered that he had neglected to get the book for her. Never mind. At least it offered him an excuse to see her again.

See her again? Why would he want to see such an irritating woman again? What was he thinking? How could his foolish heart betray him so? Why, Eleanor Kerr was by far the most exasperating, demanding, nosy, vexing, imaginative...romantic, beautiful, smart, stunning...

He let out a groan. He tried again to focus on her irksome qualities but to no avail. Her favorable qualities made themselves too apparent.

Raleigh thought back over their conversation. She hadn't been ruffled by his declaration that they were the greatest of friends. In fact, she seemed completely in agreement—certainly not displeased. But he realized that he wished their bonds surpassed acquaintanceship.

He would see her again, surely. He needed no fresh excuse, not after she demanded that he investigate Flint. And he knew she wouldn't rest until he came up with an answer for her—an answer that would satisfy her curiosity. She was a formidable presence when she chose to be, and she wouldn't be brushed off with a vague response.

He sighed. How had he let himself get sidelined into such a distasteful project?

Raleigh knew exactly how. He wanted to please Eleanor, even if it meant sticking his nose where it definitely didn't belong.

———

Two weeks had passed, and Eleanor still hadn't heard from Raleigh. Even worse, Flint Jarvis had developed the habit of visiting unannounced—and uninvited, as far as she was concerned—almost every evening. The hours between dinner and bedtime, which Aunt Daphne once used to catch up on the day's sewing for clients, were now lost to endless flirtations as she sat in the parlor and listened to Mr. Jarvis tell of his adventures again and again.

At first Eleanor didn't mind so much. She found some pleasure in watching as Aunt Daphne giggled and fluttered her eyelashes at him. Eleanor watched the years melt away from her. But as Mr. Jarvis began to repeat his tales, embellishing them so that each adventure became grander and more dangerous, Eleanor wondered if he had lost his ability—or his desire—to distinguish fact from fiction.

One evening after a particularly long visit, Aunt Daphne led her into the sewing room so they could organize their projects for the next day. She chattered so much that Eleanor wondered if her aunt was accomplishing anything.

Finally, Eleanor summoned the nerve to confront her aunt. "Aunt Daphne, don't you find it interesting how Mr. Jarvis changes his story just a wee bit with each retelling?"

Aunt Daphne set a pattern on her table. "Whatever do you mean?"

Eleanor swallowed. "Well, on Tuesday he said his last trip to Kansas City was quite ordinary. On Thursday he said he encountered bank robbers, but he merely witnessed the scene as police took them away. But today, he claimed to wrestle one of them down to the floor at risk to his own life."

"Yes, he does lead quite an exciting life, doesn't he?"

Eleanor sat at her seat and halfheartedly sorted through several spools of thread. "But wouldn't you think that he would have mentioned something that exciting on the first telling? After all, it isn't every day that one meets bank robbers. Not even in Kansas City."

"Indeed!" Aunt Daphne plopped in her chair, took out her fan, and waved it in front of her face, not in the coy manner she employed in front of Mr. Jarvis, but in the nonchalant way of a woman sincerely seeking to cool her face against the elements.

Her actions made Eleanor realize that she could be feeling a bit more fresh herself on such a heated summer evening. She withdrew her everyday fan of stiff cotton embellished with plain lace and fanned herself. Moving the hot air around helped to relieve her somewhat, although not nearly as much as she would have liked.

"Clearly we aren't concentrating on this work. It's too late, and we're too tired and excited. Perhaps I should make some lemonade," Eleanor suggested, hoping the gesture of friendship would cool off both their bodies and tempers. "Would you care for some?"

"Yes, I do believe I would."

The women rose and, after Aunt Daphne extinguished the lights, made the short journey to the kitchen. Once there, Aunt Daphne reached for the lemons.

Eleanor shooed her away. "No, no. Allow me. You sit and rest."

Aunt Daphne took her up on her offer and situated herself in the chair the cook used when she took a short break or when she shelled peas or shucked corn. "Why don't you make enough for tomorrow night, as well? Flint seems to enjoy our lemonade."

Eleanor eyed the empty pitcher fashioned of clear glass, a reminder left from the evening. "Yes, he certainly does."

"Just so you are aware, he will be stopping by tomorrow evening in time to take me to dinner. I gave Cook the night off. You won't object to getting supper on your own, will you?"

"Of course not."

"I'm sure you don't mind escaping from his stories," Aunt Daphne noted, "although I really don't think it's his storytelling that bothers you."

"I don't mind stories. But travel is only of passing interest to me, and I'm not accustomed to those who embellish their tales." Eleanor felt herself squeezing a defenseless lemon with more vigor than needed. The scent of the pulverized fruit enlivened her, yet made her feel more relaxed at the same time. She rescued a stray seed and placed it on the wooden counter.

"So you say." Aunt Daphne allowed a tense silence to hang in the air before she spoke again. "Why don't you tell me the real reason you are so opposed to my suitor. I know you're not the type to be jealous. Are you worried that if I marry you won't have a job here any longer?" Aunt Daphne asked. "If that's your concern, think nothing more of it. You have proven yourself to be a fine seamstress. Why, I do believe that you could open up your own shop if you set your mind to it."

"I have no such desire," Eleanor promised as she washed the glass pitcher, being careful not to damage the hand-painted daisies on its front.

"Good." She smiled. "For if you did, you just might prove to be entirely too much competition for your old aunt."

"Oh, really, how you do go on." Though Eleanor's observation was made in a frivolous tone, she felt flattered. Aunt Daphne was not one to dispense compliments easily, at least not to anyone who wasn't a client.

"If you're not worried about the business, then what?" Aunt Daphne pressed.

Eleanor hesitated. She wished the conversation hadn't progressed to such a point, but now that they had begun, she was obliged to finish. If she didn't, Eleanor sensed that her aunt would never allow her to visit the topic of her courtship with Mr. Jarvis in the future. "It's so difficult for a woman who lives alone with no one to look out for her best interests and well-being."

Aunt Daphne shrugged. "I don't find it especially difficult. I suppose I'm accustomed to being alone. I have learned to trust my judgment and intuition."

"Your trust is not misplaced, no doubt," Eleanor hastened to assure her as she mixed lemon juice and sugar together. "But even the most brilliant among us can be blinded by emotion."

"You feel that I am blinded by emotion?" The edgy tone of her aunt's voice left Eleanor feeling nervous.

"It's not entirely impossible, is it?" She stopped her work and turned to her aunt. She walked a few paces to her chair, knelt, and clasped her aunt's hands in hers. "Oh, Auntie, I'm so happy for you. I do so love to see you enjoying Mr. Jarvis's company. But I don't wish to see you become involved with someone who isn't worthy of you."

"I'm glad you hold me in such high esteem. Only, why wouldn't a wealthy man who travels the world be worthy of me?"

She squeezed her aunt's hands. "That's just it. Where does he get his wealth? Has he discussed it with you?" Eleanor knew her voice betrayed her hope.

"No. Of course not. Most men don't discuss their business affairs with their wives, much less with women they are courting." Aunt Daphne took her hands from Eleanor's, although to Eleanor's relief, the gesture was bereft of rudeness or anger.

Eleanor rose to her feet. "I'm sure he'll want to know all about your business. That will be a jolt for you, won't it? Having to share everything with a man?"

"He doesn't seem to place a great deal of curiosity in my business affairs. I find that fact rather comforting, in a way. His lack of curiosity only proves that he isn't interested in me for whatever income I can bring to his household. Besides, what man of his station would want his wife to maintain a business once they are—" She stopped herself short.

"*If* they are?" Eleanor didn't look her aunt in the face as she added water to the juice and sugar.

"I mean," Aunt Daphne stumbled, "if we ever are. . .uh. . .if we ever take our visitations beyond courtship."

Eleanor stopped stirring the lemonade in midcircle. "Has he proposed?"

"No, but I think he will. And I think I might accept."

"Aunt Daphne!"

"Oh, do be happy for me, won't you, dear heart? It would make things ever so much more pleasant."

Eleanor watched the lemonade settle. She braced herself before looking into her aunt's face. "Of course, I will support any decision you make in any way I know possible."

"Thank you, Eleanor."

Eleanor poured two glasses of lemonade without speaking. Raleigh had to come through for her. He just had to!

Father in heaven, I pray that Thou wilt keep my aunt in Thy care. I pray that I am wrong about Mr. Jarvis. But whether I'm wrong or right, please allow me to find out before it's too late.

Chapter 9

Raleigh was about to leave his office for a court session when he heard a knock on the door.

"Not now, Monroe," he called with enough vigor to be heard through the heavy oak. "I have no time to tarry."

Monroe nevertheless stepped just inside the door. "I beg your pardon, sir, but it's Eustis. He said he has the information you want, sir."

Eustis. Finally. It had taken him long enough. Raleigh set the court brief on his desk and consulted his gold pocket watch. He had exactly nineteen minutes before he would be forced to leave or risk being late for court. "All right. Send him in."

Eustis entered, hat in hand. "Good mornin', Mr. Raleigh."

"Good morning, Eustis." A glimpse of the man before him confirmed that he had chosen the right person. Eustis wasn't particularly handsome, and he was dressed in a style plain enough to blend in with dockworkers. "I don't mean to be short with you, but I have very little time. Please be brief."

"Yes, sir. I poked around as much as I could without stirring up any trouble. I didn't find out much. Maybe not as much as you would have liked."

Raleigh hid his disappointment with a nod. "I understand that you had to sacrifice for the sake of discretion. No one has any idea that you are working for me in this capacity, do they?"

"No, sir. I was careful."

"Good." Normally Raleigh would have sat back in his chair and offered a seat to Eustis, but he omitted the courtesy because of the shortage of time. "So tell me what you were able to discover."

"Mr. Jarvis has an office at Pier 7, but no matter when I stop by, day or night, he never seems to be there."

"Really? Then where is he?" Raleigh tried not to fist his hands. "Were you able to find out anything?"

"He seems to have a fine old time around town, Mr. Raleigh. He goes about in fine style, eating at the best dining establishments with all sorts of friends—fine-lookin' gentlemen." He shoved his hands in his pants pockets and rattled what sounded like a few coins. "Why, I think you even ate with him one day yourself, Mr. Raleigh."

"I can't deny that." Raleigh had made deliberate plans to share a meal with

79

the dapper Flint in hopes of deflecting suspicion from himself should Flint find out that someone—specifically Raleigh himself—was digging into his business. "You say he had other dinner companions this week?"

"Yes, sir. He dined twice with Miss Daphne Kerr, the seamstress who runs a shop out of her home on Cathedral Street."

"Yes." Conscious that he needed to depart soon, Raleigh picked up the court brief and held it in the crook of his arm. "She is the only female companion you noticed?"

"Yes, sir. He don't seem to pay other women any mind."

Raleigh knew his eyebrows shot up in surprise. He reset his features into a blank expression as soon as he could. "Thank you, Eustis. You have done a fine job for me. I'll remember that."

"Thank you, Mr. Raleigh." He tipped his hat and made his exit.

Raleigh was left with an uneasy feeling. Judging from the account he had just heard, Flint didn't sound as though he was gainfully employed. Perhaps Eleanor had a right to be suspicious, after all.

The following day, Eleanor arrived at the Alden home, thankful that Vera had sent word that she wanted a new housedress sewn. She had begged off making a firm appointment, truthfully pleading a full schedule already, then made a point of waiting until just before dinner to arrive in hopes that Raleigh would be back from court. If she met him, she could pull him aside and ask what, if anything, he had discovered about the mysterious Flint Jarvis.

She knocked on the door, but Monroe didn't answer. How unusual. She couldn't remember a time when he wasn't haunting the doorway. Since she was expected for her appointment, Eleanor pushed the door open and entered. She darted her gaze around the room and tried not to seem too obvious as she looked for Raleigh. At first, she didn't see him anywhere. Her heart felt as though it had sunk into her toes. She tried to tell herself the feeling was merely the result of wanting to learn about Flint Jarvis, but she knew better. She welcomed any excuse to visit with Raleigh.

Father in heaven, I pray that Thou hast forgiven me for my rudeness to Raleigh the last time we spoke. I shouldn't have let my anger get the best of me. I should not have given in to the temptation to bait him with a challenge so he would bend to my will and do my bidding. Lord, no matter what happens today, let me be conscious of Thy will, not my own. In the name of Thy Son, I pray. Amen.

Eleanor took in a breath and straightened her posture, determined that her visit would be a success on all fronts. Perhaps if she dawdled with Vera, she would be able to linger until Raleigh returned.

She headed up to Mrs. Alden's bedroom, where Vera was sure to be found.

"I just don't know what to do about Vera."

Eleanor stopped. That was Raleigh's voice! The door to the bedroom was ajar, and she could hear him speaking.

"She certainly made a fool of herself at the dinner party," he continued.

The dinner party? Why was he talking about the dinner party? That had happened more than two weeks ago. And how had Vera made a fool of herself? Eleanor had to know! She stopped short so she could listen.

Mrs. Alden's voice filtered into the foyer. "I must agree, Raleigh. I had no intention of Vera taking any interest in Mr. Jarvis. When I saw her flirting wildly with him, I couldn't believe my eyes."

Eleanor knew she was being impolite in eavesdropping. Listening to this conversation went against every good thing she had been taught. But she couldn't resist. Obviously Vera was out on some mysterious errand or they never would be talking about her in such a way.

"Good," Raleigh said. "So you'll understand when I say that if you have any regard for Vera or Daphne you'll cut off all ties with anyone having connections with Flint, including Miss Jessica."

"Jessica! But she has been my friend for years. I will not cut off communications with her." A moment of silence ensued before she added, "Jessica is not her nephew's guardian. She is not to be blamed for his actions. Although I do confess, I'm disappointed that all did not go as planned."

"Go as planned?" Surprise was evident in Raleigh's voice.

Careful not to make a peep, Eleanor brought her ear as closely as she could to the open door without being seen.

"Yes." Silence filled the room. Knowing Mrs. Alden as well as she did, Eleanor could imagine disgust with Raleigh's obtuseness registering on her face. "Didn't you suspect?"

"Suspect what?"

Mrs. Alden exhaled. "I wonder how someone as smart as you are can be so dense at times. Well, I suppose I might as well confess. Daphne and I had hoped that Eleanor, not Vera and Daphne, would take an exceptional interest in Mr. Jarvis."

"Eleanor?"

"Yes. I had hoped she would find herself to be an excellent match for him."

Eleanor tensed and watched Raleigh's face. Would his expression reveal his feelings for her?

"Daphne betrayed me, really," Mrs. Alden confided to her son. "When we discussed the party earlier, she said she was in complete agreement that Flint and Eleanor would go well together."

"The poor girl has only been here a couple of months, and already Daphne wants to marry her off?" Raleigh asked.

"I assure you, Daphne only has Eleanor's best interests at heart."

"But the sewing business—"

"I'm sure she thought that while Flint made his way abroad, Eleanor would stay in town and help her hold down the shop."

Eleanor felt her mouth twitch. Mrs. Alden knew Aunt Daphne too well.

"Mother, I can see why Daphne might be concerned about her own niece, but why would you be concerned with Eleanor's romantic affairs?"

She paused. "Because. . .because. . .never you mind. There shall be no argument, Raleigh." His mother's voice was stern. "I have a notion as to why you want to cut Flint off from us. You are jealous."

"Jealous?" Raleigh blurted. "Don't be preposterous. I am not jealous of anyone."

"Indeed, you're not? I think you protest too much, Raleigh. Everyone at the party could see that you have developed great feelings for Eleanor."

Eleanor nearly gasped with delight. So Raleigh's feelings had become obvious to his mother! Surely he would soon be making his intentions known to her, as well. A smile tickled her lips, and her foot began to tap as though she could break out into a waltz. With a show of self-control, she kept a happy sigh to herself.

"Really?" Raleigh protested. "I don't see how anyone can say that."

His words brought Eleanor back down to earth and then some. How could an utterance of just one sentence take her emotions from the heights of a mountain to the depths of a well?

"Is that so?" Mrs. Alden challenged him. "Then may I ask, whom are you trying to fool: me or yourself?"

"I—I. . ."

Eleanor could almost hear Mrs. Alden smiling. "Do you mean we sent you to Virginia and paid tuition to the law school of William and Mary all those years just so you could become tongue-tied in front of your own mother? I hardly see how you could be doing your professors proud."

A slight pause ensued, during which Eleanor imagined Raleigh drawing himself up to his full height. "Mother, you must admit, you are more intimidating than any of my professors ever were—and even most judges."

Eleanor suppressed a giggle.

"That's a fine excuse, but I will have none of that." Mrs. Alden's firm voice only proved Raleigh's observation. "Rather than meddling in the love affairs of others, I suggest that you make your intentions known to Eleanor."

Eleanor held back a gasp. So Raleigh really did have feelings for her! His mother had just admitted it, right to his face. If she could see through him, then her instincts hadn't led her astray. Again she experienced a sudden lightness of foot. She could almost imagine her toes lifting off the floor so she could float in midair.

"But I don't wish to make my intentions known to Eleanor, as you put it. You may think I have feelings for her, and I do. I am quite fond of her as a charming and beautiful companion for conversation about books and such."

Eleanor's emotions churned. The words *charming* and *beautiful*—words she had seldom heard to describe her—roiled through her head, only to be superceded by the lukewarm phrase *companion for conversation*, a term that could have applied to almost any acquaintance.

Eleanor felt her lips tighten. Yes, he had admitted a tepid partiality to her not so long ago. She couldn't accuse him of dishonesty. And what more did she have a right to ask? He hadn't mentioned courting her. How could she consider him a suitor? She shook her head. Such thoughts, running wild as they were, left her unsettled. How far had she let her feelings for him go? Too far. She tightened her grip on the fabric samples she held, conscious yet uncaring that the motion would wrinkle them.

"I believe your feelings for her run deeper than friendship," Mrs. Alden said.

Eleanor felt her pulse increase as she stopped breathing for a split second. She pressed her head against the wall by the door in anticipation of his response.

"Believe what you like," Raleigh answered, "but I have never considered Eleanor as someone I might like to court."

Eleanor clutched the woolen fabric samples even tighter, sorely testing their durability. In her heart, she couldn't be surprised by his response, but disappointment filled her nonetheless.

"And why ever not?" Mrs. Alden grilled him. "She is certainly pretty enough."

A rush of pleasure permeated Eleanor, even though the compliment was uttered by an older woman.

"I won't deny that she does have a pretty face and pleasant figure."

So he had noticed! The feeling of delight was joined by a rise of heat to Eleanor's face, making her grateful for the dimness in the empty hallway.

"And she sews a fine seam," Mrs. Alden added.

"She sews a fine seam, yes, but would she have the knowledge or experience—or even the desire—to take on the responsibilities of a lawyer's wife?" Raleigh asked.

Wife? Wife!

Eleanor wanted to burst into the room and shout, "Yes! Yes! I have the desire, and what I don't know now about being a lawyer's wife, I can learn!" Instead, she forced herself to remain standing where she was.

"Raleigh, how can you doubt Eleanor? As your wife, she would have plenty of support from the household staff, and I certainly can tell her a thing or two about how to set a fine table."

"And why are you suddenly so eager to take on Eleanor as your daughter-in-law?" Raleigh's tone betrayed his doubt. "I had no notion that you wanted me to marry."

"Of course I do, for your happiness."

"Or for your happiness, Mother? I know Eleanor and Vera get along well. I suppose you think she could encourage Vera to stay on indefinitely as your companion?"

"I doubt Eleanor holds that kind of sway over Vera."

"But it's worth a try, isn't it? Especially since your attempts to distract Eleanor from me by throwing Flint her way failed. And now that you see the folly of your strategy, you are putting another plan into progress. Are you not?" He paused. Eleanor imagined that he used such techniques in the courtroom to stymie witnesses.

"How could you accuse me of such deviousness? Why, I had no idea you were developing a fondness for Eleanor until the night of the party."

"Is that so? I may have just returned to Baltimore after an extended absence, Mother, but I think I have an idea of how your mind works. Initially, you would have liked for me to become attached to Vera since she is from a good family. Then you would have been guaranteed that she would never leave this house. But when you saw that Vera simply doesn't pique my interest, whether she's sitting by your bedside or dressed in a fabulous gown, you formulated another plan, a plan that would protect your interests should Vera eventually attract a suitor," he said. "You surmised that should I marry Eleanor she would be so grateful to be your daughter-in-law that she would eagerly do your bidding for the remainder of your days. Am I right?"

"Now that's the kind of dramatic argument I would expect from a graduate of a fine Virginia school of law. I can almost hear the jury give a collective gasp and the court observers break out into whispers and expressions of shock."

"But am I right, Mother?" he persisted.

"Of course not." Mrs. Alden's voice sounded weak.

Eleanor crossed her arms. So Mrs. Alden wasn't the champion Eleanor thought. She was simply contriving to use her as a pawn to advance her own interests! Then she remembered Mrs. Alden's remarkable ability to rise from her bed to attend the dinner party. Of course, Mrs. Alden could do most anything she set her mind to. Had Eleanor not been one of the players manipulated on Mrs. Alden's stage, Eleanor could have granted her unbridled admiration.

Raleigh spoke once more. "I can't believe you chose Flint Jarvis of all people as a romantic prospect for any woman in whom you place any regard."

"And why is that?"

"His character is suspect."

"Whatever your accusations, I don't believe them. Flint Jarvis has always been a friend of yours. Are you implying that you have poor judgment in choosing friends?" With the subject changed, Mrs. Alden's voice took on new conviction.

"You exaggerate his importance to me, Mother. He was a childhood class-mate once upon a time but hardly one of my intimates."

"You didn't object to his being invited to the dinner."

"No, but at the time, I was taking his connection to your friend Jessica into consideration, and I didn't know about his frivolous style of life," Raleigh observed.

"What do you mean by 'frivolous style of life'?"

Finally, the information she wanted to hear. Eleanor put aside her tumultu-ous emotions about her own circumstances long enough to crane her neck, so she could be sure not to miss a word. For Aunt Daphne's sake, she had to know about Mr. Jarvis. She felt her body tense.

"Since the party, it has come to my attention that Flint's source of wealth is not known. He says he is gainfully employed in shipping, yet he shows no evidence that such an enterprise supports his ability to gallivant about town every day."

"So he doesn't spend his time with his nose buried in legal briefs all day like you do." Eleanor could visualize Mrs. Alden shrugging. "Does that make him a villain?"

"I hope not."

"You may have influence in the courts, but I would think long and hard about accusing someone of wrongdoing if I were you." Eleanor imagined Mrs. Alden shaking her finger at Raleigh as she dispensed such advice.

"Indeed. And I assure you, I express my concerns to you in the strictest con-fidence." He exhaled. "I tell you once and for all, your best-laid plans have failed. I am not interested in Vera, simply because she melts into the wall, nor am I inter-ested in Eleanor; though she is a fine seamstress, that is still her station—that of a tradeswoman."

Eleanor flinched.

"Raleigh! How dare you be such a snob! I thought I reared you to be better than that. You know how well I regard Daphne, so why should I not extend the same feelings to her niece? Besides, I think Eleanor was born to a higher calling. You must remember that her family fell upon hard times through no fault of their own, darling."

"Yes, I know. But I have an image to maintain if you wish to remain in this fine home and to enjoy your current luxuries in life, Mother. Now let us not dis-cuss this anymore."

Eleanor felt her eyes tearing. How could Raleigh, the man who had shown her only kindness, suddenly turn on her and act as though she was nothing more than an insignificant fool? Perhaps she was not insignificant, but at that moment, she felt quite foolish.

Eleanor knew she couldn't face Raleigh or anyone else who mattered to her.

She spun on her heel and tiptoed through the hallway, down the stairs, and to the foyer. She looked beyond the muslin draperies out the window. Thankfully, the carriage still waited.

Monroe materialized in the foyer, seemingly out of thin air. "Miss Kerr. I'm sorry; I didn't know you were here. May I announce you to Mrs. Alden?"

"No, that won't be necessary."

"I'll tell her you're here," he insisted.

"No, I'm not here." Eleanor touched the doorknob to signal her imminent departure.

Monroe gave her a quizzical look.

"I mean, I'm here, but I need to go back. I won't be seeing anyone."

He furrowed his brow. "Are you quite sure?"

"Yes, yes. I—I left something at home. I'll be back another time." Had Eleanor still been a little girl, she would have held her hands behind her back, fingers crossed. But she had left something at home. Her pride.

As she rode toward Cathedral Street, she peered out of the carriage window as though she were seeing everything for the last time. And, indeed, she was. Or at least, that was the intent she felt by the time she reached the row house she had recently been calling home.

Once she disembarked, she rushed into the house. She had a mission, and that was to pack her bags.

"Eleanor?" Aunt Daphne called from the sewing room in the back of the house.

She composed herself, so her voice would be strong when she answered. "It is I." Eleanor made a beeline for the stairs, hoping she could escape before Aunt Daphne came in to interrogate her.

"That was a mighty short visit to the Aldens'." Aunt Daphne's voice was growing closer, and the clacking of her boot heels was becoming louder as she approached.

Eleanor hurried up the stairs. "Yes, ma'am."

"Is everything all right?"

Eleanor raced to her room, but she wasn't rapid enough. Aunt Daphne followed on her heels. Eleanor thought she seemed to move quickly for someone her age.

Aunt Daphne stood in the doorway. Eleanor had been unable to shut the door behind her without hitting her aunt in the nose. "Clearly, something is amiss. Tell me what happened. Was Vera unhappy with the patterns or the fabric you suggested? Do you want me to go by there and make amends?"

"No, Aunt Daphne. It's nothing like that. I didn't even see Vera. She was out." Eleanor threw the fabric samples onto her bed.

"Out? Out where? She never goes out."

Eleanor yanked her hat from her head. In her distraction, she forgot about her pearl-embossed hat pin, which made its presence known by scraping against the back of her head, beside her chignon. Too upset even to utter an expression of pain, she searched for it with nimble fingers and pulled it out of her hair. "I have no idea where Vera was."

"Eleanor, you're not making sense."

She fiddled with the pin with such vigor that she nearly stuck her thumb. "You're right, Aunt Daphne, I'm not. In fact, nothing about this town makes any sense. I appreciate everything you've done for me, but I can't live here anymore. I'm leaving for Louisiana next week. And there's nothing you can do to stop me."

Chapter 10

Eleanor! You don't mean that!" Aunt Daphne cried. "Surely you don't plan to go back to Louisiana. This is your home now. Baltimore." She swept her arm over Eleanor's modest bedroom as though it represented all of Charm City.

Following her aunt's hand with her gaze, Eleanor peered out of her small-ish window decorated by fresh white cotton curtains. She crossed her arms, an impulsive gesture made to help her fight unwanted feelings. Indeed, she had become attached to the city and its people in the short time she had been a part of their lives.

Taking in a deep breath, she noticed pleasant and not-so-pleasant city odors coming into her room through the open window: Cooking aromas, horse manure, and coal smoke mingled with rotting kitchen waste, musky harbor smells, flowers, and the occasional tree. It all signified life to Eleanor. Her ears picked up the other element of life in the city: sounds. A constant drone was always present. She heard horses clopping and neighing, cart wheels rumbling, and people chattering, though she could rarely distinguish their words. The exceptions were peddlers—some of them boys rather than men—who shouted the names and qualities of their wares, so their voices penetrated the air.

When she first arrived in Baltimore, Eleanor had found the noises and scents unsettling. In Louisiana, she had lived in a neighborhood of spacious homes and generous lawns, far from the hum of the center of New Orleans. Here, she was situated in the middle of a vibrant life. Not only had she become accustomed to her busy surroundings, but she would surely miss them.

"I must admit, this city feels like home to me. But I'm afraid I must return to my father's house. The time has come." Though she kept confidence etched on her face as she regarded her aunt, Eleanor heard a wistful catch in her voice.

"Don't be absurd, child. You don't want to leave now. Think of how our business is booming. Orders for Christmas dresses are pouring in so fast that you and I put together will be hard pressed to fill them all. Think of the nice little nest egg you are building for yourself, with no one's toil but your own. Isn't that something to be proud of?"

"God has blessed me. But Aunt Daphne, I know you'll find someone else to replace me in plenty of time to fill all your orders and then some."

"Where can I find a seamstress as fine as you are on such short notice?"

Aunt Daphne crossed her arms. "I'd have to train anyone else for months, and even then, she might prove not to have a whit of talent for sewing." She pointed her forefinger at her niece. "You're a natural, Eleanor."

Though Eleanor felt flattered, the pleasure of her aunt's rare compliment was deflated by her obvious self-interested motivation. Disappointment that her aunt's fondness was tinged with selfishness pricked at Eleanor's heart. "I'm sorry, Aunt Daphne, but—"

Aunt Daphne moved closer and placed her hands on Eleanor's shoulders. As her aunt moved, Eleanor could smell the faint but bland odor of the lavender sachet kept in her dresser drawers to freshen her clothes. Since arriving in Baltimore, Eleanor had come to associate the fragrance with her aunt. She had been surprised that such a vivacious woman had chosen a delicate scent, expecting her to favor lilac. But when Aunt Daphne reminded her that Eleanor's grandmother wore lavender, she understood that her wearing it was a form of remembrance.

"Please, Eleanor," Aunt Daphne said. "Think of your father. He only wanted you to come here for your health. You can't go back to Louisiana now and risk contracting malaria as your mother did. Certainly you don't wish to endure such pain as she did, even to the death."

"Of course not." Eleanor shuddered as she recalled her mother's suffering. "I wouldn't wish her type of death on anyone." She pulled away from Aunt Daphne's grasp and turned her back, so her aunt wouldn't see the tears that threatened.

"Then you see why you can't possibly go home now."

Eleanor wiped her tears away, using as little arm movement as possible in hopes that her aunt wouldn't notice. "On the contrary, it's imperative that I return home now. I'll be fine." She held back a sniffle.

"You don't know that." Aunt Daphne's voice held the confidence of a woman firm in her conviction. And why shouldn't it? Eleanor knew her aunt was right.

Having composed herself, Eleanor turned back to face her aunt. "Perhaps I don't. But it's a chance I'm willing to take."

Aunt Daphne stepped closer. "How can you be so foolish with your life? Didn't the Reverend Marks preach just the other Sunday that the human body is a temple of God? Do you want to destroy your very temple?"

"Of course not. But remember, people live in Louisiana for a lifetime at the peak of health. I believe that Papa's reaction to my mother's illness by sending me here was a bit strong. Even you would agree." She didn't wait for her aunt to protest. "I—I just can't stay in a place where they talk about people behind their backs. That's all." To demonstrate her feelings, Eleanor needed only five paces to reach the oak wardrobe that stood against the north wall. She opened the door and surveyed her assortment of ten dresses and four pairs of shoes. Assessing them, she wondered if she should send the best ones in trunks to arrive ahead of her in Louisiana.

"What? Is that what this is about? A little bit of gossip?" Aunt Daphne's words came closer together. "What did you hear? Tell me."

Eleanor eyed the dress she wore the night of the dinner party, the dress that Raleigh seemed to find flattering on her figure. On the one hand, she wanted to enshrine it as a memory of the evening—the one night when she thought Raleigh could love her. On the other, she fought a real desire to cut it to shreds then and there.

Eleanor desperately wanted to quote St. Paul's admonitions about being a busybody, but since she had learned the news from eavesdropping, she felt that to chastise her aunt would be the height of hypocrisy.

"If you are looking for somewhere devoid of rumor and intrigue, then you will soon find you have no place to live at all. I know of nowhere on earth where gossip isn't present to some degree." Aunt Daphne chuckled.

Still silent, Eleanor fingered the skirt of the dress she had worn to the dinner party. Nothing her aunt said helped to ease the hurt of hearing what was said by Raleigh and Mrs. Alden when they thought she wasn't listening. Eleanor supposed she deserved what she got for eavesdropping. Why, if her dear mother were still alive, she would have dispensed a tongue-lashing that Eleanor would have never forgotten. The idea reminded her again of how much she missed her mother.

Eleanor forced herself to bring her mind back to the present, where she could see that she had no choice but to bring out the heavy artillery. She spun on the heel of her boot and looked her aunt straight in the eyes. "Maybe not, but you won't be so amused when you find out about whom Raleigh and Mrs. Alden were gossiping. Your very own Flint Jarvis."

All mirth evaporated from Aunt Daphne's face. "Really? I don't believe it."

"Believe it."

Eleanor watched her aunt swallow. "Why would they tell you anything about Flint?"

Eleanor squirmed but summoned her resolve to reveal the truth. "I overheard a conversation. I know I was wrong to eavesdrop, but—"

Aunt Daphne flitted her hand at Eleanor. "Never mind that. Some of the best tidbits are the ones overheard. Just tell me what they said."

Eleanor took in a breath. "Raleigh said that Flint's source of wealth is questionable."

"It is not." Aunt Daphne puffed herself up so that she brought to Eleanor's mind a miffed feline. "He's in shipping. What's questionable about that?"

"I don't know the details," Eleanor answered in all truthfulness, "but Raleigh was questioning his integrity. And if you're serious about becoming Mrs. Flint Jarvis, I think you should, too. For your own good."

"Well, I think he has some nerve! I can judge Flint for myself. I don't need anyone else to interfere. Besides, I think Raleigh is just jealous. Did you know that Flint is leaving next month on a trip to India?"

"No. I'm sure that will be quite exciting for him." Eleanor tried not to grimace at the thought of a fresh batch of stories to be repeated with increasing embellishment.

"It will be. And all the while, Raleigh will be working on dry legal issues here in Baltimore. As I said, he's just envious." Aunt Daphne wasn't finished. "And as for you, my dear niece, I do believe you're jealous, too."

A chuckle escaped Eleanor's lips. "Me? Jealous of Mr. Jarvis? Surely you know I have no desire to travel, although I'm happy for him that he has the opportunity; he obviously derives such joy from taking journeys around the world."

"I don't mean you're envious of his trips. I mean you are envious of me. Here I have, without any effort, attracted the interest of a wealthy and worldly man, while you have not."

Aunt Daphne's comment stung her no less than a slap to the cheek. Eleanor wanted to blurt out that she and Raleigh were great friends but decided that she was better off not mentioning anything about him at all.

"I know what you're thinking. You're thinking that you are successful because you have managed to pique the interest of Raleigh Alden."

Eleanor remained silent but tilted her chin skyward.

"And you're going to say that Raleigh is just as important and wealthy as Flint. Well, maybe he is, but I can't imagine that tightwad doing anything more exciting than visiting an ice cream parlor." She wagged her finger at Eleanor. "And I'll bet he orders vanilla, too."

"I see nothing wrong with vanilla. It's a perfectly fine, solid flavor."

"Only you would defend vanilla!" Aunt Daphne shrugged in exasperated surrender. "You know, there's not much point in possessing wealth if one doesn't spend any of it. And if I know Raleigh Alden, he won't be spending a penny more on you than is absolutely necessary to keep body and soul together. I suppose gossiping is a cheap form of entertainment, but I prefer theater tickets, myself. And with Flint, I'm sure I'll be sitting in a box seat." By this time, Aunt Daphne had worked herself up into a frenzied state. Her voice rose in pitch and volume with each passing sentence. "Why, you and Raleigh deserve each other!"

"Aunt Daphne, please control yourself. I'm sorry I have vexed you so. I know you don't mean half of what you say."

"Don't I?"

"Well, I don't care what you say about Raleigh Alden. I have no interest in him whatsoever." Eleanor spoke the words as an honest attempt at truth, but her heart's increased thumping betrayed her tongue.

"Is that so?"

"It's true." Eleanor swallowed her mixed emotions. On the one hand, it felt good to hear Aunt Daphne pair them together. On the other, since he had betrayed her with his snobbish attitude, Eleanor didn't want anything more to do with him, even though she had to fight the feelings in her treacherous heart.

"I don't consider a snob like Raleigh as more than an acquaintance kind enough to lend me books from his personal library," Eleanor protested.

"A nice snob, eh? A contradiction of terms, indeed. I must say that after this conversation I'll have to agree that it's high time you returned to your home state. I'll send your father a telegram today telling him so. And I'll help you pack your bags."

Watching Aunt Daphne's newly developed eagerness for her to depart, Eleanor felt a sudden twinge of regret. "Perhaps I was a bit hasty. I do need to finish Vera's order."

"Never mind that. Neither I nor you will be sewing another stitch for any Alden—or for anyone who is a companion to them." With a firm motion, Aunt Daphne crossed her arms over her chest. "I won't even consider fashioning her maids' uniforms. Not even if she begs."

"But Aunt Daphne, she's your best client. Didn't you always say that a good businesswoman never lets her personal opinions and feelings interfere with a sale?"

"I said a lot of things. Things I'm beginning to regret. Besides, once I'm Mrs. Flint Jarvis, I'm not sure I'll have time to keep the shop open."

"But the shop is your life!"

Aunt Daphne set her lips firmly. "It is now, but that can change. Lots of things can change. Very quickly."

Eleanor tried not to show how upset she was at her aunt's turnaround. Couldn't she see that Eleanor only cared about her welfare? She opened her mouth to argue, but her aunt's eyes had turned cold and hard. To debate would be futile.

———

The next day, Raleigh knocked on the Kerrs' door and announced himself to their maid by handing her a calling card. After she excused herself, he remained on the stoop and tried not to let his expression reveal his great anticipation. He hadn't seen Eleanor in so long. Too long.

His mother's words resounded in his ears with the accuracy of a phonograph recording: *Everyone at the party could see that you have developed great feelings for Eleanor.* The recording continued. *I suggest that you make your intentions known to Eleanor.*

He had been an unbearable snob. He was only grateful that Eleanor hadn't been present to hear him make such foolish remarks about her station as a seamstress. Indeed, how could he have said such a thing and still call himself a Christian?

He had denied his true feelings and compounded his mistake by distancing himself from Eleanor in questioning her station. More admonitions from Mother played in his head. *I think you protest too much, Raleigh.*

If he had any doubts after speaking with his mother, the Lord made the message even more clear to Raleigh as he read his daily devotions: *"There is neither Jew nor Greek, there is neither bond nor free, there is neither male nor female: for ye are all one in Christ Jesus."* Galatians 3:28 had held no special interest or significance to him until he crossed that verse more times than he cared to recall over the past week. The Lord used it—along with his mother's wise counsel—to show him that his attitude toward Eleanor needed to change. Perhaps as did his view of many other people, as well. Raleigh sensed that the Lord would make those people apparent to him as he continued his spiritual walk.

Eleanor imagined that his profession lent itself to developing a prideful spirit, especially when a man enjoyed as many court victories as Raleigh. Ridding himself of that pride wouldn't be easy. But he resolved to shed it in obedience. Thankfully his first assignment would be easy. By reaching out to Eleanor, the blissful rewards promised to be boundless. He allowed himself a contented sigh.

He reached in his waistcoat pocket and extracted the seventeen-jewel Swiss watch that was an inheritance from Grandfather Alden. Where was that maid? Did she tarry because he had caught the Kerr ladies unaware?

Raleigh noticed the Kerrs' window box. They had made an effort to beautify the tiny patch of nature in front of the row house. The windowsill planter contained a cascade of white petunias backed up with black-faced blue pansies. English daisies flanked the box on both ends.

The front door creaked open. Raleigh looked in the direction of the sound and noticed that the maid was leaning out the doorway, wearing a cautious look on her face. "I'm sorry, Mr. Alden, but the ladies are not available at present."

Raleigh couldn't believe the maid. Surely Eleanor would be eager to see him, anticipating that he would be bearing news about Flint Jarvis. "Surely Miss Eleanor Kerr will see me."

She shook her head. "I'm afraid not, sir. Neither lady is available today."

"Perhaps I might call another time. When do you suggest might be suitable?"

The maid looked unsure. "Excuse me, sir." She disappeared again, leaving Raleigh to wait on the front stoop. He felt foolish standing alone in front of the house. Passersby looked at him as though he had taken leave of his senses.

"I'm sorry, sir," the maid said upon her return. "They were not able to provide me with a better time."

"I have no special need to see Miss Daphne Kerr, but if you might suggest a time I can speak with Miss Eleanor Kerr, I would be grateful."

"I'm sorry, sir. Miss Eleanor Kerr will be leaving for Louisiana within the week, and she will not be available to take any callers before she departs, sir."

Raleigh felt his jaw drop before he could contain himself. So Eleanor was to depart in a week's time? Without telling him? Without so much as a written good-bye? What was the meaning of this? He forced himself to regain his composure.

"Could you tell Miss Eleanor Kerr that I am here to see her on important business?" he asked. "She will understand my meaning."

The maid looked distressed but excused herself so she could comply. During her absence, Raleigh wondered what Eleanor was thinking. How could she plan to leave on such short notice and without even finding out about Flint?

The maid returned. "I'm sorry, sir, but the answer is no."

He decided to hit Daphne where she lived. "Tell Miss Daphne Kerr that I am here to settle my mother's bill."

"Yes, sir." The maid let out a tired sigh. Raleigh felt sorry for her, but he had to see someone in the Kerr household, one way or another.

Her prompt return left him with hope until she shook her head. "Miss Daphne Kerr said she has not yet tallied the latest charges, and she has asked to settle them with you when she sees you at your mother's next appointment. Good day, sir."

The faithful maid shut the door in his face before he could come back with any retort.

Some lawyer I am! I can't even find the right words to handle a delicate situation in my personal life, yet clients depend on me every day in a court of law.

Sensing defeat, he slumped his shoulders and headed toward his carriage. He felt chagrined that his driver had to witness his unsuccessful attempt to meet with two seamstresses. Thankfully, Jeters was known for his discretion.

"Where might I take you now, sir?" Jeters asked.

"Home. I just want to go home." Raleigh heard the weariness in his own voice.

In the carriage, he thought about the events that had transpired. There was no love lost between Daphne and him, but Eleanor was another matter. Why had she refused to see him? She had humiliated him, yet instead of feeling justified anger, he felt guilt. Why?

Then he remembered his conversation with his mother. She had accused him of being an unbearable snob, an accusation he richly deserved. Had Eleanor discerned his hidden emotions toward her? How could she have? He had always been careful not to reveal anything to her but kindness and friendship. Trained in the ways of the courtroom, Raleigh prided himself on being able to hide his thoughts. Such restraint could make the difference between winning and losing a case. Why did he have the distinct feeling that Eleanor knew more about him than he realized?

Yet even if she knew his feelings of superiority, certainly that discovery would not be enough to convince her to leave town abruptly. Why? Why was she leaving?

If a heart could feel a literal ache, Raleigh's did at that moment. He knew in that instant that he didn't want to lose Eleanor. Not then. Not ever. He had to get her back. But how?

An idea occurred to him.

"Jeters?"

"Yes, Mr. Alden?" he asked over the *clip-clop* of the horse's hooves.

"I've changed my mind. I'm not ready to go home yet. Take me to the harbor."

Chapter 11

Raleigh made his way to Flint's office, hoping against hope that Flint might be there.

Lord, I wouldn't be doing this except that Eleanor asked. I pray we're doing right in finding out more about Flint Jarvis.

His prayer was cut short as the carriage stopped. Moments later, Raleigh found an office front etched in gold letters with JARVIS SHIPPING, MR. FLINT JARVIS, PRESIDENT.

"At least he does, indeed, have an office," Raleigh mumbled under his breath. He turned the handle and entered.

A plain secretary who looked too thin was typing a letter. She turned from her work. "Good morning. What may I do for you today?"

"Raleigh Alden here." He handed her a business card. "I am looking for Mr. Flint Jarvis."

She took the card and read it. "I don't recall scheduling an appointment for you."

"That is because I don't have one. But I am known to Mr. Jarvis, and I'm sure he will see me if you will just let him know I'm here."

She set the card on her desk. "I'm sorry, but he isn't here."

"I can wait."

"Indeed, but you will be waiting until close of business today. We don't expect him in at all."

"Not at all?"

"No." Neither her face nor voice held any sign of apology.

"Tomorrow, then."

"I don't think so, but let me see." She consulted a book bound in black leather. "No, I don't expect him in for at least a week or two."

"But he's in town."

"I am not at liberty to say." Her voice took on an edge. "What is your business here? Perhaps his assistant, Mr. Stone, can help you?"

Raleigh tried to hide his irritation under a pleasant expression. He almost told the secretary to never mind but decided that perhaps Flint's assistant could shed some light on the matter. "Very well. I'll see him."

"Indeed? How kind of you." Her voice reeked with irony.

Raleigh bit back a stinging retort. He supposed she was only doing her job as a gatekeeper. He eyed the office door to her side that was labeled MR. LEE STONE, then watched as she thumbed through the pages once more. "I'm sorry, but his schedule for the day is full. You'll have to wait. Next week, perhaps?"

He thought about Eleanor's imminent departure. "Certainly not. My business is urgent."

She shook her head. "Mr. Stone is very strict about—"

Raleigh had had enough. Without another word, he burst into Lee Stone's office. Though he expected to find Mr. Stone engaged in a meeting or even to discover a vacant office, instead he found a man with gray hair and a matching mustache running an adding machine. The man, presumably Lee Stone, rose to his feet. "See here! What is the meaning of this?" His voice rang with a British accent. "Who are you?"

Raleigh handed him a business card. "Raleigh Alden, Esquire, sir."

The secretary was on his heels. "I beg your pardon, Mr. Stone. This man has been quite obnoxious, and he broke into your office without my leave."

Lee read the card. "Is this about some kind of lawsuit?"

"No."

"Then just what is your business with me, that you felt the need to enter my private office?"

"My business is urgent, but I promise not to take much of your time. I am a businessman as you are, and I know that time is money."

Mr. Stone waved his hand to dismiss his secretary, who nodded and shut the door behind her. He remained standing and didn't gesture for Raleigh to take a seat.

Raleigh didn't waste any time. "Where is Mr. Jarvis?"

"I say, that is none of your affair."

"I understand from your secretary that he isn't expected to be in the office over the next few weeks, yet I know for a fact that he is in town."

"I don't conduct business every day that I'm in town."

Raleigh took in a steadying breath. "Could you tell me where he is, then?"

"You seem to know his whereabouts. Why don't you go and find him yourself?"

"You don't know where he is, do you?"

"Are you here concerning Jarvis Shipping or about a personal matter?"

"Both."

"Then I recommend that you find Mr. Jarvis and discuss your business with him. Clearly, I can be of limited, if any, assistance." Mr. Stone sat back down in his seat. "As you can see, I have a business to run and accounts to balance. Good day." He leaned over his machine and punched in a number.

"But—"

"Good day." Mr. Stone's voice was firmer than ever, and he didn't bother to look up from his work.

Raleigh knew the next step would be for Mr. Stone to call in his secretary and to instruct her to summon the police. The time had come to admit that his mission had failed. Without another word, he made his exit.

"I trust your business went well, sir?" Jeters asked moments later as Raleigh climbed into the carriage.

"No, I'm afraid it didn't. Take me to the residence of Flint Jarvis on Charles Street."

The ride up the hill from the harbor took twenty minutes. Jeters had quite a time navigating the crowded warehouse district. The streets were narrow and filled with many carts and wheelbarrows. Charles Street was a desirable address, but Raleigh was taken aback by the large row house—four windows across when most had only two or three—where the carriage stopped. "Are you sure this is it?" he asked Jeters.

"Yes, sir."

Raleigh emerged from the carriage and noted that the residence seemed grand for one engaged in ordinary employment. Flint Jarvis was becoming more and more puzzling with each stop Raleigh made.

A moment later, Raleigh tried not to appear impatient when he lifted the brass door knocker, which was in the shape of a lion's head.

Flint's butler soon answered. Unlike the Kerrs' maid, he was quick to inform Raleigh that his master was absent.

"Is there a good time for me to return?" Raleigh asked as he handed the butler a calling card.

"I have no firm time to suggest, sir. Mr. Jarvis left early this morning, and I have not seen him since."

"And he didn't say where he was going?"

"I am not at liberty to say, sir."

Raleigh wondered what he meant but knew that to press the matter with a servant paid to protect his employer's privacy would be pointless. "Thank you and good day."

Thoroughly vexed, Raleigh decided he could either comb the streets of Baltimore in hopes of running into his acquaintance, or he could try visiting Flint's aunt. He decided on the latter.

"The residence of Miss Jessica Jarvis, please," he instructed Jeters.

Since Raleigh's mother and Miss Jessica had been friends for decades, Jeters knew how to lead the carriage to the brownstone home on East Mount Vernon Place. This time, when Raleigh got out of the carriage and knocked on the door, the maid granted him entrance and led him to the formal parlor overcrowded with antique furniture and bric-a-brac. He didn't have to wait long to see Miss Jessica.

"Raleigh. What brings you here?" Miss Jessica looked as well as ever. Her once-black hair was streaked with white, reminding Raleigh of a skunk. He wondered why someone so unlike a skunk would be trapped into bearing hair with such odd coloring. "Would you care for tea?"

"No, thank you, Miss Jessica. I won't be staying long. In fact, I regret to tell you that this isn't entirely a social call."

She gasped. "Is everything all right? Your mother isn't ill, is she?"

"Oh no, no. It's nothing like that. Mother is as feisty as ever, I'm happy to say."

She placed a thin hand on her lace-covered chest and sank into a red velvet chair. "I'm glad to hear it. She told me all about the dinner party. I wish I could have been there. A previous engagement I couldn't break precluded my attendance."

"Oh?" Raleigh hadn't been aware that Miss Jessica had been on the invitation list. "Well, everyone understands." He took a seat on the sofa by the picture window.

"At least I got to hear an excellent secondhand account of the party. Hearing your mother tell it was almost like being there myself."

"Yes, she does have a talent for reciting social events. I surmise that if she had been born a man she would have made an excellent newspaper reporter."

"A man, indeed. If the suffragettes have their way, women will soon have the right to vote; then who knows what liberties they will take with the country next."

"Perhaps a woman can be president one day."

Miss Jessica gasped. "Please! Don't even speculate on such a travesty!"

Raleigh suppressed a grin and changed the subject. "I'm sure Mother told you that your nephew Flint kept everyone enraptured with his accounts of travel."

"Everyone except the woman she invited him for—what is her name?" Miss Jessica rubbed her chin and looked at the ceiling. A light of remembrance touched her wrinkled face, and she lifted her forefinger. "Ah yes. The new little seamstress. Eleanor. I've got to commit her name to memory. I thought I might engage her to sew my Christmas dress. I understand she's quite good."

"Yes. Vera was very pleased with the dress that Eleanor sewed for her for the party. I thought it looked quite nice on her."

Miss Jessica's eyebrows arched. "Did you now?"

Raleigh wasn't sure what she implied. "Uh, yes."

"Your mother will be pleased that you have taken notice of Vera. Finally."

"She will?"

Raleigh didn't think it was possible for her eyebrows to rise any higher, but they managed. "You didn't realize?"

Had his mother told everyone in the world about her attempts at matchmaking? "Realize what?"

"I spoke out of turn. Don't mind me. I'm just an old lady with her ramblings. Now as much as I enjoy a visit from a courtly man such as yourself, you said this is not a social call. What is your business with me?"

"I want to know about your nephew."

Miss Jessica shrugged. "What is there to know? It's not as though he's afraid to talk about himself."

"Of that fact, I am well aware. At least as far as his travels are concerned. But he is reticent of offering any details when it comes to his job."

"So? What of it?" She touched the side of her spectacles, adjusted them lower on her nose, and looked over the top of them at him. "Don't you know that it's considered rude to pry into the nature and source of a man's livelihood?"

He didn't let her statement or her gesture intimidate him. "Forgive me, but I hope you will hear me out and give me whatever insight you can. For you see, I am out to prove that your nephew's honor is unimpeachable."

Her posture softened. "I see. And just who is questioning his honor?"

"I'm not at liberty to say. But I assure you that your trust in me will not be misplaced if you can tell me what you know."

She readjusted her spectacles to their proper position. "Very well, then."

"Miss Jessica, I was wondering what you know about your nephew's work. What does he really do to support such a lavish style of life and with more than enough time to travel the world?"

She cleared her throat. "He has quite an ordinary job."

"Indeed? A job that allows him never to appear in his office and to gallivant all day about town as though he had not a care in the world?" He tried to keep the accusatory tone out of his voice.

"You are a successful lawyer, but you have time off from your work." She sent a prolonged glance to the clock on the fireplace mantel. "Take today, for example."

"Yes." He cleared his throat. "But naturally, I do hold to a schedule. If I didn't, I would soon find myself without clients."

She looked at him quickly before averting her eyes. "I do admit that I am proud of Flint's success. He has done quite well for himself."

Years of courtroom experience led Raleigh to recognize her change in tactics as an avoidance measure. "Yes. Too well."

Her eyes narrowed. "I don't think I like what you are implying."

"Neither do I. That's why I'm hoping you can shed some light on the matter."

Miss Jessica's manner took on a cautious air. "What does his career matter to you?"

"People I am fond of might be hurt, that's why."

She chuckled, and her thin body relaxed. "I understand your fondness for Vera, but I assure you, my nephew is not a threat to you there."

Vera. Why did she keep talking about Vera?

"So if you'll excuse me." Miss Jessica rose from her seat. "I must prepare for tea. Flint is due here any minute for our weekly visit, and considering your rather impertinent questions, I suggest you depart before he arrives."

"I beg your forgiveness if my questions seem discourteous, Miss Jessica. Perhaps I am impolitic to put you in the position of responding to them." Raleigh fiddled with the brim of his hat. "But on the contrary, rather than wishing to depart, I am pleased to learn that I might have a chance to see Flint myself. I've been searching for him all day, and I came here as a last resort. It seems that the Lord has guided me to this place at this time after all."

"Don't bring the Lord into your tawdry investigation. If you have anything to say to my nephew, it won't be in my parlor. Good day, Mr. Alden." She turned her back to him and glided through the door.

"But—"

"Lacy!" Miss Jessica called.

The maid materialized almost instantaneously. "Yes, Miz Jarvis?"

"See Mr. Alden to the door."

"But if you will just let me see him for a moment, I'm sure we can clear everything up. If your nephew is the gentleman you say he is, wouldn't you welcome the chance for him to clear any doubts about himself?"

"If you insist on speaking to him, you can wait on the front porch. I will not be party to any exchange." She exited the room before he could bid her a good afternoon.

Although Raleigh felt odd standing on the stoop, thankfully he didn't have to wait long. Flint rode up in his carriage and exited with all the verve of a diplomat on an important mission. At that moment, Raleigh wished he could turn around 180 degrees and forget he had even started the whole mess. But then a picture of Eleanor popped into his head, and he knew he had to press on for her sake.

Raleigh stood with straightened shoulders, waiting in anticipation.

Flint spotted him and waved. "Raleigh, old man!" he said as he ambled up the walkway. "What are you doing here on my aunt's porch? Isn't she home?" His heels clacked on the steps.

"She's home, all right. She sent me out here to wait for you."

"How unmannerly of her. I'm surprised. Usually she has the Southern hospitality thing down pat. Well, I won't have anything to do with keeping a guest waiting outside in the afternoon heat. Come on in with me."

Flint's enthusiastic greeting almost made Raleigh feel guilty, but he knew he had to complete his errand. He followed Flint into the house.

"Lacy!" Flint called, even though no one was anywhere in sight. "I'm here!" He didn't wait for a response before motioning for Raleigh to join him in the parlor. "I was just out duckpin bowling. The last game of the season." He sat in a wing-backed chair. "A great sport. Seems to be catching on."

Raleigh nodded. John Van Sant, the manager of Diamond Alleys in Baltimore, had reduced the size of standard bowling pins that year at the suggestion of some customers. The idea was quickly evolving into an established sport. "I'll have to try it sometime."

"Yes, you must," Flint enthused as his aunt entered.

Both men rose from their seats.

"Aunt Jessica! Look what the cat dragged in. Left it on the porch, at that." He strolled over to his aunt and gave her a kiss on the cheek.

"Hello, Flint." Miss Jessica's tone was warm toward her nephew but then froze. "Raleigh." She nodded ever so slightly. "You're still here."

Flint looked from Raleigh to his aunt. "Is anything the matter?"

"Why don't you find out for yourself? If you'll excuse me." Miss Jessica exited.

Flint turned to face Raleigh. "See here, old man, what is this all about?"

"I'm afraid I am not here on a social call. I need to know, Flint, what exactly do you do to earn your income?"

"There's nothing like getting right to the point, is there, Counselor?" His expression wore a combination of amusement and curiosity.

"Time is of the essence. If I'm not able to give certain people assurances of your honor, both of us may lose everything that means anything to us."

"I'm afraid I don't understand what you mean. Furthermore, what right have you to question my honor?" The muscles in Flint's jaw tightened.

"Whether I have the right is not the question." Raleigh made sure to keep his tone level. "You can trust me when I say that once our conversation is complete you'll be glad I asked about the source of your income."

"So that is what this is about? You're concerned about where I get my money?"

At that moment, the maid entered with a tray holding tea and sandwiches.

"I didn't ask for tea." Flint's voice had lost its charm.

"I know, sir. Miss Jessica said to bring it in."

"That's fine," Flint said. "I'll serve us."

She set down the tray on a low table made of cherrywood.

"That will be all." Flint motioned for Raleigh to return to his seat, and he did the same as the maid nodded and made a silent exit.

Flint's gaze followed her out of the room. "She's burning with curiosity."

"On behalf of your aunt, no doubt. At least she will have nothing to report. Nothing that your aunt doesn't already know."

"So she is aware of the nature of your visit?" Flint's sharp tone indicated his displeasure.

"I spoke to her out of desperation. I searched all over town for you and failed to find you until now. If you had developed the habit of checking in with your office each day instead of disappearing, I wouldn't have had to resort to intruding on your aunt."

"Rudeness is never excusable. But if you must know, I have done nothing illegal. The source of my income is perfectly legitimate," Flint assured him as he poured two servings of tea into hearty cups fashioned of solid white china. "You need not worry. My honor is intact."

"Then why doesn't it appear so?" Peeved, Raleigh took his tea without sugar or cream, in spite of the fact that under more pleasant circumstances he would have asked for both.

"And why, may I ask, doesn't it appear that I am honorable?"

Trying to calm himself and to appear sociable, Raleigh took a sip of the bitter brew, then set down his cup. "Appearances count, and though you may relish the role as a man of mystery, I'm afraid Baltimore society doesn't take kindly to real-life rogues."

Flint rose to his feet. "How dare you!"

Raleigh stood. "I beg your pardon." He decided that another tactic was in order. "Flint, am I right to assume that you are a Christian?"

"Of course."

"Then may I remind you of a verse that contains much wisdom, one that I find useful as I practice law. In 1 Thessalonians 5:22, we read: 'Abstain from all appearance of evil.'"

"Are you calling me evil?"

A female voice interrupted. "No, I don't think he is."

Flint turned to face his aunt, who had just entered. "Aunt Jessica, I beg your forgiveness. This discussion is entirely improper anywhere, especially in your very parlor." He turned to Raleigh. "I ask you to leave this instant."

"You can force Raleigh to leave, but that won't solve a thing." Miss Jessica brought herself up to her full height. "Flint, you have deceived everyone long enough. It's time for you to tell the truth."

Chapter 12

As Raleigh watched the confrontation in Miss Jessica's parlor, he realized that he suddenly seemed small before the domineering woman. Flint exhaled an audible breath. "Aunt Jessica! Surely you jest."

She looked down her nose through her spectacles at him in the same manner she had exercised earlier with Raleigh. "No, I am not speaking in jest. You need to tell him everything."

Flint bristled. "But there is nothing to confess. I am a perfectly honest man who has done nothing wrong."

"Agreed," Miss Jessica said.

So Flint's aunt knew whatever secret he was keeping! Raleigh didn't like the feeling of being deceived.

"I think the fact that I am a respectable gentleman is all anyone needs to know." Flint's jaw muscles tightened.

"I believed that argument at first," Miss Jessica told him, "and I'm sorry to say now that I went along with it. But no more." Her look reminded Raleigh of a schoolmarm chastising a wayward boy for putting a frog in her desk drawer. "Clearly, Raleigh's visit here shows that the situation has changed."

Flint shook his head at his aunt. "I don't think so."

"Are you contradicting me?"

"No, ma'am."

"Good. For your mother, may the Lord rest her dearly departed soul, would find such impudence abominable."

Flint, usually so self-assured, stared at his finely crafted shoes. Seeing him so chastened seemed almost comical.

"Now then." Miss Jessica's voice remained firm. "You have a choice. Either you can tell him, or I will. Which will it be?"

As he watched their exchange, Raleigh's curiosity was piqued to a height he never could have imagined. At least he wouldn't have to wait long to have his questions answered.

Flint darted his glance toward Raleigh, then to his aunt, then back. Finally he let out a defeated sigh. "All right, then. You will feel like a fool when you find out what my big secret is." Flint's eyes had taken on a steely glint. "As Shakespeare once wrote, you are making much ado about nothing."

"I'll take that chance."

"We may as well sit down," Flint suggested.

The men waited for Miss Jessica to take a seat first. "That's quite all right. I'll leave you alone. I shall be in the garden if you need me."

The men bid her farewell, then sat down. Raleigh contemplated taking the remainder of his tea but decided the idea of lukewarm liquid wasn't appealing at the moment. He sat back in his straight-backed chair as much as was possible in hopes of putting Flint at ease.

"Care for more tea?" Flint asked.

"No, thank you."

"Suit yourself." Flint poured the beverage into his waiting cup. Raleigh noticed that hardly any steam resulted and decided he was glad he had passed on the refill. Raleigh guessed that Flint welcomed the diversion. The task kept him from having to look Raleigh in the eye.

"I recently came into an inheritance from an uncle I never knew." Flint looked at the teapot as though he were breaking the news to it rather than to Raleigh.

"An inheritance? Well, aren't you the lucky fellow? But how did you come about gaining an inheritance from an unknown relative?"

Flint shrugged. "He was a bachelor, and my mother was his only sibling. She mentioned him from time to time, but he never set foot on American soil as far as I know. He was a trader in the West Indies."

"A profitable enterprise, then."

"Very much so." Flint's gaze caught Raleigh's before he stirred milk into his refreshment. "I received a significant fortune and part of that shipping concern."

Raleigh quickly put two and two together. "Which is why you have an office at Pier 7."

"Yes." Flint took a sip of brew. "And contrary to your beliefs, I do appear there when needed."

Raleigh remembered that Eustis had never seen Flint anywhere near his office. "Not often?"

"Not often."

"I must say that is odd."

"To a real businessman, yes."

Raleigh crossed his arms, hoping the stern gesture would prompt Flint to speak out of discomfort or embarrassment. Silence didn't linger long before proving to be his friend.

"Raleigh," Flint asked as he leaned his back against the chair, a gesture Raleigh knew was contrived to feign confidence. "I must ask what development caused you to decide that you had to know about my affairs at this point in time."

Raleigh mimicked Flint by settling in his own seat. "For the woman you love. I don't want to see her hurt."

"The woman I love?"

"I know you've been courting Daphne Kerr."

"Eleanor told you."

"When you're courting as heavily as she says you have been, how do you expect to keep it a secret?" Raleigh couldn't help but expand on the thought. "Why would you even want to keep it a secret?"

"I don't. I am quite fond of Miss Kerr. In fact—" He clamped his mouth shut.

Raleigh leaned toward Flint. He placed one elbow on his knee. "Never fear. I am not Miss Kerr's guardian, and I am not here to ask your intentions. However, she is the aunt of someone I am very fond of, and I would hate to see either Kerr woman hurt by anyone." He balled his hand into a fist and propped his chin upon it.

A little smile touched Flint's lips. "Well, old boy, you say you are not her guardian, but you certainly are acting as though you were. Both women are lucky to have a friend like you."

"Then you understand my point of view."

"Yes. And I have to admire you. Not everyone would be willing to confront a man just to protect a woman who's not his wife, mother, or sister. That said, I want you to keep what I am about to tell you in the strictest confidence because I assure you, should my courtship with Daphne Kerr progress, she will be apprised of any information she needs to know."

"Understood." Raleigh sat back and nodded. "Keeping confidences is one key to success in the legal profession." He kept his lips in a straight line, so Flint wouldn't see how anxious he felt. Raleigh wondered if Flint was about to reveal that he was a smuggler, a bootlegger, or worse.

Flint returned his nod but didn't speak right away. "The fact is, I know nothing about the business, and shamefully, I seem to have no aptitude for it."

"A man of your means and wit? Surely you exaggerate."

"I'm afraid you are wrong to place such confidence in me. Oh, I tried to run the business. I assure you, I tried. But I made a mess of things. Thankfully, one of my uncle's faithful employees, Lee Stone, possessed the knowledge to make sure I didn't ruin the enterprise." He looked down at the floor in a gesture of obvious embarrassment. "Ever since he came to my rescue, I have depended on him and a circle of other trusted employees to keep my business afloat."

Raleigh hesitated. He knew the dangers of putting one's livelihood into the hands of others, even those who seem trustworthy. He had a feeling that Lee Stone would be sure to mention his visit to Flint's office and decided he'd best come clean. "I met Mr. Stone today when I went to your office in search of you." Before Flint could ask more, Raleigh hastened to add, "He seems efficient enough. He was running an adding machine during my visit."

Flint chuckled. "That sounds like Lee."

"While he seems quite competent, are you sure you're perfectly at home with the idea of giving him so much power over your business?"

Flint shrugged. "What other choice do I have?"

"For one, you could sell out."

Flint thought for a moment. "I have too much pride to sell out now that I've found I have a sizable source of income—something to pass on to my heirs." Flint's gaze met Raleigh's. "You see, I've never had that before." He paused. "I know you're smart, Raleigh. Your reputation is that of one of the most wily—and honest—lawyers in town. You can go to your practice each day with the confidence that you won't come out looking foolish."

Raleigh felt a twinge of sympathy. "Since you have shown courage in expressing yourself to me, I would be wrong not to admit that I've lost a case or two in my time."

"Of course. No one—not even you—always wins."

"No, but I've never lost a case because I whiled away all my time at local taverns."

Flint winced. Raleigh almost regretted making his observation aloud, but perhaps hearing the truth could hurt enough for Flint to change his ways.

"Maybe not," Flint said, "but you were born to wealth. Of course, you're going to succeed. You know something, Raleigh? Before I came into my unexpected inheritance, I had no way of traveling at all. I was barely scraping by at a dull job making less than eight hundred dollars a year. I had no dreams of travel, and my hours were long. Now I can do as I please with no one to answer to." His eyes darted toward the door through which his aunt had exited. "Well, almost no one."

Raleigh grinned. "Be thankful that someone cares about you. Loneliness is a terrible thing. Why do you think I pay Miss Howard to stay with Mother?"

"I suppose." Flint didn't smile as Raleigh expected. Instead, he seemed pensive. "As to not revealing everything about myself, I don't expect you to understand my point of view. And I'm sure some people doubt me, maybe even gossip about me. But I'd rather be thought a well-traveled man of intrigue than to be known as a fool—even though I can take comfort in the fact that I am a rich fool."

Raleigh took a moment to digest the information Flint had just shared. "I must say, I'm relieved to learn the facts. If I were you, I wouldn't hide behind my embarrassment any longer. So what if others run your business? I have many clients who are in the same situation."

"Do you protect them?"

Raleigh considered his question. "Not really. Most people would find my business of civil law quite dull. Just lots of papers to shuffle from one place to another, all covered with Latin phrases that few outside the profession understand.

So far I haven't been offered the chance to defend a guilty person. If I were, I'm not sure I would. I prefer to be on the side of right."

"But isn't it right to keep wrongdoers from suffering punishments that are too harsh to fit their crimes?"

"Yes."

"So isn't that part of your job? To keep everyone from discovering reality?" Flint gave him a sly smile as if to show he was in jest, but Raleigh knew that Flint believed his observation held a ring of truth.

"On the contrary, the essence of the legal profession is to find and to reveal the truth, not to diminish it." Raleigh rose from his chair. "Which is why I want you to do something for me."

When Flint stood, he adopted the posture and speed of one far beyond his years. Surely the conversation had drained him of energy. "Haven't I made enough concessions for one day?"

"I'm glad to see your capacity for wit is returning. What I want you to do will be of great benefit to you and to the one you love."

"Do you think my chances with her would be increased if she knew the facts? Do you really believe that?"

"I do." Raleigh's voice rang with the strength of the truth he knew.

"And my confession won't hurt your chances with Miss Eleanor Kerr, will it?"

"Since you have been candid with me, I owe you the courtesy of being just as frank with you. Yes, Eleanor will be greatly comforted to know the truth about you, and since I will be accompanying you to the Kerr house today, my chances with her will improve considerably." His heart did a funny flip-flop when he mentioned Eleanor's name in such close connection to his own. Somehow, it sounded perfect. Amazing, even. A wave of relief mixed with pleasure washed over him. Raleigh and Eleanor. Eleanor Alden. The combination sounded right.

"Today?" Flint's voice sounded like a jolt. "Can't this wait until tomorrow?"

"No. The sooner the better." He almost confided the fact of Eleanor's imminent departure but decided that such a ploy would make him look too desperate. Though he had gained respect for Flint during their conversation, they hadn't established trust to the level that Raleigh wanted to let Flint know just how much power he held over him at that moment.

"I don't know—"

"As much as this will benefit me, I wouldn't ask you to go if I didn't honestly believe it would help you, as well."

Flint didn't seem too happy. "If you insist."

Raleigh struggled to keep exhilaration out of his voice. "I'm afraid I must."

Flint took a moment to bid his aunt good-bye, then accompanied Raleigh into his carriage. The two men were silent during the brief trip, a development uncharacteristic for the garrulous Flint. Raleigh was grateful for the time to pray in silence.

Father in heaven, I pray that the Kerrs will see us. I try not to ask Thee for much, but please grant me the favor of Eleanor. I pray that, though this is my will, her ability to return my love is Thy will, as well. In the name of Thy Son, I pray. Amen.

If Flint was aware of Raleigh's turmoil or if he experienced any of his own, his bland expression left no indication. Almost before Raleigh knew it, they had arrived at the Kerrs'.

The maid entered the room where both women were working. Aunt Daphne had just begun sewing a lace blouse, and Eleanor was putting the finishing touches on an order she had promised to complete before leaving for Louisiana.

"Mr. Jarvis is here to see you, Miss Daphne."

Daphne gasped and rose from her sewing machine so fast that Eleanor thought she would knock over the chair. "Flint! Why, what is he doing here now? We don't have plans."

"He said he was here on business, ma'am."

"Business? Hmm. Well, tell him I'll see him immediately."

"Oh, but Miss Daphne, he brought Mr. Alden with him."

It was Eleanor's turn to drop the dress on which she was working. Made of slick satin, it slid down her legs and landed on the floor. Eleanor made a quick motion to retrieve it.

"Tell Mr. Alden to go away," Aunt Daphne said with a sharp tone.

"I tried, but it isn't working this time. Mr. Jarvis said that he won't come in without Mr. Alden."

"This time?" Eleanor asked. "He was here before?"

Aunt Daphne nodded. "Yes. I told him we wouldn't see him."

Eleanor wondered what to do. She desperately wanted to speak with Raleigh. If she didn't see him now, perhaps the opportunity would never again present itself. And she had a feeling that their business had something to do with Flint's secret. She decided to intervene. "Please, let's see them, Aunt Daphne."

"Are you daft? I thought he had hurt you."

"But he wouldn't be here with Mr. Jarvis if it wasn't important. I think we should hear what they have to say."

"Well, perhaps I can agree to see them alone."

"No," Eleanor said too hastily. "I mean, I should at least give him the consideration of one last good-bye."

"If you insist." Despite her aunt's curt words, Eleanor could see relief soften the woman's features. She never wanted to forgo an opportunity to see Flint Jarvis.

"Very well," Aunt Daphne instructed. "Escort them into the parlor. We'll be in shortly."

"Do I offer tea, ma'am?"

Aunt Daphne glanced at the clock. "No, it is too near dinner. If they delay, we can invite them for a meal. Cook is preparing roast beef tonight, so there should be enough to set two extra plates."

"Yes, Miss Daphne."

Eleanor folded the satin garment, rose from her seat, and placed it on her chair before consulting the mirror to confirm the state of her appearance. She was glad she had chosen to wear her best housedress that day. She wished she could excuse herself long enough to change into her Sunday dress but realized that to do so would make her appear too contrived—and too interested in Raleigh's visit.

She darted her gaze at Aunt Daphne and saw that she was preening with just as much enthusiasm.

"Are you ready?" Eleanor asked. "You look wonderful, by the way."

Aunt Daphne swept her gaze over Eleanor. "As do you."

Eleanor smiled. She was enjoying the truce she and her aunt had reached in unspoken agreement, so much so that she knew she would miss her once she left.

"In fact, you look so lovely today that he might try to convince you to stay," Aunt Daphne suggested.

"Oh, pshaw."

But indeed, that is what she truly desired. Psalm 37:4 popped into her head: *"Delight thyself also in the LORD; and he shall give thee the desires of thine heart."*

"Flint!" Aunt Daphne said as soon as she crossed the threshold of the parlor. "How nice to see you. I wasn't expecting you."

Not caring about Flint, Eleanor cut her glance to Raleigh. His eyes lit as their gazes met, though his expression seemed to be touched by remorse. Then she remembered how she had eavesdropped on his conversation. She wondered if regret showed on her face, as well. Though she might have appeared to be calm on the exterior, her increased pulse upon seeing him again revealed to Eleanor her secret feelings. Why had she become so vehement with her aunt and insisted on returning to Louisiana? She didn't want to go back. She wanted to stay here in Baltimore. Her new home. Where Raleigh was.

Aunt Daphne touched her hair. "I'm sorry I don't quite look my best."

"But my dear," Flint quipped, "you always look your best."

Aunt Daphne giggled like a shy little girl being asked what she wanted for Christmas. She sat down, and the others followed suit.

"So tell me what your business is." Aunt Daphne sent Raleigh a cold look.

Flint garnered her attention. "I'm aware that my style of life doesn't appear to be consistent with my income."

"Oh, that." Aunt Daphne sent Flint a dismissive wave of her hand. "Really, people are just too nosy." She sent a frigid stare to Eleanor, who squirmed.

"I'll make myself brief. My uncle left me an inheritance."

"Is this a recent development?"

"Two years ago. Before then, I—I was a clerk." Flint looked at his shoes. For the first time in memory, Eleanor felt sorry for him.

"But you're a big man in shipping now," Aunt Daphne urged.

"Yes. Yes and no. Well, I have an interest in a shipping concern, but I have nothing to do with its operations except to sign the occasional paper and review quarterly reports. And I should have admitted that from the start. I beg your forgiveness."

"What should I care about how you run your business or how you came to enter it? Such concerns belong to men, not to me."

"I would expect other women to think that, but not you." He rubbed his thumbs together but looked Aunt Daphne in the eyes. "Daphne, you are such a talented businesswoman. You know the ins and outs of your shop and can recite facts and figures from memory. Quite impressive, really."

"Quite necessary, actually."

He chuckled. "I feel like such a dimwit in comparison to you."

"A ridiculous notion."

"Not when one considers that I depend on others to operate the business that keeps feeding my wealth—wealth I never earned. Rather than a man of considerable talent and wit, you must think me a fool."

"A fool? No, I think you are one of the luckiest men I know."

"But how can you respect a man with such little talent as I possess?"

"You underestimate yourself," she protested. "As long as your business is legitimate—and obviously it is—I don't care how involved you are in the day-to-day operations, whether you or someone else runs it, or what you know or don't know. Can't you see, Flint? I don't want to be with you because of your business, but because of the man you are. And nothing will ever change that."

Relief flooded his face. "Indeed?"

"Indeed." Aunt Daphne rose.

He leaped to his feet and strode toward her. "But others might think—"

"Who cares what others might think? I don't care what kind of fool you say you are. I love you with all my heart."

"And I love you."

Frozen in her chair, Eleanor watched the couple stare into each other's eyes. She couldn't help but feel a twinge of envy despite her happiness for Aunt Daphne. Oh, to enjoy such unblemished love! If only she could rid herself of her feelings toward Raleigh!

She sighed. At least someone was experiencing a happy ending. But not her.

And it could never be her. Eleanor rose from her seat to make a silent and hasty exit. No matter how much she loved her aunt, she couldn't stand being witness to so much happiness when in only a few days her own world would change irrevocably. She would never see the one she loved, ever again.

Chapter 13

"Wait!" Mr. Jarvis's voice cut through the air in the parlor.

Eleanor stopped so abruptly that she knocked her shin into the tea table. Cups and saucers rattled together. After assuring that no china had been damaged by her near mishap, she looked up at him.

Flint lifted his forefinger. "There's more."

With the spell between the couple broken, Aunt Daphne startled as though she was regaining her senses. "There certainly is. What brought all this on, Eleanor? Why do I have the distinct feeling that you had something to do with this?" She stared at Raleigh. "And what about you?"

"Now, now, dear." Flint patted her on the hand. "That's what I wanted to talk about. Raleigh and Eleanor were, indeed, instrumental in bringing on this confession, but I don't want you to harbor any ill will toward either one of them."

"But why shouldn't I? I could have lost you."

"I'm not so sure about that, unless my own false pride had been in play. They were right, you know. I had been carrying a burden—the burden of deceit—that I knew had to be lifted eventually. I just kept putting off that eventuality. Now that everything is out in the open, I see how ridiculous I was to be worried." He turned to Raleigh. "I want to thank you for forcing my hand, old boy. You did me a favor."

Raleigh nodded once. "I'm glad, but the one you need to thank is Eleanor."

"So I was right." Aunt Daphne's tone was less forgiving. "You are the one who stirred the brew."

"Don't be so hard on your niece, my dear," Mr. Jarvis admonished. "You should be grateful that she cares about you so much."

Aunt Daphne glanced downward, and her posture softened. "I suppose. . ."

"No supposing about it, my dear," Mr. Jarvis said. "It's true."

"But Eleanor shouldn't have poked her nose into my business and dragged Raleigh into the thick of it."

"Whatever you think, won't you forgive them both? For my sake?" Mr. Jarvis implored.

Aunt Daphne's lips tightened as she thought about his plea. After a moment, she nodded. "All right. For you, I will."

"Thank you, Aunt Daphne."

"Thank you, Daphne," Raleigh added. "My mother and I hold you in regard, and we, too, want to remain on the best of terms."

Eleanor remembered what her aunt had said earlier about not wanting to sew another garment for an Alden or even for Vera. She wondered what her response would be.

"All right, then. I forgive you both for prodding into our affairs. I suppose it is better to get everything out in the open. Knowing that Flint was concerned about the way I felt, I regard him more highly now than ever."

She gazed up into his eyes, the love unmistakable. He returned her look.

"I do believe I would care for a glass of lemonade." Eleanor tilted her head toward Raleigh as she stepped to the door. "Would you like to join me?"

Raleigh cut his gaze to the loving couple and nodded. "A glass of lemonade sounds delightful." He followed Eleanor.

She hadn't counted on being alone with Raleigh but found she didn't dread the opportunity. Instinctively she headed to the back of the house, toward the kitchen, then took a turn. How could she expect someone of Raleigh's esteemed position to accompany her to the kitchen?

As Aunt Daphne had mentioned, Cook was preparing roast. Since the cut of beef was substantial, delicious cooking aromas had been swirling through the house for some hours. Inhaling, Eleanor realized she was hungry. She wondered if Aunt Daphne would ask the men to dinner. She was tempted to broach the idea but knew it really wasn't her place.

She happened to see the maid in the midst of refreshing the flowers on the dining room table. "Would you bring Mr. Alden and me some lemonade in the drawing room?"

"Yes, Miss Eleanor."

Soon they were in the drawing room, sitting across from each other in front of the unlit fireplace. Raleigh was the first to speak. "That went better than expected."

"I must say, it certainly did go well."

"You weren't surprised."

"I can't say I was taken aback, although I hadn't realized their feelings had developed to such an extent. I'm happy for Aunt Daphne, truly. And now that you have found out about Mr. Jarvis, I'm happy for him, too."

"Good." He exhaled. "Finding out about him was quite a trial."

"And I thank you. I feel so much better now. I can be happy knowing that Aunt Daphne isn't marrying someone who is suspect."

"Even though I proved you wrong by showing that Flint isn't a smuggler or worse, I admire you for wanting the best for your aunt. You are a fine woman, Eleanor Kerr."

"Thank you." Though hardly as romantic as the words she had heard Flint Jarvis exchange with her aunt, pride swelled in Eleanor all the same. Raleigh's sentiment possessed more substance. She wished she could return his compliment, but his other, unflattering words—overheard as they had been—had hurt too much. "I'm not of as great a substance as the women of Baltimore society, I'm afraid."

His dark eyebrows shot up. "On the contrary, I think you surpass them."

"Don't exaggerate for the sake of flattery, please." At that moment, the lemonade arrived, but the beverage couldn't have been colder than her tone.

"I assure you, I do not exaggerate."

She softened her demeanor. "Then thank you."

Raleigh took a full glass from the tray. "Oh, there are some pretty ladies here, some smart ones, some devout ones, some silly ones, and some who possess a few of all these traits." He shrugged.

"But none who have caught your fancy."

"None." His voice dropped to a whisper.

Eleanor took a sip of her own lemonade and found it too tart for her taste. She ran her tongue over her teeth in a vain effort to wash away the sourness as she set her glass on a crocheted doily on the table. "You left someone in Florida, then."

"No, indeed. One or two of the ladies there caught my eye, but I didn't feel the emotion—or the Lord's leading—required for me to court either with any seriousness." He took several swallows of his lemonade, apparently not minding the tartness.

Eleanor waited. Perhaps if she didn't look too eager, he would speak up and try to convince her not to leave.

"I miss some things about Florida, but now that I'm back in Baltimore, I find I feel right at home." As he continued on a monologue of the virtues of Florida versus the virtues of Maryland, she tried to keep an interested look on her face. If he had any emotion to share with her, he wasn't going to reveal it. Had she misread him so badly?

After he had nursed two glasses of the beverage, Eleanor knew she couldn't detain him longer. "I have enjoyed this afternoon with you, Raleigh, but I'm afraid this is good-bye. I am returning home next week as planned."

Following her lead, he rose from his seat. "I'm sorry to hear that we couldn't entice you to stay in Baltimore."

She hesitated. Did he really want her to stay as a romantic interest, or was he just being polite? Could she hope? "No. No, I can't." Eleanor left before he could say more. She didn't want him to see her cry.

—————

That evening as he read his devotions, Raleigh couldn't concentrate. The conversation with Eleanor lingered too heavily on his mind. Some of the statements she had made struck him as strange, indeed. Why had she asked him about other women? And what was that business that she wasn't as good as they were?

He kept reading, even going so far as to deviate from his current study of 1 Kings to flip through both the Old and New Testaments to see if he could find some words of advice. What would the Lord tell him? Nothing he landed on seemed to apply.

"I must be obtuse today." Self-disgust permeated his voice. "Who cares?" he muttered. "No one else is around to overhear me."

His mind began clicking everything into place until he remembered the conversation he had engaged in with his mother. A conversation he wished he could erase forever, but he could not. A conversation during which he was reprimanded by his mother, and rightfully so. But hadn't he made amends by doing Eleanor's bidding? He couldn't imagine any other circumstance where he would have investigated Flint. But Eleanor had asked, and for her, he did the deed.

Yet Eleanor wasn't convinced that she was good enough for him. He drummed his fingers on the arm of his chair. Someone must have told Eleanor about what he had said. He didn't bother to contain a gasp.

That had to be it! Yes!

But whom? Surely his mother would have been more discreet. She may have been upset with Raleigh, but her pride would have kept her from revealing outside of the family anything about Raleigh that shamed her.

Then who? Vera? He rubbed his shaven chin, which had grown stubble over the course of the day, with his thumb and forefinger. Could she have overheard them? But after the dinner party, Raleigh thought Vera understood that he simply felt no romantic attraction for her. Vera was a lovely woman, not mean-spirited enough to say something to hurt Eleanor, for whom she had obviously developed a fondness. He imagined Vera would miss Eleanor more than Daphne.

Monroe? Perhaps he had told Eleanor. He never seemed to hold her in particular regard. Just as quickly, Raleigh dismissed the possibility. Even if Monroe had overheard him talking—a situation not uncommon for a servant—he had not the sharp disposition to cause trouble. Yet even if Monroe had been so unkind, Raleigh doubted Eleanor would have paid him much heed. Still, if he had said something. . .

He would confront Monroe the next day. In the meantime, he needed to go to the Lord in a spirit of humility. Flint may have thought himself a fool, but Raleigh saw that he, not Flint, was the real fool.

Lord, I give Thee my false pride. Show me Thy way.

Only a few miles away in a small room in a row house in the city, Eleanor was praying just as fervently. Why hadn't Raleigh professed his love to her? She could see his feelings written on his face. And she loved him. No matter how much she fought it, she did. Seeing her aunt and Flint Jarvis that day, so enraptured with one another with a love so pure, only made her feelings toward Raleigh more difficult to deny. Yet despite the odd feeling she had as they shared lemonade together, he apparently hadn't been moved enough to make a declaration.

She knew why. No matter what his mother said, Raleigh didn't think she was good enough.

But he had said she was a fine woman. And his voice had been filled with conviction, too. He wasn't lying when he said it or wasting words on false flattery. He had really meant it.

So where did this leave her?

Father in heaven, was I too hasty in making the decision to leave here? I feel no sense of peace about my decision. What is wrong? Please, Lord, show me Thy way.

———

The next morning, Raleigh met with Monroe in his office before his first appointment of the day. "Monroe, did you by chance overhear a conversation between my mother and myself last Tuesday when Miss Vera was out on an errand?"

Monroe gazed at the ceiling as he thought, then looked at Raleigh with a gaze of deference. "No, sir. Was I supposed to?"

Raleigh tried again. "You can tell me the truth. I know you are privy to conversations around the house. If you overheard, I understand. But I need to know the truth."

"Yes, sir. But no, sir, I didn't hear anything. When Miss Vera was out, I was tending to your wardrobe. I remember."

Raleigh thought for a moment. Monroe, indeed, had tended to his wardrobe that day, and he would have been too far away to overhear them talking. So he must be telling the truth. And that meant that if he didn't overhear the conversation then he couldn't have said anything to Eleanor. "Very well, then." He was about to dismiss Monroe when he had another thought. "Was anyone else in the house that day? I know it was the maid's day off, and Cook was engaged in the kitchen."

This time, Monroe didn't hesitate. "Yes, sir. Miss Eleanor came by. I found her in the foyer. I asked if I should announce her, but she declined. She said she had left something at home and went back out to get it."

Aha. "So you didn't hear her knock?"

"No, sir."

"Did she seem upset?"

"Yes, sir. She seemed distracted. I assumed she was embarrassed about forgetting some of her work."

Raleigh's stomach knotted. If Eleanor had thought he was a snob, his conversation, never meant for her ears, confirmed her suspicions about his feelings— feelings that were part of his past, not of the love he held for her now. Shame filled his being as he thought about how he must have hurt her.

Father in heaven, canst Thou forgive me? Can Eleanor forgive me?

He kept his expression placid so as not to reveal his turmoil. "Very well, Monroe. You are excused."

So Eleanor must have let herself in, then overheard them. No wonder she was upset, and no wonder she had been acting strangely. He had to think of something. He couldn't let her go back home with anger on her mind. In fact, he couldn't let her go at all.

Eleanor arrived at church with slumped shoulders. This was to be her last Sunday in Baltimore. She would miss the Christian community she had grown to love. But she couldn't stay. Yet she still felt no sense of peace about leaving.

Aunt Daphne tugged Eleanor's gloved hand, which clutched her Bible. "There's Flint, just as he promised." She motioned for Eleanor to follow.

"Is that Raleigh sitting beside him?"

Aunt Daphne shrugged and kept walking.

Eleanor tried to put on a happy face. If Raleigh didn't return her feelings or if he simply refused to acknowledge them, then she wanted no part of sitting by him in church. Yet when she slid into the pew, she developed the distinct feeling that she had been set up, as Mr. Jarvis and Aunt Daphne maneuvered for Eleanor and Raleigh to sit by one another.

"What are you doing here? I know you have your own church. Did Mr. Jarvis put you up to this?" she hissed at Raleigh.

"He did ask me to attend today's service with him, then dine at his home afterward. I thought the least I could do to repay for my intrusions earlier in the week was to accept his invitation."

Eleanor couldn't avoid breathing in the familiar scent of bay rum he wore. She would miss that fragrance. And she would miss Raleigh. But she could never let him know. Aggravated, she opened her Bible to a random passage. Remarkably it landed on the tiny book of Jonah. She tried in vain to concentrate on the words.

Jonah. He was running away. Just like Raleigh and I are.

The thought only served to upset her more. She shut the book with more snap than holy parchment pages deserved. She took out her Sunday white lace fan and waved it over her face.

"Today's message is on the subject of denial," the Reverend Spencer began after the singing of hymns—which Raleigh joined in with vigor—and the passing of the collection plate. "Have you ever denied your love for someone?" the minister asked. "For someone important? For someone who could—and would—change your life, if only you would let Him?"

Eleanor squirmed. Surely the reverend meant the Lord Jesus. Of course, He had the power to change anything. With God, all things are possible.

To Eleanor's surprise, the Reverend Spencer recounted the Gospel account of Peter's denial of Jesus. Peter denied Jesus thrice, yet Peter became an important figure in the early church. The minister then went on to compare the love that Christians are to show one another to the love that Jesus showed Peter in the face of betrayal. After a forty-minute sermon that managed to fly with amazing speed, he ended by asking, "Are you denying someone your love today?"

Even though the love in question was *agape* rather than romantic, Eleanor couldn't help but feel that the Lord was speaking to both her and Raleigh through the sermon. She stole a glimpse at Raleigh from her peripheral vision. He kept his expression blank, but his eyes almost looked as though they were about to mist. Knowing that no modern man would want to be caught dead fighting such emotion, she stared back at the pulpit. Had the Lord gotten through to him after all?

After the benediction, Raleigh leaned toward her. "May I come by your house this afternoon?"

She nodded. Sunday dinner promised to be the longest on record.

⸺

If he had had any doubt before, Raleigh knew what he had to do now. He had to convince Eleanor to stay. There was no obstacle to their love except his own unwillingness to put asunder his pride. And what Eleanor had overheard. He flinched each time he remembered his words.

Lord, I pray that Eleanor will forgive me!

She was waiting for him when he arrived at the house. Nervousness clutched at his stomach with intense ferocity.

"Thank you for agreeing to see me today," Raleigh said.

She nodded. Her response was the appropriate one for such a noncommittal greeting, but noncommittal wasn't what he desired. "Eleanor." He didn't waste time discussing the weather or any insignificant matter. If he did, maybe he would lose his nerve—and his chances with her. He moved closer and took her hands in his. Was her heart beating as fast as he thought his was?

"Yes?"

Her encouragement gave him the fortitude to speak. "I've been a fool. I know you overheard the conversation I had with my mother. I'm so sorry for everything I said. Mother was right. I was an unbearable snob. I have been praying to the Lord, and He has shown me how utterly indefensible my attitude was. I beg your forgiveness for how I hurt you."

"So—so you know? You know that I eavesdropped?" Embarrassment made itself apparent in her expression. She stepped into the parlor, and Raleigh followed.

"I didn't put two and two together until last night."

Her face flushed. "I'm sorry I eavesdropped. How rude you must think me.

I am the one who should be apologizing to you, and indeed, I am. Can you forgive me?"

"Of course. If someone had been talking about me in such a manner, I would have taken pause to listen in, as well." He squeezed her hands. "I'm only sorry that I caused you such hurt. You have no idea how many times I have wished I could take back that day!"

"I can see that I was too hasty in judging you."

"I was not too hasty in judging you."

"What?" She tried to pull her hands out of his, but he held tightly.

"Whether you are a seamstress, a maid, or to the manor born, I knew from the day I first met you that you are a splendid woman—a woman any man would be lucky to have as his wife."

Her eyes widened, but she remained silent.

"I should have listened to my heart from the start."

"What are you saying?"

"I'm saying I don't want you to go," he blurted.

"But—but my train ticket—"

"If they won't give you your money back, I'll refund you double."

"So you're resorting to bribery?" Her tone was teasing.

He smiled. "I love you, Eleanor Kerr. And I always will."

"Oh, Raleigh, I feel the same about you. And I have for a long time. How could we have almost fallen victim to love's denial?"

"Our injudicious pride, that's how. But the Lord showed us a better way."

"We'll have to thank the Reverend Spencer."

"Indeed, I think I'll make out a bank draft to the church as soon as possible. Or at least give him a generous sum of money for performing our marriage ceremony come spring—if you will agree to become Mrs. Raleigh Alden."

She gasped. "Are you sure?"

"What kind of answer is that?" He snapped his fingers. "All right. You want me to do this the right way." He smiled and got down on one knee. "Miss Eleanor Kerr, will you do me the distinct honor of accepting my plea for marriage?"

She didn't pause. "Yes!"

"I will cable your father immediately to ask his blessing."

"I know we shall have it."

Raleigh rose and rushed to embrace her. As he brought his lips toward hers, she didn't hesitate to respond. How long he—indeed Eleanor, as well—had waited to seal their bond. A bond that pride had almost broken but that God had clearly ordained. Her sweet spirit, her soft lips, her warm embrace, her heart for God—he would relish each day with Mrs. Raleigh Alden. Forever.

Epilogue

The following spring

ook over here, please, Mrs. Alden."

Eleanor set her gaze on June. The mother of the groom had risen from her bed to appear at the wedding and looked fine in blue. Situated in a Chippendale chair that reminded Eleanor of a throne with its elegant curves, she smiled to herself at how regal—and happy—June appeared.

The new bride felt a nudge.

"Eleanor?" Raleigh smiled down at her. On this day, Eleanor didn't think it immodest to take credit for the happiness shining from his expression. "Eleanor." His voice coaxed itself into a tease. "Aren't you going to smile prettily for the photographer? After all, he's just doing his job."

"But he asked for Mrs.—" Eleanor stopped herself and laughed. The photographer from the *Baltimore Sun* wanted not to take a picture of her new mother-in-law but of her. She was Mrs. Alden! Mrs. Raleigh Alden! Her cheeks warmed. "I—I suppose I'd better get used to my new name."

"Is that such a trial?" Raleigh asked.

"No." Her voice became more firm. "No, it isn't." She smiled up at him and blinked when the camera flashed.

"That will be a beautiful picture for the society page, Mrs. Alden," the photographer claimed. "You certainly are the epitome of the blushing bride."

"Oh yes, indeed!" the reporter accompanying him agreed. Miss Leeks already had pen and notepad poised in hand. "Mrs. Alden, this is such a big day for you. Your wedding will be the talk of the town for months—even years—to come."

The nuptials had indeed been more extravagant than Eleanor had dreamed possible for her ceremony. A quiet affair with a few friends and family would have pleased her, but Raleigh and June had insisted on a grand celebration to usher Eleanor into her new life as a Baltimore society matron. "Uh, thank you."

Miss Leeks gave her a wide-eyed stare. "Do you have anything you'd like to share with our readers, Mrs. Alden?"

Eleanor looked forward to getting used to her new name, but she was still too new at being interviewed to be comfortable with talking to reporters, no matter how friendly. "I—uh—"

"Maybe you can let Miss Leeks's readers know how much we anticipate our honeymoon trip abroad," Raleigh suggested. "I admit, it took some doing to convince my lovely bride to take such an extended trip. She loves nothing more than home life."

Eleanor gazed at her new husband. "I would go anywhere with you, Raleigh."

"Such a sweet sentiment." Miss Leeks smiled. "And will you be traveling by streamship?"

Eleanor let out a breath of relief. "Oh yes! I certainly am looking forward to seeing Europe."

Miss Leeks smiled. "And will you be traveling by steamship?"

"Yes," she replied.

"Which one?"

Raleigh answered, "I would prefer to keep that a secret for now."

"A secret, eh?" The reporter's mouth twisted into a displeased line for a moment before she composed herself into a sunny demeanor. "Of course you should be permitted to be a bit mysterious about your honeymoon trip. You will fill us in upon your return?"

"Certainly," Raleigh assured her.

Miss Leeks tapped her pen against her cheek. "Could you tell us a little bit about your itinerary?"

Raleigh shrugged and gave her a half smile. "We'll be touring the great capital cities of Europe."

"That sounds so romantic!" Miss Leeks commented as she wrote. "Mrs. Alden, will you allow me to interview you upon your return? Our readers will want to know all about such a fine trip."

"Of course." At least the trip would give Eleanor something to talk about to the reporter. On this day, she felt too swept up in emotion to utter a coherent sentence.

"They'll want to know about the steamship experience, what you ate, what shipboard parties you attended, and the like."

"She'll take copious notes," Raleigh assured Miss Leeks. "Now if you will excuse us…"

"Oh certainly. Thank you for your time."

"And you, yours," Raleigh said. "Please enjoy the refreshments."

Miss Leeks and the photographer took their leave, their expressions indicating they planned to do just that.

"My, but it sounds as though I have just been given a journalistic assignment by that reporter."

Raleigh chuckled. "Do you blame her? It promises to be a fabulous journey."

"I'd be happy with any trip. Why, even if we were just going to an inn across town, that would be enough, as long as we were together."

"My sentiments exactly."

"So how do you do it?" Eleanor asked.

"Do what?"

"Handle those reporters and make them feel like they're your best friends?"

Raleigh chuckled. "Practice, my dear. Practice."

"Oh, I'll never be practiced enough to be as kind as you."

"On the contrary, I anticipate you will have many years of practice. Our love is forever." Raleigh lifted her hand, the one bearing her bright new wedding band, to his lips and back. The gesture sent a thrill down Eleanor's spine.

"Yes," Eleanor assured him. "Wherever we go and whatever we do, our love is forever."

THE
RUSE

Dedication

To the real Mr. and Mrs. Christopher Bagley

Prologue

Washington County, Maryland, 1899

Katherine Jones looked over the letter she had just penned to Otis Rath, a brave sailor fighting in the war against the Spaniards. Despite Otis's noteworthy war record and adventures at sea, she found writing to Otis much more difficult than writing to her childhood friend Christopher Bagley. Her pen flowed with no effort over the paper as she told Christopher, who was away at agricultural college, all about the week's events. They knew the same people, had been taught by the same teacher, and had attended the same church when Christopher was home. He understood her. But Otis was a stranger.

"What did you write?" Miranda Henderson asked from across the kitchen table.

Miranda kept up a lively correspondence with her cousin Matthew in the army, but Katherine was writing to a man she had never met as a favor to her beloved uncle. After the first few sentences, Katherine struggled. What could she tell Otis?

Still holding the ivory-colored rag paper, Katherine leaned her chin on her palm. "Oh, I don't know what to write. Otis and I have no acquaintances in common, and nothing exciting seems to happen here."

Miranda snatched Katherine's letter and read over it. "What makes you think he would want to read this? Who cares that you gathered more eggs than usual this week? Or what the preacher said last Sunday? Unless you think Otis is some kind of heathen and you're looking for a convert." Miranda sniffed.

"Christopher doesn't seem to mind such news."

"That's different. You've known him all your life."

"Precisely." Katherine sighed. "Maybe I never should have agreed to correspond with someone I've never met."

"Especially if your main purpose for writing is to bring him to the faith."

"No, that's not my reason. Besides, Otis says he loves the Lord. And of course I never would use war correspondence to gain a convert unless God gave me a clear leading to do so."

"And He hasn't." Miranda scooted the letter across the table back to Katherine as though it was better suited for the trash bin than the postman. "I say that if you never want to hear from your sailor again, just keep giving him a Sunday school report."

"If my letter is so boring, then you must know how to write a most entertaining missive. So tell me, what are you writing to your cousin in the army?"

"I'm glad you asked." Miranda smiled, held up the letter, and read aloud:

Dear Matthew,

This has proven to be the most exciting week I have experienced since the commencement of our correspondence! Much to the delight of the Ladies' Horsewomen's Club, I earned a blue ribbon to add to my growing collection, for my equestrian skills in jumping hurdles. My mare, Ash, was in fine form as usual, guided with my gentle but experienced and firm hand. The trophy I won is a handsome one and looks well on my bookshelf.

I have been working on my needlework to enter in the fair. The sampler, a colorful example of fine work, is almost ready. I am sure it will be recognized with yet another ribbon to add to my collection.

My room is so filled with trophies and ribbons that I do believe we'll soon need to add yet another room to the house to hold them all! But no number of accolades I can earn with my puny endeavors can ever compare to the many medals you deserve for fighting for your country each and every day. Putting yourself in harm's way is ever so brave. My heart flutters in fear to think about the danger you face. The members of the fairer sex and the men left on the home front who are unable to go in your stead are all so grateful for your courage and sacrifice.

To show my friendly and familial devotion, I am enclosing a small lock of my hair. When you look at this little memento, remember me, your dear cousin, as I remember you in fond kinship for your bravery.

Yours most sincerely,
Miranda

Katherine shook her head upon hearing such hyperbole. "I do declare, that is some letter."

"Entertaining, is it not?"

"It certainly does detail your recent accomplishments. No doubt your cousin finds such news fascinating. But I haven't earned any ribbons lately, and I'm not one to pour on the praise like you are, Miranda. Such writing comes easily to you but not to me. It's just not in my nature."

"Maybe you should follow my example and make it part of your nature, then."

"Maybe I should." Katherine stared at the words she had written to Otis, but her mind was too filled with woe to comprehend them. "Maybe I'm not called to cheer up a sailor. I should concede defeat." She looked at Miranda. "Although even if my letter was the most trite in the world, Otis would have bragging rights since he'd be getting mail. Doesn't that count for something?"

"Bragging rights, eh?" Miranda snapped her fingers. "Then why don't you give your sailor something to brag about?"

"What do you mean?"

"You've sent him a portrait of yourself, haven't you?"

"Yes, the best one I have." Katherine nodded.

"The one of you in the white lace dress?"

"That's the one."

"Good. Then all the other fellows know he's writing to a lovely brunette with big eyes. Now all you have to do is to make yourself seem just a little more... exciting."

"Miranda! Are you telling me to lie?"

"Of course not." She tapped her fingers ever so lightly on the table. "Just embellish a little. What's the harm?"

Katherine leaned back in her chair in a failed effort to separate herself from Miranda and her suggestion. "What a terrible Christian I would be if I pretended to be someone I'm not. I can't. Not even to cheer up a brave military man."

"Hmm. Well, maybe I can change your mind."

Katherine shook her head. "Never." She sealed the envelope. "If Otis doesn't want to read about the sermon, that's fine by me. He can stop writing, then."

Miranda didn't say another word. Then why did the look on her face leave Katherine wondering...and worrying?

Chapter 1

Washington County, Maryland, 1901

Though Otis had been honorably discharged from the service, Katherine's correspondence with him hadn't diminished one iota. If anything, his hints of admiration of her only increased with time.

So when a letter written in a fine hand appeared in the family's stack of mail one Tuesday morning, she felt no surprise. Only when she studied its contents did she sit down in a kitchen chair.

Otis was planning a visit. He would be arriving the next day! Katherine let out a gasp.

"Is that a letter from the sailor?" Katherine's ten-year-old sister asked, looking up from the comics section of a newspaper.

"Yes, Betsy."

"What's wrong?"

"Nothing."

"Then why do you seem surprised?" Betsy's brown eyes took on a heightened glint.

"His news is unexpected, that's why. He's coming for a visit."

It was Betsy's turn to let out a breath. "Oh! How exciting! I wonder if he wrote me, too."

Katherine flipped through the pile of mail. "As a matter of fact, he did." She handed her a white envelope bearing Otis's precise script.

"Goodie!" Betsy ripped open the letter and drew out a prize. "Look! He sent me a bookmark!"

"Oh, how lovely. I know he's proud that you are reading so well now."

Betsy began reading her missive from Otis.

Katherine interrupted with a thought. "Oh, I must tell Mother." She rushed upstairs, where Mother was folding laundry.

The older woman turned to her. "What is it, Katherine? You're running around like there's a fire, only you look too happy for anything to be terribly wrong."

"Oh no, nothing is wrong. Indeed, everything is just right!"

"Like Goldilocks in the fairy tale, eh?" Mother teased.

Katherine clasped her hands. "You could say that." She rocked back and forth with glee. "Otis is coming from South Carolina to visit us!"

Mother gasped. "He's coming all that way?"

"Yes. Can you believe it?"

Mother thought for a moment. "As a matter of fact, I can. You've been writing to him for quite some time, and I don't think the correspondence would have lasted so long after the war unless he was at least a mite sweet on you."

Blushing, Katherine took a sudden interest in the starched curtains framing her parents' bedroom window. "I don't know about that, but I do look forward to his visit."

"When is he due to arrive?"

"Tomorrow!"

Mother's expression went from pleased to alarmed. "Tomorrow? Why, we'll hardly have time to prepare any food. And we must air out Ralph's room for him. The sheets are clean, but it might not hurt to put fresh ones on the bed for Otis all the same." Mother hurried to place a pile of unmentionables in her dresser drawer. "My, but we must start right away. Get a rag and wipe the furniture in Ralph's room real good now—and dust everything downstairs, too. Especially in the formal parlor. You hear?"

"Yes, ma'am." Katherine wasn't worried. Mother was in the habit of keeping her house clean enough for company on a moment's notice.

"Oh, I do wish we had time to polish everything."

"We just polished for spring cleaning. I think everything looks fine."

"To your eyes, maybe. But you're accustomed to how things look around here. He'll be seeing everything for the first time. Oh, I wish he'd given us more notice!"

"I have a feeling he wants to see us the way we really are. I think we're pretty presentable most of the time."

Mother laughed. "I hope so. All the same, I would have appreciated more time to spruce up." She snapped her fingers. "Oh, I thought of something else."

Katherine tried not to grimace at the thought of even more work. "Yes, ma'am?"

"I'll need you to sweep the floors after you dust."

"I will." At the rate Mother was doling out assignments, Katherine feared the afternoon would melt into evening before she finished. "Um, Mother?"

"Yes?"

"After I do those chores, may I run to Miranda's for a spell? I promise to keep my visit quick, and I'll be glad to do anything else you need upon my return."

"Oh, all right. I suppose so. But make it quick, now. And tell Betsy to come see me. I'll be needing her help, too."

"Yes, ma'am."

Katherine's little sister was just about to escape to the outdoors when Katherine returned downstairs.

"Mother wants to see you," Katherine informed her.

The brown-haired girl wrinkled her nose. "She wants me to do more chores, doesn't she?"

"That's a good guess. But I'm doing my part, too," Katherine assured, holding up a dust rag. "I've got to cover the whole house. And I've got to sweep, too." Katherine knew those facts would console her sister, who hated sweeping with a passion.

"I wonder what she wants me to do."

"I don't know, but the sooner you start, the sooner you'll be done. Oh, and I'll be going to Miranda's as soon as I dust and sweep, but I'll be back to do more chores. I'd like to bake a pie tonight if I have time."

"Mother will want me to fetch the preserves from the cellar, then." Betsy's voice brightened. "Oh, and tell Miranda I said hello. Did she get her new charm yet?"

"What charm?"

"She was supposed to get a new charm for her bracelet. An aunt was going to send her a souvenir from her trip to Egypt."

"Egypt!" Katherine couldn't imagine visiting somewhere so exotic. "No, she hasn't said anything yet."

"She's hoping for a new charm, but her aunt didn't promise. It might be something else. But you can ask her." Betsy sighed. "I hope I can have a bracelet as pretty as that one someday."

Katherine grinned. "Maybe someday you will."

A short while later as she finished her dusting and sweeping, Katherine glanced at the kitchen wall clock. It told her that Miranda was likely to be occupied with her own weekly dusting. "I won't bother Miranda if I drop in. I can talk to her as she works," she muttered to herself. She slid out the back door, an early summer breeze tickling her face.

After bicycling across the road, Katherine found herself moments later visiting the Henderson house, a large brick affair complete with a carriage house and separate guesthouse.

She found Miranda dusting her family's formal parlor, a much larger room than the modest area of the Joneses' house.

Miranda stopped her chore and urged Katherine to take a seat beside her on the velvet sofa. "I have to say, you seem excited."

Katherine sat—but not still. "I am! You'll never guess what news I have!"

"What?"

She took Miranda's hands in hers. "Otis is coming here for a visit!"

Miranda took her hands out of Katherine's. "After all this time?"

"Yes. Can you believe it?" Katherine had to suppress herself from clapping.

"No. Yes. I mean, I don't know." Miranda embraced her. "Oh, Katherine! This is wonderful! Do you think he means to court you?"

"I—I don't know. Perhaps." She averted her gaze to a blue Oriental rug.

"How splendid!" But her friend's exuberance only lasted a moment before her mouth opened into an uncertain circle. "Uh-oh."

Katherine froze. "Uh-oh? What do you mean?"

It was Miranda's turn to avert her glance. She studied her hands. Even though Miranda was merely engaged in household drudgery, she nevertheless wore her ubiquitous gold charm bracelet that Betsy had mentioned. Miranda also wore two rings. One was set with a sapphire and the other with a pearl and two diamonds barely visible to the human eye. "I'm afraid there's something I have to tell you."

Katherine sat beside Miranda. Fear engulfed her, but she had to know the reason for Miranda's sudden change of mood. "What?"

Miranda took a minute to compose herself before she spoke. "You know how I think—in fact I know—you're a fine woman. Any man would be fortunate to court you."

Such flattery from the self-absorbed Miranda pricked Katherine with suspicion. She let her friend continue unabated.

"And I know how you've always wanted to play the banjo and harp, and that you wish you had kept up with your dancing skills, that you long to play the piano like a graduate of Juilliard, and that you wish you were as good with horses as I am."

Katherine sighed. "Yes. That would be nice, wouldn't it? But alas, it is only a dream. And I certainly don't see what this has to do with Otis's visit." An uneasy feeling overcame her, leaving her with a sudden desire to flee.

Miranda kept her riveted. "Yet you are so accomplished in your own right. You sew a fine seam, and your cooking is rivaled only by your dear mother's."

"You're making me blush. Please, don't flatter me." Her friend's compliments, while she knew them to be sincere, alarmed her.

"But it's true! And Otis should appreciate all those fine things about you. And he'll appreciate you even more when you show him how well you play the harp, ride a horse, play the piano, and dance."

"I beg your pardon?" Katherine felt the color run off her face. "When I show him what?"

Miranda cleared her throat. "All the things you said you always wanted to be."

"But, Miranda! I only shared those thoughts with you in confidence. Of course it would be wonderful to be so accomplished, but developing those skills takes work. Years of work. I haven't made the time or effort to earn the right to claim any of those talents. And I never would."

"I know you wouldn't."

"So. . ."

"So I—well, you know I was writing to Otis, too."

"Yes, you kept that no secret. And he is a free man. He can write to anyone he likes. But I still don't see the connection you seem to be trying to make."

"Otis never detailed our correspondence to you?"

Katherine shrugged. "I see no reason why he owed me any explanation about your letter exchange. As I said, he's a free man, and I trust you as a friend."

Miranda blanched. "Your trust was not misplaced. Not exactly. In fact, I said nothing but flattering things about you."

"You talked about me? I can't imagine why. Not after you chastised me about my letters being a bore. Whatever could you have said about me that he would find enthralling?" An unwanted thought struck her mind. "Unless. . .oh, Miranda, you didn't make up wild stories about imaginary accomplishments of mine, did you?"

When her friend didn't rush to reassure Katherine, she knew they were both in trouble.

"Miranda!"

Miranda grimaced and then lifted her finger in a victorious way. "Never fear. I didn't exaggerate. Not much."

A groan flew from Katherine's lips. "Why did you feel the need to exaggerate at all?"

"Well. . .I wanted to cheer him up. And believe you me, I did! I told him how wonderful you are and about your many talents," said the matchmaking friend.

"And about how brave he is, no doubt."

"True."

"That I don't mind. All of our military men are courageous and daring. But why did you have to make up stories about me?"

"I didn't. Exactly." Miranda blushed. "Well, maybe I did. I just wanted him to like you even more than he already did. You. . .you do like him, don't you?"

"Well, yes, but I didn't mean for you to intervene on my behalf."

"I meant well, you know."

"I know." Katherine summoned her patience. Miranda possessed a kind heart, but her interpretations of right and wrong were often painted gray. "But surely you knew that the truth would come to light one day."

Miranda drummed her fingers on the edge of the sofa and studied them. "Looks like 'one day' has finally arrived. But I wouldn't worry if I were you. Once Otis sees you and how charming and accomplished you really are, he's certain to love you just as much as I do. Even more so."

Katherine tried not to be too harsh in her admonishment. "Oh, Miranda, you always did love a good romance. But honestly, you never should have tried to lead Otis to believe I'm anything more than I really am. He's sure to feel letdown when he sees me in person." Katherine felt her heart descend into the depths of her stomach in disappointment.

Miranda let out a horrified breath. "No, you mustn't let that happen. You have to convince Otis that you possess all the talents I mentioned."

"You mean, convince him that I can actually do all the things that have only been a fantastic notion for me all these years?"

"Of course. How much time do we have?"

Fear struck her. "None. He'll be here tomorrow."

"Tomorrow!" Darkness cast a shadow on Miranda's face, but she soon composed her lips into a sunny smile. "Well, we'll just have to get working on you right away."

"No, Miranda, we've got to confess the truth to Otis. We can cast our bread upon the waters and pray for his pardon."

"No! No, you can't. How will that make me look in front of him? He's bound to pass judgment on me and tell all my friends. I'll look like a fool." Miranda's breathing became noticeable.

"I don't think so."

"That is one place where we disagree, Katherine, and I don't want to take a chance. Please, since you are my dearest friend in the world, you have to help me. Why, if anyone found out I had embellished the truth, I would just lie down and die."

"Oh, Miranda, you exaggerate."

"See? You're already saying it. You're calling me a liar, even in casual conversation."

"No, that's not what I meant."

Miranda withdrew a lace handkerchief and brought it up to her eyes. "I only did it for you. I only want you to be happy. And you were, weren't you? Otis is very fond of you. Fond enough to visit. Maybe even fond enough to court you."

"But I don't want his love if it's based on a lie."

"It won't be. I promise."

"I'm not so sure—"

Miranda sniffled. "Oh, you must not say anything to Otis or anyone else. I promise I'll help you. I'll do anything. Please keep my secret. If people think I'm a liar, my reputation would be ruined, and I'll never be able to find anyone to marry me. Ever. My future would be dismal. My whole life would be nothing but a shambles. No one, male or female, would trust me again. I'd be destined to spinsterhood. Please don't ask me to be a spinster forever, Katherine! I'd rather die!" Miranda had worked herself up into sobs, her blond curls bobbing up and down as her shoulders shook, and she blew her nose into the cloth. "Please, I beg you not to force me to be a spinster!"

Katherine knew she was asking Miranda no such thing, but her friend's antics stunned her into silence. Miranda, always one for the dramatic, nevertheless accepted as unvarnished truth every word she uttered. She believed that Katherine would ruin her life if she let on to anyone that any word bearing a shade of dishonesty had ever escaped Miranda's tinted lips. Katherine's heart stung her chest with pain upon seeing her friend's distress.

"Oh, please, Katherine? Can't you just let on that you possess all these talents, just for a while? After all, he won't be here long, will he?" Miranda blew her nose once more.

"He didn't give an exact time. I don't suppose he could leave his business more than a couple of weeks at the most."

A little smile curved Miranda's lips. "Good. Well, if it's too much for you to convince him entirely, maybe you can hint that you are quite accomplished, just as I said."

"You have more confidence than I do." Katherine's mind whirred at the thought of her plight.

"There's a reason for my confidence. Never fear, Katherine. I have a plan."

Chapter 2

That afternoon, Christopher stopped by the Joneses' house to return a cup of sugar his mother had borrowed from Mrs. Jones. Happy to see her friend, Katherine poured them both lemonade and suggested they sit under the oaks in the backyard for a time. Christopher seemed all too happy to take Katherine up on her suggestion, a fact that gladdened her. A nagging thought that if Otis came courting she wouldn't be able to visit with Christopher with such spontaneity anymore shot through her mind, but she dismissed such dreary thoughts.

"I have good news," she told him well into their visit.

"Oh?" His blue eyes took on an interested light, and he leaned toward her slightly in his wicker chair.

"Remember Otis?"

"Otis. Yes." The excitement left his voice. "The sailor. Are you still writing to him?"

"Yes. I told you that."

"You did? How about that."

Katherine tried to ignore his lack of enthusiasm. Christopher usually wasn't so forgetful. Why was he being like this? She made a deliberate effort to fill her voice with life. "Well, you shouldn't mind. After all, you always told me how much you appreciated my letters when you were away at school."

"Yes, but that's different." He winced.

"I don't see how—"

"Never mind. So what's your news?" Christopher's mouth straightened. He didn't look happy.

Katherine hesitated but pressed on. "He's coming for a visit."

Christopher's eyes widened, then narrowed. "Is that so? How about that. When?"

"Tomorrow."

"So soon?" He leaned back in his chair. "You seem relaxed about the whole thing."

"I've already swept and dusted, and with Mother and Betsy working along with me, there's not much else left to do, really. He can take us as we are. Well"—she felt her face flush—"sort of."

"What do you mean, sort of?"

137

Katherine paused. After taking in a breath to prepare herself, she revealed Miranda's plan to Christopher.

"Miranda has convinced you to do what?" Christopher's blue eyes lit with surprise and anguish.

His obvious disapproval left her disconcerted. "I know it sounds wild, but she only got in this mess because she was trying to help me. Now I feel obligated to help her get out of it."

"I don't think he'll ever believe it, Katherine. I think you should tell him right away, the minute he arrives. You don't want him to be disappointed, do you?"

"No. But I won't disappoint him. I've always wanted to be a skilled horse-woman, a ballerina, a banjo player, a harmonica player, and a harpist. I'll just have to accomplish all these skills a little earlier, that's all." She brightened. "That gives me an idea. You're accomplished on the banjo."

"Yes?" His tone revealed how leery he felt.

"So will you help me? Please?"

"How?"

"Your part is easy. Just teach me one tune on the banjo. That's all."

"One tune is not going to convince him that you are accomplished on the instrument." Christopher settled in his seat like an immovable object and swirled the melting ice in his glass.

"Miranda promised to change the subject before he can ask me to play something else."

Christopher didn't answer right away, which gave her hope. But then he shook his head. "I want to help you, but I can't. I just can't. I'm sorry, Katherine. You're on your own this time."

"You can't?" Vexation and hurt crossed her expression. She rose from her chair and took the glass from him. "It was nice to see you, Christopher, but I must bid you good day. You see, I must bake a cherry pie for my visitor."

Christopher watched Katherine walk into her house and slam the back door behind her. He knew everything was not fine. Would it ever be?

The idea that this Otis fellow planned to come in and sweep Katherine off her feet filled him with ire. Christopher had been planning to ask Mr. Jones if he could court Katherine. They had known one another since childhood, so Christopher didn't anticipate a long courtship. He only wanted to be betrothed long enough for Katherine to plan a wedding. Knowing that Katherine didn't want to put on airs, he imagined his bride would want a simple day. A few words uttered by the preacher in front of their closest friends and family, followed by a short reception featuring one of those big tiered cakes that the women liked to bake. Katherine wouldn't demand an elaborate or expensive honeymoon trip either, although he wanted to give her the best few days of her life. If they married in the fall after the harvest, they could steal away to a nice hotel in Washington, D.C., perhaps. They could see the monuments and take in a little history. The thought brought a smile to his lips.

All too soon, he recalled why these plans would have to be delayed. Perhaps they would have to be forgotten. The idea that Katherine might never be his speared his heart.

What had happened to Katherine, the sweet girl he knew and loved? Why was she letting Miranda wrap her up in a scheme to fool a correspondent she didn't even know? Well, she hardly knew. He balled his hands into fists and relaxed them.

Father in heaven, I pray for patience.

As soon as he sent up the silent prayer, Christopher knew the answer. Katherine was sweet. Too sweet. Which was why Miranda could put on a few tears and melt Katherine's resolve. Miranda was taking advantage of their friendship, and he didn't like it. Not one bit.

Patience, Lord. Please.

The ride back to the Bagley farm seemed to take longer than usual. Once he arrived, he took a moment to compose himself before he went into the kitchen. "Christopher, you're late for supper," Mother pointed out the instant he entered.

Christopher shut the back door so it thumped to a close with a gentle rap. He didn't mind his mother's reprimand. Though her tone was always serious, he knew her firm hand was a sign of her desire to make sure he never wavered from conducting himself in the way a country gentleman should.

"Your daddy's already getting me another load of wood for the stove."

Guilt visited him as he realized he could have brought his mother fresh fuel for the fire if he had arrived a few moments earlier. "Yes, ma'am. I didn't mean to be late." He looked beside the stove and noted the sparse state of the wood box. After he had returned home from college, he soon realized his parents expected him to resume his chores. Upon reflection, he surmised that such an expectation seemed fair. His brothers and sister had left home to marry in past years, leaving Grandpa and his parents at home. Long past his sixtieth birthday, Grandpa possessed vigor, but he could hardly be expected to perform Christopher's chores.

He glanced at Mother, who was at that moment setting the kitchen table with the everyday dishes painted with blue flowers he had known since childhood.

"Mother, I'll get you a couple of extra loads of wood after supper." He took off the brimmed hat that had protected his head from the warm sun and hung it on the wooden peg beside the door.

"I'll excuse you this time. Just don't make a habit of it. You might have been able to run wild and do as you pleased at school, but you're living by my rules now," Mother reminded him as she set a spoon on the table. "Now get washed up." She tilted her head toward the basin as though Christopher no longer remembered its location, despite the fact it hadn't changed in his lifetime.

He suppressed a chuckle. "Yes, ma'am."

"So how are the Joneses?"

"Fine. Just fine. Mrs. Jones thanks you for the return of the sugar, even though she said you didn't need to bother."

Mother nodded.

"Is that beef stew I smell?" While Christopher wanted to know, he also welcomed a way to distract his mother.

"Sure is. So did you see Katherine?"

So much for distractions. "Yes, ma'am."

"And what is the latest news with her?"

"Not much. Her correspondent from South Carolina is coming for a visit."

Mother stopped stirring the stew long enough to look him in the eye. "Her correspondent? That sailor you told me about?"

"Yes, ma'am."

"I would have thought she stopped with that letter-writing nonsense after the war was over. I hope he doesn't think he can just swoop in here and take over everything."

"I don't know what his plans are, Mother." He sat down with a sigh.

Grandpa chose that moment to shuffle into the kitchen. "What plans?"

"Katherine's correspondent is coming for a visit."

"Oh." Grandpa shrugged. "Well, that shouldn't bother you none, Christopher. I doubt he can offer you much competition." He sniffed the air. "I've been waiting for some of that good stew, and I think I smell your yeast rolls cooking, too, don't I, daughter?"

Mother nodded. "Yes, Papa."

"Good." Without fanfare, Grandpa sat down at his regular place at the table. Christopher judged by his slow movements and lethargic expression that he had just awakened from his afternoon nap.

Mother set a pan of rolls on the coolest part of the stove. The light brown tops were shiny. He had often watched her brush the bread with beaten egg whites. He didn't know much about cooking, but he supposed that extra step was what resulted in the sheen that made the bread look so appetizing. Obviously she had prepared the bread to her usual perfection.

Christopher heard Daddy kicking the bottom of the back door, a sure sign that he had a pile of chopped wood in his arms and couldn't open it himself. He hurried to assist him. "Sorry, Daddy. I was planning to get some wood after supper."

Daddy released wood from his arms and let the split logs fall into the metal box. "You can take a turn next time." He smiled.

"Yes, sir." Christopher returned to his seat. The milk in Grandpa's glass looked appealing. He poured himself a glass from the green pitcher Mother had left on the table.

Mother set a bowl of stew in front of Grandpa. Christopher observed Grandpa watching the steam rise and looked at him in amusement as the older man surveyed the food, a satisfied expression on his face.

Christopher didn't listen to the banter of the others as he ate his beef stew, bread, and ice-cold milk. All he could think about was Katherine and how they had corresponded while he completed his studies at Maryland Agricultural College. His plans to court Katherine were dashed when Katherine asked him to participate in the ruse Miranda had cooked up to fool the war hero.

He didn't know which part of his visit to Katherine's upset him more—the request for him to help her fool this Otis fellow or her apparent attachment to the sailor who was important enough that she wanted to make him think the best of her.

Otis hadn't seemed so threatening when he was safely tucked away—far away—on a navy ship. Once he was discharged, he seemed so distant in another state way down south. But now that he was coming to see them, well, that was another story. If only Christopher could put a stop to the visit!

But what should stop Otis from visiting? Christopher knew he had no right to dictate to Katherine with whom she chose to correspond or if and when that person should come up to Maryland.

What a fool he had been not to realize that the correspondence could evolve into romantic notions. Not that he blamed Otis. Who wouldn't take a chance in flirting with a woman of such beauty? He thought about Katherine's big brown eyes, smooth skin, and glossy dark brown hair. The image of her face had kept him motivated at college when he felt lonely and wanted nothing more than to go back to the home he knew and loved. Now that he had returned home, apparently the situation had changed and he could no longer depend on resuming his relationship with the woman he had loved since he was a boy.

"Another glass of milk, Christopher?"

He lurched back into reality. "Oh. No thanks, Mother."

She set the pitcher back on the table and sent him a look that told him he was being too quiet. He could only be grateful for her discretion in not prying. Spooning into a square of warm bread pudding laced with cinnamon and bulging with raisins, Christopher allowed his thoughts to wander to Katherine and her dilemma.

How could Katherine have developed a love for this interloper rather than him? If anyone's correspondence should have developed into mutual love, it should have been the one they had shared. Christopher and Katherine had exchanged letters when he was away studying. He hadn't written flowery words or poetry to her. He had hoped she had some idea about the feelings he harbored for her. But judging from her actions, she did not. If only he had made his feelings known! Maybe then this usurper wouldn't have proven to be such a temptation for the only woman he had ever loved. The only woman he could love.

Lord, why is Katherine tempted away from me? What can I do? I don't want to lose her. I don't think my life would be as happy without her.

His chest tightened in anger even as he tidied up his hands with a napkin. Maybe all this was happening because the Lord knew Katherine wasn't right for him. As a friend, perhaps. But not as a wife. How could she ask him to help her fool Otis, a stranger she'd never met?

Christopher set his spoon in the empty dish, wishing he hadn't been thinking such dark thoughts so he could have enjoyed the delicious treat. He noticed that Mother had held back two extra desserts for later, but he nursed no hope of enjoying either. Grandpa was sure to sneak them both before the next day. Sighing, Christopher rocked back in his chair so only the back two legs balanced on the floor.

"Christopher!" Mother's voice cut through the air. "Where are your manners? You're liable to put a hole in the floor rocking back like that."

He set the front two legs back on the wide plank floor, making sure to be gentle with the motion lest he dent the wood. "Yes, ma'am."

Still, his mother's worries about her floor were the least of his. He couldn't imagine how the little bit of rocking he might do could ruin pine floors that had seen his parents through twenty-nine years of marriage. The thought made him realize how lucky they were.

If only he had spoken up to Katherine sooner! Then he could have looked at the whole scenario with amusement. Katherine had always wanted to dance ballet, ride horses at an expert level, and play the harp, harmonica, and banjo. Everyone knew it. But for Miranda to tell Otis such fantasies! And for what? Some man who didn't care about Katherine. At least, not as much as he did. And always had.

Christopher knew that Katherine never would have written such embellishments on her own; she was much too sweet for that. But now that her so-called friend had written Otis that she had mastered so many accomplishments, Katherine was in a bind. He could understand why Katherine didn't want to embarrass Miranda even though she deserved it. Yet the fact that Katherine didn't want to get her friend in trouble only made him love her all the more.

He wanted to send up a silent prayer that she would make a fool of herself. Such action would serve her right for agreeing to make that poor sailor think she could do so many things. After all, she was a consummate cook and an expert in the domestic arts. Those talents were far more important to the enjoyment of everyday life than being an expert horsewoman or playing the harmonica and banjo. But she couldn't see that, he supposed.

Temptation to pray for her downfall prodded him.

Lord...

Lord, please make Katherine see that she doesn't need to change a thing about herself. Help her to see her true value, that she doesn't need to put on a show to protect a friend. I know her good-heartedness is what got her into this mess, Lord. I ask Thee to protect her in these coming weeks. In the name of Thy Son, I pray. Amen.

He knew the prayer he uttered in silence was far more loving than his original thoughts. Even better, the peace he felt in his heart told him that he meant every word. Whatever happened during her correspondent's visit would be in God's hands. He would have to make himself content in that knowledge.

Chapter 3

The next day, Katherine heard the sound of horses' hooves thudding and carriage wheels turning against the dirt road leading to their house. The impending arrival of a guest left her with a sense of anticipation and fear. The visitor had to be Otis. She peered through white cotton curtains adorning her bedroom window and watched the hired carriage, drawn by two black and brown horses, come to a stop. It shook as its occupant moved to the side and then disembarked.

Otis emerged. Katherine remembered the small portrait she possessed of him and had always hoped it was not an image that flattered its subject too greatly. As his picture promised, he had coal black hair and dark eyes, but his complexion looked much paler than she anticipated. And he appeared to be shorter than she had envisioned. Instead of the hulking war hero she expected, he seemed slight, though he bore a paunch. In a moment of guilt, she set back the curtain. Though spying wasn't her habit, realizing he wasn't quite as she anticipated ahead of time would keep her from making a face of disappointment or doing something else that might cause embarrassment to him—or to herself.

The thought stirred her to peek once more.

To her surprise, a collie emerged behind him on a leash.

"He brought a dog? I don't remember him mentioning a dog." The animal, though cumbersome in size, looked cute with a coat of long black, white, and tan fur, a pink tongue moving back and forth with his panting. He barked as if to announce his arrival.

Standing beside the carriage, Otis inspected the house, but Katherine couldn't tell from his expression whether or not the two-story white clapboard structure with its black roof and matching shutters met his expectations. She watched him look over the landscape, knowing his gaze would rest upon the lush green lawn that she had run across time and again as a girl. He would also view large, mature trees. She allowed herself a smile when she remembered how often as a child she had climbed those trees, much to her mother's worry.

His gaze wandered to her window. She scooted to the side so he couldn't see her. As soon as he occupied himself with paying the driver, she resumed her observation unencumbered.

He picked up his trunk without huffing, so apparently he was stronger than he appeared. She decided that was good, since he looked as though the slightest breeze could pick him up off his feet and blow him all the way back to Charleston. Katherine couldn't help but notice that compared to Christopher, robust and muscular from years of working his family's farm, Otis looked downright weak.

Christopher! She let out a puff of air so strong that it threatened to move the curtain. She was mad at him. She had to remember that.

Otis approached the porch. Katherine rushed down the stairs and into the kitchen so he wouldn't realize she had been watching him. He would tap the front-door knocker, and she would emerge from the room as though she hadn't thought a thing of his impending arrival. Better yet, he might think she was cooking something delicious. As a first impression, such an idea wouldn't hurt.

Katherine had just crossed the threshold when the knocker sounded.

Sitting at the kitchen table, Mother stopped sorting through a jar of buttons long enough to look at the clock. "Is it two o'clock already? That must be your friend. My, but time flies."

"Yes, ma'am."

Katherine's sister, Betsy, grinned. "Katherine's got a beau! Katherine's got a beau!"

"Not true!" Katherine objected.

"Enough of that, Betsy," Mother scolded. "I'd better not catch you saying any such thing again."

"Yes, ma'am." Betsy glanced at the floor.

Katherine wondered if Mother would respond to the second knocking on the door. Mother was quick to put her question to rest. "Well, don't just stand there. Answer the door!"

"Do I look well enough?" Katherine touched the side of her smooth brown chignon. She had selected her Sunday dress to wear for Otis since he would be seeing her in person for the first time. The frock, a bright yellow reminiscent of spring daffodils, complemented her dark hair and olive-toned complexion. Since she and her mother had just sewn the dress from a new pattern the past spring, she felt confident she appeared as fashionable as any of the ladies Otis might know in Charleston.

"Yes, you look very attractive in that dress, and you know it," Mother assured her. "And I see the pink is still in your cheeks from where you pinched them just now."

Katherine blushed, no doubt producing red in her cheeks not unlike the roses in Mother's flower garden.

Mother chuckled. "Such affectations were popular in my day, as well. You must really be out to impress your correspondent. Now run along and answer that door. You have accomplished the trick of not appearing too eager, but now you are in danger of making him think we are not at home, or worse, that you are lazy."

"Oh, we can't have that!" Nevertheless, Katherine walked with a dignified gait. In her own letters to Otis, she had portrayed herself as a lady. She was determined that the reality of their visit would match her letters, if not Miranda's exaggerated descriptions. She smiled as she opened the front door.

Otis tipped his hat. "Good day. You must be Katherine?" His sparkling dark eyes told her he wasn't disappointed by her appearance. He formed the words with a rich Southern accent that she discovered to be appealing. She found she wanted him to say her name again and again.

"Yes. And you are Otis." Her voice sounded colorless when compared with his drawl, but he didn't seem to mind.

"Indeed."

"It's lovely to meet you after all these years." She stepped aside for him to enter.

The dog barked. "Yes, yes," Otis said. "You are Miss Katherine's gift, if she will accept you."

Katherine gasped. "For me?"

Otis nodded. "Yes. For you. You wrote to me how much you love animals, and I thought a large farm such as yours would have plenty of room for this little mutt to roam."

"I wouldn't call him little." Katherine got down on her knees and rubbed the dog affectionately. He yapped and licked her cheek. "Or a mutt."

"He likes you."

"And I like him." She smiled and hugged the collie around the neck.

Otis chuckled. "I would agree, now that you mention it. He's but a pup, yet judging from his parents, collies both, he shall grow to a right fine size. I haven't named him yet."

"Oh, we shall think of a name together!"

Mother chose that moment to join them in the parlor. She stood a few feet behind Katherine. "Good afternoon."

Betsy bounded in behind her, beaming from ear to ear. "A dog!" She rushed to the collie and rubbed his neck. "She's so cute!"

"She's a he," Otis said. "And you must be Betsy."

Remembering her manners, Katherine made the proper introductions.

"Welcome. I am so glad you will be staying with us awhile," Mother said. "Along with your pet."

"Oh, he's not my pet," Otis said. "He is my gift to Katherine."

"I know you won't mind, Mother," Katherine interjected.

"Not at all. We have plenty of room for a dog to roam." Mother smiled.

Betsy patted the dog's fur. He panted and almost seemed to smile at the little girl. "This is the best gift ever!" She beamed at Otis.

"I'm glad you like him." A pleased expression covered Otis's features.

Mother didn't let the dog distract her from her duties as hostess. "I know your trip was long and arduous, Otis. Might I provide you with refreshment?"

"I made a cherry pie yesterday," Katherine added. "I used my own preserves."

"My, but that sounds tempting. I do insist on having a slice, if you would be so kind," Otis said. "But if you ladies don't mind, I'd be much obliged if you would allow me to place my trunk in my quarters so it's not in everyone's way here in the parlor."

"Never you mind about that. Mr. Jones will show you to your room when he comes in from the fields." Mother swept her hand toward the door on the side of the parlor that led to a staircase. "But just so you know, yours is down the hall, first room on the right."

Katherine hurried to open the door for Otis. "That was Ralph's old room. He's off at college."

"He didn't return home for the summer?"

"No, he's taking classes. He wants to graduate a semester early if he can," Katherine said. "He's engaged to be married. Remember how I told you?"

"Oh, yes. I do remember you mentioning that. Well, I promise to take good care of his room in his absence."

"I'm sure you will," Mother said. "Come, Katherine, help me dish up the pie."

"Can I take the dog for a walk?" Betsy asked.

"That's *may* I take the dog for a walk," Mother corrected.

Betsy nodded. "May I take the dog for a walk?"

"That's better. As long as you promise to be careful," Mother admonished.

"I will! What's his name?"

"We haven't decided yet," Katherine said. "Do you have any suggestions?"

Betsy thought for a moment. "Well, he is big and fluffy. Maybe Furry?"

"Furry." Katherine scrunched her nose. "I don't know. Doesn't have much of a ring to it."

Betsy thought again. "Mother said something about him having plenty of room to roam. Maybe Roamer?"

"Roamer. Hmm," Katherine said.

"I think Rover would be better," Mother suggested. "What do you think, Otis?"

"Rover is a fine name for a dog of this nature."

Katherine agreed. "Rover it is, then."

Betsy smiled and headed out the door with Rover.

"I see you've made someone happy," Katherine noted to Otis as she showed him to the parlor.

"I'm glad. But what about you?"

"Oh yes. Who wouldn't like such an amenable animal?"

Katherine followed her mother into the kitchen. "So how do you like him?" Though she felt confident Otis wasn't within earshot, nevertheless she whispered.

"I think he seems mighty nice. No wonder you corresponded with him so long."

Katherine reached for the metal door of the top shelf of the stove. She often took advantage of this closed compartment just above eye level. It kept food warm and soft, but it wasn't so hot that it cooked food further. Retrieving the pie, she breathed in its fruity aroma. "I hope he's not too disappointed in me."

"Whatever would give you such a notion?"

Katherine set her pie on the pine table so her mother could slice it. "I don't know."

"Well, get that idea out of your head. Any man who'd be disappointed in you would be a fool anyhow."

Katherine grinned as they took the pie in to the parlor to serve their guest. They found him sitting on the horsehair sofa. He looked comfortable, as though he belonged there.

Katherine set the tray on the coffee table. "I brewed some tea this morning. I remember you writing me that you like a nice glass of iced tea in the afternoon. I even added a sprig of mint, just as you told me you like."

"Thank you. How kind of you to remember my little idiosyncrasies." He took a taste. "Ah! Refreshing."

He seemed to enjoy the sweet treat, complimenting Katherine on her pie. In person he proved as amiable and charming as he had in his letters. She was certain Father would like him, too.

Then again, would he? Perhaps Father wouldn't like Otis at all. Once he was discharged from the navy, Otis had gone back to work in an office. From the looks of him, he had never picked up a hoe or milked a cow. Christopher, on the other hand, felt at ease with anything having to do with farming.

"Do you like to hunt?" she blurted in the middle of his discourse on his aunt's latest trip abroad.

"Hunt?" Otis chuckled and sliced the pie with his fork. "Why would you want to know such a thing? Surely hunting doesn't interest you."

"I must say, Katherine, what did possess you to ask such a question?" Mother asked.

"I. . .uh. . ." Katherine didn't want to admit that she had been thinking about how Christopher loved the outdoors. Hunting was one of his favorite fall and winter activities. "I know how much Father loves to hunt, and I thought maybe the two of you could try it some time."

"In that case, yes, I do hunt from time to time." His eyes twinkled. "Mighty fine pie. Mighty fine." He took another bite.

"Thank you."

Pie consumption notwithstanding, Katherine waited for him to elaborate about his hunting trips, but no details seemed to be forthcoming. Christopher, on the other hand, would have launched into a story about his latest hunting experience. She suspected Otis's enthusiasm for the sport was lukewarm at best. She wondered how Father, an avid hunter, would greet such news.

Considering the notion seemed foolish. So what if Father and Christopher shared a love of hunting? There was no requirement that any suitor of hers would have to love the sport, even though they did eat game throughout the winter as part of their survival. Still, she supposed in a large city like Charleston, people didn't have to eat game—at least not game they shot themselves—to get through a long, cold winter. What winter there was in Charleston. Otis had written to her about the palm trees and how a body could be comfortable year round in a temperate climate. Why, they hardly had any snow at all down there. Certainly no more than a few flakes.

She visualized a picture of her Maryland farm covered in a blanket of white, as revitalizing as a fresh cotton sheet on a hot July night. She couldn't see such an image where palm trees grew.

An unwelcome portrait of the times she and Christopher took sleigh rides in the snow came to mind. She tried to shake these images from her head, but they persisted. There would never be sleigh rides with Otis. Not in the tropics.

Why am I comparing him to Christopher? Otis is charming and gentlemanly in his own right. What is wrong with me? Christopher is a childhood acquaintance. That is all he ever could be.

An alternate voice in her mind argued, *A childhood acquaintance, yes, but then, why can't you get him off your mind?*

Mother's quiet voice interrupted. "I understand Otis is quite a writer."

Katherine forced herself back into the conversation. "Oh yes. Not only are his letters quite entertaining, as you already know, but of course his poetry is, too." Katherine shot her guest a look. "I hope you don't mind that I have shared some of your verses with Mother and Father."

"No indeed. I am flattered that you think my scribblings are worthy of such notice."

"Maybe you'll decide to write a book one day. One of my other friends—Christopher—wants to write a book." Now why had she said that?

"Christopher. That name sounds familiar." Otis paused in a thoughtful manner, but he didn't seem perturbed. He nodded. "Ah yes. Weren't you corresponding with him while he was at the university?"

Had she told him that? "Yes. Yes I was. He's just a childhood friend."

"I think it's endearing that you've kept in touch all these years."

"That's not so hard," Mother pointed out. "He lives just down the road." She cocked her head eastward toward the Bagleys' farm.

Katherine would have let out a groan if manners had permitted. Why did Mother have to be so helpful? She did her best to recover. "I have always tried to encourage him. He wants to write a history book or an important biography some day."

"Is that so?"

"Yes, and I think he will succeed. He's quite brilliant in all subjects."

"Indeed." For the first time, Otis seemed vexed.

"I—I know you're very smart, as well, Otis," Katherine added.

"Thank you for that." Otis set his empty plate on the table.

"Might I offer you another slice of pie?" Mother asked.

Otis patted the striped vest that covered his belly. Katherine confirmed her first observation that despite his willowy frame Otis's abdomen appeared portly for a man under the age of thirty, but she decided extra layers of fat lent him a look of prosperity.

She set her mind back on the query at hand. "Christopher's father needs him on the farm, and he's studied agriculture so they can grow crops more efficiently. But I do hope he will take time to write his book. Maybe in the winter when the work on the farm is less taxing."

"Oh, there's always something to do on a farm. The livestock don't take a break in the winter," Mother said. "They still expect to be fed. And the cows must be milked twice a day, and of course there are always eggs to be gathered."

Otis pondered Mother's observation. "Now that you make mention of such tasks, Mrs. Jones, I must say, farming does sound quite different from a normal business. I suppose I had never given working the land for a living much thought. I don't have it in my blood, as they might say."

Katherine hadn't thought about the idea that her friend harbored no love for farming. Her family had occupied their piece of land for three generations. Her grandfather Jones had granted parcels of acreage to her uncles for their own home sites, and she expected they would further divide up the land so her cousins could live on the same site in peace and comfort.

Katherine had never thought about living anywhere else or adopting any lifestyle other than that of a farm wife. What if Otis really did think he might cart her off to South Carolina? Would she be happy amid palm trees and in sweltering heat most of the year, even if they did decide to live near the Atlantic Ocean where she could wet her feet and enjoy the cooling effects of the water? Katherine had never seen the ocean. She had only seen pictures of it in books. If the photographs were to be believed, the water met the sky in a never-ending mass. She pictured a scene of uninterrupted blue on blue. What would it look like in reality? She shrugged but kept the idea to herself. Living near a vast body of water held no special appeal for her. The idea of seeing the ocean in real life felt akin to traveling to Europe one day. Both offered a distant fantasy that might be tempting but not appealing enough to pursue with determination.

"So what is your favorite chore, Katherine?" Otis asked.

She jerked back into the present. "Chore? Oh, I suppose I don't mind baking. Although it's a bit warm to undertake too much kitchen work at present."

Otis nodded his head toward his empty dessert plate. "You certainly display a knack for baking."

Katherine smiled at his approval. As her mother extolled Katherine's talents in the kitchen, she resumed her daydreams. She had always pictured herself helping her husband—whoever God planned for her—on a farm. She would assist in tending the livestock, making sure the chickens were fed, the cows milked twice a day, and the pigs slopped so that they would fatten nicely for butchering. She could almost smell salt-cured ham, aromatic slabs of bacon, and fried fatback.

Her thoughts returned to her imaginary future husband. She would help him plant peas, corn, turnips, potatoes, and strawberries in spring. As she thought, she could almost feel plowed dirt give way beneath her shoes. Disturbed from its rest, the dirt left little particles on her feet in protest. After tending to the gardens throughout the summer, Katherine would help with the harvest. She anticipated spending weeks canning the harvested vegetables and making jelly and preserves—strawberry from the small patch they would keep and grape from a few vines she would maintain of deep purple Concord grapes. Like the Proverbs 31 woman, she would keep her family well fed over the winter months.

At night, she would relax by crocheting blankets, mittens, hats, and scarves for her own children and extras for any babies her friends might be expecting that year—just as she was stitching a pair of white booties for the baby Vera's sister Alice expected to arrive soon. She would sew clothes from colorful fabrics she had ordered from the *Wish Book* or saved from patterned flour sacks. When snow covered the ground, she would embroider a fine seam so the family would have fresh linens for the summer. She would bake for Christmas and inhale the scent of a freshly cut cedar tree decorated with strings of popcorn and peppermint candy sticks. Her children would find nice round oranges and walnuts in their Christmas stockings, and each would have a new pair of mittens and socks she fashioned herself.

"My, Katherine, but what are you thinking about?" Mother interrupted.

She startled. "Oh, nothing. Just about crocheting."

"Crocheting? Oh yes, you must show Otis that blanket you're fashioning." Mother leaned toward him. "It's the most beautiful shade of red. I am trying to convince her to enter it in next year's fair."

"Perhaps she should."

The fair. Was there such a thing in Charleston? She wondered what life in Charleston would be like in comparison. Perhaps she would be expected to patronize a seamstress instead of buying fabric and a sewing pattern from the dry goods store. Maybe a laundress would come to her house to wash her clothes and iron her linens and Otis's shirts. Katherine had to admit that was one chore she wouldn't miss. Standing over a heavy, hot iron while trying to coax wrinkles out of starched cotton wasn't her idea of a fun way to pass an afternoon. Nor were sweeping and dusting, two chores that always seemed to beckon. Maybe having others to help in the city would be a blessing.

But then she thought about how her friend Vera once told her about the rank odors of Baltimore: manure, garbage, too many people crunched together. Katherine stole a glimpse at her beloved front yard, flush with magnolia trees that stood fifty feet high and were covered with waxy, dark green leaves. The back and both side yards were equally majestic and offered a lush array of trees that God Himself had planted before her grandfather's birth. She recalled the sweet, cool, fragrant breezes that descended from their boughs.

Though Otis never wrote in so many words that he planned to court her, she suspected that he wanted to visit her home in Maryland in part to see if she would one day make him a good wife. After all, they had been writing letters to one another for years and she had not, as of yet, been spoken for.

She wondered how many trees Charleston could hold in a yard. Few if any, she imagined. Could she make herself content with a window box planted with small flowers, maybe petunias? She wanted to scrunch her nose at the thought.

Light shone through Mother's spotless windows and fresh curtains. Who wanted to smell foul odors all day when the country offered open air and sunshine? Then she remembered how she adored newly picked vegetables and fruits. Vera had once mentioned friends in Baltimore who rented a plot of land so they could have a garden. Imagine! Even then, she couldn't see how a city garden could hold the capacity to produce much of a crop. She speculated that Otis was wealthy enough to purchase a house with a yard that could be called spacious in a city. Yet at the same time, she imagined that on such limited space, she could put up a few jars of jelly at most.

What about meat, milk, and eggs? She'd have to purchase those at a market, she supposed. In any town, raising her own chickens and cows would be out of the question.

She held back a sigh. No wonder city women had garden clubs and society meetings. The city offered nothing for them to do all day!

At that moment, a chicken that had ventured closely to the house clucked, a sound she heard through the open parlor window. The clucking seemed to beg her to stay.

What is the matter with me? Why are my thoughts running wild? What has this visit from Otis put in my head?

She knew as soon as the questions entered her mind. His presence introduced new possibilities for her future. Possibilities she had never considered.

"But of course, though farming is not for me," Otis explained to Mother, "I give farming and farmers my highest respect. Working the land is a noble profession."

"I'm sure that's what Katherine thinks, don't you, Katherine?" Mother prodded.

"Indeed!"

"Is that all you have to say?" Mother chuckled and shook her head. "You'll soon find my Katherine is seldom so silent."

Katherine felt her cheeks flush. "I'm sorry."

"Never you mind," Mother assured Otis. "She'll start talking soon enough."

Katherine resisted the strong urge to turn her gaze up to the ceiling and back, but such a motion would only make her seem to be the little girl her mother portrayed her to be.

"With all due respect, Mrs. Jones, I find Katherine's speech to be quite charming."

Mother sent him an approving smile.

Flattered, Katherine ventured an observation. "One good aspect of farming is that you have a chance to rest a little in the winter, along with the land."

"Hello! Do I hear voices in the parlor?" Father's tenor grew a little louder with each word as he made his way toward them from the kitchen.

"Yes you do, dear," Mother called.

Father crossed through the archway.

"Father!" Katherine rose to her feet. "Otis is here."

She noticed the contrast between Otis's pressed suit and Father's denim overalls. His shirt had started out the day crisp and clean, but now the sleeves were filthy and the collar filled with dust. Out of consideration for Mother, he had wiped the mud from his boots, but the smells of the outdoors hung about him and wafted into the parlor, mixing with the pristine and feminine atmosphere of the formal room.

Otis rose. "Good afternoon, Mr. Jones."

Katherine couldn't help noticing that Otis, on the other hand, could have posed for a gentleman's shaving lotion advertisement in a fine periodical. Not a hair strayed out of place. The part in the middle looked so straight that it could have been the model for a schoolchild's ruler. His deep-hued hair shone, and his fashionable dark mustache had been tamed into place with a liberal application of wax. His white collar held so much starch that there was no danger of it bouncing out of place. Likewise his dark suit could carry him into the finest dining establishment with ease, complemented by shoes that appeared never to have journeyed a mile.

She could only hope that her father would be impressed by Otis's immaculate appearance. He peered at the young man standing by the sofa, but what Katherine saw in his eyes didn't bespeak overwhelming approval. In fact, she couldn't discern by the look on his face what Father thought. She wondered why.

"Oh yes. The war hero and avid letter writer. Afternoon, Otis." Father took off his hat, spotted with sweat on the brim, and wiped his brow. "We've heard good things about you from our Katherine." He smiled and extended his hand in greeting. Then he looked at his dirty, sweaty palm and decided to wipe it against soiled denim overalls. "Uh, maybe we'd better shake another time."

"I don't mind a little dirt." Nevertheless, Otis withdrew the right hand he had offered. A shadow of relief crossed his face. "I was just remarking to the ladies how I think farming is a noble profession."

"A noble profession." Father seemed to contemplate the notion. "I reckon it is at that. Only I don't feel like I look so noble at the moment." A chuckle escaped his lips.

"That's quite all right, Mr. Jones. Sometimes office work doesn't leave one looking, or feeling, so noble, either." Otis broke out into an affable grin. For that, Katherine felt grateful.

"Why don't you wash up and let me fix you a big piece of cherry pie?" Mother suggested to Father.

"The one Katherine baked?"

"Yes, sir," Katherine answered.

"Sounds good." He winked at his daughter and then exited, intent on his task.

Katherine allowed herself a grin. Food. Sustenance, especially a cherry pie with delightful red fruit filling and a buttery crust, could turn many an acquaintance into a lifelong friend.

Since he had been promised a treat, Father didn't dawdle but returned right away.

"I'm not surprised you baked the pie yourself, Katherine," Otis observed. "Your cooking skills are indeed splendid."

"And that's only the beginning," Father promised. "Katherine will be preparing fried chicken for dinner tomorrow. You'll see then that she can also make a superb cake."

"I'll look forward to that." Otis patted his belly.

"I understand you brought us a collie? Betsy seems quite enamored of him," Father observed.

"Yes, indeed." Otis smiled.

Father nodded, and both men soon were talking about the merits of the breed.

As the afternoon waned, Katherine could see that despite Otis's difference in outlook on life he was a brother in Christ and showed respect to her parents. By the time five o'clock rolled around and the cows beckoned for their second milking of the day, Father seemed to embrace Otis—if not wholeheartedly, at least as well as could be expected for a man he had met only that afternoon.

Who could ask for more?

Chapter 4

Later that night, Katherine knelt beside the twin bed, fat with quilts sewn by her mother and her mother's mother. She kept her favorite on top. The red, white, and blue octagons alternated in a pleasing patriotic pattern. Even though early summer weather meant the coverings weren't needed for warmth—demonstrated by a pleasant breeze that blew in through crisp curtains—she liked to keep them on her bed for the familiarity and comfort of home. Never mind that she kicked them off the bed during her sleep and had to straighten them each morning.

Before she shut her eyes so she could concentrate, she glanced at her shelves. Her book collection was sparse but meaningful to her: a copy of the King James Version of the Bible and several well-known novels. On the next shelf down was a collection of display dolls—four in all. Two had been gifts from an aunt as souvenirs from trips: A Cajun doll hailed from faraway New Orleans, and a Betsy Ross doll reminded her of history lessons she learned about Colonial America. The third—a blond Southern belle she named Rosemary and had begged for over the course of several months—had been a Christmas gift. And the last—another Southern belle who could have been Rosemary's sister—she had bought with money she had earned from picking berries and selling them at the market in town one summer. She had named the fourth doll Cherry. She wondered if Otis would mind if she brought her doll collection to South Carolina, or if he would think her babyish for wanting to hold on to mementos of her girlhood. She knew Christopher wouldn't mind. Most likely he could recall the story behind each doll.

Christopher. There he was again, occupying her thoughts.

Closing her eyes and bowing her head, she would remember to thank God for His bountiful provision and for Otis's safe arrival in Maryland. The stiff braided rug was digging into her knees. One day, she would own a soft rug so she could pray in comfort. Or at least, relative comfort. She shifted her position and pondered Otis. As she expected from their lively and lengthy correspondence, he fit right in as though he had been living with them all his life. And there she was, planning to make him think she was accomplished in a number of pursuits. Maybe she shouldn't push her plans forward. Not even for Miranda. Was her idea of friendship misplaced?

The next day, Katherine heard a horse clomping up the drive. She pulled back her curtains and was surprised to see Christopher ride up on his gray and black horse, General Lee. To her shock, her heart lurched. What was Christopher's mission?

Just as quickly, her excitement turned to vexation. No doubt he had come to visit Otis, to see what he was like. Why, Christopher even carried a gift. Judging from the shape of the wrapping, the offering was a jar of Mrs. Bagley's famous damson plum preserves!

Like a Ferris wheel going around and around, her emotions for him softened. How nice of him to be so thoughtful.

Thoughtful because he was curious. Hmm.

Wishing to change out of her plain housedress and into something that made her feel more presentable for company, she hurried to her oak wardrobe, which offered six dresses. She had worn her fashionable yellow one yesterday, so that wouldn't do. A beige Sunday dress complemented her slim frame but was much too showy for everyday.

She regarded the remaining four clean housedresses. The first was the color of a soft pink rose petal. The second would be considered more fashionable, but it had been sewn from a less showy but good sturdy natural cotton. The third and fourth were too heavy for spring wear, so she ignored those and opted for the more fashionable lightweight garment. Slipping into the cream-colored dress in a hurry, she then pulled on her stockings and tied up her boots. With deft fingers, she twisted her hair into a chignon. The result was agreeable. Her hair looked like a soft, dark pillow framing her face, with wisps falling attractively along each side. She pinched her cheeks in the right places to heighten the pink color and bit her lower lip a few times. Pleased with the result, she hurried downstairs to greet the men.

They were chatting like old friends before she even set foot across the parlor threshold. Christopher appeared to be relaxed as he swayed back and forth in the rocker. Otis looked nonchalant, poised on the sofa.

Her stomach lurched. Had Christopher already told him about Miranda's plan? But no, Otis looked too congenial to have just experienced disappointment. She sent Christopher a fearful glance, but the look he returned to her indicated no intrigue. So he wouldn't betray her! Or did he hope she would change her mind and go back on her plan? She imagined the second scenario was more to his liking.

At that moment, Otis regarded her with widened eyes and a softened countenance. Apparently he still felt her appearance was agreeable. Christopher's clean-shaven jaw tightened when he eyed Otis watching her. Certainly he wasn't jealous!

Christopher's gaze traveled Katherine's way, and his blue eyes lit with pleasure. His unspoken approval was enough to make her reconsider her plans to fool Otis.

Almost.

After the men rose from their seats and the three exchanged greetings, Katherine took the remaining vacant chair, a blue overstuffed model favored by her father. She felt grateful since its presence meant she didn't have to choose to sit beside Otis as Christopher sat by himself across the room. Still, they were close together since the formal parlor was small.

As the threesome talked about little of consequence, Katherine compared the two men. Otis was a polished gentleman, just as his letters had indicated. But Christopher was both polished and more down-to-earth. While he didn't dress in a manner as formal as Otis did, he still conveyed confidence that seemed to make Otis's expensive and fashionable attire much less important than Otis likely meant for them to be. Christopher put on no affectations, employed no exaggerated mannerisms, and no flattery fell from his lips, but his ways communicated genuineness that Otis somehow seemed lacking.

Wouldn't it be funny if I ended up sending Otis home and then was courted by Christopher?

Until that moment, she hadn't thought of Christopher in romantic terms. She wondered how the idea, so remote before, suddenly struck her without warning. She had never thought of him as anything more than a fond friend. So why did she suddenly become aware of his gentle manner and the way he looked at her when he thought she wouldn't notice?

"I read something of interest in your local paper today," Otis ventured late in the conversation. "An evangelist is planning to visit the area."

"A common occurrence this time of year," Christopher pointed out.

"Indeed. So do you plan to go to the revival meetings?" Otis inquired, looking at Katherine.

"Um, I hadn't thought much about it one way or the other. We go to church every Sunday, and we always have a revival for a whole week come summertime."

Otis cleared his throat. "Faithful attendance to one's place of worship is commendable, to be sure. How long has your pastor served your church?"

She thought for a moment. "Ever since I was a little girl. I vaguely remember the first pastor. He retired long ago. Rev. Michaels is the only preacher I truly remember."

"I see. Then I suggest you might find interest in discovering for yourself how another man of the cloth approaches the religious questions of the day." Otis's statement seemed to be a challenge.

"Sure. But I still don't think there's a minister alive who can outpreach Rev. Michaels," Christopher opined.

Otis chuckled. "I'm sure this evangelist won't give Rev. Michaels any competition. But why don't we go to see him all the same?"

"Well, if I weren't willing to engage in adventure, I shouldn't have a houseguest from another state, I suppose. All right, then. Let's go." Her heart increased in its beat as she took a risk. She turned to Christopher. "You'll come along, won't you?"

He looked surprised. "Me? Are you sure?"

"Of course I'm sure. It wouldn't be the same without you."

"Well, then. Why not?" Christopher smiled.

Katherine felt much too happy that Christopher had accepted. She decided not to ponder what that might mean. At least not at the moment. She could worry about it later.

"Are we still on for the concert sometime during my stay here?" Otis asked, interrupting her musings.

"Concert?"

"Yes." Otis looked at her quizzically. "Surely you won't mind that I make mention of this in front of your friend Christopher, since he is certain to be included in your plans."

"Uh, of course."

"Oh well, perhaps you are not aware, Katherine. Miranda said in her correspondence to me that I must visit Maryland sometime—"

"She said that?" No wonder he had decided to make the trip.

"Why, yes." He continued undeterred. "And she said that when I did all of you would put on a concert. Wouldn't that be splendid?"

"Uh, splendid indeed."

"I certainly hope that event comes about. She suggested that I might add a song or two on the piano. I've been practicing several of my favorite tunes ever since her missive arrived."

"How sweet of you," Katherine noted.

"Yes, how sweet." Christopher didn't sound as sincere. He crossed his arms.

If Otis was bothered by Christopher's aside, he didn't let them know. "Miranda also mentioned that your church will be putting on a talent show later this month. Perhaps the concert among friends will be good practice for that event, as well."

"Indeed." Katherine hadn't given the talent show much thought. Now Otis was recruiting her to take part. If he wanted her to participate, she would do so to please him.

"Christopher will be invited to the concert, certainly?" Otis prodded.

"Of course, Christopher will be invited." She looked at him. "And you will be playing the banjo for us all, won't you?"

"I thought you were talented at the banjo, Katherine," Otis said. "So, Christopher, perhaps the two of you will be playing a duet?"

Katherine wasn't sure why she felt her face flush. "No, Christopher and I haven't had a chance to practice a duet. Although that does sound like a fine idea for another time. No, I plan to play the lap harp."

"Ah yes. The lap harp," Otis said. "I'm sure you'll sound like an angel."

Christopher chuckled with so much suddenness that he nearly spit. Katherine would have poked him in the ribs had he not been sitting too far away for such a reprimand.

"I fail to see why that is so amusing," Otis remarked.

"I'm sorry. It's just that—that—"

Katherine held her breath, waiting to hear what he might confess.

Christopher looked at Katherine and then back to Otis. "I've known Katherine since we were both little, and I've seen her look less than angelic at times."

"Christopher!" Katherine huffed.

Otis chuckled. "I'm glad to hear you are human. I'm not sure I could live up to the expectations of a true angel."

"I'm sure you could try." She crossed her arms. While Christopher could have revealed her secret, she wasn't sure she was happy with his confession that she was less than perfect, even though she was well aware of her flaws. To hear the fact expressed out loud by a friend was disconcerting, somehow. She decided to deflect to another tangent. "But speaking of an angel, Betsy will be tap dancing in the show."

"I can't wait. First, you must tell me, Christopher, about Katherine's not-so-angelic moments," Otis prodded.

"Certainly you don't want to hear some boring old story about my childhood," Katherine protested.

"Oh, a little harmless fun couldn't hurt. I know you have a sense of humor, Katherine," Otis pointed out.

"I have the perfect story!" Christopher launched into one of his favorite accounts about how the class bully dipped her pigtail into an inkwell.

"That happened with a girl and boy at my school, too," Otis countered. "Seems children everywhere have the same thoughts."

"Apparently." Christopher chuckled. "But did the girl at your school break her slate over his head?"

Otis thought for a moment. "No, I think she cried and told the teacher."

"Not Katherine. She fought back. Wally had a bruise on his forehead for a week." He laughed.

"Mother wasn't so amused," Katherine pointed out. "She had to cut off three inches of my hair. For the longest time, I felt like a boy." She groaned.

"I'm glad to see your hair grew back. No one could mistake you for a boy now," Otis observed.

She flushed. "Thank you."

As the men shared other amusing childhood anecdotes, Katherine sat in silence. Yes, it was going to be a long visit, indeed.

Chapter 5

As General Lee trotted down the path, Christopher barely noticed the lush trees dressed in the peak of their emerald finery or the scent of the crisp open air with its mixture of fresh plant odors and earthy animal aromas. He was much too pensive to take in the familiar, though beloved, surroundings along the road.

The dilemma he faced left him with a sense of unease, and he didn't know what to do about it. He desperately wanted to expose Miranda's misguided plan, not because he desired to be judgmental, but for her own good. What had gotten into Miranda, wanting to put on airs for this acquaintance, a man Katherine knew only through letters? He admired Katherine's desire to protect her friend, but he couldn't condone the deception.

Christopher had known Katherine all her life. And here was this stranger, an interloper, being treated as though he mattered more than anyone else. Christopher pictured Otis leaning back on the divan in a relaxed posture that stated his special standing at the Joneses' place. Christopher found himself glowering at the dirt road. The image of Otis made him want to spit.

In just a day, Otis had settled into the Joneses' house and acted as though he was their social director, religious adviser, and royal guest of honor. Sure, he seemed like a nice fellow on the surface, but anyone could act all high and mighty when no one knew him from Adam.

He wondered what Otis was like at his home in South Carolina. He said he had a job at an office somewhere in Charleston. He dispensed such a fact with the air of one who served President Roosevelt. Christopher could see that his rival fancied himself important. Well, maybe he was important. Maybe what he did in his office was more important than slopping pigs and milking cows every day.

With that thought, he tightened his grip on the reins.

Christopher could never deny that anyone who wore a suit to an office, which no doubt Otis did, could appear more dashing and handsome than a man in overalls. He looked down at his plain cotton shirt and pants. Since he had dressed with the intention of pleasing Katherine, he had made sure his clothes were clean, but they certainly weren't expensive. Not even store bought. He had donned his best everyday shirt and pants. From his available wardrobe, Christopher couldn't have dressed better. Maybe Otis could get away with sitting around all day in a Sunday suit. He was a stranger after all. But if Christopher had worn his Sunday suit to see Katherine, she would have thought him peculiar. Possessed of a fever, even.

Christopher tried to shake the image of Otis out of his mind, but he couldn't. He kept remembering how the other man looked as though he was wearing something out of a *Wish Book*. The most expensive suit they manufactured, in fact. And his gold cuff links, octagons with scalloped mother-of-pearl edges, were engraved with three scripted initials bold enough to be seen from across the room.

Christopher sighed. He had scrimped and saved to afford college tuition. Though he looked forward to a bright future, he didn't anticipate a life filled with luxury. His dressy cuff links were unetched, silver-plated ovals that he only wore once a week to worship service. The contrast between the cuff links alone made him see that he could never give Katherine a life in which she could afford to buy luxurious frivolities. Even if he could, where would Katherine go donned in fine silk and crocheted lace every day? Worship service at church and the occasional wedding celebration called for fancy attire; for the most part, though, farmwives chose sturdy, serviceable dresses, since they engaged in chores for the better part of the day. Delicate fabrics and excessive amounts of lace wouldn't survive long on a woman who toiled in a steaming hot kitchen and smelly chicken coop.

Christopher ducked to avoid a low-hanging tree branch, but his thoughts remained uninterrupted. If Katherine stayed on the farm with him, she would never know days of relative leisure. She deserved a life filled with garden club meetings and with luncheons where the women gossiped and played games and enjoyed indulging in afternoon teas. But if she chose life on the farm, she would have to work. Truly Katherine deserved better than an existence filled with drudgery as Mrs. Christopher Bagley.

Lord, what is Your will? Just a month ago, I was certain You would have blessed my marriage proposal to Katherine. Now she's got another man visiting her and her family, and her mother seems to like him a whole lot. Even Mr. Jones doesn't seem to be immune to Otis's charm and flattery. I admit to the sin of envy, Lord. I wish I could be in Otis's place, to be able to see Katherine anytime I like. I long for her, Lord. I wish Your will was for me to marry Katherine. I have wanted that for a long time. But if it isn't, I'll let her go. I promise.

Even as he promised, Christopher felt his stomach tighten as though it had been wrapped in bailing twine. He knew he was being too hard on Otis. If the newcomer hadn't been a serious rival for Katherine's affections, Christopher might even have liked him. He seemed intelligent and nice enough for a city dweller. But he couldn't like Otis. He just couldn't. If this was a test from God, it was one he was failing. Miserably.

Christopher approached the redbrick house he had called home since infancy. Grandpa stood on the front stoop, waving for Christopher to hurry.

"Coming!" he called.

Grandpa nodded and went back into the house.

Christopher studied the low-lying sun on the horizon and realized that supper would be ready soon. He wasn't sure he could eat. But for Mother's sake, he would try.

———

"Vera, I'm really having second thoughts about this concert," Katherine admitted the next day as they enjoyed a glass of iced tea over the kitchen table at the Sharpes' farm.

"Just tell Miranda."

"Don't you think I've tried? No matter how much I protest, she only makes me feel like I'm not her friend unless I go along with her plan. You should see how she can turn on the tears."

"I can imagine. She can really make you feel like the world's going to end if she doesn't get her way, can't she?"

"Yes, and you know I've never been one to deal with guilt well."

"Neither do I, or maybe I'd have the courage to confront her." Vera sighed.

"Looks like us two sissies have to put up with this plan, then. I really do appreciate your help, Vera. I have to say, I am looking forward to the day Otis goes home."

"What a shame. I take it you two aren't going to be courting, then?"

"He's never said the first word about it. And to tell you the truth," Katherine confessed, "I'm glad. He's nice and all, and he even brought me a dog—"

"A dog?"

"Yes. A beautiful collie. We named him Rover. I must say, Rover has made fast friends with Betsy. She plays with him more than I do."

"No doubt Rover has helped Otis find his way into Betsy's heart, too."

"I think so," Katherine agreed, setting her empty glass on the table. "But she's always been fond of him. He pays attention to her and sends her little trinkets from time to time."

"He'll make a good father one day."

"I'm sure."

"Just not for your future children?" Vera prodded.

Katherine shook her head. "No, not for my future children."

Vera sent her a knowing smile. "Then Christopher must have won after all."

Katherine felt her face redden. She wished she had left a swallow of tea in her glass to cool herself off. "I don't know. . . ."

Vera laughed. "All right. I won't say another word. Besides, we have more immediate concerns. Namely, this issue of the harp."

"I know. I'm sorry Miranda told him that I could play the harp. And I'm even sorrier she talked me into trying to pretend I can."

Vera's sigh reminded Katherine of how her mother sounded when she was a little girl and had forgotten to feed the animals. "So, what song did you order?"

" 'I Send My Heart Up to Thee!' That won't be too hard to mimic, will it?"

Vera sent her glance to the ceiling and back. "It won't be easy."

"You'll keep your promise, won't you? You'll teach me how to move along with the notes so it looks like I'm playing? For Miranda's sake?"

"You know, Katherine, I think it would be much easier if you would just learn the song and play it for real."

"Learn the song?" The idea sent chills of uncertainty up her spine. "But what if I make a mistake and hit a sour note? Or even worse, what if I forget the tune altogether and have to come to a grinding halt?"

"So what if you do? Then at least everyone will know you were playing for real. And anyhow," Vera added with such haste that Katherine wondered about her sincerity, "that won't happen."

"I don't know," Katherine said. "In spite of my reluctance to go along with Miranda's suggestion, I still think she had a good idea. I want to make sure the performance is error free. It's a good thing you can sight-read music so easily."

"For the first time, I wish I couldn't." Vera sighed.

"You do think you can learn it by the time they're expecting me to play, don't you?"

"Yes. I just hope for Miranda's sake—and yours—that no one will realize the sound of the music is coming from the next room." Vera freshened both of their glasses of tea from the pitcher she had kept sitting on the table.

"I think it will be close enough." Without adding more sugar, Katherine took a sip of her freshened beverage.

A terrible thought occurred to Katherine. "Do you think your sister's harp will sound the same as the harp I'll be playing?"

"I doubt anyone will notice. It's not as though we'll have a professor of music among us." Vera scrunched her lips. "Are you sure you want to go through with this?"

"I absolutely do not want to go through with this."

Vera's eyes widened.

"But I must," Katherine assured Vera before she got too attached to the idea that the plan had changed. "But only for Miranda's sake. I never would have thought up such a scheme myself."

"I doubt you would have. You have a bright mind but not a scheming one. If Miranda had only used her brains for good and not for mischief, we would all be happier."

"True. But Miranda doesn't mean any harm. I know she doesn't. She's just the playful type."

"You're too forgiving."

"Maybe I am. But I'd rather be known as too forgiving than too judgmental."

"So there's no way I can talk you out of this wild idea."

Katherine shook her head.

Vera put up both hands in surrender. "Oh, all right. I can see there's no drumming any sense into that hard head of yours. But I want you to know that the only reason I'm going along with this is because I know the concert will delight Alice and her husband."

"You're a good sister to Alice. And a wonderful friend to me."

"I can only hope my gesture of friendship won't be the ruination of you." Vera pointed her forefinger at Katherine. "You are taking a mighty big chance of making a fool of yourself in front of everybody we care about. I know you have no idea how to play the harp. Does your family even own one?"

"Uh, that's another thing. I was hoping you could loan me yours so I can practice at home. I'll borrow the one in the music closet at church to use that night. I'll only need yours until Otis goes home." She crossed her arms. "I know that fine instrument has been sitting idle ever since you went to Baltimore."

Vera set her gaze toward the parlor even though the harp wasn't visible from the kitchen. "I admit I haven't plucked the first note on it since I got back. Mrs. Alden preferred the pianoforte. For once, I was glad I had suffered through lessons with Mr. Montgomery all those years."

Katherine remembered the stern teacher and concurred with Vera's sentiment. "I imagine Mrs. Alden misses you."

"I'm not so sure. I think she's happy with her new daughter-in-law."

"Well, you have much better things to do than to be a companion for an elderly woman and her grumpy son."

A wry grin crossed Vera's lips. "I imagine Raleigh is much less grumpy now that he's found love."

"Hmm. Maybe so." Katherine realized that Vera had adroitly led her onto another topical terrain. If she didn't recover, she'd leave without the treasured instrument. "So you'll let me take the harp? I promise to take the best care of it in the world."

"Oh, all right. But you must promise to return it as soon as Otis goes home."

"Of course." Katherine rose from her seat and embraced her friend.

"Won't you have another slice of peach preserve pie, Otis?" Looking pleased, Mother sliced her knife through a thick slab of iced dough and cut into the meats of soft fruit baked to a deep orange hue.

Otis patted his stomach. "Oh, I don't know, Mrs. Jones. I already ate one mighty big slice. And your fried chicken and mashed potatoes were simply splendid. I don't believe I've ever tasted such marvelous yeast rolls since the days I was a boy eating Sunday dinner at my dear grandmother's." He looked skyward and lowered his voice to a somber tone. "May the Lord in heaven rest her sweet soul."

Mother straightened her lips into a respectful contour for a moment, then turned the corners of her mouth upward. "So you must have another roll in memory of your grandmother."

"I think I'll take the pie instead." He offered his dessert plate. "Thank you mightily."

Katherine suppressed a smile. Since his arrival, Otis had ingratiated himself to her mother by complimenting her appearance, housekeeping, and cooking. He had made friends with her father by fishing with him and helping tend to the livestock. And he still looked quite stylish and smart while doing so. She had expected him to wear his best clothes at first but to relax later in the visit. Yet to her surprise, Otis didn't seem to own any clothing that wasn't the latest fashion. Even his everyday clothing looked as though it had been sewn by an expert tailor using the finest fabrics. She marveled at his style.

Nevertheless, Katherine could see through Otis's affected appearance and flattery even if her mother could not. She realized he was trying to impress her by gaining her parents' approval. Judging from Mother's eager motion in placing another large slab of pie on his plate, Otis's plan could be labeled a success.

Father didn't smile as he stirred three teaspoons of sugar and a generous stream of cream into a cup of rich black coffee. "Didn't Christopher perform well in church last night?"

"Christopher?" His name slid onto Katherine's lips more easily than she meant. Otis peered at her from the corner of his eye. "Yes. He always sings well. Don't you think so, Otis?" She sent him a smile she knew to be too bright.

"I hadn't heard him sing before last night, but I'll take your word for it."

Katherine twisted her lips. Otis had perfected the art of withholding compliments from Christopher.

"Yes, Christopher always sings for us at the midweek service. We missed him while he was away studying at college. He's a fine boy," Father added.

Katherine tried not to cringe. She knew this was her father's way of advising her not to make a decision too quickly. She felt heat rise as a flush of embarrassment covered her. She looked at Otis. If Father's observations perturbed him, he didn't show it. Perhaps his preoccupation with flattering Mother covered his vexation.

Relieved that Father's remark hadn't started an unfortunate strain of discussion, Katherine picked at her sliver of pie and occupied her mind with other thoughts.

Immediately after Sunday school, Katherine rose from her seat. Miranda had been eyeing her all through the lesson, and Katherine wanted to make her escape before her friend could snag her. No doubt Miranda wanted to involve her in yet another scheme to fool Otis. Katherine's plan almost worked, but Miranda caught up to her before Katherine could avoid her without being rude.

"How is it going with Otis?" The man in question had carried a discussion on a minute theological point past the class hour and, just out of earshot, was making a brilliant argument before a rapt circle of their peers.

Miranda ogled him dreamily. "He certainly is dashing, isn't he?"

Katherine glanced at him. "I suppose, in his way."

"And smart." She stole another glance at the former sailor, then turned back to Katherine. "You don't seem impressed."

Katherine deliberately kept her eyes from focusing on Otis and held her voice to a near whisper. She motioned for Miranda to join her in walking to the sanctuary. "He's nice enough. He even brought me a beautiful collie."

Miranda took in a breath and kept pace. "He did? How marvelous."

"Yes, he is a gentleman. But. . ." Katherine didn't want to tell Miranda that her war hero couldn't hold a candle to Christopher.

"But what?"

"Never mind. What did you need to tell me?"

"How did it go with the harp?"

"Vera agreed to help."

"I knew she'd come through." A mischievous light glowed in Miranda's eyes and just as quickly dissipated. "But now we have another problem. Remember, he thinks you're an expert horsewoman."

"Oh no. I forgot all about that." Katherine groaned. She looked her friend in the eye. "Miranda, this has gotten out of hand. I think we have to put a stop to it and confess all to Otis."

"No! Please don't!" She ground her heel in the floor.

"Then what am I to do?" Katherine peered at the front of the sanctuary and noticed that Otis had moved away from their friends and now occupied himself by conversing with her parents, since they had already taken their seats in a pew. Christopher, donned in a rich blue robe, had already positioned himself on the third row of the choir loft.

"That's what I wanted to talk to you about. I have a plan."

Katherine clutched her Bible. "I'm afraid to ask."

"Don't worry. My idea is brilliant. If I may say so, you and I could be mistaken for sisters from a distance. So I have a simple plan. Next Thursday, when are your parents sure to be in the house—or at least nowhere near the stables?"

Katherine thought. "A little before lunch, I suppose."

"Good. I'd like to come to the barns then. If you could dress in your riding habit, I'll do the same, and we'll look very much alike. At that point, all I have to do is take Ash out and jump a few hurdles. After that, I'll disappear into the barn.

Then you come out, pretending you're the one who performed the jumps."

"I don't know. I don't think I like such an idea."

"Oh, please? For me? I promise you I'll never ask another thing of you in my entire life!"

Katherine sent her a reluctant nod and then hurried to sit beside Otis in the pew. Miranda strode to her place in the front row of the choir loft. They had just seated themselves when the pianist struck the first note of "Amazing Grace."

Katherine tried to concentrate on the sermon and sing with focus, but her mind was elsewhere during most of the service. As the benediction was said, she resolved to make amends by paying full attention the next week and at the Wednesday evening prayer service.

To Katherine's surprise, after worship, Christopher caught up with her on their way out of church.

She stopped by an aromatic rosebush near one of the front stained glass windows and eyed his Sunday suit. Though not as fine as Otis's, the cut flattered his muscular, trim, and tall form. "You slipped out of your choir robe fast enough."

"I hurried on purpose, I must confess. I have to talk to you."

Katherine looked toward the dispersing crowd of women dressed in colorful Sunday dresses and men in their best suits. Her parents were still lingering with a few of the other congregants. From all appearances, Otis didn't mind chatting with one of the engaged women from their Sunday school class. Katherine wouldn't be missed, at least not for a few moments. She turned her full attention to Christopher. "All right. What is it?"

His stare brooked no room for play. "I saw you talking to Miranda."

"So? Miranda's my friend."

"I know you both too well. Katherine, I wish you wouldn't go through with her ridiculous plan."

"I know it seems ridiculous to you, and maybe it is. But haven't you ever done anything ridiculous for a friend?"

Christopher thought for a moment. "Maybe when I was a boy, but not recently. No doubt, I'm not as sentimental as you are about your friends."

"Perhaps not."

"Being a loyal friend is an admirable quality." He smiled and touched her arm briefly. The unexpected contact sent a pleasant shiver through her. "I just don't want to see you suffer for your sacrifice in giving in to Miranda's misguided plans."

"Miranda doesn't mean any harm. I'm sure all will be well."

"I wouldn't be so quick to caution you if I thought following through with her scheme would be good for all concerned. But in my view, the whole idea is pointless. As much as it pains me to say it, anyone can see that Otis fits right in with you and your relations. I don't care what Miranda says. I don't think you have to prove anything to him."

"Maybe you're right, but I promised Miranda I'd go along with her. And even if I have to suffer a little, I wouldn't be a good Christian witness if I went back on my word." Her resolve wasn't inwardly as strong as she made herself appear, but she didn't want Christopher to see her waver. With a deliberate turn, she set her gaze toward her family and felt thankful when Mother motioned for her to join them. "I've got to go. See you soon." She rushed toward Mother and relative safety.

Christopher watched Katherine depart. He wanted to hasten to her, to make her see reason, but he remained frozen in place. He was left so irritated by the exchange that he couldn't bring himself to move. During church, he had been even more vexed to see Katherine sitting by Otis. No matter what Christopher did, it seemed he couldn't win.

Grandpa tapped him on the shoulder. "There you are, boy. We've been looking for you."

"Sorry, Grandpa. I had to talk to Katherine."

Grandpa rubbed his chin, touching a bit of gray stubble that he had missed in his efforts to shave that morning. "Yep, that Katherine girl is a mighty fine young woman. Too bad she's let herself get carried away by that Otis feller. He's a fancy dresser, all right. Too fancy. Anybody can see he don't belong in these parts."

"That's what I've been thinking."

"Yep. I been watchin' him. He talks a fine streak. Flatters every woman around. Every man, too, for that matter. Even had some kind words for me this morning. But I don't know. He seems just a little too slick. Yep, a little too slick. He reminds me of Homer James. He almost got ahold of your grandma, you know. But she saw through him. With a little nudge from me." When Grandpa winked, Christopher noticed that the sharp blue color of his eyes hadn't diminished since Christopher was a boy.

"But how can I help Katherine see?"

Grandpa watched the Joneses and Otis board their buggy. "I don't reckon I know right off the top of my head, son. But the good Lord in His wisdom will show you how. Just you watch."

"Watching is pretty hard, Grandpa."

"Sure it is. Just be careful you don't watch too long or hard, lest you wait too long to take whatever action needs takin'."

"I'll try not to." Still, as Christopher and Grandpa walked toward the Bagleys' buggy, another thought occurred to the younger man. An even worse thought.

What if the tricks end up leading Katherine straight into Otis's waiting arms?

Chapter 6

Your *Wish Book* order arrived!" Mother's voice, traveling from the kitchen to Katherine's room early that morning, carried a mixture of anticipation and curiosity.

Katherine set her boar-bristle hairbrush on her oak vanity and rushed down to the kitchen. Since she hadn't taken time to secure her hair into a chignon, loose locks flew outward as she hurried. She couldn't let Otis see her open the box or even let him see the package. What if he guessed she had ordered sheet music? And what if he asked her to play the song for him, then and there? He was the persistent type, just liable to make such a request. If he did, he'd find out all too quickly that she couldn't play a note on the harp.

How she wished she had the courage to tell Miranda they had to call the whole thing off! She remembered the times she had tried, to no avail. Miranda would only succeed in crying and making her feel terrible.

"That's a mighty flat box," Mother noted as Katherine reached for it.

She nodded and departed before Mother could stop her or ask questions.

As soon as she returned to her bedroom, she unwrapped the package. The paper smelled crisp and new. The sweet smell of fresh ink greeted her nostrils. She studied the picture on the cover. A beautiful blond woman was pictured, with cheeks as red as apples and a subdued-looking mouth that appeared ready to burst into song. Katherine opened the music and stared at the notes.

"Hmm. Not too much of a challenge. At least not for someone as experienced at the harp as Vera. I'll bet if I go over to the house now, she'd play it for me." Since she'd completed her before-breakfast chores, Katherine knew she could slip out for a few moments without too much chastisement from Mother.

Turning to the round vanity mirror, she looked at her reflection and deemed the results of her toilette acceptable. With a quick motion, she pinned her chignon into place and set off down the steps to leave for her friend's house.

"Good morning, Katherine." Otis had already sat down at the table, waiting for Mother to serve him a helping of scrambled eggs and bacon.

"Good morning, Otis. And a fine day it is, too. If you'll be so kind as to excuse me, I have an errand to run. I must see Vera."

Mother lifted her spoon and shook it at Katherine. "At this hour?"

"She's an early bird. No doubt she rose hours ago," Katherine assured her as she bounded through the back door.

"But, Katherine, you must have a bit of breakfast."

"I will, later. I promise." Katherine rushed to set her bicycle upright, placed the sheet music in the basket, and headed off for Vera's.

On the way, her growling stomach objected to the fact that she had left without a bit of her mother's scrambled eggs. But her task was too important to allow her to stop for sustenance.

The aroma of spicy pork sausage cooking on the stove tempted her palate as she skipped up the stairs to the kitchen of the Sharpes' farm.

Vera's slackened jaw and widened eyes revealed her surprise. "Uh, good morning, Katherine. You're making the rounds mighty early."

Alice scooped up a sausage patty as she and Katherine exchanged pleasantries. Expectant motherhood agreed with Alice, who was an older version of fair-haired Vera.

Vera nodded toward the package Katherine held. "What have you got there?"

"The sheet music, silly. Just like I told you."

Vera didn't crack a smile. "Oh. Well, maybe we can take a look at it after breakfast. Will you have some sausage and eggs?"

Katherine sat down at the table. "Why, how kind of you. You know, I am a bit hungry, so I do believe I will accept your offer."

As they ate and chatted, Katherine hardly tasted the sausage and eggs. After the meal, Katherine asked Vera if she would play the song.

"My, but judging by the way you hurried through your meal, this must be the most exciting song ever," Alice observed. "Mind if I listen with you?"

"Of course not," Katherine said.

Vera escorted them into the parlor, where the lap harp awaited. Vera studied the music for a moment, nodded her head, and began to play.

Though Alice hadn't been informed about the significance of the sheet music, Katherine listened in anticipation. As expected, the song was delightful. When Vera finished playing, Katherine clapped. "Oh, Vera, that's beautiful!"

"Indeed it is," Alice agreed. "Won't you play it again?"

"Of course." Vera gave Katherine a knowing look. "Katherine, why don't you go into the kitchen and fetch me a glass of water? If you would, please."

Katherine wondered about her friend's sudden thirst and then realized what she meant. She wanted Katherine to hear how the music would sound coming from another room, since that was their plan.

"Vera, can't you wait for a glass of water? Honestly!" Alice protested.

"I don't mind, Alice," Katherine assured her all too quickly. "Might I fetch you a glass, as well?"

"No, I'm fine, thank you." Alice settled into her seat and rubbed her expanded abdomen.

As Katherine poured Vera's water in the kitchen, her elation over the music drifting in from the parlor vanished. Vera had been right. There was no way the music would sound immediate enough to fool their audience. If only she had listened! Exhaling in defeat, she steadied her emotions and reentered the parlor with a glass of cold water and a smile.

"That was just as beautiful the second time," Katherine told Vera.

"Indeed, yes," Alice agreed. "What a lovely song, Katherine. I can see why you're excited about it and wanted to share it with Vera. Certainly you plan to learn it yourself."

"Yes. If Vera will teach me." Hearing the lack of enthusiasm in her own voice, Katherine realized her zeal for Miranda's plan had long since abated. The depth of the web of deception Miranda had woven was materializing. Yet rather than the clever spider awaiting a reward for a well-spun snare, she felt like the foolish fly. Silken words felt like threads of barbed wire, encasing her in a trap from which no desirable means of escape offered itself.

"Just be sure you do." Alice smiled. "I'll leave you girls to your visit. Sewing awaits me. Don't dawdle too long, Vera. The eggs need to be gathered."

"Yes, Alice."

Oblivious to Katherine's inner turmoil and Vera's part in the plan, Alice exited the parlor, humming the tune.

"Oh, Vera, you were right. My idea will never fool anyone. What am I going to do?" Katherine wailed.

"Just what I told you that you should have done all along. Learn the song."

"But I don't have time."

"Of course you do. If you work at it."

"Will you help?"

Vera handed her the sheet music. "Do I have a choice?"

───

"After all this time here, I can't believe I have yet to hear you pluck the first note on the harp," Otis observed.

Katherine peered at the ground long enough to show Otis she had no intention of responding. Otis, Katherine, Vera, and Christopher had formed a group, making their way to their respective buggies. They had just passed a delightful evening among their favorite crowd, hosted by the parents of their mutual friend Lily.

"Oh, believe it," Christopher muttered.

Katherine poked him in the ribs and gave him a warning look from the corner of her eye. So far Christopher had been a true friend. He hadn't betrayed her, even though she'd been nervous all night that he might say something to Otis to make him suspect Katherine wasn't all that Miranda had portrayed her to be in her letters. But Christopher hadn't so much as hinted that anything was amiss.

Not that he was a big talker in any event. He'd been quiet all night. Katherine saw him observing Otis from time to time, but Christopher never challenged Otis on any of his opinions, even though some of his ideas were citified or poorly supported, at least to Katherine's way of thinking. Katherine knew Christopher hadn't changed so much since he went away to school and had now returned to make a life for himself on his family's land. Perhaps Christopher didn't say a great deal because Otis wouldn't be here long. Or maybe because Christopher didn't like Otis much. He never mentioned it, and Otis had never wronged Christopher; she, though, sensed that Christopher was wary of him.

"So how much longer are you going to keep me in suspense about your talent as a harpist?" Otis asked.

"Not too much longer, I hope. I want to be sure I have a special song prepared for you. I've been practicing with Vera." There. She had stuck as closely as she could to the truth. That should help. "Isn't that right, Vera?"

"Yes, that's right." Even Vera couldn't deny the truth of that statement.

Katherine sent her a grateful look. Regret at following Miranda's schemes was starting to take its toll. She wanted to please Miranda and Otis, too. Yet the burden had become wearisome.

"Are you sure you can't play something for me in the meantime? I don't mind if I have to hear a sour note or two as you practice." Otis stopped beside the Joneses' buggy.

"Or three or four," Christopher chided.

"Christopher!" Katherine admonished him.

"I'm sorry. You'll have to pardon me, Otis. I've known Katherine so long I forget sometimes she's all grown up and I shouldn't tease her."

"As long as Katherine doesn't mind, I suppose." Otis sounded grumpy. Then, as though remembering where he was, he composed his expression into a grin. "My, but you have a nice church." He observed the landscape. "And such nice countryside here. I'm tempted to extend my stay."

"You're certainly welcome to do so," Katherine blurted.

He smiled. "So which one of your many talents will you be displaying for the talent show next week, Katherine?"

Katherine stiffened. She had been so busy worrying about the harp and her lack of expertise in horsemanship that she had forgotten all about the talent show. Well, she didn't forget, really. Not entirely. But she didn't think of herself as one of the contestants. And now Otis had made it clear that he expected her to take part. At least Christopher and Vera were in on the ruse so they wouldn't blurt out something embarrassing. Still, she wasn't sure how to answer.

"Why don't you try all of them?" Christopher winked.

Katherine shuddered. How could he suggest such a notion? Didn't he know Miranda's reputation was at stake? Certainly she couldn't be expected to betray her friend. Poor Miranda would be devastated if Katherine went back on her word.

If only she could go back in time and convince Miranda that trying to deceive Otis wasn't a good idea. Then she recalled how Miranda had cried and carried on to the point that Katherine felt helpless to deny her. Even if she could turn back the clock, she would make the same decision to help her friend. A decision that was looking less wise with each passing moment.

Otis chuckled. "If she did, the show would last all night, and she'd be the only contestant!"

"At least you'd win, Katherine," Vera noted.

Katherine nodded. Otis meant his observation as a compliment, but she hardly felt flattered. Instead, guilt crushed her soul. She cut her glance to Christopher. He looked pensive. She swallowed, glad to arrive at their buggy. While she wanted to climb in, the others looked at her, awaiting an answer. "Uh...I...uh...I hadn't thought much about entering the talent show. I thought I'd just watch."

"What?" Otis protested. "And deny everyone the pleasure of seeing you perform? I won't hear of it."

"I'm sure it's too late. Mrs. Watkins must have everyone lined up by now."

"No, it's not too late," Christopher assured her. "In fact, they'll take entrants up to the last minute."

She kept from shooting him a mean look. "I don't know. . . ."

"Then it's settled," Otis said. "You'll enter." He snapped his fingers. "I have a splendid idea. Why don't you dance a fine ballet number for the show, and I'll play the piano for you? I'm sure if I put my best foot forward I can learn a number before then. And certainly you can, as well."

A mixture of gratitude, surprise, and guilt shot through Katherine. "You'd do that? You'd play the piano for me?"

He bowed. "I'd be honored."

Katherine wished he weren't such a gentleman. "Otis, I have a confession to make."

As soon as the words left her mouth, she could sense a spark of electricity between Vera, Christopher, and herself. She felt her face turn several shades of hot red. "Speaking of the ballet, I'm afraid I'm out of practice. I wouldn't dream of dancing in front of the whole church."

He looked disappointed. Katherine glanced at Vera and Christopher and saw disappointment on their faces, as well. How had she managed to let everyone down in one fell swoop?

Otis recovered first. "Oh. Well, I can't expect you to keep all of your skills up to their best level at all times, and I'm sure the church members would concur. But never fear. You still have many talents to offer the show. And I can still help. I know a musical number calling for the banjo, harmonica, and piano. Perhaps we could perform a duet. You could play the harmonica and banjo as you indicated, and I can accompany you on the piano."

Katherine could see that Miranda had dug a deep hole for her, and she was teetering over the edge, about to fall into the abyss. Learning a few ballet moves surely would have been easier than mastering not one but two instruments. She had to think quickly. "That is indeed a splendid notion, Otis. And once again, I appreciate your willingness to accompany me. That is so sweet and kind of you." She thought she heard Christopher emit a small snort. "But I have a better idea. Why don't we instead provide background music for Christopher to sing a solo?"

"Oh yes indeed!" Vera chimed in. "Katherine, I think this is one of the best ideas you've had in a long while. What do you say, Christopher?" She turned to Christopher, eyes shining. "Why don't you enter the show and perform with Katherine and Otis?"

It was Christopher's turn to hesitate. "But I hadn't planned to enter the talent show."

Assuming that since Vera supported the idea, she would help her, Katherine thought it politic to add, "As you pointed out earlier, there is practically no deadline. You can enter moments before the show starts. Oh, you must enter, Christopher." She tapped Vera on the shoulder. "Why don't you play along with us? I think we might even win!"

"Maybe I shall," Vera agreed. "Katherine's right. With this pool of talent, we may win!"

"Win indeed," Otis observed.

"Since I have a chorus of insistence, I see that I shall not escape your begging and pleading until I agree to perform." Christopher's voice betrayed a mixture of regret and anticipation.

Otis spoke up. "I feel I must point out that banjo music hardly works with a piano and a harp. Perhaps a simpler solution would be for me to teach you a piano duet, Katherine. Since you are competent on the harp, harmonica, and banjo, surely one song on the piano would be an easy accomplishment for you." He turned to Vera. "And you can still accompany us on the harp."

"Oh, of course. Katherine is a marvelous pianist," Vera said. "What do you say to Otis's idea, Katherine?"

"I don't know about 'easy,' but I think I can manage." Katherine held back a relieved sigh. Striking a few piano keys had to be less taxing than managing the banjo and harmonica simultaneously. She sent him her sweetest smile. "All right. I'll do it."

Chapter 7

In spite of his best efforts not to express vexation, Christopher slammed the door on the way into the kitchen after he arrived home. "Hello, Grandpa."

Grandpa nodded. "Hello, Christopher." Instead of his usual crisp voice, Grandpa's words sounded muffled.

He eyed his grandfather, sitting at the table and swallowing. "Sneaking a piece of pie?"

"Don't tell your mother. She's been trying to get me to cut back on desserts, but I won't stand for it. I've lived this long without watching what I eat too close. I reckon the good Lord will see fit to let me live a few more years. And if He doesn't, then I figure I'll be with your grandma sooner than I thought."

Grandpa shuffled to the sink pump and rinsed the dish, washing away evidence of apple pie crumbs. He turned to his grandson. "But you. Well, you're young and another matter altogether. So why are you so angry?"

Christopher tried to think of a way to avoid admitting the truth. "Who says I'm angry?"

Grandpa wiped the plate with the dry dish towel and slid it into its proper place in the kitchen cabinet. "Look here, young man. I've known you since you were nothin' but a little red thing squallin' at the top of your lungs. I know when you're mad. Besides, I slammed a door or two in my day myself." He winked. "So does this have something to do with that sweet little Katherine and the competition from South Carolina she imported for you?"

"Competition? He's no competition for me."

"That bad, huh? Well, I know a thing or two about women. They haven't changed all that much since I was a young buck. You've just got to get in there and show her what's best for her, that's all." He shuffled to his seat, plopped down, and situated himself in comfort.

Christopher took a nearby chair. "And just how will I do that when I'll be singing along with his piano playing?"

"Say what?" Grandpa twisted his index finger in his ear.

Christopher wasn't sure whether to laugh or get even madder. He decided to take the middle road and keep his unwelcome emotions in check. "I got roped into performing with him at the talent show." He relayed the rest of the story.

Grandpa thought for a moment. "Well, I'd normally observe that a situation like that would put him in a superior position. He could be tempted to flub-de-dub on the piano so you would stumble in your singing."

"Oh." Uneasiness visited Christopher's stomach. Such a thought hadn't occurred to him.

Grandpa lifted his forefinger to get Christopher's attention. "But he won't do that. Not with Katherine playing along with him. So I think you came out on top after all, my boy."

Grandpa's encouraging words gave Christopher pause to consider what other good could come out of the situation. "At least Otis won't have Katherine all to himself."

"True. Except when he is teaching her the piano duet."

"Oh, yes. I hadn't thought of that." Christopher's depression returned.

Grandpa winked. "But there's not a thing in the world to stop you from being at every possible practice. So what if that means you might have to hurry through your chores. Skip supper, even. But maybe if she has to feed you, she'll feel sorry for you and pay you more mind. That mothering instinct comes out real quick. It worked with your grandma."

Christopher laughed. "That's what you always say."

"And you can believe it."

"I don't know how much mothering Katherine wants to do. I'm thinking I would have been better off if I had agreed to go along with her plan of deception."

"Now wait just a minute here. It's not Katherine's plan of deception but Miranda's. She's the one who's keeping the pressure on Katherine to make her keep on going along with this silly game."

"You're right. Katherine is not a deceiver at heart. And she never will be. She's too good for that. Too kindhearted for her own good. Every time she tries to wiggle out of the ruse, Miranda cries. She makes Katherine feel really bad. It makes me mad just to think about it."

"What do you think made Miranda decide to tell all those stories anyway?"

Christopher thought for a moment. "I don't know, but I have a feeling Miranda never thought Otis would make the journey all this way to see us. She thought she'd never get caught, I suppose."

"I've seen Miranda in action. Now she doesn't think I'm looking. She thinks I'm too old to notice or to be noticed. Maybe she's got a point there."

"Grandpa, that's not so."

The older man held up his hand. "Don't you go arguing with me, son. I'm just saying that people say things in front of me they wouldn't dare utter in front of their parents. And I've seen that Miranda friend of yours brag within an inch of her life. Gets carried away, she does. I suppose she can't help it. Don't know why she feels she has to brag so much, though. She's a right pretty girl. Well off, too, judging from all the jewelry she likes to wear all the time. Guess she just wants attention. But to drag poor Katherine into it, that's just wrong."

"I know. And I wish she hadn't," Christopher said.

"Well, she's trying to do a good turn for a friend, and I suppose I can't fault her so much for that. But as for you, two wrongs don't make a right. You're doing the right thing not to be a part of the scheme. They'll all learn. But I have a feeling they will have to learn the hard way."

"As much as I don't like this Otis guy. . ."

"Yep, I never much cared for competition either. He seems nice. Too nice."

"That's just it. I can't find anything wrong with him. He's charming. And there he is, right in her house. She doesn't stand a chance." Christopher sighed. "Maybe they should be together. Maybe I'm the one interfering in God's plan."

"I doubt it. Just be sure to be around when she falls. You only have a short time left before he has to go back to where he came from. Those days will pass much sooner than you think."

Christopher remembered Otis's hint that he'd like to remain in Maryland longer. "I don't know. I'm afraid he's taken such a liking to Katherine that he wants to extend his visit. What's wrong with that man? He told Katherine he had a business to tend to. But I don't see how he'll get anything done playing around here forever. Doesn't he ever do a lick of work in his sorry life? Of course," Christopher ranted, "he's using the excuse of the church people and the appeal of the countryside as reasons to stay longer, but I can see right through him. The snake." He cut his glance to his older relative, who had always been his mentor. "Can you take a guess, Grandpa?"

He shrugged. "Maybe he's independently wealthy."

"Maybe so." Christopher remembered the expensive-looking suit he wore to the gathering that night. "He certainly dresses in clothes that look like they were store bought. And not from just any store but a fancy city tailor."

"Yes, I have to admit, Otis cuts a fine figure. But you look better than he ever could even when you've got on dungarees with pig slop all over 'em. Of course you do. You take after your old grandpa." He wagged his forefinger. "Not that your mother was any slouch in her day either. Don't tell your father I said so, but she had quite a few offers before he came along and stole her heart." Grandpa rocked his chair back on its hind legs. "But your daddy has made her happy, and they gave me and your grandma you and your brothers and your sister. I'll always be grateful to him for that." He nodded. "Yep, one day I hope you can look back on your life with as much satisfaction as I have in mine."

"I'm not sure I will if Katherine decides to abandon me for Otis."

"Maybe you should speak up now before she sets her mind for good."

"Why bother? I can't compete with Otis."

"With that kind of attitude, you never will win at anything." Grandpa's frankness caused Christopher's heart to skip a beat. "Unless all she wants is money. And you won't be giving her a whole lot of that out here on the farm."

"Maybe not, but she'll always have plenty of fresh air and enough to eat. Besides, Katherine isn't like that. Money never interested her. Sure, I know she wants enough so she won't have to worry, but she never seems to care about fine things like some other women. Like Rosette Sims, for one."

"The flirty little brunette who likes to wear her dresses a little lower than she should on top and a mite too short on the bottom?"

"Grandpa! I didn't think you'd notice such things."

"I might be old, but my vision's still good."

"As a matter of fact, she did come to mind. She always wears the most elaborate hats and too much jewelry for all occasions. Even more so than Miranda."

"I see you've noticed her, too, then." Grandpa chuckled.

"I don't mean to be prideful, but Rosette has sent interested glances my way more than once." Christopher cleared his throat. "I've never paid her any mind."

He knew why. He was still too much in love with Katherine.

———

The evening of the harp solo arrived. Vera had planned the small gathering of friends as a way to entertain her sister who was still in her confinement, so she had asked the guests to bring dishes to share, as well.

As Katherine crossed the threshold of the Sharpes' kitchen, lap harp in hand, she couldn't remember a time when she had felt more nervous. Well, maybe during the play in her senior year of high school, when she blanked out on her lines and had to ad lib, thereby adding new meaning to the word *comical*. Too bad the skit had been written as a drama.

"Are you ready, Katherine?" Vera greeted her. "You certainly look splendid enough to perform at a real theater!"

"Thanks." She looked down at her dress. "So do you."

Vera blushed. "Hardly. But thanks for the compliment."

Otis entered behind Katherine, carrying a load of food. "Good evening, Miss Vera."

She sent him a pleasant smile. "Good evening, Otis."

"Pardon me for getting right to the point, but I confess this load is a bit heavy. Where shall I put all this food?"

"Over on the table in the dining room, if you'd be so kind. I'll arrange it later." She pointed to a table where other guests had already placed many succulent dishes.

"I'm surprised you couldn't follow the aromas, Otis," Katherine chided. "Everything smells so delicious, Vera. You must have prepared your famous chicken casserole."

"Indeed I did."

"And everything does smell scrumptious," Otis agreed.

As he hurried to comply with Vera's instructions, Katherine whispered to her friend, "I wish I felt as confident as you say I look."

"You have no reason to fear."

Katherine wasn't so sure, and the anxiety in her voice betrayed her sentiments. "What will happen if I falter? I'll look like a fool in front of Otis and Christopher. . . ." She shook the thought from her head.

"I wouldn't worry if I were you. Most people don't know enough about playing the harp to realize any mistakes."

"I don't know."

"You have learned your song well. We certainly practiced enough!" Vera looked toward the door. "Besides, judging from the looks of what Otis brought in, you outdid yourself on the quantity of food. No doubt quality, as well."

"I hope so. I cooked all day. Cherry pie, nutmeg cake, vegetable salad, potato salad, even fried chicken. Otis did a lot of taste testing, and he approved all the dishes."

"I can't wait to try everything. Come, let's go greet the others."

Katherine nodded. She managed to relax as she talked to her old friends and got caught up with their lives. Though life moved slowly on the farm and proved predictable, she still enjoyed hearing about each person's joys and mourned with each sorrow. She tried to make her way over to Christopher, but he spent most of the evening with the men, most likely talking about the latest market numbers and other details of running a farm. Though she found the talk fascinating, the men considered numbers and such more their domain, so she tried to look as though she wasn't paying them much mind.

She caught Christopher's eye once or twice, and though he looked congenial enough, he never did manage to finagle his way near enough to her to share a thought or two. Funny, she had missed him while he was away at school, but since his chatty letters always kept her informed, she didn't think much about his expected absence at gatherings. Now that he was always in the same room, she realized how much her fondness for him had grown over the years. Too bad he considered her nothing more than a childhood friend.

Where did that thought come from?

"Why, Katherine," Miranda noted, "if I didn't know better, I'd think you were blushing."

"You must really like Otis a lot," Lily observed.

"He is nice enough." Katherine didn't want to be ebullient about her guest. Otherwise, her friends might get the wrong idea. On the other hand, she didn't want to be too harsh. Why invent a failing just to show them that her heart refused to flutter when he entered the room?

"Maybe you'll be moving to South Carolina before you know it," Lily speculated.

"Now, now, let's not jump to conclusions," Katherine said. "I have no thought in my mind of making any such decision. Otis and I have become acquainted through the exchange of letters. That is all, and that is all I think it ever shall be."

"He hasn't hinted at more?" Miranda's eyes were wide.

Katherine shrugged. For the first time, she wished Otis had flirted with her. Then she would have a story to share amid blushes and shy whispers. But as it was, she did not. She swallowed. "As I said, he is a kind houseguest. He will be returning to his home soon."

"I see." When Miranda turned her head to eye Otis, her pearl earrings dangled in stride. She fanned herself with a much higher degree of energy than the weather required.

Even Katherine had to admit he cut a fine figure in his tailored clothes.

"He is quite stylish," Lily noted. "But he has nothing on my Wilbur." She sent her fiancé a smile that caught his attention. He smiled back.

Katherine held back a chuckle. Only Lily would say that Wilbur appeared superior to Otis. She looked over at Christopher. He held his own against every man in the room. Every man she knew, for that matter. Even Otis.

"Well." Vera approached from the kitchen and looked at the overburdened table. "It looks like everyone is here. I say it's high time we ate."

Alice's husband offered grace, and they began.

Katherine wasn't worried about dinner. She knew she could hold her own in cooking. For once, she felt relaxed and took time to relish the feeling as she sampled the dishes her friends had brought.

"This cherry pie is mighty good," Christopher remarked later over dessert. "I'm told you made it?"

"Yes I did. I'm glad you like it."

"I sure do." He grinned. "Your cooking certainly has improved since your teen years. I remember when you brought rock-hard biscuits to a church potluck dinner."

She groaned. "Did you have to remind me?" Still, she cherished his memories. Christopher's observation only brought to light the history they shared, something she never could have with Otis.

Seeming to sense her thoughts, Otis interjected from his perch on the other side of the divan, "Yes, this pie is wonderful, Katherine. I don't remember a time I've tasted better. And Christopher, you must try the nutmeg cake, too. It's absolutely splendid. I had the privilege of being with Katherine as she cooked, so I have already sampled every foodstuff she made. I can assure you, each dish is absolutely exquisite."

"I'm sure." Christopher didn't look too happy.

"What amazes me, Miranda, is that you never told me about this particular skill. Frankly, I think cooking well is much more useful than being able to sing and dance. Much more practical, certainly."

"Katherine is talented in a number of areas, as Miranda told you," Christopher said. "Katherine is much too modest to boast about her skills and talents. Then again, I've known her a long time and I am well aware of her many gifts."

"Thank you," Katherine said softly. Christopher's kind words meant so much more than any flattery from Otis could have.

Dinner passed all too quickly. Wariness returned later as Katherine went before her friends. Since they were show-offs, the friends played and sang for each other to rousing applause. Miranda took the opportunity to sing an opera tune that impressed all, even Katherine. Upon the song's completion, Otis clapped the loudest. Miranda curtsied several times to resounding applause.

"I know you brought that harp for a reason," Christopher said to Katherine. "Let's hear you play."

"I agree!" Otis said. "She's been practicing with Vera, and I haven't heard her pluck the first note myself.

Katherine swallowed but obeyed their prodding and took her place in front of them.

Father in heaven, I know I don't deserve Thy mercy, but I ask for Thee to stay with me as I perform tonight.

Once Katherine hit the first few notes, she remembered the rest of the song with ease. She even forgot she had an audience of almost everyone in the world she cared about, and as she plucked, she enjoyed listening to the music she created. She almost couldn't believe it when the end of the piece was greeted by unstinting applause and smiles from her friends. She felt pleased and relieved. Vera had been right after all. Learning the song was much more rewarding than pretending to learn it. And her conscience was clear.

Father in heaven, I thank Thee for seeing me through.

Chapter 8

After the concert, the group relaxed, seated around the room, and talked among themselves. Otis broke off with Christopher and approached Katherine as Vera excused herself to chat with Miranda.

Katherine gave him a look that she knew expressed her nervousness. She wasn't sure what to expect.

To her surprise and delight, he offered a smile. "You played superbly, Katherine. Even better than I anticipated. And I assure you, that's saying quite a lot."

Katherine smiled, feeling genuine delight in a performance well executed. As Vera had foretold, the effort had been worth the reward. "Thank you."

Otis rose from his seat. "If you'll excuse me, I must say a few words to Miranda. Surely she is to be congratulated for her superb rendition, as well. She certainly chose a challenging aria and delivered it flawlessly. Why, she could pass for someone trained in such arts."

"Yes." The fact she felt no jealousy surprised Katherine.

"Is she?"

"Is she what?" Katherine shot a glimpse Miranda's way.

"Why, trained in the art of opera, of course."

"Oh." Katherine tried to recall. "I believe she took lessons some years back. A voice teacher traveled from town to town, giving lessons every week or so. I didn't take advantage of the opportunity, I'm sorry to say."

"That is not to be regretted. Your talents are many." He nodded once. "Now to congratulate Miranda."

Katherine wasn't alone for long, because Christopher soon walked up beside her. "For once, I concur with Otis. Your talents are indeed many. I must say, your performance just now was splendid."

Katherine noticed that Christopher's congratulations sounded heartier than Otis's had. His words seemed to convey that he was happy she had finally learned to play the harp after years of wishing she could. "Yes. Learning that song—really learning to play it—taught me a lot. I have to give Vera credit for being patient enough to teach me."

"Yes, Vera is a good friend to you."

She nodded and looked over at Otis. He was engaged in animated conversation with Miranda.

Christopher's gaze followed hers. "Otis seems to have made a new friend here."

"Yes."

His dark eyebrows shot up, drawing her attention not only to his surprise but also to his clear blue eyes. "You don't seem to be bothered by his apparent interest in your friend."

"Should I be? I've always maintained that Otis and I are just correspondents. Nothing more."

Christopher didn't seem to mind her admission and changed the topic. Yet she hardly heard what he said as she recalled the trickery regarding the horsemanship that Miranda had planned over her protests. Katherine had decided to make one last attempt to call it off. "Excuse me, Christopher. I have something to say to Otis and Miranda."

"Oh?" His mouth straightened. "You don't want to hear about how Reddy got out of the pen and scared Mr. Crawford half to death?"

"Again?" She shook her head. "That bull has never been one to be controlled, has he? How many times has he gotten out of that pen?" Nevertheless, she drew out her lace fan and cooled herself with it as she stood in place, a sign of her willingness to listen to his tale of mock woe.

Christopher laughed and finished his story, embellishing the details and making much of the fact that his neighbor Homer, known to be equal parts bully and coward, fell facedown in the mud while trying to escape the ranting beast, hurting only his pride but leaving a splotch of wet dirt on his dungarees. Though glad for the amusing interlude, Katherine excused herself from Christopher as quickly as she could when he was done.

She made her way through the gathering, weaving through couples as well as clusters of friends chattering about the latest news. When Katherine reached the couple, Miranda was throwing her head back in mirth. Her earrings dangled with the motion.

"Oh, do let me in on the joke. I always like a good laugh," Katherine said.

Otis's response didn't convey the deference to which Katherine had become accustomed. "Perhaps I should wait until we arrive at your home. I would be remiss if I allowed Miss Miranda to listen to my story again. I never like to bore anyone."

"Oh, you could never bore me, Otis," Miranda insisted. "Do retell the whole story from start to finish. And don't you think of leaving out a single detail on my account."

"Are you sure you'd like to hear me tell my tale again?" Otis asked.

"Indeed."

"All right, then. If you will not take no for an answer." Otis grinned and then related a story about his office that didn't seem all that amusing to Katherine, but Miranda laughed again as though she had heard it for the first time.

Katherine wished she hadn't insisted on hearing the story. She took her cue from Miranda and chuckled at the right times. Encouraged by their attention, Otis relayed yet another event, one mildly amusing to Katherine but apparently of great interest to Miranda.

"You are aware that Katherine is an expert horsewoman, are you not, Otis?" Miranda asked when the subject of Miranda's success in horse shows was broached.

Good! An opportunity!

"About that—" Katherine said.

"Yes, indeed," Otis interjected, lifting his forefinger as though he were a college professor about to make a point that would be included on the examination. "You made that quite plain in your letters, Miranda."

"Oh, but I could never compete with Miranda. And I wouldn't want to." Katherine sent a flattering look Miranda's way.

Miranda fanned herself with enough gusto to cause her overloaded charm bracelet to clink with fury. She batted her heavy eyelashes at Otis. "Well, I do have my share of ribbons and praise for my skill. Katherine has complimented me many a time."

"Coming from another expert horsewoman, that must mean a lot," Otis said.

"About that expert horsewoman business," Katherine managed, "I must admit, I'm not quite as skilled as you may have been led to believe. In fact—"

Otis swatted his hand at her and looked at her as though she were a child speaking out of turn. "Our Katherine is the modest one, isn't she?" Otis asked Miranda. "I can see why she's so popular."

"I prefer to say that I am blessed with many friends who are kind to me beyond what I deserve," Katherine said. "Take Miranda here—"

"Yes, Miranda does seem as though she would make quite a good friend," Otis observed, sending a pleasant smile Miranda's way. "Perhaps you should come along and watch Katherine as she demonstrates her skill to me sometime. I was thinking of asking her if we could meet tomorrow, perhaps."

"Tomorrow would work well."

"Good. By all accounts, you would appreciate the chance to watch, since you will know how hard she works to hone her equestrian skills."

Miranda didn't miss a beat. "I'd love to be there. I'll see what I can do. As you know, I'm always up for an adventure." She sent Katherine a sly smile that Katherine was sure escaped Otis's notice. "Seeing Katherine and her horse would be quite impressive, but now that I recall my schedule for tomorrow, I regret my entire afternoon is engaged." Miranda let out a larger-than-life sigh. "I'm afraid I shall miss seeing her. Another time, perhaps." The sweet countenance she conveyed to Katherine left no hint that Miranda had any other intention.

Katherine suppressed a groan. Try as she might to confess, an admission wasn't going to take place. Not with Otis and Miranda dominating the conversation as they were. To speak now would only serve to embarrass Miranda. The thought of her friend's tears and recriminations left Katherine with a sorrowful feeling. To reveal all would embarrass Miranda and cause her to break her promise. Katherine couldn't find it in her heart to do either. Any courage she had mustered to speak the truth evaporated. "Excuse me, but I think I'll have another glass of punch."

"Where are my manners? I should have noticed your cup was running low and pardoned myself so I could freshen it for you. Please forgive my breach of courtesy." Otis reached for her cup.

"Not at all." Katherine noticed that Miranda's cup and Otis's were half full. She was tempted to deny him, but he took the cup, leaving her alone with Miranda. Katherine saw an opportunity too good not to pursue. She cleared her throat and started speaking so quickly that her words almost ran into each other. "Miranda, maybe we should call off the whole plan regarding the horse tricks."

Miranda's eyes widened as she shushed Katherine. "Don't speak so loudly. Someone will overhear."

"That wouldn't be such a disaster, I'm beginning to think." She pursed her lips and looked at the tips of her shoes. "I really think we should call it off."

"No. Please. I don't want to lose face in front of Otis. Not now."

A thought flashed through Katherine's mind. "You like him, don't you? You really like him."

Miranda blushed. "He can see me ride—as myself—another time."

Otis returned with two full cups of punch. "I beg your pardon, ladies, but the line for the punch was unbelievable for such a small gathering. Mrs. Sharpe let the bowl run dry and had to replenish the supply. I do believe the entire assembly ran out of punch at the same time." He handed Katherine her cup. "But the wait does mean that I can offer you a beverage freshly prepared."

"Thank you. That is splendid." Miranda said.

"Yes," Katherine said as she accepted her cup. "Splendid."

"As for the wait, never worry for a moment, Otis," Miranda hastened to assure him. "Katherine and I were sharing entertaining confidences, were we not, Katherine?"

"Um, yes. Confidences indeed."

Otis chuckled and took a sip of his drink. "Ah, the whisperings of the fairer sex. Intrigue we men shall never be privy to nor understand."

"Indeed you shall not!" Miranda teased. "For we women need to maintain a few mysteries to keep ourselves interesting to you men, do we not?"

"I'm not so certain. I would venture a guess that you would remain interesting to us, mysteries or no."

As Miranda giggled, Katherine felt her eyebrows rise. Did she ascertain something in Otis's tone that revealed he held a mystery, as well? She wondered.

"I'm here!" Miranda called out the next day, catching Katherine at the stables as planned. Seeming to be oblivious to the drizzle that had fallen on and off throughout the day, she flashed Katherine a winning smile. She dismounted from her dappled gray mare and swept her hand over her red cropped riding jacket and formfitting riding pants. "How do I look?"

"Great." Katherine looked down at her own outfit, which mirrored her friend's. "We look almost identical," she had to admit.

Katherine looked back toward the lake and saw Otis approaching, carrying a wooden bucket. He'd been fishing with Father for the better part of the day. No doubt she would hear many stories about his successful trip.

Miranda hissed, "That's him! If I don't hide, Katherine, he'll see us dressed alike and know something is amiss!"

Panic seized Katherine. She watched Miranda head into the barn. The plan was set to commence.

Katherine turned toward her visitor and put on her most cheerful face. "Hello, Otis!"

He quickened his pace, approaching her with increasing speed. When he drew close enough to speak to her without raising his voice, Katherine noticed the dank smell of muddy water, wet grass, and fish. He seemed not to notice that outdoor aromas clung to him, a fact that Katherine found amusing in the usually immaculate Otis.

"I came here as soon as your father and I ran out of bait and called it a day. We had an excellent time. I caught an exceedingly large trout that should feed the whole family for one meal at least." He extracted the fish from the bucket and showed it to her.

Katherine concentrated her thoughts on how the fried fish would taste, its flaky meat tender and buttery. "That sounds wonderful. I can fry it up for you tonight."

"Good." He held up the fish for his own inspection and studied it, a boastful look upon his countenance. "I'll dress this fellow here as soon as I see you jump. I don't want to tarry, though, as it wouldn't be fair for me to leave your father with all the work to do. He's at the house now, dressing his catch." Otis, much to Katherine's relief, returned his own catch of the day to the wooden bucket.

She nodded and ducked into the barn. Miranda saw Katherine enter and delayed leaving long enough to make Otis think Katherine had mounted the horse. Then she trotted out in style.

Katherine watched as Miranda and Ash jumped the practice hurdles, one right after the other, in a fluid motion. Still hidden in the barn, Katherine gasped in awe. If only she could make her horse jump in such a way!

Katherine had relaxed until they approached the last hurdle. She watched as

186

the horse slipped. Miranda pulled on the reins, but her efforts proved futile. She lost her hold, fell off the horse, and landed on her side on the ground.

Katherine didn't think about what could happen as she sprinted toward Miranda. No matter how embarrassed she would be, no matter how much pride she would have to throw aside, she didn't care. She had to make sure her friend was all right.

From the corner of her eye, Katherine noticed that Ash had stumbled but recovered. Well-trained and faithful animal that she was, the horse stood beside the hurdle and whinnied, watching what would become of her mistress.

Otis ran to Miranda in the meantime. "Katherine!" he called, obviously not realizing the deception at first. Raw fear made itself evident on his face. He really did care about her! Her heart soared, then plunged.

Reaching Miranda first, he knelt beside her, although she had already recovered and was sitting upright on the ground. He looked into her face. "Miranda?" He paused. "Miranda! What is the meaning of this?"

Chapter 9

Katherine could hear the anger in Otis's voice. Guilt shot through her. If he was angry, he had every right to be. The ruse had been exposed, and Otis was about to discover that he had been duped.

All she could do was try to make amends.

Katherine bounded to their sides. "I can explain."

Otis stood and helped Miranda rise to her feet. He pointed to Miranda, and then to Katherine. "You. . .you two are dressed alike. Why? What's going on here?"

Otis's glare stole Katherine's courage. "I'll explain later. We need to tend to Miranda now." She took her friend's hand. "Miranda? How are you?"

Miranda nodded before a wry grin bent her lips. "I've felt better, but I'll be fine."

"Are you in any pain?"

"No."

"That's a relief." Katherine exhaled. "You're standing, and that's a good sign. Try to move your arms and neck. Can you?"

Miranda lifted her arms and rotated them back and forth. To show how well she had recovered, she danced a triumphant little jig. Katherine clasped her hands to her chest. "Praise the Lord!"

Christopher and Vera approached, scaring Katherine since, too absorbed in Miranda's plight, she hadn't seen or heard them. "Mrs. Jones said ya'll were out here. What's going on?"

Otis's face darkened. "What's going on? What's going on? I have been deceived; that's what's going on."

Christopher shot Katherine a look that conveyed both chastisement and fear.

"It's all my fault, really," Miranda rushed to elaborate. "I took a little fall. Nothing unusual in this business. Everything's fine now. Please don't concern yourselves with me."

Christopher's eyes filled with compassion. "I'm so sorry, Miranda. Is there anything I can do to help you?"

"You can help me recover my pride, I suppose. If that's possible." Miranda laughed, a sure sign she had returned to her ebullient self.

Christopher nodded. "Good. But perhaps we should postpone our talent show practice to another day. Apparently none of us are in any state to practice our musical number at present."

"Oh, Christopher!" Katherine said. "I'm so sorry. I forgot all about our practice today. And Vera, I apologize to you, too. Look, we can find some way—"

"Never mind, Katherine." She looked as though she felt sorry for her friend.

Otis glared at Christopher. "You act as though you know what happened here."

"No, Christopher and Vera had no part of this," Katherine explained.

"Be that as it may," Otis said in a controlled voice, "I am very vexed with you, Katherine. I may not be the sharpest pencil in the box, but I can see what's going on here. You and Miranda dressed alike, and you let her use her skill to make me think it was you who was jumping hurdles. Is that right?"

Katherine looked down at the ground. "I'm afraid so."

"It's all my fault, Otis."

Katherine breathed a sigh of relief. Finally Miranda was ready to confess and Katherine was free.

Otis turned to Miranda. "Your fault?"

"Yes. I wrote all those things about Katherine, knowing she wasn't as skilled as I claimed. I never thought you'd visit, but when you did, I panicked. I thought up this whole plan, and I begged her to go along with me in the ruse. She tried and tried and tried to get me to change my mind, to come clean, to confess everything right away, but I was the one who resisted." Tears rolled down her cheeks. She sniffled.

"There, there, now." Otis patted her on the shoulder.

Miranda nodded and took a handkerchief from her jacket pocket. "I—I was too prideful and didn't want to be embarrassed. I didn't want you to know I had lied. I'm so sorry."

"I see that you are," Otis cooed.

Miranda looked up at him with tear-drenched eyes. "Can. . .can you ever forgive me?"

"Of course I can."

"And can you forgive me?" Katherine interjected. "Like Miranda said, I didn't want to be a part of this. I was only going along with it for Miranda's sake, and I'm sorry I didn't have the fortitude to stand my ground."

"What she says is true. Katherine was being a friend to me," Miranda agreed.

"In that case, yes, I can forgive you, too, Katherine." Otis turned back to Miranda. "I can't believe you both went to all this trouble just to impress me."

"To impress you? I suppose you could look at it that way, yes," Miranda said.

"But you shouldn't have risked your life, my dear," Otis said.

"I did no such thing. The hurdles were easy ones. I admit I was surprised when Ash faltered." She looked down at the ground and pointed. "That's the culprit."

They all observed a patch of mud.

Christopher studied it. "That's enough to throw anyone." He sent Katherine a comforting look and touched her on the shoulder briefly but drew his hand back before anyone else noticed.

"The mud was concealed by grass," Miranda said. "I know because I didn't see it myself; if I had, I would have led the horse around it and not attempted that last hurdle. No one could have predicted that Ash would falter. And it's not as though I have never fallen. The only thing that's hurt on my account is my vanity." She chuckled.

"Perhaps, but I must say, despite your good intentions, I am quite upset by this development. I never meant to cause anyone to tell a lie. That distresses me greatly. Perhaps since I have proven to be such a negative influence, I should pack my bags and leave."

"Leave?" Katherine asked. "Otis, I know this has all come as a shock to you, but please do not resort to hyperbole."

"I'm not so sure I am. I will have to think about what my next course of action will be. Maybe I should take the train out on Monday morning."

"But what about the talent show? Will you stay for that? Please?" Miranda implored.

Otis set his heels firmly in the ground. "I don't know if I can be convinced."

"At least watch us rehearse," Katherine suggested, hoping he might change his mind.

Otis withdrew his pocket watch and looked at the time. "It's only two o'clock. I should have time to get to the train station to purchase my ticket if I leave right away."

"Two?" Christopher questioned him, withdrawing his own watch. "I'm afraid your timepiece is not accurate, Otis. My watch says it's already a quarter to three, and I have mine set by the jeweler according to railroad time."

"Then your watch should certainly be accurate." Otis harrumphed. "I did notice my watch seemed to act in a sluggish manner before I departed South Carolina. Apparently its performance has not improved since then." He set the hands to the proper time.

"Then it's settled. You don't have time to do anything about your return trip today. You may as well stay for the rehearsal," Katherine pointed out.

"All right, then." He didn't seem too upset that his plans to leave had been derailed. Katherine had a feeling his suggestion had been more bluster than intent.

"Good!" Miranda took him by the arm, a development that seemed to please Otis.

The group walked back to the house in silence. Katherine became immersed in her thoughts. Even though the incident with Miranda had tarnished her relationship with Otis, Katherine was glad they had committed to participating together in the talent show. That meant she could be close to Christopher when they practiced for their performance.

The afternoon had told many a tale. At the pivotal moment of despair, Christopher, not Otis, chose to comfort her. In that instant, Katherine realized that she had ignored a treasure living right next door. She knew she could love Christopher as more than a friend. But after her mistakes, could he ever return her feelings? If he couldn't, she knew she would be getting what she deserved. She had done wrong out of a desire to please a friend.

Now she could see beyond any doubt that what her friend had asked of her was wrong. She never should have let herself get involved in Miranda's schemes. In her heart, Katherine knew that Miranda hadn't acted to embarrass Katherine intentionally. In fact, Miranda had the highest stake in making sure the ruse was a success. But in hindsight, Katherine discerned that she shouldn't have let Miranda define their friendship. She should have stood up for herself and insisted they come clean about Miranda's letters to Otis. She had learned so many lessons during Otis's visit: the limits of friendship, the importance of courage, and where her heart lay in regard to Christopher.

Then fear struck.

Heavenly Father, has my misguided attempt to help Miranda caused me to lose Christopher forever?

Otis left them to join Father in dressing the catch. As Vera, Miranda, Christopher, and Katherine crossed the porch, Katherine suppressed her disturbing thoughts. Nothing would be gained if the practice for the talent show proved to be a similar disappointment because she was distracted.

Mother regarded them as they entered the kitchen where she was in the process of rolling smooth, creamy dough for dinner rolls. Katherine took in a deliberate breath, inhaling the appealing scent of fresh yeast that filled the kitchen.

"My, but we have quite a crowd here," Mother observed. "How is everyone?"

Christopher answered first, followed by the others' exchange of pleasantries. Mother offered glasses of refreshing mint tea and cups of coffee. As they relaxed for a few moments in camaraderie, Katherine felt eternal gratitude that no one mentioned the mishap with the horse. Nervousness seared her throat as Otis entered, but he busied himself with a quick cleanup at the washbasin and then excused himself to his room. She had the distinct feeling that since he had made no mention of the mishap at that moment he planned to let it pass. She breathed a sigh of relief. At least he had shown her a small portion of mercy.

"Is everyone ready for practice?" Otis asked after he had taken a brief interlude to freshen himself. Katherine couldn't help but notice combed hair, clean clothes, and the aroma of spicy shaving lotion, no doubt applied to impress Miranda.

She cut her glance to Christopher. He still looked unsullied in a crisp white shirt and blue and white seersucker pants. Vera's encounter with the outdoors left her equally unspoiled, appearing in white and yellow as she did. Even Miranda, dirtied as she was from her fall, beamed so brightly no one would notice how much mud her pants had accumulated.

"I'm more than ready to begin," Katherine offered. "Mother, would you care to watch us perform?"

"I wish I could, but I'm too busy with this dough at the moment. Do play loudly enough so I can hear, will you?"

"Of course." She managed a smile.

As they rehearsed their numbers in the parlor, Katherine noticed that Otis's mood improved. He played with more gusto than usual. She found the development to be no surprise. Miranda provided them with an enthusiastic audience, clapping in resounding approval whether or not they had missed notes. Every once in a while, Mother called out encouragement from the kitchen.

Betsy bounded in from playing outdoors, with Rover following closely. "I heard the music. It sounds so pretty!"

"Thank you," Otis said.

Mother appeared. "Do I hear that dog scampering around in here?"

"Sorry, Mother," Betsy answered and shooed the dog outside.

"Betsy," Mother warned, "you know Rover can't be here in the parlor. Please try to do better."

"I will." She shut the door behind Rover.

"That dog has taken up the worst habit of coming in the house," Katherine said.

"He does that because he loves me," Betsy informed her. "He wants to be where I am."

"That's all well and good, but as far as I'm concerned, he belongs outdoors," Mother reminded her.

"I know. I'll do my best to keep him outside." Betsy scampered to where Miranda sat and took a place beside her. She fingered Miranda's charm bracelet. "Did you get the charm from Egypt yet?"

"Not yet." Miranda smiled. "I am hoping Aunt Tilly can find one in the shape of a pyramid, but of course such a trinket might not be available."

"I hope she finds one. I know it will be pretty if she does."

"Speaking of pretty, what are you going to do for the talent show?"

"Tap dance."

"Oh, that sounds nice."

"Mother is going to play for me." Betsy turned a sunny expression to Otis. "Are you ready to play in the talent show?"

"I'm not sure. I may not be here."

Betsy's chin nearly hit her chest. "Why not?"

"This is news to me, too, Otis," Mother pointed out.

"Oh, please stay, Otis!" Betsy implored.

"I think you should, especially now that I've heard you play. You're so wonderful with music!" Miranda added. "I just don't know what we would do without you in the talent show. Why, I told everyone at church how talented I know you to be, and now they're all eager to hear you perform."

"Is that so?" Otis's chest puffed up.

"That's so." Miranda batted her eyelashes in his direction. "Oh, please say you'll stay."

Otis paused, much to Katherine's amusement. He was playing up his act for all it was worth.

"Please?" Miranda and Betsy asked in unison.

"Oh, all right." Otis smiled.

"Yay!" Betsy clapped her hands. "So will you play another song for me?"

Since Miranda never professed to Otis that Katherine could play the piano, Katherine had nothing to prove. She felt as relaxed as she could, considering that, as she practiced her song, she still felt Otis's eyes watching her. As they continued, she missed a few easy notes and soon realized she wasn't up to form, but they made progress on the musical number. After a half hour, she felt satisfied that they had accomplished as much as could be expected for one day.

"Why don't we call it a day on this music?" Katherine ventured.

"So soon? I was enjoying the show," Miranda objected, though not with vigor.

"Perhaps you will see your way clear to watching us rehearse tomorrow," Otis suggested.

"That is a thought." Miranda smiled. "You've done very well. If I may be so bold, I'm wondering if you might like to take a break and let me entertain you with a song."

"Absolutely!" Otis said. "Will you allow me to accompany you on the piano?"

"That would be my pleasure."

"Your request? Perhaps 'Hello, My Baby.'"

"That's a popular song, indeed, but hardly one that suits my voice."

"What was I thinking? Of course that wouldn't be a suitable tune for your feminine voice."

"Do you know 'Havanaise' from the first act of *Carmen*?"

"You have certainly named a challenging song," Vera observed.

"Indeed it is. I'm not sure I can do Miranda justice with my accompaniment, but I shall try," Otis said.

Miranda took in a breath and executed the difficult operatic number without a flaw. Such was her skill that even Mother stopped her work long enough to enter the room to hear Miranda sing. When she completed the number, the resulting applause from everyone in the room was genuine.

"I think we could give the others some competition at the talent show," Otis said.

"I think we could." Miranda giggled, then composed herself. "Present company excluded, of course."

Otis glanced at the others. "Of course."

Somehow, he didn't sound convincing.

———

Horses' hooves pounded against Maryland dirt as the Bagleys' buggy journeyed to the Sharpes' farm after rehearsal.

"Christopher Bagley, you certainly are not very good company today." Sitting in the seat beside him, Vera poked him in the ribs.

"Ouch!"

"Sorry. I don't know my own strength."

"Sure you don't." Christopher rubbed the place in his side where Vera's elbow had prodded. "Another one of those and I won't be able to sing."

"As if you can concentrate with Katherine around."

"I'll only permit you to say such a thing since you are like a sister to me, Vera."

"I'm so glad that's what you think. Someone has to tell you to wake up and hear the rooster crow."

He glanced at the unsightly curves of the horses' rumps, their hindquarters moving back and forth in rhythm, and the trees that lined the path. Anything to keep from facing Vera—and the truth she was bound to reveal.

"I know what you were thinking," Vera continued, undeterred. "You were thinking that Otis was too much competition for you. Well, if you can't see after the way he treated her today that he is totally and completely out of the picture, then you need a good whack between the eyes with a frying pan."

"And you think you're just the one to do it?" Christopher teased as they turned into the drive.

"Someone has to!"

"Maybe you should tell Katherine what you just told me and see what she has to say about it." As soon as he uttered the dare, he regretted his words. What if Vera called his bluff and really did tell Katherine? What then? He cleared his throat. "Uh, if you have a right mind to. But I think she'd laugh in your face."

"Cry with relief is more like it. I know she's sorry she pulled all those stunts just to protect Miranda."

Christopher brought the buggy to a stop in front of the Sharpe house.

"It's a shame Miranda planned such a scheme." Vera's feet hit the ground, and she let go of Christopher's hand after he assisted her in disembarking. "Truly a crying shame. Katherine really is talented."

"I wish she had said something to Otis right off the bat, though, instead of waiting," Christopher said.

"We both tried to encourage Miranda to be honest once we found out what happened," Vera said. "But you should have seen her let loose with the tears. She put on quite a performance to keep us both involved in her plan."

Christopher nodded. "Knowing Miranda's penchant for drama, I don't doubt it a bit."

"I think Katherine has learned her lesson about the limits of friendship. I know I have."

Chapter 10

Four days later, Katherine peered through her kitchen window. She watched Vera dismount from her bicycle and lay it on the ground near the porch. "Is it time for rehearsal again?" They had been practicing often over the past few days. Katherine enjoyed the time she spent near Christopher, but she never admitted that fact to anyone. Not even Vera.

Mother dried a drinking glass. "Yes, it must be. I thought you said they'd be over directly after lunch. They're right on time."

Betsy entered. "Mother, may I go to the general store and buy some candy?"

"I don't know." Mother eyed her. "I had no idea you had so much extra money. Aren't you saving up for Christmas?"

"Yes, but I have two extra pennies I can spare. Please?"

"Well, you've done a good job with your chores lately. I suppose you can go, but take Rover with you."

Betsy smiled and ran out the door, almost running into Vera.

Sheet music in hand, Vera rushed into the house. "Hello, Mrs. Jones."

"Hello, Vera. Nice to see you again." Mother set the glass in the proper place in the cabinet.

Vera nodded, and Katherine noticed her breath came in shallow and fast spurts. "Katherine. Are the others here yet?"

"Not yet."

"At least we don't have to worry about Otis, since he's right here."

Katherine shook her head. "No, he isn't."

Vera's nose wrinkled. "Whatever do you mean?"

"I haven't seen Otis all morning. He didn't have lunch with us. How about you, Mother? He tells you everything. Have you seen him lately?"

"I haven't, as a matter of fact. You know, he doesn't talk much to me anymore." Mother eyed Vera. "I declare, it looks to me like there's been some sort of spat, but Katherine won't tell me a thing for love or money. Now, you wouldn't happen to know about any unfortunate event that might have transpired, would you, Vera?"

"Oh dear, Mrs. Jones, you are putting me in quite a pickle."

"That's what I thought." Mother rubbed her dish towel in a vigorous circular motion against a defenseless plate. "Hopefully one day she'll see fit to confide in me."

"If I hadn't had a spat with him before, I'd certainly have a right to now,"

Katherine noted, handing her mother a newly washed plate. "You'd think since he is staying right here with us that he could be on time for practice. But I suppose not."

"If his lack of punctuality at the past two rehearsals are any indication of his dedication to our cause, he may not show up at all," Vera opined. "I wonder why? He seemed so enthusiastic about performing in the talent show before."

"I think I can guess. I have a feeling he's practicing a number for the talent show with Miranda," Katherine noted.

"Really?" Mother nearly dropped her plate. "I admit they made a wonderful team the other day when he played the piano and she sang such a lovely opera number. But what about you? Does he plan to leave you out in the cold?"

"No, I think he plans to be part of our act," Katherine answered. "I just believe he thinks he's so good he doesn't need to practice." Having completed her task, she squeezed water out of the dishrag. "And we have all noticed how he's been absent from the house lately."

"He did go fishing with your father yesterday, so of course we didn't see him much," Mother reminded her.

"Yes, he has developed quite a fondness for fishing, I must admit," Katherine said.

Mother placed a spoon in the drawer. "And that's to our advantage, too. I've enjoyed eating fish more often since he's taken up the hobby."

"I'm not surprised to hear you take up for him, Mother. He does love to flatter you." Katherine untied her apron.

"Katherine! You are being mighty hard on poor Otis."

Father chose that moment to return from his errand at the general store. "What's this about poor Otis?"

"We were discussing his unexplained absences from the house lately," Mother informed him.

Father set down his sack of goods and gave Mother a quick kiss on the cheek. "Yes, I've noticed that, too. Didn't want to make mention of it, though. Wonder what's gotten into that boy?"

Katherine gave Father her rapt attention. She could tell by his voice inflection that he had some idea. But to her disappointment, he only took a seat at the table and made no further effort to reveal his notion to them.

Vera cleared her throat. "I hate to be the one to tell you this, Katherine, but Lily said he's been at the Hendersons a lot lately."

"The Hendersons?" Mother asked. "Whatever is the attraction there?"

"So I was right after all." Father chuckled. "I believe her name is Miranda."

"Well, of all things! To think he'd abandon our beautiful Katherine for the likes of Miranda Henderson!"

Katherine tossed her apron on the peg fashioned just for that purpose. "Oh, he didn't abandon me, Mother. He and I were never more than acquaintances who enjoyed a vigorous exchange of letters."

"But I thought his real intention of visiting us here was a desire to court you," Mother protested.

"Maybe it was, at first. And maybe I thought a little bit about the idea myself, just in passing, mind you. But long ago, I decided I didn't want to take things further with him."

"Really?" Father prodded.

"Really. I have no desire to live so far away. If I moved to South Carolina, I'd hardly ever see you at all. And Otis doesn't live on a beautiful farm. I don't know that I'd like living in a city like Charleston so much. Why, Hagerstown is too big for me."

"You do have a point," Mother said. "I don't want you to move, either. But I do want you to be happy."

"Me, too," Vera added.

Katherine's heart warmed to hear those closest to her express their fondest wishes for her welfare. "I have discovered that Otis does not hold the key to my happiness."

Father grinned. "I think Christopher is practicing with Katherine more than necessary for a church talent show."

So Father had noticed! Could it be so? "Oh, but it's a complicated number," Katherine explained.

Vera giggled.

"Well, I certainly don't object if he wants to spend a little extra time with you. I've always liked Christopher. I had no idea you weren't interested in Otis. I'm like your mother. I thought the possibility of a courtship was the reason he made the trip up here to start with."

Katherine sighed. "Well, maybe at one time I thought Otis was exciting. And maybe he is. But he just doesn't hold any romantic interest for me. And now that I think about it, I doubt that he ever did."

"Did you enjoy the revival meeting?" Mother asked Otis and Katherine as they talked around the kitchen table after the first meeting.

"Yes. The pastor was wonderful," Otis said.

"But not as wonderful as our pastor," Katherine added.

"I'm glad you didn't make me go," Betsy opined, looking up from her book.

The clock chimed nine times.

"That reminds me," Otis said. "My pocket watch has been running slow. Let me see how it's doing." He reached into his vest pocket. A stricken look crossed his features.

"What's the matter, Otis?" Katherine asked.

He didn't answer right away but patted around his vest pocket. "It's not here."

"What?"

Otis patted more frantically. "My money clip. It's gone!"

"Gone?" Mother asked. "Are you sure you had it?"

"I never leave home without it."

Betsy, Katherine, Otis, and Mother searched the house for the money clip, even eliciting Father's help. The clip was nowhere to be found.

"Someone must have taken it at church," Otis concluded.

"Otis, do you know how ridiculous that sounds? Why would anyone at church take your money clip?" Mother said.

"Why indeed?" Father noted. "Although I'm sure no one at church took it. When did you see it last, Otis?"

"Actually, I didn't have it at church, come to think of it. I slipped my offering in my pants pocket and left my money clip here."

A collective sigh could be heard in the kitchen.

"Let me check my room now." He returned moments later. His face looked pale. "It's not there."

"What do you mean, it's not there?"

"It's not on the table where I left it."

"Then where could it be?"

"I don't have any notion. I must have dropped it somewhere." Katherine could see by Otis's demeanor that he didn't think any of them took it.

"This means you won't be able to leave, right?" Betsy asked, her eyes wide. "Maybe you can stay with us forever?"

"Oh, I think I shall wear out my welcome long before eternity." Otis chuckled. "But I am charmed by your sentiment all the same. Besides, I can always have more money wired."

"Never you mind about that, Otis," Mother said. "You are our guest, and we'll take care of you. One way or another."

"I'm sure we'll resolve this matter soon. Why don't we keep looking? Perhaps I dropped it on the floor."

The family scoured the house to no avail.

"I can't imagine what happened, Otis," Mother said.

"I'm so sorry," Father added.

"No, I beg your pardon for causing you worry," Otis said. "It is far too late now to vex ourselves any longer about it. No doubt the money clip will show itself in the light of day. Maybe in the yard."

"Maybe," Katherine agreed. "I hope so."

The money clip did not show itself in the yard or anywhere else the following day, in spite of continued efforts to find it.

"This visit certainly has started to see its share of odd circumstances," Otis noted. "First I find I've been deceived; then my money clip turns up missing. I'm almost afraid to speculate on what might happen next."

"I understand why you're upset, Otis," Katherine told him. "I would be, too, if my money were missing. But there's nothing we can do about it except keep looking and praying."

Otis let out a harrumph. "All the same, I'll send away for funds from home. They should arrive soon."

Despite Otis's grumpy manner, Katherine felt sorry for him. No matter what, he didn't deserve to lose his money. She had an idea what might have happened to it but didn't feel at peace about confronting the person who might have been the perpetrator. That would have to wait until the right time.

The following day, practice for the talent show went well, especially since Otis had decided to grace them with his presence. They ran through their performance several times without any noticeable flaws. For once, Katherine felt as though they might be recognized with a prize at the talent show.

Otis didn't agree. "I noticed we were a little off on the chorus today, and the flaw never was corrected to my satisfaction. I suggest we practice our songs one last time."

Katherine felt too tired, both physically and mentally, to resume playing, but she responded the only gracious way she knew how. "That. . .that seems like a good idea."

Even without Vera present to play along with them, the practice went well.

"I'd say after this session, Otis, you have two excellent chances of winning the competition. You should be proud."

"Hmph. No matter what the outcome, I will share the glory with someone else."

The clacking of heels against hardwood floors greeted them. "Lemonade, anyone?"

Katherine couldn't remember a time when she had been so glad to see her mother. She held a silver tray on which rested drinking glasses and a pitcher of the cold beverage.

Mother smiled. "It's such a hot day that I thought you might like some additional refreshment."

Otis took a glass. "Thank you, Mrs. Jones."

Miranda held out her hand to accept a glass. A look of panic crossed her face when she studied her blank wrist. "My bracelet!"

"Bracelet?" Katherine asked.

"It's gone!" Miranda clutched her wrist as if the motion would cause the bracelet to reappear.

Katherine's stomach lurched. She wished there were a doubt as to whether or not Miranda had worn a bracelet, but she knew her friend had indeed included the jewelry in her day's ensemble. She recalled the charms tinkling together when the group met outside before coming into the house to rehearse.

"I can't replace some of the charms I had on that bracelet. I have to find it!" Miranda's voice grew high pitched.

"I'll help you," Otis assured her.

Katherine spotted Betsy playing a game of fetch with Rover. "Have you seen Miranda's bracelet?" she called to her sister.

Betsy watched Rover running with a stick in his mouth, then turned toward Katherine. She shook her head. "No. Why?"

Betsy looked innocent enough, but Katherine approached her while the others searched the house and yard. "It's missing."

"I'm sorry. Do you want me to help you look for it?" Betsy pushed a loose lock of hair off her face and tried to weave it back into her braid.

"You can. Or you can tell me where it is."

Betsy's brown eyes widened. "But I don't know where it is."

"Just like you don't know where Otis's money clip is?"

"Money clip?" She shook her head back and forth rapidly. "No! I don't! I promise."

Katherine bent down and looked her sister in the eyes. "Betsy, remember the extra money you said you have? Where did it come from?"

She pouted. "I—I saved it up."

"But what about Christmas? I know you don't have a lot of money, and if you keep spending it, even if only two cents at a time, there won't be much left over for gifts."

"Yes, there will. I promise. I'll help you look for the bracelet."

Katherine stopped her. "So you're saying you don't know where the bracelet is?"

"No, I don't."

"Are you sure?"

"Why should I know?"

Katherine didn't know how she could say what she meant. "Well, it's pretty. I know you like it."

"But I wouldn't take it. That's what you're saying, isn't it?"

"No, not really," Katherine protested.

"Yes, you are. I'm not stupid." Hurt filled Betsy's eyes. "I didn't take the bracelet or the money clip. And I never would. I never would take anything that didn't belong to me. I can't believe you would think that!" Tears threatened.

Betsy could be mischievous, but Katherine sensed the child was telling the truth. Betsy had admitted she didn't want Otis to leave, but she didn't fidget or avert her eyes when confronted with the question of the money clip's whereabouts. Nor did she flinch when questioned about Miranda's bracelet. "All right.

I believe you. I'm sorry I even asked. You know I love you very much, but even the most wonderful person in the world can be tempted. And you have to understand that we are all concerned. Things are turning up missing around here. Things that shouldn't be. Doesn't it seem strange to you?"

"Yes." Betsy nodded. "But I didn't take anything."

"I know that now. I'm sorry I asked. Can you forgive me?"

Betsy hesitated.

"Pretty please with sugar on top?"

A little smile crossed her lips, and she nodded. "Okay, then."

Katherine hugged her little sister. "So do you have any idea at all what might have happened to Miranda's bracelet?"

"No. I really don't. But I'll help you look."

"It's a deal."

The sisters exchanged an embrace.

They were interrupted when Christopher tapped Katherine on the shoulder. "Hey, aren't you two going to help us look?"

"Of course. Please, Betsy."

Betsy headed in the direction of the driveway.

Obviously picking up on Katherine's tense mood, Christopher asked, "What was that about?"

"I was asking Betsy if she knew anything about the bracelet. I was especially concerned because Otis's money clip went missing the other night."

Christopher's eyes widened. "I wonder how something like that could have happened?"

"I don't know, especially in our own house."

"And you thought Betsy might know something about it?"

"Well, she did want him to stay." She decided not to mention that Betsy wanted their guest to stay forever.

"I don't think Betsy would hide Otis's money clip. And I don't think she's all that interested in Miranda's bracelet."

"Well, she did admire it once; that made me think of her, but I know now she didn't take either item. Then who did?"

"I don't know. I wish I could solve the mystery." He motioned for her to join him in continuing the search for the bracelet. They both kept their eyes on the ground. "Do you mind if I ask you something?" he inquired a moment later when they were out of earshot of the others.

"No."

"You said Betsy wants Otis to stay. I know he pays attention to her and gives her little gifts, and she's taken to Rover very well. So it's only natural she'd want Otis to stay. But what about you?" His voice softened. "Will you miss Otis when he's gone?"

She didn't answer right away. "Well, I suppose I will. He's a nice enough fellow."

"Oh. But you don't want him to stay on indefinitely?"

"No," she admitted. "Is it that obvious?"

"No, not to anyone but me. You've been nothing but kind to him."

"Well, yes. As I said, I like him well enough, but not as a suitor, if that's what you mean."

"That's what I mean."

Katherine looked up at him and saw a light in his eyes she hadn't seen since Otis's arrival. Could he be feeling the same way about her that she had been feeling about him? It couldn't be possible. Could it?

"Come on," he said, breaking into her thoughts. "Let's see if we can find the lost objects."

Chapter 11

Even after an intense search, they hadn't produced either lost item, but the losses were the last thing on Christopher's mind as he made his way home later.

Katherine is free! Katherine is free!

As he rode home, Christopher whistled, something he hadn't done in a long while. Come to think of it, he hadn't whistled a happy tune since Otis arrived in Maryland.

Christopher had a feeling that Katherine's change of heart had something to do with Miranda. Yes, Otis had been all too forgiving of Miranda and seemingly less tolerant of Katherine's part in the ruse—started by Miranda, no less—than Christopher had thought would be the case once all was revealed. Yet Miranda had flirted her way into Otis's heart, which no doubt explained his response. Christopher had been watching Katherine around Otis since his arrival and noted that she never seemed to warm up to him much. Rover's presence seemed to gain Otis a place in Betsy's heart rather than Katherine's.

Maybe Katherine did love Christopher after all. Enough not to let another man take away her affections. If only that could be so!

From the looks of things, the way Otis and Miranda stayed near one another during the search, Otis had decided to court Miranda and she would accept. Christopher wasn't surprised. Miranda and Otis had never missed a chance to converse with one another since they first met.

Christopher harbored no regrets about Otis's visit. Now that Katherine had seen Otis in person and sparks had failed to ignite, she would be more than happy to pursue other interests. His conscience could be clear when he asked Mr. Jones if he would be welcome to court her. He could barely contain himself.

Moments later, after he had put General Lee in his stall for the night, Christopher walked to the house. The tuneless but happy melody still played upon his lips as he bounded up the steps to the veranda.

"Well, I'd say from the sound of that whistlin' of yours that practice went mighty well this afternoon." Grandpa rocked back and forth in his wicker rocking chair, taking advantage of the cool evening air as was his habit.

"Very well. Very well indeed." He decided to share what happened with Grandpa. Stopping in his tracks, he leaned against one of the Greek Revival columns. "I do believe Otis and Miranda both have a gleam in their eye for each other.

Wouldn't surprise me one little bit to find out they're courting."

"It wouldn't surprise me, either," Grandpa noted.

"You saw the way they act around each other, too?"

The older man resumed rocking. "I think everybody did. Except Otis. Thank the Lord, he finally came to his senses. Now you can make your move. Find out what Katherine really thinks of you."

"I will, Grandpa. I will."

Christopher shot through the door and ran up the stairs to the small attic room where he had spent many childhood hours and would remain until his wedding day, when he would take ownership of the parcel of land on the east side of the farm that his father had promised would be his. On that acreage, Christopher would build his own little house for his new wife and anticipated family.

He took out the small typewriter and placed it on the well-worn desk from his boyhood, sized for a younger student rather than a man. Placing a piece of paper on the roller, he looked at the blank page.

He typed, "Chapter One."

"That certainly was an uplifting service." Katherine's voice sounded light, as though she had just indulged in a drink of fresh, cool water.

Christopher kept pace beside her as they headed for the buggy. He had been hesitant to ask his father if he could borrow the buggy every night that week. Thankfully, Daddy didn't seem to mind.

"Yes, the sermon was rousing," Christopher agreed. "So rousing I almost forgot the heat."

"On a muggy night like this, I doubt anyone can forget the heat for long." Katherine fanned herself with her Sunday-best fan, a frothy affair with feathers on the handle. She had told him once, some time ago, that the fan had been a gift from a cousin who loved to travel the world. Christopher could see by how Katherine waved it back and forth with such force that she really was trying to cool herself, rather than putting on a flirtation for his benefit. "Nor can I forget our troubles," she added. "I wish we could find the money clip and bracelet."

"Me, too. So strange how both disappeared without a trace."

"I don't understand it. But it's a wonder Otis hasn't hightailed it out of Maryland for good. He must think all of us are liars. First we put on a ruse; then his money clip turns up missing."

"I'm sure he thinks nothing of the sort."

"Still, it's mysterious."

Christopher shrugged. "It's entirely possible that Otis lost his money clip somewhere and Miranda lost her bracelet, too. After all, she's been wearing it for some time, and the latch could have loosened over the course of the afternoon."

"True. But I wish we could find the lost items."

Christopher didn't want to linger on the mystery. Instead, he caught a firefly, making sure not to tighten his palm enough to hurt the bug. Stopping in his stride, he opened his palm and showed his prize to Katherine. The little insect blinked for them once, then twice, before it flew into the darkness.

"You haven't changed a bit." Katherine shook her head as they resumed walking.

"Sure I have. I used to collect them and put them in a jar. With air holes, of course."

"Of course." She giggled.

"Now I just let them go. Isn't that better?"

She laughed. The sound of such joy left Christopher with a warmed heart. How he had missed having Katherine all to himself. Now that Otis had made it a habit to escort Miranda home each night, Christopher felt so light he could have flown to the moon and back, if such a thing had been possible. The fact that Katherine had agreed he could escort her home each evening made his time with her more precious.

With Christopher's assistance, Katherine boarded the buggy. The touch of her warm hand left him with a pleasant tingle. He wished he could prolong the contact, but to try to do so wouldn't be proper. Instead, he made his away around to the other side of the buggy and then leaped onto the seat.

Katherine didn't waste time once the buggy got moving with a jerk and a start. "So, what did you think of the sermon?"

How could he answer? He wanted to hold on to his manly pride so he didn't admit out loud—even to Katherine—how much the evangelist had touched his soul. Since childhood, he had considered himself a Christian. Yet the minister made him see what Katherine had been telling him all along for so many years. That thankfulness for God's loving care was key to a Christian's joy. He could almost feel his burdens lifted. Suddenly, he knew that everything important in his life would work to God's glory if he surrendered all to Him.

"I found it comforting that he said Jesus will lift my burdens. Just like you said," he conceded.

"Of course it's just like I said." She tilted her chin upward in a self-satisfied manner.

He grinned in amusement, then turned serious. "The pastor has convicted me."

"Really?" Even in the dark, he could see her mouth slacken. "How?"

"You were there years ago when I accepted Christ as my personal Savior."

"How well I remember. You're a good man, Christopher Bagley."

A delightful shiver ran up his spine as he sensed the depths of feeling behind her words. "You know, God has been doing all the work in my relationship with Him. He's been listening to my petitions, answering prayer, and walking with me. And I never have hesitated to call on Him in times of trouble."

"Aren't we all quick to call on Him in those times?" Katherine's soft voice sounded tinged with regret.

"I suppose. But He keeps walking with me. Like last night."

"Last night? What happened?"

He hesitated. "I haven't mentioned this to anyone else." He stopped. Would she think him silly?

"You can trust me with any confidence. You know that."

"I think I can." He cleared his throat. "I started on my book. I have almost written the first chapter. Or typed it, rather."

She gasped. "Why, Christopher! That's wonderful! I just knew you'd write that book one day."

"Well, it's hardly written yet." He chuckled.

"I know, but chapter one is a wonderful start! Do tell me what it's about!"

"It's a work of fiction."

"Fiction? I thought you'd write a biography."

"I might. But I want to write a fictional story first. A story of family and what it's like to live here in Maryland."

"Not too exotic," she teased.

"No, but from my heart. And if no one wants to publish it, that's fine. I'll keep it, and my grandchildren can read it one day."

"Grandchildren. The thought seems so far away. But family is something to be thankful for. Maybe you can serve God by focusing at least some of the story on how your characters walk in faith."

He remained pensive for a moment. "Come to think of it, that's a great way to serve Him. Not that I could write a fictional story about the people around here, especially our two families, without mentioning God."

"Amen. He has given us so much."

"That's what the pastor has impressed upon me this week."

"Me, too. I see now that I don't thank Him as often as I should."

"I don't believe it."

"Then I have a proposal for you. Why don't we agree to thank the Lord for three extra things each day? And we'll talk about it every night, being accountable to one another."

He thought for a moment. "That's a wonderful idea. Let's do it."

———

After bidding Christopher farewell for the evening, Katherine stepped over the threshold and shut the kitchen door behind her.

"Katherine?" Mother called from the sitting room. "Is that you?"

"Yes, ma'am." Katherine ventured in to see her mother. She found her sitting in her rocker. Mother set the book she was reading in her lap and looked up.

"How did the meeting go tonight?" she asked.

Father, sitting in an overstuffed chair beside Mother, looked up from the newspaper crossword puzzle he was in the process of completing. "Was it much like the one last night?"

Katherine nodded. Her parents allowed her to travel to the meeting with Christopher rather than them, a sure sign they didn't mind her spending time with him. "Very much. The pastor was very lively and entertaining."

Father tapped his pencil against the newsprint and looked at Mother. "It sure sounds like he hasn't lost much of his energy or zeal. Maybe we should go."

"Maybe we should. If you don't mind us following you along," Mother teased.

"Mother, how many times do I have to tell you Christopher and I are just friends?"

Katherine's parents exchanged a look. She decided not to ask what they were thinking.

———

Christopher and Katherine rode in the buggy headed for home after the last night of the revival. Christopher glimpsed at the church one last time as they left the churchyard. The little chapel lacked the stained glass of fine places of worship in the city, but the church held its weight in inspiration. Looking ahead, he watched the sun, only beginning its descent on the horizon, turn the clouds pink, perhaps clothing itself in a soft blanket as it tucked itself in bed for the night. He held back a chuckle. Being around Katherine was causing him to make poetic observations.

He would miss taking Katherine to and from the meetings. On this night, she looked especially pretty, wearing a dress she told him she had sewn just the past week. She had already worn the dress to Monday night's meeting, but he didn't mind seeing it again. None of the women he knew except Miranda could go a whole week without repeating. Besides, mint green went well with Katherine's dark hair.

"A lot of people went up to the altar tonight, didn't they?" Christopher mused.

"Yes. I think this week has been a great success. And we can count it a success, too, since we've been inspired to increase our prayer life. What did you thank God for today?" Katherine asked.

"I thanked Him for the pink blanket He made for the sun."

She peered at the sky. "It is pretty, isn't it?" Then she started. "Why, you didn't thank Him for that today. We're looking at it now."

"I thanked Him just now. Doesn't that count?"

She twisted her lips and cocked her head. "But what about earlier today? What did you thank Him for?"

He didn't hesitate. "You."

"And I thanked Him for you," she admitted. "What else?"

"For enough food to eat and my family."

"Same here."

"We certainly do think alike."

"Yes, but you know, we need to expand. Both of us need to come up with something more original."

"Remember, Solomon said there's nothing new under the sun," Christopher pointed out.

"There's nothing new that God hasn't seen, but we can at least show Him we're thinking beyond the basics. Don't you agree?"

"Yes. I accept your challenge. I'll expand my range of thankfulness tomorrow. And the next day. And the next." A thought occurred to him. "Don't I get any credit for my pink blanket idea just now?"

"Yes, that is pretty original. Especially for a man."

"Hey, what's that supposed to mean? Are you saying men aren't supposed to appreciate a good sunset?"

"No, of course not." She giggled.

Christopher joined her mirth, enjoying their easy rapport.

He brought the team to a stop in front of her house, then, after jumping down himself, helped her disembark from the buggy.

Katherine looked at the house and noticed that her parents' bedroom light shone. Otherwise, the house was dark.

"A penny for your thoughts," Christopher prompted.

"Do you think they're worth a penny?" she quipped.

"More than that, I'm sure. So what are you thinking?"

She paused, wondering if she should share. "I'm just speculating on whether Mother will be looking out the window at us shortly."

He chuckled. "No doubt she will be."

"Let her look. There's no place I'd rather be than here with you tonight." She paused.

"I feel exactly the same way."

As he took her in his arms, she became aware of the cinnamon aroma of soap that always hung about him, a pleasant but subtle reminder that he was near. His body near hers felt warm, but despite the heat, she didn't mind. As though God read her thoughts, He sent a breeze their way at that moment. The cooling air wafted through her cotton dress.

Christopher grasped her more closely. He gazed into her eyes, and she studied his, lit as they were by the moonlight. He slowly brought his face toward hers. As their lips met, Katherine realized this was a moment she had been waiting for all of her life. She wanted the kiss to last forever.

Chapter 12

The night of the talent competition arrived. Katherine felt as ready to perform as she ever would be. Not that she could concentrate much on the talent show. Her thoughts lingered time and again on Christopher's kiss. Every once in a while, she brought her fingers to her lips, remembering the sweet touch of his lips. She wondered if he thought of the kiss, too.

She hadn't seen Christopher since the night he had kissed her. Her heart pounded with anticipation of seeing him again. She was ready early for the show. Though she tried to appear relaxed, the urge to peer out the window time and again overtook her. Finally, Christopher arrived in his buggy right on time, looking dapper in his dark Sunday suit. She was glad she had decided that night to wear a dress he had said was his favorite—her mint green frock.

Still, for the first time, she felt awkward in his presence. "Are you ready for the show?" Her question sounded weak to her ears, as though she were trying to make conversation where there was none.

"Yes." His terse response wasn't characteristic of him, either.

Christopher must have thought the kiss was a mistake. Or is he just feeling awkward? We have been friends for so long. Will romance be easy for us?

As Christopher helped her onto the buggy, Katherine noticed once more how manly his strong hand, roughened from farm work, felt on hers. She wanted him to linger in the touch, but as soon as she was seated, he hastened to take his place beside her. His posture looked stiff rather than shouting the easygoing confidence to which she had become accustomed from him. "I promised Vera I'd take her, as well. So we'll be going by her house next."

Katherine nodded. Maybe the fact that they planned to pick up Vera on the way would help. Her company would surely ease the awkwardness.

She eyed a boy riding up the driveway on a horse that was as black as midnight. "Look! It's a stable hand from the Sharpe farm."

Christopher brought the buggy to a halt. "He seems to be in a hurry."

"Is everything all right?" Katherine asked the stable hand as soon as he drew within earshot.

"I think so. I have a message for you, Miss Jones." He handed her a missive written on Vera's ivory-colored stationery.

Nervous, Katherine opened the letter and read aloud:

My dearest Katherine,

Forgive me. Alice's time to deliver her baby has come, and I must tend to her. I am so sorry I cannot play the harp with you at the show tonight. I have summoned the midwife, but I don't expect the baby to arrive before morning. I will send news of the baby's birth. Please put on your performance without me. I know you are sure to do me proud!

With love from your faithful friend,
Vera

"Oh, Christopher, I don't think we'll win without her."

"We're not there to win. We're there to be a part of the evening," Christopher reminded Katherine.

"Yes, I suppose you're right." She grimaced and folded the missive.

At that moment, Mother and Father hurried out of the house.

"What is it, Katherine?" Mother wanted to know. "Is everything all right?"

"I hope so. Alice's baby is coming. The midwife should be there by now." A worried tone entered her voice. "I didn't think she was due to deliver for another two weeks."

"Give or take two weeks is perfectly fine," Mother assured her. "Predicting such things as the birth of a baby isn't an exact science, you know. The details of life are best left to God."

"Yes, I have learned that more than ever recently," Katherine noted. "But I do wish the baby had waited a little longer. Just a few hours. Vera's harp added so much to our song."

"I doubt the baby knows anything about your harp music," Father teased.

"True." Katherine smiled.

"Will you still perform in the show?" Mother asked.

"Yes. We'll give it our best try," Christopher answered.

Katherine knew what she needed to do. "Father, will you lead us in prayer for Alice's baby?"

"I thought you'd never ask." He prayed for Alice's health, for the baby's safe arrival and future, and for Alice and Elmer as they would become new parents on that night.

A cloak of silence embraced them as they contemplated Father's prayer.

Mother broke the silence. "If the two of you are planning to be on time for the show, you'll need to get going!"

"So we shall." Christopher smiled and tipped his hat in the direction of Katherine's mother.

"We'll see you there," Father said.

"And we'll be rooting for you," Mother added.

"Thanks!" Katherine waved at her parents as the buggy left the yard.

The horses trotted well and swiftly. Once they arrived at church, Christopher unharnessed his horses and took a moment to feed the faithful beasts a sugar cube apiece. He patted General Lee on the nose. "There's more of this where that came from, fella."

The steed whinnied.

Katherine turned and saw Mrs. Watkins standing near the entrance to the sanctuary. She motioned for them to come closer, using quick little movements that bespoke urgency. "She seems like she wants to see us in a hurry. Let's go."

When they met Mrs. Watkins, they could see the expression she wore wasn't happy.

Christopher tipped his hat at the older woman. "Good evening, Mrs. Watkins."

After they finished exchanging greetings, Katherine couldn't stand the suspense. "If I may mention it, you look a bit upset, Mrs. Watkins. Is everything all right?" A terrible thought occurred to her. "You. . .you didn't hear that anything untoward has happened to Alice, did you?"

Mrs. Watkins's eyes widened behind her spectacles. "Alice? Alice Sharpe?"

"Yes, ma'am."

"Oh, no. Why?"

"She's delivering her baby tonight," Katherine informed her.

Mrs. Watkins gasped. "Already? I just can't believe how time flies."

"Yes, ma'am. Vera sent us a message. She'll be with Alice and won't be performing with us." Katherine sent Mrs. Watkins a pleading look. "I hope we can still be in the show."

"Oh, certainly. Certainly." Mrs. Watkins nodded. "That shouldn't present a problem. Although Vera is so sweet and talented. I'm sorry she'll be missing out on this opportunity to perform for us."

"Me, too."

"What I have to tell you does concern the show, however," Mrs. Watkins said. "The chairman looked over the finalized roster of performers and decided at the last minute to make a change in the rules. That change affects you."

Katherine held her breath, even though she wasn't surprised by the chairman's actions. Mr. Perkins was a known grump, and he seemed to take pleasure in creating the greatest amount of uproar over the smallest details.

"When he looked over the roster, Mr. Perkins noted that Otis was participating in two acts. Were you aware of that?"

Both nodded. "We were told that would be fine," Christopher elaborated.

"It would have been, had I been in charge. But I'm afraid Mr. Perkins sees things differently. When he noticed that Otis was participating in two acts, he ruled that in fairness to the rest of the competition Otis could only perform once."

"Does Otis know this?" Katherine asked.

"Yes, and that's where you come in. I asked him what we should do, and he has chosen not to accompany you but Miss Miranda Henderson."

"Oh," was all Katherine could manage to say.

"I'm so sorry," Mrs. Watkins said. "I wish there was something I could do, but I'm afraid my hands are tied."

"That's fine, Mrs. Watkins," Katherine assured her. "We're glad you told us as soon as you could."

She smiled, and her posture softened with obvious relief. "Thank you for being so cooperative. Of course, I would expect as much from two of my best Sunday school students."

"Yes, ma'am," Christopher and Katherine responded in unison.

"Well, I must be moving along. Lots to do, you know." She scurried into the social hall.

Left with Christopher, Katherine noticed that although he hadn't said much to Mrs. Watkins he wore a dark expression.

He shook his head. "If that doesn't beat everything I've ever seen. Leaving us stranded like that."

She searched for consolation. "Otis can't be blamed for his decision."

Christopher crossed his arms. "Is that so?"

"Not entirely. I concede that perhaps he can be faulted for choosing to perform with Miranda instead of us. After all, he had made a pledge that he would play the piano with our act." She hurried to add, "But he apparently also made a promise to Miranda. And he was put in an untenable position at the last minute. What could he really do? After all, you and I are performing together, whereas without him, Miranda would be all alone. And he had no way of knowing that Alice's baby would come tonight so Vera wouldn't be performing with us."

"True. But I still say he's a snake."

Katherine laughed. The sound of her mirth brought a sideways grin to Christopher's face.

"I can see it's just you and me, then."

Why did that sound so good? "Yes," Katherine said. "It's just you and me."

"And together, we'll do just fine."

"Yes. Together, we'll do just fine."

"Are we changing our act so that you're now a parrot?" Christopher teased.

Katherine caught on without hesitation. "Are we changing our act so you're now a parrot?" She mimicked a squawk. "Polly want a cracker!" She let out two sharp whistles.

Christopher laughed. "That's pretty good. Maybe we should change our act after all."

"Uh-uh. I think you should sing instead. I just hope my solo accompaniment can do you justice."

"Sure it will."

"Just in case, let's sneak into the Harvesters classroom and do a quick run-through on the piano. Shall we?"

"We shall."

After going through the song twice, Katherine was pleased. "Well! That doesn't sound quite as horrid with my playing alone as I anticipated.

Christopher chuckled. "You always could cheer me up."

She giggled.

"Now let's go in there and knock 'em dead."

"Christopher! I'm not sure that's what we should really say about a church performance," she teased.

"At least we'll all be headed to a good place," he countered.

She shook her head and sent him a lopsided grin. "You're incorrigible."

"From you, I'll take that as a compliment."

"That you may."

Their mood lightened, Katherine and Christopher were prepared to enjoy the talent show. They sat in the audience near the front, along with the other participants. Betsy sat beside them. She twiddled her thumbs and rocked back and forth, a sure sign she was nervous.

Katherine looked for Miranda and Otis but saw neither of them. She decided to concentrate on the notes she would need to play so their act could be a success.

Soon the strong scent of lily of the valley drifted Katherine's way from behind, a scent that always hung about Miranda. Katherine felt a tap on her shoulder. She turned to see Miranda.

Miranda tightened her lips, and a light of regret emitted from her eyes. "Did Mrs. Watkins see you?"

Katherine nodded.

Miranda sighed. "I'm sorry about your act. Otis didn't want to let you down, but he didn't feel he had any other choice."

To confirm Miranda's proclamation, Katherine caught a glimpse of Otis. Indeed, he looked sheepish and sent her an apologetic shrug. Remembering what she had told Christopher, as well as her resolve to act with kindness toward Otis, Katherine made sure no disappointment displayed itself on her features.

"Will you still be performing?" Miranda's concern seemed genuine.

Katherine nodded. "Don't worry. Christopher and I can make do, but without Otis, you would have been much worse off than we would, with no accompaniment at all."

Miranda's body relaxed with obvious relief. "And besides, you have Vera. Where is she, anyway?"

"Uh, we don't have Vera. She's with Alice. The baby is coming soon. Sometime tonight."

Miranda gasped but followed with an enthusiastic, "Oh, how exciting!" before Mrs. Watkins shushed the audience.

Katherine turned toward the stage and watched the performances. She wasn't disappointed. All of the acts were entertaining, and many were executed with professional competence.

As the show progressed, Katherine speculated silently on which act might win the blue ribbon and, as an added incentive, a certificate for two free dinners at the Hagerstown Inn. Katherine thought surely four-year-old Mary Lou, with her moppish dash of blond ringlets, was a shoo-in with her ballet performance. But after seeing Jim Bob's unicycle and juggling act, she decided maybe Mary Lou would have to be content with the red ribbon and bag of penny candy. Surely a little girl would prefer a sack of sweets to a meat loaf dinner, anyway. Then again, who could ignore the outrageously funny skit that several of the high schoolers presented? She was only glad she could sit on the sidelines and not be called upon to judge.

Next followed Betsy and her tap dance. Katherine whispered encouraging words to her before she took her turn. Christopher winked, and she giggled in return.

Dressed in light blue with a large matching bow, her dark hair fashioned in sausage curls, Betsy rivaled Mary Lou in attractiveness. Even better, she performed a flawless rendition of her tap dance, hitting each note just right. Mother was in fine form with her accompaniment, as well. After the song, Betsy curtsied prettily, curls falling back into perfect place. Her smile made her look like a seasoned performer. Katherine couldn't remember a time she had been prouder of her little sister. The audience clapped and whistled.

Later, Miranda sang her aria without missing a note. Otis delivered a performance on the piano that expressed the emotion of the music in a flawless fashion. The conclusion of their number was greeted by applause so great that Katherine thought the building might burst.

She felt nervous now that their turn was nigh, but Katherine knew that singing to God's glory took first place. The money raised from the sale of tickets was to be donated to a nearby orphanage in the name of the church and of Jesus Christ. How much more glory and honor could there be?

Mr. Perkins rose from his seat and took center stage, as he did between each act. He clapped along with the audience until their applause ceased. Mr. Perkins then launched into his introduction. "And now, ladies and gentlemen, we come to our last act for this evening. Miss Katherine Jones and Mr. Christopher Bagley will be performing a medley of song for our entertainment and enjoyment. Please give them a warm welcome!" He clapped, and the audience followed suit.

Katherine felt self-conscious as she took to the stage. She almost wished she hadn't worn her conspicuous mint green dress. She glanced at Christopher, who stood straight, gazing upon the audience as though they were in for a great treat.

She suppressed a smile. Christopher really was a performer!

She scooted onto the piano bench and unfolded her sheet of music.

"Good evening, ladies and gentlemen," Christopher said. "Tonight it is my distinct pleasure to perform a popular melody known as 'The Blue and the Gray' or 'A Mother's Gift to Her Country' written by Paul Dresser."

Christopher nodded to let Katherine know he was ready to begin singing. She played a brief introduction. He sang in a perfect baritone, hitting every note with precision:

"A mother's gift
To her country's cause
Is a story yet untold.
She had three sons,
Three only sons,
Each worth his weight in gold.
She gave them up
For the sake of war,
While her heart was filled with pain.
As each went away,
She was heard to say,
He will never return again.

"One lies down near Appomattox,
Many miles away.
Another sleeps at Chickamauga
And they both wore suits of gray.
'Mid the strains of 'Down to Dixie'
The third was laid away
In a trench at Santiago.
The Blue and the Gray.

"She's alone tonight,
While the stars shine bright,
With a heart full of despair.
On the last great day
I can hear her say,
My three boys will be there.
Perhaps they'll wait
At the heav'nly gates,

On guard beside their guns.
Then the mother true,
To the gray and blue,
May enter with her sons."

Katherine could hear a few sobs and sniffles from the audience as she played, but she dared not look up lest she miss a note. Moments later as she took her bow, Katherine couldn't see a woman in the house who could boast a dry eye. Mrs. Watkins shook with sobs. Mr. Boyd blew his nose with a hearty snort into a red bandanna. Katherine wasn't surprised. The citizens of the region had been greatly impacted by the War Between the States and the recent conflict in Cuba.

Christopher sent Katherine a slight nod, prompting her to play the first chords of "Dixie." Without a moment's hesitation, the crowd stood in respect to the anthem of the Confederacy. By the time Christopher had completed the last chorus, all the men seemed to be holding back tears. Everyone seemed to remember the losses, the bravery, the horrible realities of war. Hitting the last note, Katherine knew that no matter what the outcome they could not have performed better that evening.

But victory didn't matter. Her reward was Christopher's smile. He motioned for her to join him by his side. Katherine curtsied; then he took a bow. Applause resounded in wave after wave. Katherine eyed the judges conferring. As she and Christopher returned to their seats, she knew the decision would soon be announced.

As the judges continued in their deliberations, each person who participated in the show was invited by Mrs. Watkins and Mr. Perkins to go back up front and take bows to fresh rounds of recognition for their hard work and valiant efforts.

Katherine eyed her parents sitting near the back, dressed in their Sunday best. They sat near Mr. and Mrs. Bagley, dressed in their Sunday finery, as well. All four parents clapped as though they'd seen a professional production in New York, instead of their own children performing in the little church they'd visited weekly their whole lives. Then again, maybe pride in their own children and the fact that Christopher and Katherine had performed well before people who cared about them all was the reason for the older people's enthusiasm. Certainly Christopher and Katherine's act was more meaningful to their parents than any big production staged by strangers would have been.

Katherine eyed Christopher's grandfather sitting as far up front as he could, right behind the performers. He looked younger than his years in his Sunday suit, and he wore a yellow rose in his buttonhole. No doubt he had plucked the special bloom himself from Mrs. Bagley's flower garden. She let out a giggle as the elderly gentleman, a veteran of the War Between the States, filled the room with the noise of a shrill and approving whistle.

Mr. Perkins nodded for all to return to their seats and then took the white envelope from the nearest judge. With an exaggerated gesture, he polished the lenses of his reading spectacles. The audience watched as though the action were the most fascinating thing one could ever witness. After he positioned his glasses in their proper position on his thin nose, he extracted a silver letter opener from his vest pocket. He sliced open the missive with a careful gesture. Clearly relishing his role as announcer, he placed the opener back in his pocket and with a flourish extracted a piece of white paper from the envelope. When Mr. Perkins looked over the results, Katherine thought he might make the announcement then. She held her breath.

Instead, he folded the paper, held it in his hand, and spoke to the audience. "I am happy to announce that there are no ties for any of the positions. The judges have reached decisive verdicts on all counts." He grinned at the judges, and they nodded. "First of all, let me say that everyone here tonight is a winner. I think we as their audience have demonstrated our appreciation and sentiments by our vigorous applause."

"Hear, hear!" a man shouted, amid a chorus of new praise.

Mr. Perkins nodded as a signal for the audience to quiet themselves. "Now to announce the winner of our honorable mention ribbon."

Whispers of speculation could be heard rippling across the audience.

He paused and then looked over the performers sitting in the front part of the audience. "Honorable mention goes to Miss Betsy Jones for her marvelous dance!"

The audience clapped in approval. Betsy pouted with disappointment at coming in so far from first place but saw Mother's chastening look and quickly formed her lips into a winning smile. She took her ribbon with a curtsy and returned to her seat.

"Very fine. Very fine." He cleared his throat. "And moving right along now, our fourth-place winner is—Mr. Jim Bob Boyd and his amazing unicycle!"

Jim Bob sauntered up to accept the ribbon. The semifrown he wore demonstrated his lack of enthusiasm for his prize. Nevertheless, he nodded toward the audience and mumbled thanks to them and to the judges before he returned to his seat.

"Thank you, Jim Bob, for a fine performance." Mr. Perkins cleared his throat. "And now for our third-place winner. The yellow ribbon is awarded to a vocal performance."

Katherine took in a breath and prepared to go up to the stage to accept the ribbon. With such fierce competition, she and Christopher were lucky to be recognized with a ribbon at all. And a yellow ribbon would look nice in her room, reminding her of a successful evening.

She sent Christopher a little smile, which he returned. He shifted in his seat.

Surely he had come to the same conclusion as she and was preparing to accept his ribbon.

"And the yellow ribbon is awarded to—Miss Miranda Henderson for her rendition of 'Havanaise' from the first act of the opera *Carmen*!"

It took Katherine a moment to recover from the surprise announcement. She settled back in her seat and clapped, stunned. She watched Otis and Miranda rise and stride toward Mr. Perkins to accept the ribbon.

After they arrived on the stage, Mr. Perkins presented the prize to Miranda as Otis remained positioned beside, yet still slightly behind, her. Composed as always, Miranda curved her mouth into a pleasing expression that would have led the casual observer to believe she had been awarded the first-place trophy and ribbon. Though pleasant, Otis's grin looked tighter and more constrained than Miranda's. Katherine knew him well enough to realize he was doing his best to conceal disappointment.

Both Miranda and Otis emitted a hearty round of thanks to the audience and to the judges before taking their seats. Katherine had a chance to whisper congratulations to the couple before Mr. Perkins resumed making the announcements.

Katherine relaxed. Since Miranda and Otis placed so low, there was no chance she and Christopher would be recognized. She could enjoy vicarious victory for a friend instead. The pressure was off.

"We're getting closer and closer to announcing the evening's winner, folks!" Mr. Perkins teased.

Katherine refrained from shaking her head. Any other day of the week, Mr. Perkins seemed to revel in his reputation as a grouch. Tonight, he clearly enjoyed playing the part of the jolly announcer. "I must say, I am in wholehearted agreement with this next decision. Our next winner deserves the bag of penny candy from Dooley's Dry Goods Store and her big red ribbon."

Speculative whispers filled the room.

Mr. Perkins continued. "Who can forget such a sweet rendition of the art of ballet? May I see little Miss Mary Lou Evans?"

Mary Lou giggled and bounded up to the stage. Mr. Perkins held out both the red ribbon and the sack of candy to the little girl. She ignored the ribbon and grabbed the candy.

Amid chuckles and aahs from the audience, she pulled on the string, trying to open the bag. Her mother rushed up to retrieve the little girl, the candy, and the ribbon. Mrs. Evans smiled and instructed Mary Lou to thank everyone, which she did in prompt obedience. The pair exited the stage amid laughter and new applause.

"She certainly deserves that big bag of candy, doesn't she, folks?" Mr. Perkins prodded.

More chuckles and applause ensued.

Mr. Perkins gazed over the audience and sent them his broadest smile. "And now for the big moment, folks. The award of the blue ribbon and this lovely engraved trophy." He studied the engraving on the silver loving cup and read, "In Recognition of the Finest Performance of 1901, Blessed Assurance Church Talent Show, Organized by the Ladies Missionary Society in Support of the Kent County Alms House, First Prize for a Talent Performance."

The audience applauded.

"This seems like a fine moment to thank the Ladies' Missionary Society for staging an evening of superb entertainment for us all. Ladies, will you please stand?"

Mrs. Watkins and the rest of her contingent stood and accepted their accolades.

After the clapping died down, Mr. Perkins looked inside the cup. "And not only will the first place winners have this lovely cup to keep forever, but in appreciation for the efforts of the grand-prize winners, the Hagerstown Inn has included a voucher for two fine dinners!"

He paused, and on cue, everyone applauded.

"Now, is everyone ready to hear who will be our grand-prize winners for this evening?"

Shouts of "Yes" filled the room.

"Then don't let me keep you waiting any longer." He took in a breath. "I am pleased to say that this fine prize goes to Mr. Christopher Bagley for his fine performance of 'The Blue and the Gray' and 'Dixie'!"

As even more applause thundered, Katherine gasped. She knew Christopher had outdone himself, and she hadn't made any mistakes in her accompaniment. Yet she had no idea he would walk away with the prize.

"Now that we have those dinner vouchers, we have an excuse for a night out." Christopher winked.

Katherine moved aside so he could receive his award, but he took her hand, insisting that she receive the award along with him.

After they took to the stage and bowed before the audience, Katherine noted that even Otis and Miranda appeared to be pleased with the outcome of the contest. When Mary Lou waved to them, a red, sugarcoated gumdrop was pinched between her forefinger and thumb.

Chapter 13

The night air felt refreshing against Katherine's face as she and Christopher made their way to the buggy after the show. Stars winked at them from a cloudless sky.

"Were you surprised we won?" she ventured as the buggy pulled out of the church lot.

"A little. I didn't think I was the best singer there tonight."

"I thought you were. If anything, my poor accompaniment dragged you down."

"Now I know you're fishing for compliments since everyone around thinks you're marvelous at the piano."

She giggled. "Okay, maybe I wouldn't mind the occasional compliment. Is that so bad?"

"I suppose not." His sigh was one of contentment. "This night can't get much better."

"Yes, this time has certainly been one filled to the brim with excitement. Probably more excitement than I've seen in my lifetime."

"Maybe things will slow down and get back to normal soon."

"I hope so. I think." Katherine grinned.

They approached the turnoff to the Sharpes' farm. "Do you think we should stop by and see how Alice is doing?"

Katherine hesitated. "I doubt the baby has had time to arrive yet." She looked longingly at the house.

"Come on, Sadie. Giddup, General Lee." Christopher clicked his tongue and pulled the reins to instruct the horses to turn left.

"I can't believe you're doing this."

"I know you can't stand the suspense. Besides, if the baby hasn't been born yet, we'll just go on home," he said. "Alice won't know we've been by, but I'm sure Vera will be glad we stopped in to check on the family."

"I'm sure Elmer is nervous, too," Katherine observed. "After tonight, he'll be a father."

Moments later, they pulled in front of the house. Katherine jumped off the buggy, holding the loving cup all the while.

A ragged-looking Vera answered their knock on the back door.

"Uh-oh. It looks like you're still in the middle of everything," Katherine observed. "I guess we shouldn't have stopped by this late. Tell Alice I'm sorry we disturbed all of you."

Vera waved them into the kitchen, shaking her head. "You're not bothering us. The baby arrived just minutes ago." She kept her voice low.

"That's wonderful!" Katherine gasped. "Tell us! Is it a boy or girl?"

"It's a boy." Vera beamed. "They named him Paul Victor."

"Small victory?" Christopher asked only half jokingly.

Katherine thought for a moment. "That's right. *Small* is the meaning of the apostle's name."

"I hadn't thought of that, and I'm not sure Alice did, either." Vera's facial expression looked thoughtful.

"I'm sure throughout his life he'll enjoy triumphs both large and small," Christopher remarked.

"Aw, what a sweet thought." Katherine smiled.

"I think I'll share that with Alice," Vera said. "Once she wakes up, that is."

"Speaking of sleep, we'd better let the proud new aunt get some shut-eye." Katherine tugged on Christopher's sleeve. "Let's go."

"You'll do no such thing!" Vera stopped them with her voice.

"Huh?" Christopher asked.

"Not without telling me about that trophy."

"Oh. This." Katherine had been so involved with the conversation that she had forgotten she was holding a rather cumbersome prize.

"You won, I see." Vera beamed.

Katherine nodded.

"You don't seem too happy."

"Oh, we are," Katherine assured her. "You know something? Winning a prize seemed so monumental only moments ago, but in light of a new birth, a talent show seems inconsequential."

"Inconsequential or not, I am so sorry I left you out in the cold at the last minute," Vera apologized. "But obviously, you didn't need me."

"Yes, we did need you. But we both realize your absence couldn't be helped," Christopher said.

"That's right. We both wish you could have been there. You worked just as hard as the rest of us."

"So tell me all the details." Vera became breathless with anticipation.

"First of all, Mrs. Watkins greeted us at the door with a terrible surprise," Katherine explained.

"Oh?"

"Otis was snatched out from under us."

"Well, not exactly snatched." Christopher told Vera the story.

"I can't say that I blame Otis," Katherine admitted. "Miranda would have been all alone without him."

"True," Vera said. "Oh, I feel so terrible. Even worse now."

"Silly goose! Would you have me blame little Paul for putting us through so much trouble?" Katherine joked.

"So tell me who else won."

Katherine decided to have a little fun by dragging out the anticipation. "Betsy won honorable mention."

"Good for her!"

"She was a little disappointed, I have to admit."

"There's always next year," Vera said.

"That's what I told her," Christopher said.

"Jim Bob took fourth with his unicycle and juggling act."

"Mmm-hmm."

"Miranda and Otis took third."

Vera's eyes widened. "She just took third place? I can't believe it! What happened? Did Otis flub on the piano?"

"No, we can't lay the blame at Otis's feet—or should I say, hands," Christopher quipped.

Katherine chuckled. "I admit, I was shocked. Her voice is so beautiful, and I've never heard an opera number that she couldn't execute with great success."

"I concur," said Vera. "So who took second?"

Christopher answered. "Mary Lou. She danced a ballet piece."

"Aw, I'll bet that was the sweetest sight!"

Katherine nodded. "And you know who took first prize!"

Vera clapped as though she had just heard the news for the first time.

Christopher finally intervened, speaking in a hushed tone. "Ladies! Do you want to wake the baby?"

Vera looked embarrassed, and Katherine stopped in midbob. "Sorry."

"It's hard to believe we do finally have a baby to consider after all these months of waiting." Vera held her voice to a loud whisper. "I'm so happy for you. See, you didn't need me after all."

"I missed you, though." Katherine waited for Christopher to concur. When he didn't take the hint, she poked him in the ribs as inconspicuously as possible.

"Oh, yes. I missed you, too."

"It's a sin to tell a fib," Vera reminded him, although she sent him a half grin. "You two make a great team. Why can't you see that? Do I have to be the one to tell you?"

"You don't have to be the one to tell us," Christopher responded, "but I don't mind hearing it." He looked into Katherine's eyes.

"All right, you two lovebirds. Time to be on your way. Some of us have real responsibilities." With a waving motion of both hands, Vera shooed them toward the door.

Katherine covered her face and pretended to be fearful of Vera's mock ire. Yet she couldn't resist one keen observation as she exited over the threshold. "One day it will be your turn, Vera."

The blond shrugged. "I'm in no hurry. All in the Lord's good time." Sending the couple a smile, Vera shut the door behind them, but Katherine glanced back in time to catch a wistful look on her friend's face.

Katherine turned to Christopher. "You know, I do hope she finds someone soon. She deserves someone of her own."

"She's helping with little Paul. That should be enough to keep her hands full. And her sister's bound to appreciate what she's doing."

"Of course Vera's appreciated. But I'd like to see her have her own family. She'd be a great mother. If only some man could see it."

"Women! You and your matchmaking!" Christopher looked to the sky and back, shaking his head. "No bachelor is safe around any of you."

"And that's the way it's supposed to be." With her hand in Christopher's, Katherine leaped to her seat.

They passed two neighboring farms, the silence interrupted only by jangling harness and plodding hooves. They soon arrived at the Joneses' farm. Katherine enjoyed being by Christopher's side to the extent that she was sorry to arrive home.

"Oh, I meant to ask but forgot in all the excitement," Christopher said. "Did you find the missing money clip? Or the bracelet?"

"No, and even worse, I'm missing an earring, as well. I could have sworn I left the pair on my dressing table, but I can only find one now."

"That's too bad."

"Yes, and it was my favorite, too. I just can't imagine why someone would take all those trinkets. We've never had this problem before."

"Maybe Otis pretended his money clip was missing so no one would suspect him when he took Miranda's charm bracelet. As a memento of her, of sorts."

Katherine knew Christopher didn't mean what he said. "If Miranda were a real schemer, she might have taken Otis's money clip and then pretended her bracelet was missing. But of course, she would never do such a thing." Katherine sighed. "Neither Miranda nor Otis is the culprit, I'm sure. We're grasping at straws."

"Too bad Sherlock Holmes isn't around to help us out."

"I'm sure he could unravel the mystery. But more likely, it's no mystery at all. Just carelessness on Otis's part to make him misplace his money clip. And perhaps a loose clasp on Miranda's bracelet. My earring could have fallen off because of a faulty clip. Who would need only one earring?"

"True."

"It's coincidence. That's all." She thought for a moment. "I've already confronted Betsy, and she told me she didn't take anything. I apologized for thinking it was her."

"So you believe her." Christopher's tone showed he saw no reason not to believe Betsy.

"Yes. But the other day, she had extra money, and I never got a satisfactory answer as to how. And she has always admired Miranda's bracelet. Asked about a certain charm, even."

Both of them sat in uncomfortable silence until they arrived at the Joneses' farm. Still, Katherine didn't want the evening to end. She noticed the light was on, an indication that her parents had arrived home first.

After Christopher walked her to the front door, she thought of a stalling tactic, a way to keep him near her a few more moments. "Mother made apple pie today. Would you care to join me for a slice?"

"I reckon I would. I seldom get to eat dessert at my house. You know, apple pie—or any pie, for that matter—doesn't last long with Grandpa around."

"Better get some of that dessert while you can then." She winked.

Just then, the front door opened and out bounded Rover. The dog nearly knocked them both down.

"Now scoot, Rover!" Father called after the dog. "No more getting in the house!"

"Aww, poor dog!" Katherine sympathized.

"Poor dog, nothing. He knows better." Father pointed out.

Katherine watched the dog exit to the side yard.

"Come on in, kids," Father offered, holding open the door. He glanced at the loving cup Katherine held and let out a low whistle. "I have to say, that's something!"

"Yes, I wanted you and Mother to see it up close, but I'm going to let Christopher keep it. After all, he's the one who charmed the audience with his singing."

"I think you should keep it, Katherine." Christopher offered.

"I'll hear nothing of the sort."

Christopher grinned. "Oh, all right." He glimpsed at the side yard. "Uh, if you'll excuse me, sir, I want to see something."

"Of course."

Katherine watched as Christopher kept his eye on the dog. "What's wrong?"

"I'm not sure, but I think I saw something in Rover's mouth. Let's follow him and see what he does." Christopher didn't wait for her to respond but hurried after the collie.

"What do you think is the matter?" Father asked.

She handed him the loving cup. "I don't know, but I'm going to find out." Katherine followed Christopher.

An instant later, both of them watched as the dog dug a hole and dropped a shiny object into it. He was just about to cover it up when Christopher shooed him aside. He bent over and took out a shiny silver spoon. He held it up for Katherine to see. "Well, look at that."

"Mother won't be happy to see her good spoon out here in the dirt."

"A little soap and water will take care of that. But more important, see those little mounds of fresh dirt?" He motioned to several areas. "It looks like Rover's been busy. I have a feeling I know what's in most of those holes."

Katherine suddenly had a feeling, too.

"Would you bring me a lantern and your mother's gardening shovel?"

"Of course!" Katherine hurried to the shed and retrieved both objects.

Christopher was petting and consoling the dog upon her return. She handed him the tool and lit the lantern. Feeling sorry for the animal, she petted him as Christopher dug. Rover barked in protest at having his treasures disturbed, but as Katherine smoothed his fur and spoke to him in sympathetic tones, he calmed himself.

As Christopher plowed into the dirt, he found several shiny objects. Otis's money clip, with the money still attached, Miranda's bracelet, and Katherine's earring were among them. The items bore bits of dirt as testimony to their adventure but otherwise were in pristine condition.

"What a relief!" Katherine placed her hand to her chest. "But that still doesn't explain Miranda's bracelet. She never took it off while she was in the house."

"Let me see something." Christopher tried the clasp. As soon as he shut it, the clutch fell open once more. "See? It's just as I suspected. The clasp was weak. Miranda must have lost it."

"And Rover found it."

"Maybe she'll thank him."

Just then Otis arrived from escorting Miranda home. Katherine and Christopher called out to him.

"Look. We found your money clip." Katherine held up the prize.

"Marvelous!" Otis's grin nearly reached the sides of his face. "And Miranda's bracelet?"

Katherine held up the sparkling bangle. "Right here. And my earring, too."

"So we finally know why the dog was so eager to get in the house," Otis observed. "He wanted to get his clutches on anything shiny."

"Apparently," Katherine agreed. "Now we'll have to be serious about keeping him outside, or well supervised at all times if he does happen to venture indoors."

"I'm sorry my gift has caused so much disturbance," Otis said.

"Don't be sorry. I love Rover, and so does Betsy." Katherine sighed. "Betsy. I asked her if she took the money clip. I feel so terrible about that now."

"Betsy?" Otis asked. "What made you think of her?"

"Well, she had extra money for no reason, and she always liked Miranda's bracelet."

"Extra money? Oh." Otis looked down at the ground and back.

"Why, yes." Katherine grew suspicious. "You wouldn't know anything about that, would you?"

Otis's mouth formed a regretful line, and he winced. "I'm afraid I do."

Chapter 14

Katherine looked at Otis in surprise and noticed that Christopher wore a similar look of disbelief. How could Otis know anything about Betsy and her extra money? Surely he had given her gifts from time to time but always in front of the adults. Besides, he had advised her to save her pennies each time. So what could he mean?

Christopher was quick to take up the line of questioning. "So you were giving her money. Why?"

"She was doing me a favor."

"A favor?"

"She was, uh, delivering letters to Miranda for me. I paid her a nickel for each letter she delivered."

"Oh!" Katherine blurted.

Otis took Katherine's hands in his. "I'm so sorry, Katherine. I must admit I had thoughts first along that we might court. But then I met Miranda, and I felt an inexplicable connection to her. Like we are kindred spirits. Not that I don't think you are a fine woman. You are. Any man would be happy to have you as a wife."

"Any man but you," Katherine teased and then turned serious just as quickly. "I know, Otis. You have no need to apologize to me. I have enjoyed our correspondence, and I will always be glad you and I are acquaintances. But like you, I feel no longing beyond that."

"Thank you. I hope you are not upset with me for partaking of your family's kind hospitality all this time."

"Of course not. You have been a blessing. And I think it was God's plan for you to find Miranda. I've never seen her happier."

Otis beamed.

Father approached the group. "What's going on out here?"

Christopher showed him the holes the dog had dug.

"Rover was our thief," Katherine said. "He's the one who took the money clip, the bracelet, and my earring."

"He had just taken off with this spoon, but we caught him red-pawed," Christopher added.

The group chuckled.

Father whistled. "I was so eager to get him out of the house that I didn't even see the spoon. Well, I'd say this calls for a celebration. In the form of delicious apple pie."

"I'll say," Christopher agreed. "Just let me get these holes filled back in, and I'll be right there."

"I'll stay here and hold the lantern," Katherine offered.

Father agreed, and he and Otis went back into the house.

A few moments later, Katherine and Christopher went back into the house, where the promised pie awaited them.

"I understand you found all our treasures," Mother noted.

"Yes. We've got to keep the dog out of the house." Katherine chuckled. She remembered that she wanted to apologize to her sister. "Where's Betsy?"

"She's gone to bed. It's been a big night."

"Do you think she's asleep yet?"

"I doubt it. Why?"

"I just want to go up and speak to her a minute." Katherine excused herself and made her way to Betsy's room. She had shut off her bedside light.

"Betsy?" she called softly.

"Is that you, Katherine?"

"Yes." Katherine turned on the light.

Betsy squinted. "That's bright."

"Do you want me to turn it back off?"

"No. I'm not sleepy." She sat up in bed, her brown curls falling around her shoulders, reaching well past the top of her cotton nightgown. The little girl, with her flawless complexion and pink cheeks, reminded Katherine of a child in a fashion advertisement in a ladies' periodical.

"I just want to tell you something. Congratulations on taking honorable mention at the talent show."

"Thanks." Her tone betrayed her lack of enthusiasm.

"But there's something else. Guess what?"

"What?" Betsy perked up. She loved a mystery.

"Guess what we found?"

"The bracelet?"

"Yes! And the other things, too!"

Betsy clapped. "Where? Are you going to make me guess?"

"Not if you don't want to."

"Maybe a squirrel hid them in a tree."

"Close. Rover hid them in the yard."

"Rover?" She giggled. "Smart dog."

"Too smart, it seems. Apparently he was eager to get in the house because every time he did, he took something shiny."

"This means I was to blame, at least a little, then." She hung her head. "Are

Mother and Father mad at me?"

"No, I don't think so. No one can watch the dog every second. But we all have to be more careful about letting him get into the house."

Betsy nodded.

"And Otis explained where you got that extra money. He said he was paying you to take letters to Miranda."

"He told you?"

"Yes."

"I'm surprised. He told me not to say anything." She hesitated and then blushed. "I—I hope you don't mind."

"No. Why should I?"

Betsy shrugged. "I guess I thought you two were sweet on each other. But then it looked to me like you think a lot more of Christopher than you ever did of Otis."

"I know you like Otis. Is that okay with you?"

"Sure. I like Christopher even more."

Katherine smiled. "I have to admit, I do feel better now that I understand the full picture of where you got your extra money. Thank you for forgiving me for even asking you if you could have taken anything that didn't belong to you."

"You're welcome. I always get blamed when something goes wrong."

"The plight of the youngest." Katherine chuckled and then hugged her sister. "Thank you for understanding. I promise to trust you always, from now on."

Betsy nodded. "Is Otis mad that you know about the letters?"

"No. I don't even know why he kept it a secret. We wouldn't have minded if he wrote to Miranda. But please don't keep secrets from us anymore. I'm sure that's what Mother will tell you once she finds out about this. Okay?"

Betsy nodded. The two sisters exchanged one last hug, and Katherine put out the light, wishing Betsy a good night and sweet dreams.

A moment later, Katherine joined the others.

"Is Betsy asleep?"

"Not yet. But she will be soon." Katherine took her place at the table.

"Christopher says you two stopped by Vera's," Mother noted. "She has some news?"

"I wouldn't tell her until you came back." Christopher pushed back his empty dessert plate.

"Yes she does."

Mother leaned forward. "What's the news?"

"Alice delivered a little boy safely. Both of them are fine. His name is Paul Victor."

"What a lovely name. Maybe we should all have a second piece of pie in celebration."

"I'll take you up on that offer," Father said.

"Me, too," Christopher chimed in.

Father sent Katherine an approving look. Suddenly she was aware that no matter how many fishing trips he had taken with Otis, no one could ever replace Christopher in Father's heart.

"I think I've had quite enough excitement—and pie—for one night," Otis said. "Time for me to hit the hay."

Mother slid pieces of pie onto Father's and Christopher's dessert plates.

"With your permission, Mr. and Mrs. Jones, I'd like to take dessert with Katherine in the parlor."

"Why, of course," the parents agreed.

Mother smiled. "I'll be bringing in some lemonade in a moment."

Katherine couldn't see letting her mother wait on her, hand and foot. "Don't trouble yourself. Let me."

"If you insist."

Katherine poured the sweet liquid into two clear glasses that had once belonged to her grandmother. Though Christopher was fond of dessert, she wondered why he wanted to take her in the parlor to enjoy it. The setting seemed so formal.

As they exited the kitchen, Katherine thought she caught a glance exchanged between her parents. Did they know that something was about to happen? Katherine didn't dare think it to be so. She took in a breath.

Once they entered the parlor, she was glad Christopher had chosen such a setting. Though Katherine had been in the parlor often—mainly to dust it once a week—she looked at the room with fresh eyes that evening, perhaps because the night seemed to offer a new beginning.

Moments later, she and Christopher were settled into the sofa, as much as one could settle into unforgiving black silk cushions sewed with covered buttons and stuffed with rigid horsehair. As they partook of their pie, they recalled the evening's entertainment, reliving the highlights of their favorite acts.

"I think we can count this as a successful night," Christopher observed.

Katherine concealed her nervousness. Surely he hadn't summoned her here just to mull over the evening's events. "Too bad everyone couldn't win at the show," she managed.

"We all had fun, though."

Katherine finished the last of her lemonade. "I guess that's really what counts in the end." She sighed. "And to think, on this night, God brought a new life into the world."

Christopher nodded. "Each new life is a miracle, that's for sure."

They sat in companionable silence for a few moments.

Christopher broke the quiet. "Maybe this evening can be even more significant, with your consent."

She was glad she'd finished the lemonade. Otherwise, she might have been most unladylike and spit it out in surprise, certainly not an auspicious end to any evening. "Uh, what do you mean?" Time slowed for Katherine. Her heart beat faster, and her hearing became acute.

He set down his plate on the coffee table. "I have to admit, I was disappointed when I first learned Otis would be visiting."

"Really?"

"Yes. I was jealous. Especially after you and Miranda went to such lengths to impress him."

She felt a flush of chagrin. "And I tried to drag you along with me. I am truly sorry for that, Christopher. I will never ask you to do such a thing again. Not even for Miranda. But I think the trick with the horse was what clinched the relationship between her and Otis."

"If that was her plan, it certainly worked. Are you sorry?"

"No! I hope they live happily ever after."

"Just like in the fairy tales, huh?"

"Sort of like that."

"That's a good idea. I'll do the same."

"Are you still keeping our agreement to thank God for three blessings each day?" Katherine asked.

"I sure am. Tonight in my evening prayers, I'm going to thank Him for the birth of Paul Victor, for the success of the talent show, and for you."

Katherine felt herself blush. "I'll do the same. Except I'll thank Him for you." Feeling perhaps she spoke too boldly, she continued. "And I'll add a fourth thanks. That we solved the mystery."

"Yes, that is something to be thankful for." Christopher cleared his throat and set down his plate. He drew closer to Katherine. "Enough about all of that. I have something else to ask you. Something I've been wanting to ask you for a long time. Something I had planned to inquire about before Otis entered the picture."

She felt her heart beating once again. "Oh?"

"You mean to say, you had no idea of my interest in you?"

"As a friend, yes." Her heart beat faster.

"Of course I value your friendship, and that relationship is a fine basis for my growing feelings for you. I suppose I'm not a man of great and flattering words like your friend Otis. I'm not as skilled in making my real feelings known." He swallowed. "I didn't want to ask you to commit yourself to me while I was still in school, so I didn't plan to speak to your father until after I graduated. Then, when I came home, I discovered Otis was arriving in town and even staying at your house."

Katherine took in a breath. No wonder Christopher had been so distressed!

"I never meant to cause you any concern."

"You know something? Now that all is said and done, I'm glad Otis visited. You've had a chance to sort out any romantic feelings you might have harbored for him, and he for you. You'll never have to look back and feel a trace of doubt."

She considered the wisdom of his words. "True. I know that Otis can never be more than an acquaintance. In fact, I doubt we'll resume our letter-writing relationship after this. Make no mistake. I'm not angry with him.

"Understood." Christopher let out a happy sigh, then took her hand in his.

She trembled in happiness at his touch. She found she couldn't speak, an unusual plight for her.

"Katherine, I'm hoping you'll allow me to ask your father if I may court you with the earnest intention of our future marriage."

She took in a breath. "By all means, don't delay! Ask him as soon as possible!" She looked into his blue eyes. "Not that there's any doubt as to what his answer will be. I know how fond he has always been of you."

"Really?"

"Really. I could tell he never was rooting for Otis."

Christopher chuckled. "That's good to hear." He stopped, returning her gaze. "I love you, Katherine. And I believe in my heart that I always have."

"You know something? I believe in my heart I have always loved you, too. I just needed to come to my senses, that's all. At least I didn't have to fall off a horse like Miranda to see the light." She smiled.

"Please don't. I always want you to take care of your sweet self." He brought his face closer to hers.

Their lips met, the reality far exceeding the anticipation in joy.

Epilogue

Finally, the day Katherine dreamed of so long had arrived. The day she would become Mrs. Christopher Bagley! To her eyes, the church had never appeared more beautiful, decorated as it was with fragrant summer flowers and lit with long tapered candles, even though evening would not approach for hours.

Katherine watched her mother, dressed in a blue summer frock suited to the mother of the bride, begin her walk up the aisle, escorted by Ralph.

Katherine, knowing her turn would arrive soon, smoothed the white lace that decorated her white silk bodice. Vera had assured her repeatedly that the train kept its proper fall. Katherine dared not move too much lest she spoil the effect.

Katherine's first bridesmaid, a cousin from Virginia, took her turn walking up the aisle.

Katherine clasped her father's arm as she stood behind the church doors, ready to make her entrance for her walk down the aisle. Christopher would be waiting for her. She anticipated seeing the light in his eyes, knowing his expression of happiness would mirror her own.

Her second bridesmaid, another cousin, entered the sanctuary.

Katherine thought about their plans. Christopher had promised her a honeymoon trip to Washington, D.C. She hadn't been to the city since a family vacation years ago. She remembered feeling as though she was in the middle of a grand place. But to tour the city again with her beloved husband by her side; why, the thought was too delicious!

Her third bridesmaid, Lily, took her turn. The time drew near. Katherine could only think of Christopher. He would be her husband in a few moments. And she would be a wife. *Lord, I pray I will be a worthy wife for Christopher.*

Miranda and Otis, wed the previous month, were visiting from Charleston. When they had visited earlier, Katherine had seen the glow of love reflected on Miranda's face and Otis's, as well. How happy she felt that they had wed and were there to witness her nuptials.

Katherine watched as Vera stepped through the doorway, taking her turn walking up the aisle. While her friend made a beautiful maid of honor, Katherine hoped that one day soon Vera would be a bride.

"Are you nervous?" Father whispered.

"No. Nothing else has felt so right."

Father's eyes misted.

She squeezed his hand. "Father, stop it, or you'll make me cry."

"I know you'll be living only three miles away, but you won't be my little girl anymore."

"You never need to worry, Father. Christopher will always take care of your little girl."

They exchanged a tender smile and then took the first steps that would lead to Katherine's new life.

Vera's Turn for Love

Dedication

With love to Carrie, Kathie, Sally, and Vickie

Chapter 1

W"ho is that man?" Vera Howard whispered in Katherine Bagley's ear. The church social hummed with voices, but Vera didn't want to eye the new man too closely. Trying to conceal her interest, she cast her gaze over other parts of the social hall. A picture of Jesus as a child hung in one corner by an arched window. A few feet away, little girls tried to outperform one another on the upright piano. She watched one group of friends after another as they talked—anything to keep from setting her stare on the irresistible stranger. No need to let the object of her curiosity, with his wavy black hair, flashing blue eyes, and fine form, suspect he had attracted her interest. True, the twentieth century had dawned, but discretion never went out of fashion.

"You want to know about that man?" Katherine's mouth slackened, and her brown eyes grew wide. "Vera! I've never heard you ask such a question!"

Heat rose to Vera's cheeks, yet she couldn't resist taking a second peek at the dark-haired stranger. At that moment, he laughed with a gusto that showed his enjoyment of the conversation. She liked a man who could laugh without inhibition. Who wouldn't be drawn to such vitality and comeliness? Suddenly fearful of swooning, she took a seat, being careful not to let any punch spill on her cream-colored dress. "I don't suppose I should have asked."

Katherine sat beside her and nudged her in the ribs. "No, of course you should if you want to know. It's just that you shocked me because you've never asked about a gentleman before this moment. Tell you what. Let me see what I can discover for you." She finished her punch, set down the cup, and rose to fulfill her promise before Vera could object.

Katherine was right, Vera thought. She had never been especially intrigued by any new man at church. Of course, men she didn't know joined their church or just visited from time to time—comely men at that. But they were usually accompanied by a pretty wife and several young children. This man appeared to be alone.

Vera eyed Ethel, who was known to be seeking a suitor. No doubt Ethel would bat her long black eyelashes at him all too soon. Vera, with a slight frame and face she thought pleasant enough but not beautiful, decided that she didn't stand a chance against such a bold and coy rival. Withholding a sigh, Vera fanned herself against heat that seemed to increase as the crowd grew more animated. Or was she hot with emotion?

Katherine returned and sat in the empty seat beside Vera. The brunette leaned toward Vera. "I found out who your mystery man is." Katherine's eyes glowed with excitement. "It's Byron Gates."

"Oh." Vera felt a flush of embarrassment. Katherine had said the name as though she should have known the significance of one Byron Gates. But she had no idea.

"Byron Gates!" Katherine emphasized his last name.

Vera set her empty punch glass on a nearby windowsill beside two other abandoned glasses. "Gates. Gates. Hmm."

Katherine nudged her. "From Gates Enterprises in Baltimore. You lived in Baltimore. Surely you know of the family." Her voice rose in pitch, colored with indulgence and impatience.

Chagrined, Vera thought until she remembered. "Come to think of it, I do believe my employer in Baltimore was invited to their home for a reception once. But that reception was held in honor of people I didn't know, so I wasn't included. I never did learn more about the Gates family." She shrugged. "I was just a paid companion. I had no reason to socialize with them."

"Well, you do now." Katherine slipped a glance Byron's way. "I have a heart for no one but Christopher, but I would venture a guess that the other girls here would think you quite lucky."

"Lucky?"

"Yes. Haven't you seen how he's looked your way more than once tonight?"

Vera thought she had caught Byron stealing furtive glances at her as he maintained conversations with others. Until Katherine had mentioned it, Vera had attributed the observation to an overactive imagination. Or wishful thinking. "I've tried not to notice."

"He's noticed you. You know how love can catch one unawares. Deep feelings can start with just a look."

"Like with you and Christopher, perhaps?" Vera teased.

Katherine eyed her husband, standing at a small distance from them with a group of mutual friends. The love in her eyes surpassed all verbal expression. "Perhaps."

"Nevertheless, let us not speculate about love on my part or Byron's. I haven't so much as spoken to him yet. I might find him most disagreeable." She had a feeling she wouldn't.

"Once you stop swooning, you can decide." Katherine studied Byron from the corner of her eye. "I don't advise passing judgment based on someone's appearance because it's the heart that matters, but. . ."

"But?"

"He is dressed in quite a style and carries himself in a manner that exudes confidence. Do you think he may be just a bit worldly?"

"Maybe a bit, at least in comparison to us out here in the country. Why do you mention it?" Vera asked.

"Just make sure he's not too worldly. I know you would never want to have a romantic relationship with someone who doesn't share your love for the Lord."

"True. I believe I would be much happier with a godly man," Vera answered with vigor.

"Good. That's what I knew you'd say." Katherine smiled. "Come now. Let's see Clarence."

"Clarence?" Vera studied the tall, dark-eyed man with chestnut brown hair. He stood erect, cocksure of himself as always. "What does he have to do with all this?"

"Everything. Byron is here visiting him."

"My, but you do work fast."

"Out of necessity," Katherine said. "Did you see Ethel watching him like she's an owl and he's a rat?"

Vera wasn't certain she liked the idea of Byron being compared to a rat, but the allusion to prey wasn't lost on her. "Ethel eyes all the new men like that. And some of the old ones, too."

"I know." Katherine squeezed Vera's hand with urgency. "Let's show Mr. Byron Gates someone much prettier. There's no time to lose. Ethel is moving closer, as though she plans to strike at any minute."

Vera looked toward her rival and saw that Katherine was right. Still, Vera tried not to look too eager. She did want to meet Byron but had no desire to run over the top of Ethel to do it. Besides, Vera wasn't the most flamboyant woman in the room by any means. Certainly someone with more fire in her appearance would attract a bachelor whose residence in Baltimore and association with Clarence suggested sophistication.

The closer they got to Byron, the faster Vera's heart beat. As Vera and Byron were introduced, she noticed Ethel casting a narrow-eyed look her way.

"I am enchanted to meet you," Byron said in greeting.

"Enchanté." She nodded and wondered how she had managed to form a welcome in French. If one was to utter a greeting comprised of only one word, at least the word should be sophisticated. She treated herself to silent congratulations.

He moved closer, bringing with him a clean scent of shaving tonic. "Ah, so you respond in French. Did you study abroad?" The way he cocked his chin in her direction showed that she had gotten his attention.

Vera suppressed a giggle. Study abroad! Hardly. She was merely a farm girl who was once a companion to an elderly Baltimore lady. Now she was home, helping her sister tend to her small son.

"Don't let her fool you with the errant foreign word. Vera's from around these parts, and she hasn't ventured far," Clarence offered. "The farthest she's ever been is from Hagerstown to Baltimore."

"Clarence," Katherine chastised him, "Vera may not have traveled far from this county, but she is able to hold her own against any sophisticate."

Clarence tilted his head and seemed to be holding back an urge to say something unpleasant. Vera tried not to wince. Obviously Clarence wasn't thrilled by the prospect of her conversing with his friend from out of town.

"So you've been to Baltimore, eh?" Byron's eyes lit, and he focused his full attention on Vera. "Visiting friends?"

"I did more than visit." Despite Katherine's enthusiastic support and encouragement, Vera struggled to maintain a favorable posture and a lilt of confidence in her voice. "I lived with the Aldens."

"The Aldens." Byron gave the briefest of pauses before recalling the name. "You must mean the lawyer Raleigh Alden and his mother, June?"

Vera nodded and looked at the points of her shoes.

"Vera was June Alden's companion, but now she's home helping her sister, Alice," Katherine pointed out.

Vera was not ashamed of helping her sister. Still, she wished that her former status as nothing more than a paid companion had to be mentioned, June Alden's high regard for her notwithstanding. Vera held back another wince. Immediate honesty was the best policy.

There's no point in putting on airs, only to have the wind knocked out of my sails.

"Had I known the Aldens employed such a lovely companion, I might have ventured there a time or two myself," Byron told her.

Vera looked quickly into his blue eyes, then sent her gaze back down again. Byron was a bold one.

———

Byron whistled as he made ready to retire for the night. He couldn't remember a time when he had met any woman in a church social setting who had captured his imagination with the liveliness of the delightful Vera Howard. In fact, he couldn't remember having been in a church setting lately. The thought shamed him.

No wonder he had recently felt his life spiraling downward. He remembered how he had been spurned by one of Baltimore's outstanding debutantes, a certain Miss Elizabeth Josephine Reynolds. Elizabeth wasn't the greatest prize of Baltimore society, so her rebuff of his advances had taken him aback. Her refusal hadn't been delivered with the practiced skill of a popular debutante either. No, she had laughed in his face. Had he been such a rake as all that?

Apparently his reputation was not the best, and the social set in Baltimore knew it. He desired a woman of fine breeding and a high level of patience who would share his future responsibilities in running his father's manufacturing interests. Was this type of woman to be found?

He thought about his office and the responsibilities he had left at home. He wasn't afraid of work, but he wished the promised position offered more than worries and columns of numbers. The idea of sitting all day at a desk, working over accounts, managing inventory, vexing about how to keep workers happy with their pay while earning the company a profit, being sure the quality of goods was maintained, and then overseeing their shipment out from the Baltimore docks on time—none of these chores lent themselves to his particular interests or talents. Why couldn't his father have been a prosperous merchant so Byron could use his charm to sell fine goods? Or perhaps a lawyer with a position for Byron in his firm, since Byron could debate with the best of them?

Byron's father had already reminded him that his days of few responsibilities were numbered. "I am looking forward to passing the torch of Gates Enterprises to you, my eldest son. My boy who has grown into a fine specimen of a man."

As Father made the announcement, meant to be a supreme compliment, Byron had tried to appear enthusiastic. He even managed a smile. But his zest for running the family business ran cold.

Too restless to sleep, he took a seat in a corner chair and laid his head back against the leather. His thoughts wandered back to his childhood friend Daisy Estes. A man who flirted with as many women as Byron expected the occasional refusal, but he never worried. Not only did most women succumb to his engaging manner, but he also imagined that one day he could count on Daisy to marry him if all else failed. At least that's what he had assumed for years, until he and Daisy realized one day that they could never step over the romantic line. Still, he felt hurt that she had turned her attentions to Horace Moore. Plain, dull Horace. Byron couldn't imagine his lively friend, so coquettish in her manner, saddled with such a bore. If she wouldn't become Mrs. Byron Gates, couldn't she at least have displayed better taste when she rebounded?

Even worse, he hated the thought of disappointing all four of their parents. The Estes and Gates families had always been friends, with the elders remarking what a fine match Byron and Daisy would make one day. They spoke not in jest.

Against his will, Byron recalled God's commandment: *"Honour thy father and thy mother: that thy days may be long upon the land which the Lord thy God giveth thee."*

Though his parents had no intention of forcing a marriage, Byron felt a sense of duty toward them. How could he, their eldest son and heir to the family business, not abide by their fondest wishes? As for being close to God—Byron had hardly been a monk, but he still kept the Lord's wishes in the back of his mind. Church teachings he learned as a boy were more than happy to oblige, popping into his head whether beckoned or not.

Clarence chose that moment to burst into the bedroom. "There you are, old man. I must say I'm surprised to find you here. I can't believe you are retiring for the night already. Unless you in fact plan to change clothes for another round of festivities."

"Festivities? Are you saying you know a place where celebrations of life are beginning anew?"

"I know of none. I was hoping you did."

"I'm not the one with connections here."

"True. No, old man, I'm afraid I know of no other place to go now. They roll the sidewalks up at five o'clock, to be sure. We must make our own entertainment out here in the country. Not that we're too shabby about that. But you can hardly expect our humble establishments to be as active as the big gaming halls and places of frolic that you might find in the city. In fact, by local standards, a church social is considered a fine night of vigorous entertainment." Clarence sighed. "My, but I do miss the gala atmosphere of Baltimore."

"Yes, we did have a fine summer last year, didn't we? But surely you don't neglect to see the charms of your home."

Clarence surveyed the room and shrugged. "I suppose."

"I find the country quite charming indeed."

"Really? I'm surprised you're not bored already. Unless. . ." He sent Byron a cunning look. "You sly dog. You've found a woman, haven't you?"

Chapter 2

Byron crossed his arms, shifted in his seat, and studied Clarence. As usual, his friend had ventured a correct guess. Relishing triumph, Byron allowed a smile to slip upon his countenance. "As a matter of fact, I have found a woman."

"I knew it!" Clarence rubbed his hands together and grinned. "I can see by the cat-that-swallowed-the-canary look on your face that you're confident she returns the favor. But why should I doubt it? You seem to find a woman anywhere you go." Since the bedroom had but one chair, he sat on the side of Byron's bed and positioned his foot on top of the mahogany rail left exposed by the blue bedspread.

"You exaggerate, my friend. I confess that this woman is not the usual type I pursue. She is very charming and a lovely woman indeed, yet in a way that displays no affectations." Byron looked into space, thinking of Vera. "I have drawn the distinct conclusion that this is one woman I shall never forget."

"A woman you shall never forget, eh?" Clarence rubbed his chin. "I'm thinking back on all the women you spoke with at the social."

"You'll be thinking a long time, then. People out here are quite friendly, and I spoke to many this evening."

Clarence chortled. "Friendly, yes. But I've never seen the women quite as friendly as they were tonight. They were drawn to you like bees to honey, old man. I can only stand nearby and hope some of your charm rubs off on me—or that I can be around to mend the hearts you break."

"You sell yourself short, Clarence. Besides, women—and fellows, as well—will always be fascinated by the new man in town. That's not to say you're old hat, but you certainly are well-known around these parts. I, on the other hand, am a stranger. To them, my story is new."

"Everything you say is indisputable. But remember, I've seen you operate in the city where you are well-known." He tilted his head and sent Byron a mischievous look. "I've always admired you for how you can charm any woman you have a mind to. So who is your latest victim?"

Byron felt the smile slide back to his feet. He cringed. "Victim?"

"A willing victim, no doubt," his friend hastened to assure him. "So who might the lucky woman be?"

Byron wished Clarence wasn't staring at him, waiting for an answer. So women associated with him were considered victims, eh? Byron resolved at that moment to improve his reputation. He took in a breath and held it as if to affirm his resolution.

"My, but she must be quite a prize. Let me guess." Clarence rolled his gaze upward and tapped his chin with his forefinger. "Is it Carolyn?" Clarence leveled his eyes toward Byron.

"The brunette with the red fan?"

"That's the one. She's quite a catch. I've had my eye on her myself for a while. I do say your appearance around these parts might liven things up and prod her not to wait too much longer to choose a suitor."

"She's that popular?"

"You didn't notice? She held court most of the night." Clarence smiled, and a mischievous twinkle sparked in his eyes. "I know. Maybe we can make a game of our little competition."

"Sorry, my friend, but we'll make no sport of Carolyn's affections. No, I have someone else in mind."

"You want to make sport of another's affections?" Clarence shrugged. "One woman is as good as another for games, I suppose. Who, then?"

"No, I will not make sport of this woman's affections. I have resolved to change my ways."

Clarence whistled. "She must have made quite an impression."

"Yes. And I won't make sport of any woman's affections, for that matter."

"This change is quite sudden. I'm not sure I like it," Clarence said. "I'll take a guess. Is she a redhead?"

"No. She's a blond."

"A blond, eh? Now who could that be?" Clarence crossed his arms and thinned his lips in thought. A mischievous light struck his eyes as he snapped his fingers. "I know. It must be Rosetta."

"That harebrain?" Byron grimaced.

Clarence chuckled. "So she's witty. Then surely you must have your eye on Jane."

Byron shook his head.

Clarence let out an exasperated breath. "Then who, man? There was no other blond. At least, none worthy of the attentions of a man such as yourself."

"Really? If you think that, then surely you didn't see Vera Howard."

Clarence's mouth slackened. "Vera Howard? You must be out of your mind!"

"Why ever do you say that?"

"Because, she's. . .she's a wallflower, that's why. Hardly ever utters a word. As quiet as a church mouse. And speaking of church mice, Vera is certainly at home in a church. She's banging on the door every time it opens."

"Some men would consider quiet restraint an asset in a woman and be delighted with a woman who considers church attendance more than a duty and an obligation—but a joy."

"I wouldn't take you for a man who values silence."

Byron bristled. "I'm not. And as long as I'm with Vera, I don't have to be. She and I had quite a lovely conversation."

"Indeed? Then her personality must undergo a transformation when she's with you. Not that I find such a development to be a complete surprise." He smirked. "Vera is inexperienced and no doubt flattered easily by your attentions. However, I must point out that she clearly is not your type."

Byron tried not to take offense at Clarence's observation. Though he knew his friend didn't mean to insult him, the truth hurt. He considered the possibility that the Lord was speaking to him. How long had He been trying to get Byron's attention? Too long, no doubt. Byron had finally reached the point where he was willing to listen, even if that meant he wouldn't like much of what he heard. "You were wrong about her being quiet, at least in my company."

Clarence shook his head. "Perhaps she seems talkative to you, but based on everything I've seen, she's a shy little thing. Don't take my word for it. You'll find out soon enough. The moment she slaps you across the cheek when you try to steal a kiss." He chuckled.

"Am I really such a rake as all that?"

"A rake? Why, many men don't mind wearing such a label. Don't you know the term holds a hint of intrigue and romance? Women love that sort of thing, you know."

"Women who care not a whit about home and family," Byron observed.

"Oh, so that's what you care about now, old man? Then maybe this mouse, Miss Vera Howard, would make you a fine, timid little wife."

"You need spectacles, my friend."

Clarence chuckled. "No indeed, my friend. You are the one who could use assistance with your vision and discernment. The apple of your eye tonight is dull. She is at present serving as a nanny to her infant nephew, Paul Victor, since her married sister, Alice, is once again in a family way."

"Alice Sharpe?"

Clarence nodded. "She'll be going into her confinement soon enough. And your Vera will be busier than ever."

"I'm sure she'll find plenty of time for me."

"Then you'd better hurry. Once Alice ties her down with two little brats, Vera will be hard-pressed to call her life her own. Not that she has much of a life now."

Byron opened his mouth to protest, but Clarence beat him to the punch. "I have a proposition for you."

"Oh?" Byron leaned forward in his chair.

Clarence hopped off the bed and moved closer to Byron. "I'll bet you can't get Vera to agree to marriage within six months."

"Marriage in six months? That's not a small wager."

"Not too large for a betting man such as yourself." Clarence leaned against the mahogany bedpost.

"I wish you wouldn't offer such temptation. You know my betting days are behind me. Even if they weren't, I could never toy with such a sweet woman as Vera."

"Toy with her? *Toy* is your middle name."

Byron swallowed. "But you know why I came here."

"To visit me, your old friend, of course." Clarence's tone told Byron he spoke only partly in jest.

"Of course. But also to cultivate new and better habits. I really do want to change."

"Perhaps, but that doesn't mean you must pursue the dullest woman in the county. You won't be happy if you're bored, and you'll only return to your old ways."

"But I won't be bored. My interest in Vera Howard is genuine. She intrigues me. And I plan to see if I can eventually coax her into a courtship."

Clarence laughed. "Surely you can't be serious."

"I am indeed."

"Suit yourself. But at least we can make the process more interesting."

Byron was almost afraid to ask. "How?"

"I'll make you a wager, but not a serious one. If you manage to begin courting Vera Howard within six months, I'll take you to a tavern at my expense to celebrate your victory."

The idea of betting on his future on a whim disgusted Byron, but he couldn't help himself. He had to learn the rest of Clarence's scheme. "And if I don't?"

His friend didn't hesitate. "You'll have to treat me to a night of gaming in Baltimore."

Byron didn't answer right away. Whether he won or lost the bet, he didn't want to go to either a tavern or on a night of gaming. He shook his head. "No. You can bet, my friend, but you'll be betting alone."

"Bold, yes. Too bold if you ask me," Alice said a few days later, after Vera told her about the encounter at the church social.

Each day, the two women took advantage of the quiet interlude after lunch dishes were gathered and washed. Usually Vera enjoyed those moments of conversation and catching up with one another. But on this day, for the first time since her return to Washington County, Vera wished she had found something else to do instead of talking with Alice after lunch.

"Do you think such a sharp tone is good for the baby when you're trying to rock him to sleep?" Vera offered out of genuine concern and the desire to soften her sister's criticism.

"You're right." Alice looked up at Vera and then back to Paul. Rocking in the chair and holding him in a blue blanket, Alice looked as though she posed for a talcum powder advertisement.

Vera rocked back and forth in the chair across from Alice. "I don't know. I rather liked Mr. Gates's straightforwardness. After all, it's not every day I meet a new man who is free with compliments."

"Free with flattery for you and every other woman who crosses his path, I'll venture," Alice cautioned.

"I'm not sure I would pass such judgment yet. I may not be the most beautiful woman in any given gathering, but surely you don't mean that I am so ugly that no man would flatter me." Vera picked up a ball of twine and a tiny crochet hook from the basket beside the chair.

"Of course not, sister dear. I didn't mean to hurt you. I just am very aware that you aren't wise in the ways of the world and of men." Alice rubbed her son's cheek.

"And you are?" As soon as she blurted out the words, regret filled her soul. "I'm sorry. I didn't mean that."

"I know." Alice looked up and sighed. "I suppose I would have been more insulted had you implied that I know all too much about men. Besides, we are sisters, and if we cannot be frank with one another, then we don't have much of a relationship, do we?"

Vera tried to concentrate on a stitch, but in her distress, her work wasn't up to its usual quality. "It would break my heart for that to be so."

"Then let me continue to be forthcoming with the truth for your own good. How much do you know about Byron Gates?"

"Not much," she admitted. "Only that he's charming and handsome. Quite pleasant, really."

"Of course he is. He's a carefree bachelor. No doubt he uses smooth words to captivate all the ladies. And that is why, my dear sister, he is not a suitable match for you," Alice cautioned. "I advise you to stay away from Byron, and I expect you to heed that advice."

"How do you know so much about him?"

"After you mentioned him to me on the evening of the social, I had Elmer do some digging for me."

"Alice! You certainly didn't waste any time. Why are you worried? I don't even know Byron. At least not very well." Vera tore out the stitch she had just crocheted.

"True, but you have never expressed interest in any man before now."

"That's just what Katherine said," Vera noted.

"And she is a lifelong friend of yours. So you can see why I believe that my fears are not unfounded."

"Fears?"

"Yes." Alice sighed, a sad look reaching into her eyes. "I'm afraid I don't like what Elmer told me about your Mr. Gates."

"What did he discover?"

"Byron Gates is a known rake, cad, and gambler. No honest woman in Baltimore will have him, and neither should you. I recommend strongly that you stay away from him. And Elmer agrees."

Vera didn't answer. She could only hope the reports about Byron were wrong.

Chapter 3

Later that night, Vera thought about her sister's admonition. Though the Sharpes lived in the country, Elmer had friends nearby who once lived in the city, and they would be in the know about Baltimore's prominent families. Vera had no reason to doubt that what he had discovered about Byron held the truth. Surely his reputation as a rake and gambler was deserved.

Vera let out a distressed sigh. She had seen handsome faces and even bon vivants before, but Byron possessed an indefinable quality that attracted her. And yes, she was naive about men. No wonder her sister had expressed concern about her becoming involved with Byron Gates. But Vera didn't lack discernment and wisdom.

I don't care what Alice says. If Byron comes to church this Sunday, that will show me and everyone else that he is nurturing his spiritual life. I don't care what his reputation is. I want to find out about him for myself. I'm going to talk to him anyway.

Vera looked out over the lush Maryland countryside that was the Sharpes' farm. Her sister had finally permitted her to accept Byron's request to share a picnic lunch, however grudgingly, as long as she and the baby accompanied them. Over the past few weeks, Vera had noticed that Byron never seemed to miss a chance to converse with her at church and to hover nearby at local social gatherings. Though to be bold was not her way, Vera gave him enough encouraging glances that he finally asked her if she'd consent to promenade with him on the next sunny day. To her surprise, Alice and Elmer gave their permission that night. She remembered writing a reply to Byron's request, which contained her pledge to prepare a basket lunch.

Vera peeked at her sister. Despite her reluctance to allow Byron near Vera, Alice had been kind enough to keep herself out of earshot most of the day. Yet she lingered closely enough to the couple on their outing that there would be no question they were fully chaperoned and that all was proper. Her infant son, Paul, had proven to be an agreeable and quiet companion. Sitting underneath an oak tree, Alice played with him, cooing all the while. Seeing the picture of her sister's happiness, Vera couldn't help but fantasize about what her own eventual marriage and motherhood would be like.

"I do believe this is the best fried chicken I ever put in my mouth, Miss Howard."

She regarded her own leg of fried chicken. The coating had cooked to a golden brown, and pinprick-sized dots of black pepper promised a well-seasoned entrée. The juicy meat didn't disappoint. Though she knew a compliment was deserved, she wasn't sure how to respond to such hyperbole. "Indeed, sir? Then you must not have eaten too much chicken in your lifetime."

"I beg your pardon, but I have," he responded without a shade of defensiveness. "I am quite well traveled. Would you like me to tell you all about Spain?"

Spain! Imagine, being so well traveled. She thought about her own sheltered life and how she had seen nothing outside of her beloved Maryland. How could she expect to keep a worldly man such as Byron interested in her trivial doings? Then she remembered sage advice given by Aunt Middie long ago: *To be fascinating, open your ears and use them!*

Vera leaned closer but made a conscious effort not to lean too near. "Yes, I would love to hear about Spain."

He launched into a fascinating account of the sights of the distant land and then moved on to descriptions of other places about which Vera had learned only in books. By account's end, she was shaking her head in amazement. "How marvelous to be so well traveled."

Byron looked into the sky. "But I have so many other places I want to go. Greece, Cyprus, Egypt."

Vera caught her breath. "I can only dream of such strange lands."

"Then dream with me." He looked at her, but his tone took on a faraway pitch, as though he were traveling to a place beyond their immediate circumstances and taking her with him.

The thought gave her goose bumps. "Oh, how I would love to dream with you."

Propping himself on one palm, he tilted himself closely enough to her that she could breathe in the scent of his manly shaving water. That he desired to bring himself closer to her filled her with vitality. She could feel her eyes open wide with interest.

"I can show you the world if you're willing to go along with me," he persuaded.

Vera took a sudden interest in her buttered yeast roll. She could never travel with her lunch companion except as Mrs. Byron Gates, and it was much too soon for either of them to contemplate such a proposal.

His voice retained persuasiveness. "You would like to travel, wouldn't you, Miss Howard?"

She bit into her roll with what she hoped looked like a ladylike motion. She could only imagine listening to his soft, masculine voice telling her the history of each landmark.

"Certainly you would," he answered for her.

"One day, perhaps," she managed.

"I can't say that I blame you for not wanting to commit to me as a traveling companion—yet. Perhaps we might take some time to learn more about each other." He drew his hand closer to hers but stopped short of touching it.

Vera shot a glance toward Alice. Almost as though she knew Vera's thoughts, Alice gave her a warning look. Vera couldn't decide whether to move her hand back to the folds of her skirt. She looked into Byron's face and decided to keep her fingers right where they were. She cleared her throat. "How?"

"I suppose you have observed that I haven't let you out of my sight whenever we're in the same room together."

Vera giggled, drawing Alice's unwanted attention once more. Vera averted her eyes and set their gaze upon her linen-clad knees. "I would not be so immodest as to think you were so very interested in me."

My, but he must think me a ninny from the way I sound! She held back a cringe.

He chuckled, filling the air with the mirth of kindness. "Immodest? Why, I should think you have suitors standing in line."

A shiver of pleasure coursed through her upon hearing such flattery. Vera lifted her lace fan and waved it before her face, even going so far as to bat her eyelashes. She had never flirted so boldly before, but try as she might, she couldn't stop herself. "I can see why you are such a popular bachelor in Baltimore. Surely the ladies there swoon over you."

To her surprise, he tensed. His countenance took on a hard expression, and he turned his gaze from her face, looking instead at a distant grove of trees. She followed his stare but saw nothing out of the ordinary that would call his attention to the foliage. Fear shot through her as she placed the fan back on the blanket.

"Is anything the matter, Byron?"

He looked at her, but his eyes appeared to be vacant, as though he didn't really see her. "No." His tone wasn't convincing.

"I—I'm so sorry. You must think me much too bold and brash. It. . .it's much too brisk today for a fan. I don't even know why I brought it."

"Perhaps you care to fan away the rumors about me that you obviously heard?"

"Rumors?" she blurted.

"Now you're the one who's being coy."

She set down her fan and looked at him without smiling. "All right. It's true. I have heard that you are quick to flirt with many women and that your favorite pastime is gaming."

"And yet you still don't mind sharing lunch with me?" He searched her face with a probing look.

She averted her gaze to the blanket and then looked back at him. "Was I a fool to take a risk?"

"I hope not. In fact, I am hoping to prove to you and the rest of the world— and even more importantly, to God—that I want to come back to the fold."

Her heart beat with happiness. "Really?"

"Yes. I regret my youthful follies. Not to mention, I have grown tired of them. As the apostle Paul wrote in his letters, there comes a time when a man must put away childish things. And while gaming and flirting might seem to be adult pursuits, they are childish."

She took a moment to contemplate his words. "Perhaps with wisdom so hard won, you should consider the ministry."

His laugh sounded pleasant. "I am neither called to nor worthy of such a high pursuit. However, your compliment will be one I shall revisit in my memory many times." He grew serious. "Thank you for your willingness to show me a Christian spirit, flawed as my past is, when surely your past, present, and future are—and will be—as white as a fresh cotton sheet on a summer day."

"Now you are the one who places too high a regard on a person." Unaccustomed to such flattery, she waved her fan in front of her cheeks once more.

"Are we experiencing a sudden rash of heat?" he teased.

The flush of warmth she felt made the fan even more necessary. "Yes. Yes, we are experiencing a sudden rash of heat."

"Really?"

"I assure you I never play the coquette. At least, I never normally do. I mean, I didn't until today. I—I. . .oh, I don't know what I mean." Waves of chagrin flowed through her. She couldn't look at him, not at all. She rose to her feet. "If you're done with your meal, I suppose we had better be packing up what remains of the lunch. The baby needs to go down for his afternoon nap soon."

Returning to Clarence's from the picnic, Byron didn't hurry the horse. He wanted to contemplate the time he has just spent with Vera. Even though her sister had been within earshot, entertaining the baby, he could sense that Vera's emotions toward him grew. Based on what Clarence had revealed about her and given Vera's expressed chagrin at being just a mite coy that afternoon, she wasn't one to flirt indiscriminately. He had found her expressions beautiful and her witticisms fascinating. Having always protected his heart, Byron didn't remember a time he had known love—at least, not the kind of love that could sustain a marriage. But Vera was unique. Whenever he neared her, he could envision wanting to stay with her for a long, long time.

If only he had not been so quick to throw away a perfectly respectable reputation with shenanigans well-known to all. How could someone such as Vera be expected to think of him as anything but a cad—a man entirely unsuitable for her?

Try as he might, he had become all too aware that ridding himself of his past mistakes was not going to be easy. People with vicious tongues, jealous of the Gates family's position and wealth, were all too eager to keep accounts of indiscretions alive. Would his past one day catch up with him, sweeping Vera from him?

Even worse, Byron knew his family had other plans for him. Plans he didn't much care to have come to fruition. He didn't see how Vera, a countrywoman not raised to join his social set, could possibly fit in that picture.

Turning into Clarence's drive, Byron tried to put on a happy face. No point in sharing his worries with his friend. He had a feeling they would come home to roost soon enough.

———

Alice said nothing during the journey from the picnic place to the farmhouse. If anything, she demonstrated the epitome of the charmed matron as long as Byron remained in their company. Only later, after Vera had bid Byron good afternoon and Alice had put down her child for a nap, did she seek out Vera in the informal parlor.

"There you are. You seem chipper." Alice took a seat in the overstuffed brown chair across from Vera's.

"I'm always chipper." Vera ran her feather duster over the lamp shade with more enthusiasm than she usually displayed for dusting.

"Not quite as chipper as you are today. So tell me, what puts you in such a good mood? Or shall I say, who?" Alice inclined her head in Vera's direction. "Let me guess. Byron Gates is responsible for your carefree demeanor."

Vera sat in a convenient chair but kept the feather duster in her hand. "I confess it. Byron is the source of my pleasure."

"And many other women's. I knew that letting you picnic with him was a mistake. I pray you haven't fallen into his treacherous web."

"How can you discern that he has woven such a web? You hardly know him. I daresay you don't know him as well as I do."

"Not that your acquaintance is one of longevity."

"True." Vera flinched.

"I'm sorry, but I worry because of Byron's sudden eagerness to court you."

Vera fingered the crocheted doily on the right arm of the chair and studied the pattern. "You think he will ask to court me in earnest?"

"In earnest, you say. That only proves you have been contemplating the possibility."

Vera looked back to her sister's face. "What if I have? Am I such an ugly ninny that no man would ever want to court me? Is that what you think?"

"You know that's not what I think. Granted, you know as well as I do that you have a reputation as a wallflower, but many a wallflower has journeyed to matrimony with great success. So please, humor me, will you, dear? Let me have Elmer ask Clarence if Byron's intentions are honorable. Our families are both on friendly terms, and I know Clarence would have no reason to lie. Elmer, I assure you, will find out all we need to know with the greatest discretion."

"I don't know. . . ."

Alice leaned toward Vera and set her gaze into her eyes. "What are you afraid of? That your new interest is not as honorable as you hope?"

Vera held Alice's gaze but rooted her heel in the floor. "No. I am not afraid. Have Elmer ask him. And I want to know as soon as possible what Clarence has to say."

Chapter 4

The following day, Byron returned to the Stanley house from an errand in town. To his surprise, Clarence greeted him at the door with the air of a child awaiting a gift from a doting grandparent. "You'll never guess what happened today."

"I don't know, but I can say you look happy." Byron hurried up the porch steps and tried to think of what event could put such a smile on Clarence's face. "Perhaps someone who owed you a debt came by to repay?"

"Now that would have been good news. But sadly, that isn't so."

"What, then?"

"Perhaps you'd better sit down." Clarence gestured his friend inside. "Let's take a seat in my study."

Byron followed Clarence to a room where he had traveled many times—the study near the back of the house. Stale tobacco smoke and the scent of Clarence's usual citrus shaving lotion mingled to remind visitors that the room was his haunt. He took a seat in his favorite black leather chair, and Byron selected a Chippendale intended for visitors.

The suspense was weighing on Byron. "All right, tell me."

Clarence lit his pipe. "Byron, my good man, you are obviously making serious progress with our wager on Miss Vera Howard."

The news was welcome to Byron, but he tried not to convey any emotion. "What do you mean?"

"I mean, I had a visit from her brother-in-law today. Elmer Sharpe."

"Oh." Byron's voice sounded flat, even to his ears. This had happened before. First he would garner the attention of an attractive woman, enjoy a mild flirtation; then a key relative would get wind of his attentions and ask probing questions. More often than not, such a visit signaled the end of his tête-à-tête with the woman in question. "What did he want?"

"I'll give you three guesses, and the first two don't count. He wanted to know if I think your intentions toward Vera are honorable."

Byron remembered Clarence's insistence on betting. He held his breath and tightened his fingers around the chair arms. "So what did you tell him?"

Clarence inhaled on his pipe and then refreshed the tobacco with a light. The aroma of quality leaves filled the study. "I'm your friend, am I not?"

"Yes. So what did you say?"

"Do you think I'm a fool, man? I told him that of course your intentions are honorable."

Byron brightened. "You did?"

Clarence laughed. "You sound like a little boy on Christmas Day."

Byron wondered if the comparison was all too apt. "I do thank you for speaking kindly of me to Vera's brother-in-law."

"Kindly. Yes." Clarence smirked. "Oh, I feel badly about my little fib, but it's all in good fun."

"But Clarence, you did not tell a fib. My intentions toward Vera are indeed honorable. She means more to me than just a little fun. I've told you that."

Clarence looked down his pipe stem at Byron. "I feel sorry for you, then. Her sister isn't going to be happy about the prospect of your courting Vera. Granted, I sang your praises, but Elmer is quite astute. No doubt his visit here was prompted by whatever he heard about your past. I also have no doubt that he'll share whatever he finds out about you with his wife."

"Oh." Byron stared at his boots.

"You have a right to be disconcerted," Clarence admitted. "Alice is very protective of Vera. You'll have a long row to hoe, indeed, to get on her good side."

———

Vera sat at the table and watched an argument ensuing in the kitchen of the Sharpe farm. Alice pressed her fingers into a mound of dough with vigor. She refused to turn her eyes toward her husband.

"I don't care what Clarence says, Byron Gates is known as a man about town in Baltimore, and I see no reason to think he's changed just because he's in the country. If anything, he's liable to believe our Vera is more naive than the women in the city, and he'll try to take advantage of her just as sure as the sun will rise tomorrow."

"Now, now, Alice." Elmer consoled her from his place at the table. "You don't know that. Perhaps Byron has come here as part of a process of invoking real change in his life."

"And you don't know that," she retorted.

Up to this point, Vera had witnessed the exchange as she deboned chicken for use in a rice dish. She set down the butcher knife. "Please don't be vexed, Alice. You need to take care of yourself and of the life you carry."

"It's too late. I'm already vexed." Alice kept kneading the dough.

Elmer intervened. "Vera is right. Alice, I know you are not yourself, thanks to your delicate condition, but please, do not resort to histrionics in an effort to control your sister. She has served you well all this time. Isn't she allowed to find a little happiness for herself if that's God's will?"

Vera never expected to find such a strong ally in her brother-in-law. She let out a little gasp. "Thank you, Elmer."

"I would think my own husband would defend my viewpoint," Alice rebuked him, her eyes narrowed. "With his reputation, Byron Gates surely is not the man for our Vera."

"Alice, I know you want what's best for Vera, but you also want what's best for our children. You're worried about losing her, aren't you?" Elmer looked at Vera.

Alice nodded. "All right, I'll admit it. I don't want to lose Vera." Alice looked at Vera, her eyes soft with the love and concern of a sister. "Can you blame me?"

Vera responded to Alice with a loving look in return, though she remained silent.

"Of course I don't blame you for not wanting Vera to leave," Elmer agreed. "But we can hire a nanny if need be."

"How can you be so callous?" Alice asked. "A nanny would never love our children as much as their own flesh-and-blood aunt! Isn't that right, Vera?" Alice's large eyes reminded Vera of a sad puppy.

"Of course, that's right." Vera swallowed and kept her focus on the chicken. Leaving the love and security she enjoyed at her sister's house was a drawback to any romance she might find, but if she was ever to have her own life, she would have to look at the transition as a new and exciting step in God's promise for her future.

Elmer raised his hands in mock exasperation and let them fall back on his lap. "Women!"

The sisters chuckled, but as soon as the moment passed, Vera turned to serious contemplation. *Father in heaven, do not let me become a source of contention between this couple Thou hast joined together. I am torn about my feelings for Byron and my place in Thy world. Please show me what is Thy will.*

"What are you thinking, Vera?" Alice interrupted.

"I was praying."

"You'll be needing lots of prayer if you think you can tame Byron Gates." Alice stopped working the dough long enough to study Vera. "Surely I'm not the only person you've talked to about Byron. You're so enamored that you can hardly contain yourself."

"Have I been as silly as all that?" Vera set a leg bone on the table.

"Perhaps not," Alice admitted. "But have you talked about Byron to anyone else?"

She stopped her task long enough to consider the question. "I did mention Byron to Katherine."

"And what did she have to say?"

Vera didn't answer right away. "Well, she did say he's quite handsome."

"Even the men have noticed that," Elmer noted. "Whenever Gates enters a room, the other young bachelors look at him with daggers in their eyes. I'd say they view him as unwelcome competition, to be sure."

"I don't mind admitting that Mr. Gates is handsome, although he wouldn't hold any appeal for me even if I were still single," Alice said. "But whatever your opinion of his countenance and form, appearances are not everything."

"I agree," Vera said, "and I would never choose a companion based on attractiveness alone. Katherine knows that."

"So Katherine had no reservations?" Alice stopped manipulating the dough.

Vera swallowed. "I wish I didn't have to tell you this, but as soon as she saw Byron's worldly appearance and bearing, she advised me to be sure he loves the Lord before I become too attached to the idea of romance."

"I knew Katherine to be wise. Good for her for speaking the truth." Alice smiled and rolled the dough into a ball.

"Byron told me during the picnic that he wants his mistakes to stay in the past and that he wants to pursue a closer relationship with God. No doubt that since he'll be seeking God, his behavior will adjust itself accordingly and will be above reproach now and in the future. True, it is never wise to stray from God, but judging from Byron's attitude, he has repented and is eager to return to God's standards for his life. And as for me, I want to give him a chance."

Vera remembered the picnic, and how Byron's presence had made her tremble with delight. "I may as well tell you that I did invite him to accompany me to church as long as he remains here."

"Church, eh?" Elmer laughed and looked at his wife. "I don't see how you can object to that, Alice."

She shot her husband a look. "I do not approve. Ensuring oneself of a regular escort is fine and good for a young woman, but Byron's presence is sure to discourage more fitting suitors."

"It's just church," Elmer countered, "and no other suitors have made their intentions known."

Vera felt the sting of Elmer's comment.

"It's not as though Mr. Gates made himself known. You had to seek out Clarence to learn his opinion of Mr. Gates's intentions, remember?"

"Of course." Elmer's voice displayed uncharacteristic irritability. "Instead of complaining, Alice, you should be thanking me that I sought to protect Vera from any man who might be using worship in the Lord's house as a ruse for meaningless flirtation."

"I don't think he is. As I said, he really is trying to change," Vera volunteered.

"That's what Clarence indicated, as well," Elmer agreed. "Gates's willingness to turn away from a sinful life should make you happy, Alice."

"Of course I'm happy for him," Alice agreed. "But, Vera, I doubt that the Lord expects you to take every errant sinner you meet under your wing."

"I'm not taking every errant sinner under my wing," Vera replied. "Just Byron."

Late Wednesday afternoon, Byron entered the dining room of the Stanley house for dinner. He was surprised to find Clarence reading a newspaper at the table. Normally he had left for his card game by this hour. "Good afternoon, Clarence."

Upon spying his friend, Clarence set the paper on the table and studied him. "What brings you to the table so early?"

"I might ask you the same question."

Clarence shrugged. "Coughs and colds kept two of our card players away. We called off the games." He peered at Byron. "Your turn."

Byron slid onto his seat and nodded to the servant to fetch his drink. "Midweek church service. I don't want to be late."

"Church? On Wednesday night?" Clarence asked Byron. "Since when do you care about going to church in the middle of the week? Isn't once a week enough to fulfill one's religious obligation?"

"I wouldn't call my attendance an obligation at all. I find it rather pleasurable." Byron straightened his tie. "Especially since I discovered that Vera attends midweek services."

Clarence leaned his chin against his palm. "So from now on you'll be going twice a week."

"I've been going twice a week. You just haven't noticed."

"I noticed you've been turning down my invitations to Wednesday evening card games. Now I know why. But church, old man?" Clarence tugged at his collar as though the motion would help more air enter his lungs. "Stifling."

"Am I right in assuming you don't care to join me?"

"Right you are." He leaned back in his seat as a servant set down a bowl of squash soup before him.

"Too bad. You might meet a woman there yourself."

"I know all the women in that church, and I have since I was a boy. There's no fresh face there for me."

"Then go for the sermons," Byron suggested as he was served his own bowl of soup. "Even in midweek, they are quite inspiring. I didn't know the Bible contained such depth. There's much more to it than the Ten Commandments."

"As if you could recite even five of them."

"I can now."

Clarence shook his head. "I'm astounded. And this is all because of Vera Howard. Whatever do you see in that little mouse?"

"If you have to ask, you don't understand love."

"Love?" Clarence chortled. "Isn't it a little too soon to call whatever it is you're feeling 'love'?"

Byron realized that, according to convention, he shouldn't be blurting his realization of such potent feelings even to his best friend. The thought occurred to him that giving his feelings such weight was premature. But he knew that whenever he came near to Vera, he lost all sense of place and time. Only she, with her beauty and sweet spirit, existed for him. As long as he could see her, little else mattered to him. No other woman had made him feel that way. Not even Daisy, whom he had known since childhood.

"Most likely you would label my feelings infatuation," Byron conceded to Clarence. "And perhaps they started out that way. I did feel an initial flush of longing when we first met. Yet this time, it's different. Unlike my notice of ladies in Baltimore, with Vera I am not ready to give her up and move on to my next—and more compliant—conquest. I would like to remain with Vera as long as I can."

"Forever?"

"I cannot say so yet. But I do find her intriguing. She's unlike any other woman I've met."

"You keep saying that, but you can't prove it by me."

"Must I prove anything to you, Clarence? Really, she is pure and sweet and beautiful in a wholesome way."

"Wholesome. Not a quality you usually look for in a woman, and certainly not one I seek."

"Then maybe if you gave someone like Vera a chance, you'd appreciate a woman who listens to your stories. Vera always listens to mine." Byron smiled, remembering how mesmerized she had been by his accounts of foreign travel.

"I wonder how long that will last?"

"You are too cynical."

"I prefer to think of my attitude as one of caution. What if you flirt with her and you discover she's not the lady you thought her to be?"

"She is every bit an innocent," Byron protested with more might than he intended. "You, having known her all her life, should be aware of that."

Clarence shrank. "Yes. All right, I admit it. If you were to discover anything sullied about Vera Howard, I would be shocked."

"So how can you even suggest she's anything but the greatest of ladies? Why, if you weren't my friend, I would acquaint you with my fist for giving expression to such a thought."

"I understand that you're not yourself, befuddled as you are by Vera; I've seen women like her before, and so have you. A member of the fairer sex who has little experience can often become enraptured by the attentions of a man of the world. She thinks she wants to remain virtuous but is soon swept away by his charms, and then. . ." He let his voice taper and then sighed as though he were remembering a few misadventures of his own. "If you can convince her you're in love, you may be in for a most interesting evening."

"With some of the women I've known in Baltimore, perhaps. But Vera won't be as willing to part with her virtue in exchange for a few sweet words."

Clarence thought for a moment. "I do admit, Vera is more devout than most. You're in for a challenge, my good man. Perhaps that's why you find her to be such an intriguing enigma."

Chapter 5

Later that evening, Byron arrived at the Sharpe farm to drive Vera to church. She greeted him at the door, looking ravishing as always. By this time, he knew the color of all her dresses; tonight, she had donned his particular favorite, a pink frock that made her blond locks seem brighter, brought out the roses in her cheeks, and nipped her small waist.

Lest he make her feel uncomfortable, he didn't allow his appreciative gaze to linger on her too long. "I'm here yet again to drive a beautiful lady to church. Byron Gates, reliable escort extraordinaire!" He bent low at the waist and swept his arm in a grand gesture, hat in hand.

"A beautiful lady?" Vera blushed.

"Yes, you and no one else." His voice softened, and he drank in Vera's loveliness until he felt the presence of another. He looked beyond Vera to see her sister standing a few feet away in the parlor, holding the baby. Her expression was hardly agreeable. "Good evening, Mrs. Sharpe."

"Good evening." Spoken through tightened lips, the salutation sounded forced.

Her terse expression surprised him, since Vera's sister had been pleasant immediately after the picnic. And Clarence promised that he had praised Byron when Elmer made inquiries.

Still, Byron had been greeted in such a manner before in houses where he was wearing out his welcome. Had he already stepped over the line with the Sharpes? Or had his reputation merely preceded him? He decided not to consider either possibility, especially since he had been a gentleman at the picnic and committed no romantic crime by escorting Vera to and from church each week.

Elmer emerged from another part of the house. "Good evening, Byron." Elmer's tone conveyed warmth, the type of warmth that told him he understood Byron. Had he been as much of a rogue in his younger days as Byron had been? Byron couldn't be sure, but he was glad to have an ally. An important one at that.

"Good evening to you, Elmer. I trust all went well with the birth of the new foal last night."

"Yes, though for a while, it was touch and go. But the little horse is a beauty, just like his mother."

"Indeed." Byron remembered another beauty. He gazed once more at Vera, the lovely blond before him. He couldn't help but find her tempting. Yes, he had

264

come to rural Maryland to change, to rid himself of his roguish ways. So why had he run into Vera? Was she really so appealing, or was he simply too attracted to women of any persuasion to know what—or who—was right?

He could meditate on the possibilities all day and never find the answer, so he decided to focus on the present. "We had best be leaving, lest we be late for the service."

"Yes, I do hate to walk in late," Vera agreed.

As they traversed the lawn, he halfway listened to her talk as he helped her onto the buggy for their brief journey to church. The habit of lending only a fraction of his attention was a practiced skill he had developed from listening to many women chatter. He found most of them to be content with the occasional nod, making him wonder whether they cared if he listened to them or not. Just as he granted himself a mental pat on the back for his sly ways, guilt stabbed him. Hadn't he just thought to himself how he found Vera fascinating? Then he should be willing to listen to her. At that moment, he vowed to mend his ways.

Open ears offered a pleasant surprise. Vera proved herself well versed on the topics of the day and even offered opinions that could stand up to logic. Not like the other women he'd known. His off-and-on attention in the past had yielded information about Paris fashions and the cost of Irish lace. Vera didn't seem to concern herself with such trivialities, yet her style of dress looked impeccable. Even better, Vera sought and listened to his thoughts and opinions. She grew more fascinating by the moment.

They reached a point of companionable silence, a fact that didn't bother him and didn't seem to vex her either. With a side-glance, he observed the sheen of her blond tresses, the high color in her cheeks, and the enthusiastic turn of her pouty lips. Temptation reached fiery tentacles around him.

He wondered if she struggled, too. He suspected she did. More than once, he had caught her viewing him, then looking away so quickly that he knew she hoped he hadn't noticed. Blushes and intense fanning were other indicators to him that Vera burned hot underneath her cool exterior. Reading such hints had become an accomplishment, one that served him well as he pursued flirtations in the past. Remembering they were on their way to church, he resisted the urge to pull the carriage off to a grassy patch on the side of the road so he could kiss her.

"A penny for your thoughts," she ventured.

He startled. "A mere penny?"

She laughed softly. "I might have more in my purse, but I would hate to divert money from the collection plate."

"Well, we can't have that, now can we? Especially for such a poor investment as the content of my thoughts." He turned serious. "I doubt you'd want to know what I'm thinking."

"Oh, but I do." Her eyes widened.

"What would you say if I told you I was thinking about what it might be like to kiss you?"

She gasped, her expression a mixture of pleasure, surprise, and uncertainty. "Mr. Gates! Are you always so bold?"

He sent her his most appealing sideways grin. "I find I am not bold at all in the presence of homely women."

She fanned herself and stared at passing trees. "I do not give out my favors frivolously. Not even for a comely and sophisticated man such as yourself."

"I know you don't. That fact makes you all the more appealing in my eyes."

She fanned herself with renewed vigor. "I declare, how you do make me blush!"

"So there is a bit of the coquette in you, after all."

"The coquette in me doesn't show herself too often. In fact, she can disappear just like that." Vera closed her fan with a decisive snap and placed it in her lap. "Now to be perfectly serious. I will not kiss anyone but the man who will one day be my husband."

"Really?" Relief that Clarence was wrong about Vera's fortitude as well as a feeling of disappointment presented themselves. He covered his inner turbulence with a quip. "What a quaint notion."

"I don't find it quaint at all. Good morals are always in style," she pointed out.

He noted the white clapboard building on the horizon, its painted steeple pointing toward heaven. "Indeed. I suppose our timely arrival at church is proof positive of that fact."

"Yes, and not a moment too soon, either."

"Now really, I am not uncouth," he assured her. "And to prove my point, I promise to be the perfect gentleman from now on. I won't even broach the subject of a kiss again without your leave."

"If I were playing the coquette, I would venture the observation that your resolution is regrettable."

"Yes, it is." He tried to keep his stare from her full lips. "Regrettable indeed."

Clarence was waiting for Byron when he returned from escorting Vera to church. He sat on the porch, rocking back and forth, and motioned for Byron to join him. "So how did things go with the little mouse?"

He flinched and then leaned into a porch column rather than taking comfort in sitting in an available wicker chair. "I wish you wouldn't call her that."

"Call her what?"

"A mouse, of course. Must you sound so condescending?"

"So sorry, old man." A twitch of his lips revealed Clarence's apology was less than sincere. "So how did it go? Did you kiss her?"

Byron debated whether or not to tell Clarence the awful truth. Not so long ago, he wouldn't have hesitated to change the subject, or even to exaggerate so it would appear that Vera couldn't resist his substantial charms. "I didn't try."

"You didn't try?" Clarence didn't bother to conceal his shock.

Byron folded his arms. "No. I broached the subject, but she wasn't willing. I promised I'd be the perfect gentleman, and I will continue to do so."

Clarence sniffed. "I would think someone as naive as Miss Howard would have fainted with delight at the prospect of your attentions. Surely you are not losing your touch?"

Byron bristled in spite of himself. "Vera is not just any woman. She's different from the others, just as I told you. Her refusal only proves me right."

Clarence chuckled. "You had better hope she's not too different. Or else you'll lose the bet."

"I've told you, there is no bet." Byron's voice sounded as irritated as he felt. He stopped himself before he could say anything he might regret.

Clarence laughed and rose from his seat. "Come on in, old man. Let's call it a night."

Byron made a show of looking at the stars. "In just a moment."

"Planning your next strategy?"

"No, I'm only gathering my thoughts."

Clarence shrugged. "Whatever you say. Are you and I still meeting tomorrow morning for our horseback ride?"

"Of course. I'm looking forward to that."

Byron turned to look at the night sky and heard the door shut behind his friend. The solitude left him with a sense of freedom and weightiness combined. He prayed he hadn't offended Vera with his boldness. For the first time, he noticed that he truly was concerned about his behavior in relation to a woman—Vera.

Lord, guide my relationship with Vera.

He took in a breath. Had he just prayed? How many years had transpired since he tried to communicate with God? Hadn't he been a boy wearing pajamas, kneeling by the bed? He remembered the simple prayer his mother listened to each night. "Bless Mama. Bless Papa. Bless Katie. Bless Jenny. Bless Billy. Bless Gertie. Bless Bobby. And bless Bitsie. And thank Thee for Thy gracious mercy. I ask Thee in the name of Thy Son, Jesus. Amen."

Byron grinned. His parents were both blessed with good health despite their advanced years, still abiding in that same house. His brothers and sisters—now known as Katherine, Virginia, William, Gertrude, and Robert—were grown and living in various forms of contentment. Long ago, the cat had met her reward—a paradise of soft pillows and unlimited catnip and cream, according to Mother.

Ah, for those years of untarnished joy. Perhaps that's what Vera possessed that appealed to him so much, aside from her obvious physical attributes. The beauty of fresh innocence. He realized more than ever that he would not be the one to sully such loveliness in any way.

Chapter 6

Days later, Vera quivered with anticipation as she and Byron approached the Sharpes' house after the Sunday morning worship service. Looking at her lap, she was pleased to see that her blue summer frock looked fresh despite the heat. Only two small strands had freed themselves from her chignon. She consoled herself with the hope that they didn't make her appear too mussed.

She stole a glance at Byron. He appeared as handsome as ever, with his refined good looks and posture that bespoke genuine confidence. On their last encounter, she had summoned all of her strength of will not to allow him to kiss her, and she knew she had to be vigilant in resisting his charms. Would he try to kiss her again? She hoped so. And she hoped not. For if he did, she didn't know what she might do.

Lord, grant me strength.

The Sharpes' buggy pulled in right behind them. No doubt, Alice had insisted they not lag too far behind, insuring that Byron act as the perfect gentleman. Vera had avoided talking to Alice about Byron since Wednesday night, but she wouldn't be able to hold off her sister's probing questions forever. The women knew each other well. Alice surely had sensed that something had happened between Byron and Vera. True, the fact that he mentioned kissing changed everything, showing Vera that Byron did harbor romantic notions about her. Her own response to the idea told Vera that her feelings for Byron had traversed onto new ground.

She didn't want the time with Byron to end. "Won't you join me for Sunday dinner?" she asked. "I baked a pudding for dessert."

"A pudding? What flavor?"

She twisted her lips into a wry grin. Surely he didn't care what flavor as long as they were in companionship. Realizing he was jesting, she shot back, "What flavor do you like?"

He shrugged. "Oh, let me see. Mango. Pineapple. Cricket."

"Oh, you!" She tapped him on the arm and laughed with more gusto than she had felt in some time. "If you want to wile away the afternoon with us, you'll have to settle on plain old vanilla and thank the Lord for it."

"Vanilla it is, then." Vera noticed that his gaze fixed on the Sharpes disembarking from their vehicle. "Are you sure your sister won't mind?"

"You are my guest, and I'll be doing my part in the dinner preparations, so there."

Byron chuckled. "You are getting bolder. I hope your family won't blame your high spirits on my influence."

"If they do, I'll thank them. It's about time I developed high spirits." She nodded once and took the hand he offered to help her descend from the carriage. His strong grip made her feel secure. Somehow, she knew that even if she tripped his powerful arms would shield her from a fall.

Alice approached, holding the baby. "Thank you for escorting my sister to worship, Mr. Gates."

"My pleasure, Mrs. Sharpe."

"And you should be happy that I invited Mr. Gates to dine with us." Vera put on her most agreeable smile.

Elmer joined Alice. "You did? Good. It's about time you had Sunday dinner with us, Byron. We men can talk while the women fix dinner."

Byron grinned back. "Yes, I'm always primed for a good discussion concerning the news of the day."

Though Alice's demeanor indicated she wasn't thrilled with Byron's inclusion in their dinner plans, she didn't comment. Grateful, Vera confined her conversation to the contents of the sermon and the details of preparing the meal.

Over roast beef and mashed potatoes, Elmer kept Byron talking, and Vera appreciated that her sister refrained from saying anything unpleasant to their guest. Byron complimented every dish and raved over how smart little Paul already appeared. Vera could see by the way Alice's expression softened during those times that Byron's charms were working their wonders.

Vera knew Alice didn't want her to make a poor match, hence her reticence to accept Byron unabashedly. She prayed Alice would change her mind. At least Elmer was on her side, and Paul, in his innocence, smiled and gurgled at Byron. Vera enjoyed witnessing the connection Byron made with the youngest Sharpe. She sensed that Byron's magnetism could easily turn from attracting women to coaxing his children into obedience.

"Time to do the dishes, Vera," Alice said even before they partook of dessert.

"Oh, but I promised Byron some vanilla pudding." She suppressed a little laugh.

"Let me help you with the dishes, dear," Elmer offered.

"Thank you, Elmer." Vera made a mental note to do something nice for Elmer the next time the opportunity presented itself. "I'll dish up the pudding. Might we take dessert in the parlor?"

"Of course," Elmer said quickly. "Would you feel too put-upon if Alice and I had our dessert in the kitchen?"

In spite of mild objections and agreements whispered hastily by Alice to Elmer, Vera soon found herself alone in the parlor with Byron. She had brought in the pudding along with coffee on a tray and set the refreshments on the table.

Alice and Elmer could be heard conversing in the kitchen.

"Seems like Alice and Elmer are having a good time. Maybe they're glad to get away from us," Byron joked. Just as quickly, his expression grew wistful. "Aren't they lucky to be so in love after all this time?"

"They haven't been married so very long. Only six years. But you're right. Love can expire long before that."

"I suppose not having the pressures of fast-paced modern city life can add to one's contentment." Byron took a taste of the promised vanilla pudding.

Vera froze in place, watching for his reaction to the dessert. To her delight, he shut his eyes and smiled dreamily.

"Mmm. That is some kind of good!" He looked at her and took another spoonful.

"Do you think I could please you if I baked a pudding every day?"

"Forever."

She caught something in his gaze that told her he was serious, but just as quickly, the telltale light left his eyes and he composed himself. Feeling a flush of mixed emotions, she hoped her own expression didn't reveal too much.

He cleared his throat. "On another topic, I've been observing you for a while now in a variety of situations. Will you let me in on a secret?"

"A secret?"

"Yes. You are so much at peace. Surely it isn't because you're so sheltered from the world?"

She felt her face grow hot. "I—I suppose I am what one would call sheltered. Surely much less worldly than the women you usually meet."

"You can trust me when I say that you compare most favorably to other women."

"Really?"

"Really. You need not seem so surprised." He paused. "Although I wonder if you wouldn't mind leaving your protected world for a trip now and again. When last we spoke, you indicated you were eager to hear about my travels."

Relieved that he had shifted the subject, she decided the best course of action was to begin a vigorous debate. "Yes, I do enjoy your stories of adventure."

He took a sip of coffee. "No doubt. Being a companion to a lady who remains in her bed at home most of the time as you were in Baltimore, and now helping your sister here in the country—well, neither situation lends itself to adventure."

"Maybe not the type of adventure you consider. But my life is exciting enough for me. I am enthralled each day to see how Paul has grown, how much progress he is making. I see Alice and Elmer's happiness at the prospect of welcoming the new life she is carrying. I am thankful for the work I have to do, for the ability to read my Bible. In everything, I see the wonder of God's creation. That, I assure you, is more than enough excitement for me."

"So it is not excitement you seek in the traditional way, but peace."

"Yes. Do you mind that terribly?"

"To my surprise, I don't."

She laughed. "I would still like to travel someday, although in the safety of modern conveyances. I'm not sure I'm one for an African safari or for climbing mountains in Switzerland."

"I've been on both types of expeditions, and though they were intriguing, I have no special desire to repeat them." Tasting his coffee, he seemed to ponder her words. "So where do you find your peace?"

"I was hoping it would be obvious that it is derived from my faith."

He didn't consider her question long. "Yes. I suppose it is."

"Nevertheless, I'm sorry you felt the need to ask. Am I such a poor ambassador for Christ?"

He set down his cup. "Indeed not! It is not your witness that is to blame for my obtuseness. Rather, it is my failure to see what is plainly in front of my face. Forgive me."

"Of course."

Relief evidenced itself in his small sigh. Then his expression tightened. "I hope you will continue to be so patient with me when I make my next confession."

"Confession?" Hadn't she heard enough bad revelations about Byron? What else could be left? She braced herself and forced her voice to sound strong. "What is it? You can tell me."

"Thank you for your confidence." He paused. "After some thought and prayer, and under duress, on Wednesday morning, I'll be taking Clarence to Baltimore for a few days."

"Oh?" Though she tried to hold it back, she knew disappointment expressed itself upon her face.

"Yes," Byron answered. "I shall miss accompanying you to the midweek service."

"As will I. But I must ask, why are you taking Clarence to Baltimore at this time? Is there a particular reason?"

"It's to settle a wager."

"You made a bet with Clarence?"

"No, although he thinks I did, and he refuses to be convinced otherwise. I can see by his persistent references that he won't rest until one of us declares victory or defeat. So I have decided simply to treat him to a night on the town so I can be released of this perceived obligation."

"Knowing Clarence, I have no doubt he would resort to trickery to gain a night of entertainment."

Byron chuckled. "I must take the blame since my past caused Clarence to believe I would be eager to bet. I pray that the tentacles of my past are short ones and that I can soon embark on a trouble-free future. May I beg your indulgence and patience?"

"Of course. I will put my trust in the Lord that He will walk with you as you write the end of the dark chapters in your life. I will pray earnestly for that to happen, by your leave."

"Yes. Please do pray. I plan to resist temptation, but in the thick of it, one's resolve can weaken."

At that moment, Vera said a silent prayer that he would hold strong.

Chapter 7

An hour later when Byron went into the Stanley house, Clarence called out to him from his study. Byron joined him.

Clarence grinned at him from his usual chair and set down his paper. "Well, well, well. You're later than usual, old man. I had to dine alone. Does that mean Vera invited you in for dinner?"

He nodded as he took a seat.

"You don't seem as enthusiastic as a man should when he's making such fine progress. I thought she was nearly falling all over herself to get you accepted by her sister. What happened? Was Alice rude to you at dinner?"

"She wasn't too friendly, but I think she was beginning to warm up to me by meal's end."

"Ah, that old Gates charm. Why am I not surprised?" His face fell. "Uh oh. I suppose this means I'll be the one paying for the night on the town."

"Oh no you won't. That's what I wanted to tell you. I know you won't rest until this idea of a bet is settled, and no matter how many times I tell you I have no intention of betting on my wooing of Vera, you insist we still have a wager."

"Now, am I as slippery as all that?" Clarence clucked his tongue.

"Worse."

Clarence laughed. "I suppose I am. So what is it you want to tell me?"

"To be rid of the idea you have of a wager, I want to offer you a night on the town in Baltimore and call it even."

Clarence joined the fingertips of both hands and touched his clean-shaven chin. "You're conceding? What a disappointment. Things are getting interesting."

"Interesting for you, perhaps, but I desire nothing more than to rid myself of this albatross." Without thinking, Byron looked at his chest as if expecting to see a dead bird hanging from a rope around his neck.

"Have you no pride?" Clarence jested.

"Not anymore. At least not the type of pride that causes me to worry about losing and winning bets."

"All right, then. I'll be more than happy to spend a night out with you. I'll need a few days to settle matters here, and off we'll go."

"I thought as much, which is why I didn't plan to leave until Wednesday. I'll write and let Mother know we'll be staying at the house."

"Have you told her about your country mouse?"

"No." Byron flinched. The notion of telling Mother she could forget her dreams of Daisy as her daughter-in-law was not something he anticipated with glee.

"I wish I could be there to witness the day Vera Howard meets the formidable Mrs. Gates. I wonder how little Vera will seem beside the sophisticated Miss Estes?"

"They are a contrast, certainly. But Mother will come around. Once she realizes how Vera and I feel about one another and that Vera would make anyone a fine daughter-in-law—not to mention, my wife—she'll be pleased."

"I still can't believe you've maintained any interest in Vera after all she's put you through."

"All she's put me through?"

Clarence shuddered. "That's right. Forcing you to sit through boring sermons and church socials, refusing to let you kiss her, and then acting as though she's better than you just because she can listen to the preacher drone for hours without her eyes glazing over. She should be on her knees thanking you for bringing some life into her boring existence. Before you came to visit, I assure you, she was the perfect little mouse. No man wanted her. And no other man ever will."

Byron felt the blood rise to his face. "I've decked men for lesser insults." He balled his right hand into a fist and punched it once in his open left palm.

Clarence blanched. "I beg your pardon. I suppose I didn't realize that this is not a game to you anymore. She's really gotten to you, hasn't she?"

"Yes," Byron admitted.

"And so quickly, too. I never thought I'd see the day." Clarence shook his head. "It's always hard to see a good man like you succumb."

"That's the problem. I'm not a good man. But I will be. You'll see."

———

"Soup's wonderful," Elmer commented later over supper. The three were dining late, having already put the baby to bed for the night.

"I do believe it is every bit as good as the roast you served for dinner," Vera observed.

"Did you really taste it?" Alice added salt to her bowl of soup. "You seemed too interested in Mr. Gates to take in much of what you were eating."

"Yes, I'm surprised you even realized you ate roast," Elmer teased.

"Just barely. Although I am pleased that he enjoyed the pudding."

"Pudding. Yes," Alice remarked. "So just what did the two of you talk about while you were in the parlor?"

"Alice, can't you let them have a little privacy?" Elmer chided.

"When he admits he wants to court her and stops pussyfooting around, then they can have some privacy," Alice said.

Vera couldn't believe Alice even considered the possibility. "Are you saying you wouldn't mind?"

Alice gave a slight shrug. "He is charming, I must admit. But he hasn't won me over yet. Not completely, anyway."

Vera exchanged hopeful looks with Elmer.

"I worry," said Alice, "because he didn't seem to be in the best of spirits when he departed this afternoon."

"Oh. That." Vera hesitated. "Well, he's going to Baltimore for a spell, and I don't think he's happy about it."

"Doesn't want to leave you, eh?" Elmer ventured before drinking down his milk.

Vera's face flushed hotter than her soup. "I'd like to think that's part of the reason, but he isn't happy about why he's going."

"Not bad news, I hope," Elmer said.

Alice didn't echo his sentiment in words, but as a concerned expression crossed her face, she stopped eating.

"Not really. He has to take Clarence out for an evening."

"Oh, he has to, does he?" Alice's voice rose with suspicion. "If he's taking Clarence Stanley to Baltimore, that can only mean trouble."

"I'm aware that cities have a reputation for harboring evil, but that doesn't mean they will be doing anything wrong," Vera said.

"You know Clarence better than that. Even if Byron Gates's reputation were pure white, it's unlikely Clarence would be up to much good," Alice objected. "Did he tell you where they were going, or what their plans are?"

"No."

"Then I wouldn't trust either of them."

"Maybe you wouldn't, but I trust Byron," Vera said. "I think he is trying to change his ways and I'd like to give him the chance to show me that he means what he says."

"If you want my opinion, I think there's a chance he's putting on an act for you, Vera, and chasing other women behind your back," Alice said. "Why else would he develop this sudden need to go to Baltimore?"

"He could very well have some business to attend to while he's there," Elmer pointed out. "After all, his family still lives there, and that's where his family business is based."

"True, Elmer," Vera said. "I have no doubt he'll accomplish some business while he's there. And all will be well after he entertains Clarence this one night."

"So you would like to think," Alice noted. "I don't enjoy being cynical, but what if you're wrong?"

"Of course I wouldn't want to have a suitor court me if he's only putting on an act. But I have taken your advice to heart, Alice, even though you don't think I have been listening. I have been praying for discernment. I truly believe the Lord will show me if Byron proves false."

"Perhaps, but He also gave you an earthly sister to guide you. Vera, you should be grateful for a sister like me. I don't want to see you fall into the hands of a cad."

"Our Lord is a God of second chances. Even seven times. And seventy times seven. You don't seem to be willing to give Byron one."

"I appreciate your compassion, but you are too naive to know what is best for you," Alice said. "With Mother and Father gone, you need our protection."

"Yes," Elmer agreed, "but only up to a point. After all, Vera lived on her own in Baltimore, and she conducted her affairs without reproach while she worked there."

Alice paused only momentarily. "I suppose you're right. I'm sorry, Vera. I really do mean well."

Vera nodded. "I know you do. And I'm grateful to have a sister who cares."

That night, Byron wanted only to retire early, but Clarence was too excited by the prospect of the trip to sleep. He insisted that they engage in a game of chess.

Byron moved a knight and watched Clarence promptly capture the piece. "Good move."

"If only you concentrated on chess as much as you seem to be preoccupied with Vera Howard. I must confess, I am amazed by your persistence with her."

"Why is that? Am I a known quitter?" Byron moved a pawn.

Clarence studied the board and spoke without moving his eyes from a bishop. "No. But you are not known to change your ways for any woman. And while I must say I envy your fortitude in wanting to turn over a new leaf, do you think God would want your motive to be so you could capture a woman? It looks suspiciously like that's just what you might be doing."

"Is that so?" He watched Clarence make his next move.

"Yes." Clarence leaned back in his leather chair and crossed his arms.

Because the criticism came from a trusted friend, Byron took no offense. Rather, he contemplated the possibility while only halfway studying the chessboard. "Yes, I can see why it might appear that I'm not sincere in my motives. And you're right that no man should use God as a means to fulfill earthly desires. But I came here to visit you without knowing Vera at all. And I had already decided even before I boarded the train to come here that I wanted to seek a life that showed respect to God. No longer do I want a life of useless frivolity."

"And Vera has helped you stay on the new course."

"I don't deny that. Isn't the fact that she inspires me to her credit?" Byron moved a pawn, not caring whether or not the move would sacrifice the piece in short order.

"I suppose," Clarence conceded. "She always did impress me as the type more suited to a convent than a dance hall."

Byron looked to his friend. "She would consider that a compliment, although

I know you don't mean it as such."

"Instead of letting those silly Baltimore debutantes discourage you, old man, why don't you seek a more adventurous type? Someone who's nothing like Vera. She doesn't fit your style."

He lifted his forefinger, mimicking a schoolmaster. "Correction. She didn't fit my style. But she does now."

"You've changed that much?" Clarence moved a pawn.

"I'd like to think so. And for good reason," Byron said. "It's not as though my former life was bringing me joy and comfort. Disgrace and disrespect was more like it."

"Maybe you should enter the ministry."

"Maybe that's the bet I should have taken instead of the one you offered."

"Ah, but ministers aren't supposed to be betting men."

"True, they are men of faith." Byron advanced another pawn even though he wasn't sure that was the best move.

Clarence captured the piece. "I'm surprised Vera has managed to hold your attention all this time. I must have underestimated her charm." He fingered the white pawn that was his prize and then set it back in its proper place in the wooden box from whence it came. "But I'm even more surprised by the way you seem determined to change your lifestyle and attitude. Why, it appears you truly can no longer concentrate properly on a simple chess match."

"I must let you win once in a great while," Byron responded. "After all, you have been kind to show me your hospitality all this time."

"Let me win indeed. Just for that, this will be the shortest, most devastating match on record." A mischievous glint that bordered on the vengeful entered Clarence's eyes.

Byron's lips contracted into a wry grin. "That's the spirit. Now the match will start to get interesting."

"Care to place a bet?"

"No." Byron didn't even let a hint of mischief or mirth color his voice. "No, I don't."

"Pity."

"I have much more important matters to occupy my mind."

Clarence's eyebrows shot up. "You mean, something—or someone—other than Vera Howard?"

"I sent a letter to my father about my intentions."

"Your intentions? Are you saying you intend to court Vera Howard?"

Byron captured a knight. "Regrettably, despite my success with Mrs. Sharpe today, I don't think I enjoy enough good standing to entertain such a prospect. At least not yet. No, it's about another change in my life. One that I think will please him indeed."

The following day, Byron was surprised to receive not a letter but a wire from his father. The elder Mr. Gates was not known for extravagance, so the costly form of communication indicated the message contained a matter of import. As he read it, Byron's hands shook, an uncommon occurrence for one so confident.

Whereas Father had splurged on the telegram, the economy of words was evident. Yet they said enough: *Daisy Estes.*

Chapter 8

A few days later as Byron readied himself to go to Baltimore, he tried to keep his mind off Daisy Estes. How could Father have come up with such an unfeeling response to his letter—her name appearing on an impersonal telegram?

When he heard a knock on the door to his room, Byron expected his visitor to be a maid bearing freshly laundered linens. "Come in."

"Sorry to disturb you, sir, but this just arrived." Clarence's valet handed him a letter bearing Father's precise handwriting.

Not surprised that Father chose to follow up his initial correspondence, Byron nodded and accepted the missive. He took a seat in the leather chair and waited for the valet to exit before he read it:

> *Byron,*
>
> *I trust you received my wire and that the name* Daisy Estes *gave you pause as you waited, no doubt, for this letter to arrive. I realize you needed this time in the country to reflect upon your life. As you know, I am pleased that you have finally realized the time has come for you to throw off the ways of carefree bachelorhood to seek the more fulfilling rewards of marriage and eventual fatherhood. Not only is a man of your position expected to make such plans, but also, indeed, to do so is his duty to God, country, and family.*
>
> *While I am on the topic of religion, your mother was thrown into ecstasy by the news that you are seeking our Savior in a real way. Indeed, I was forced to retrieve the smelling salts to prevent her from swooning. I trust the next time you have news of such import to share that you will caution your mother to remain seated.*
>
> *But I digress. The Savior has blessed our lives with His abiding presence, and you know that we believe Him to be more than just a genie in a bottle to grant our wishes, however worthy those wishes might be. I pray your spiritual journey is not a trivial pastime for you but one that will increase your richness of life.*

Byron paused in his reading and cringed. Father's observation, in its truth, hurt. He tapped the letter on the arm of the chair before he resumed reading:

Now as for richness of life, I have a word of caution for you regarding this little diversion you have found for yourself in the fresh country air. I am quite aware of and embarrassed by the outcome of your most recent flirtation with Miss Reynolds. Her rejection of you is widely known, though I skirt the issue and provide nebulous answers just shy of lying to protect what's left of your reputation whenever any of our acquaintances hint of anything less than honorable. I only pray your poor mother isn't exposed to stories of your tomfoolery. Surely the refined ladies she befriends are either unaware of your mischief or are too polite to inquire.

I can't help but wonder if the incident with Miss Reynolds is at least part of the reason why you have taken on this sudden and unexpected interest in religious matters. Regardless of how He chooses to reach you, I shall not complain.

Yet I caution you not to confuse spiritual and physical matters. I implore you to remember that a flirtation with a country mouse is all in good fun, but do remember that a fine woman, Daisy, is here at home, waiting in the wings for you. Rather than spurning her by carrying on out in the country, you should be grateful her father is a friend of mine and that the two of us—as well as your mothers—anticipate the joyous day when our two families will unite through your marriage.

I hope and pray that you will reflect mightily upon the content of this letter. I look forward to seeing you when you arrive here in town this Wednesday.

Yours,
Father

Despite the fact he was in danger of being overheard by servants in the area, Byron let out a groan that reached all four corners of his room. Perhaps he should have made things clear as to where he stood with Daisy before he left town. Then again, avoiding unpleasant situations and news had been part of his old life—before Vera.

Flirting had seemed so amusing at the time, with both parties exchanging flattering words that lifted the spirits. Harmless trivialities, indeed. Or were they? Apparently not. Perhaps the pastor of Vera's church was right. Coy words, empty promises whispered under the moonlight were corrupt because they could lead to carnal sin and emotional pain, both with long-term consequences. When he first heard the sermon, Byron thought the pastor was making much ado about nothing. But now that Father's letter was in his hands, he could see that he had created a most undesirable situation for all concerned. A situation that was not going to resolve itself with ease.

He had to make amends. He knew how, but he didn't like the prospect. If only he could find another way.

Hearing the clomping of a horse's hooves on the dusty path leading to the Sharpe farmhouse, Vera kept her hands in the dough as she kneaded but still managed to get a peek.

She recognized the black horse with a star-shaped spot around his left eye as Byron's and knew that the man of whom she had grown fond had come for a visit. "Byron!"

Wishing she hadn't blurted out his name, she scanned the portions of the dining room and hallway she could see through the open kitchen doors and sent up a prayer of thanks that she didn't see Alice, nor did she hear her sister protest Byron's approach. Alice, now well into her confinement, had taken on the habit of stealing an afternoon nap. Surely she and little Paul were both sleeping soundly. Elmer, out in the fields, would have little to protest in Byron's presence and was unlikely to leave his work this early.

Vera wiped her sticky hands clean on a damp cotton cloth and wondered if she should entertain a man with such a passive chaperone in the house, but to awaken Alice was taking a chance that, without Elmer's softening presence, her sister would encourage Byron to depart. And for him to make an appearance, Vera sensed he had something important to tell her.

Not willing to appear too eager, she busied herself with an imaginary spot on the counter until he knocked. As soon as he did, she rushed to greet him. "Byron. I didn't expect to see you again before you left for Baltimore. Is everything all right?"

He tipped his hat. "Vera, I beg your indulgence for my unexpected visit. I hope you will overlook my boldness and allow me a few moments with you?"

Did he really think he had to ask? She retained her composure. "Of course."

She realized the time had come to relocate since he still stood on the back stoop, hovering in the kitchen doorway. "Might I pour you a glass of lemonade? Perhaps we might sit out in the yard under the trees where it's cooler."

"That sounds like a fine idea to me." He looked past Vera into the house. "That is, if my presence won't offend your sister."

"She's asleep, and besides, I think you might have assuaged her heart a little the last time you were here. Especially since little Paul took to you so well." She decided not to repeat Alice's worries and speculations about Byron's trip to the city.

Respecting propriety, Byron waited on the porch while Vera made haste to pour lemonade. The couple then settled with their refreshments on stiff wicker chairs under a large oak tree with outstretched branches. For a few moments, they sat in companionable silence. A soft breeze blew against Vera's face. The air was welcome after her work in the hot kitchen all afternoon. She listened to the wind blowing through the leafy oak trees that dotted the yard.

The mixed-breed dogs, Spot and Peanut, inspected Byron and sniffed at his knees, asking for pats on the head before they ran off to romp on their own. Mouser, the cat who lived up to her name, took a well-earned nap on a vacant chair.

Having befriended the dogs, Byron stared off into the blue sky with its feathery white clouds. Was he trying to discern shapes in the cloud formations? She smiled at the thought that a grown man like Byron, so full of self-assurance, would be playing a boyish game. She sighed. Amid such peace, all felt right with the world. If only she could freeze the moment in time and enjoy it longer.

She discerned that such a wish was not to be as she watched Byron set his empty glass on the patch of lawn near the chair.

"Might I offer you another glass of lemonade?" she asked.

"Oh no, thank you, although the offer is tempting."

She looked at him. His words conveyed pleasantness, yet his facial expression had tensed. Obviously his visit involved more than letting her know he would be staying in the country a few more days, along with passing the time with refreshment and conversation. She wanted to ask what he was thinking but held back, sensing that he would reveal his meaning to her soon.

Byron's glass tipped to its side. Vera made no move to retrieve it since the grass had cushioned its fall. Byron didn't seem to notice the minor mishap. The obtuseness was unusual for him.

He cleared his throat. "Vera, I have something to tell you."

"Oh." She wished she could have uttered a more intelligent response, but anything she could say of any content would be groping in the dark. "Does your news have something to do with your trip?"

He nodded.

"You—you'll be returning soon?" She hoped her question didn't cause her to appear bold or, even worse, desperate.

Byron's expression didn't convey such an interpretation of her words. "Yes, that part of the plan hasn't changed. The visit will be brief."

She kept herself from breathing an audible sigh of relief. Curiosity piqued, she continued. "You'll be seeing your family, I assume. And all is well with them, I hope?"

He hesitated.

"Unless it's none of my concern," she rushed to apologize. "I didn't mean to pry. Forgive me."

"No, you're not prying. That's a perfectly sensible query. And yes, I will be returning to my childhood home. My parents inherited the town home from my grandparents. I can't imagine it not being occupied by some of the Gates family."

"My family has been in this area for generations, as well. I know exactly what you mean."

"I do look forward to my visit with family. And of course, I have a few pressing business matters to attend to while I'm there. As you undoubtedly have learned, work takes no vacation."

She considered the batch of dough she had just prepared and remembered the other chores awaiting her. "How right you are. In that event, I wish you a wonderful visit and smooth resolution of your business affairs while you are in Baltimore."

"Thank you."

She perceived he had more to tell her. What could it be? She took the opportunity of silence to express her own thoughts. "I cannot tell you how gladdened I am that you stopped by today. You have offered me a most pleasant diversion."

"And you have done likewise for me."

Silence visited once more. She could feel the electricity between them. His feelings for her had grown. Though she had turned down his request before, now she longed for a kiss.

Chapter 9

Vera wondered if Byron felt the same. Did he want to kiss her as much as she yearned for him? She couldn't discern from his facial expression what he was thinking.

Alice's warning that Byron might be going to Baltimore to seek a sinful type of fun pulled at her mind. Vera didn't doubt that plenty of women in the city would enjoy his attentions. Yet he wasn't acting like a man in a hurry to visit another woman.

"I hope you don't mind my saying that I will miss you enormously while I'm away." Byron leaned toward her and looked into her eyes.

"No." Her voice was but a whisper, though his sentiment heartened her.

"Will you miss me just as much?" He sounded shy, somehow.

His vulnerability, uncharacteristic for Byron, emboldened her to take a chance. If he was toying with her, the response she gave would tell. If he had developed true feelings for her, she would learn that truth. She was ready for that certainty, whether it meant admitting Alice was right and putting all thoughts of Byron out of her mind once and for all or if it meant she could think of spending her life forever with him.

"Yes. I will miss you terribly, too. Do say you'll be returning as soon as your business in Baltimore is complete."

Her throat constricted, and she became conscious of her beating heart. She searched his face for signs of his authentic feelings. His eyes widened, and the corners of his mouth turned upward, though not too much. No matter how cool he tried to portray himself, she could see in that instant that he yearned for her as much as she did for him.

"I dreamed of such a response. I couldn't leave without your assurance that I had not mistaken your communication during our last meeting—that you indeed want me to return."

"Yes." As soon as her admission left her lips, she realized how bold she sounded. An attack of shyness forced her gaze to the ground.

"Then, yes. I promise I will return as soon as my mission is accomplished."

There was something in the tone of his voice she didn't like. She sought to discern his hidden meaning. "Mission? I thought you were entertaining Clarence. But now you're making your trip sound more urgent. Is it?"

"I'm afraid it is." He hesitated.

Vera watched his body tense. He tightened his jaw. As she waited for him to speak, Vera's thoughts ran wild. He said his family was doing well, so apparently no close relative suffered from an illness. But what about Byron himself? Had he developed odd physical symptoms that were causing him to seek a doctor's advice?

"Are you ill?" she blurted out.

A stunned look crossed his face. "Ill? But no." He pursed his lips. "Please forgive my lack of attention. What I have to say is not easy."

"Whatever it is, I will do my best to understand." She waited for him to enlighten her.

He hesitated.

Her mind played out another scenario. He had mentioned business. Was his family concern in trouble—a turn of events he didn't want to admit? Did he think he would be less desirable in her eyes if his business had fallen upon hard times?

"If your troubles are financial, please know that I only ask the Lord each day for enough."

"As the Lord's Prayer instructs us."

She nodded.

"I admire your attitude about money, Vera. Many women do not share your philosophy. But I can assure you, money is not my worry."

"Then do tell me," she begged. "My mind has already filled with too many unthinkable possibilities. Whatever do you mean by your mission?"

"I—I must visit a lady of my acquaintance."

Vera stiffened. "A lady?" Alice had never missed an opportunity to warn her that Byron had unfinished business with a number of women, so why was she surprised? She forced herself to remember that at least he trusted her enough to be honest. A lesser man would have hidden his reason for going to the city. "You're planning to visit a lady?"

"Yes. A nice, respectable lady. A lady who both of our families hope will join me in marriage."

Vera gasped. "Oh." She couldn't remember a time she had felt more distress, but she didn't dare express it. She had already made a fool of herself as it was. Her humiliation was such that at that moment she would have welcomed Alice's appearance to interrupt this conversation, even if she were bearing her most stern look and admonition.

Vera straightened herself in her chair. "You are a free man. You do not need my permission to see anyone you wish. I hope your visit with her is all you anticipate it will be." Had Vera been a woman of demonstrable emotions, she would have burst into tears, her voice quivering. But having been reared to be strong, she was able to maintain her composure. "So you are. . .promised. . .to this woman?"

Please, Lord, don't let it be so!

Byron wasted no time in consoling her. "No. Please don't think that. If I were, I never would have pursued any type of relationship with you. Unfortunately for our parents, neither the lady nor I wish to marry. At least, not each other."

Surprise, relief, and confusion reared their heads, leaving her in turmoil. "What? I'm afraid I still fail to understand."

"She has already told me that she has another beau who's been pursuing her."

"And that doesn't bother you?"

"Not in the least."

Not in the least. When had Vera heard four more lovely words? She couldn't recall. "Well, it's settled then, isn't it? You and she have agreed to part ways." Her voice sounded too hopeful, reflecting the unwelcome jealousy she felt.

"There were no ways to part. At least, not as far as I'm concerned."

"Really? Then how could your parents have come to the conclusion that the two of you were betrothed?" She paused. "I'm sorry. I'm not passing judgment. I'm trying to make sense of what you're saying."

"And rightfully so. If I am going to live my life as an honest man of integrity, as I hope to do from now into the future, I must be truthful in all of my dealings. Thank you, by your sweet spirit, devotion, and example, for encouraging me to that end." He sat back in his chair but didn't look at her. "I am putting myself at risk of sounding ungentlemanly by saying this, so please keep it in confidence. I'll begin by saying that I've known Daisy since we were children."

Vera didn't speak but held back her disdain. The fact that her rival had a name didn't ease her mind at all. She wished she hadn't heard the name. Vera concentrated on the fact that Byron was taking her into his confidence and kept listening.

"Our mothers thought we looked cute together when we were little, so they thought it would be a fine idea if one day we were to wed. No one paid attention to their plans. Even when we were older, both of us assumed our mothers would realize their fantasies were just that—idle dreams. We were sure once we made our intentions known to others, all plans would be forgotten. But they weren't."

"So you and Daisy never had romantic attachments?"

"Nothing beyond some unfortunate flirtations now and again. Neither of us took them seriously."

"Women are tenderhearted, Byron. Suppose Daisy did take you seriously?"

"But she didn't. I know her." His lips thinned into a firm line before he resumed his explanation. "Daisy has a good reputation, yet she is a flirt, often inviting the attentions of men. She is just as quick as any man to offer a flattering phrase or two."

"Oh!" Vera wondered how unsophisticated she must seem when Byron remembered Daisy. She tried not to wince.

"So you can see why Daisy is not for me. I would prefer someone. . .someone more reserved." He looked into her eyes. "Someone like you."

Vera didn't know what to say. She returned his feelings and wanted to admit it, but the words wouldn't leave her lips. She couldn't remember a time when she had been sorry that her mother had reared her to act in the reserved manner of a true lady. Her training had become so ingrained that she found it impossible to be bold at such a moment. When Byron spoke, dissolving her need to respond, she felt grateful.

"I trust you will keep this confidence to yourself." The tone of his voice indicated he didn't doubt she would.

"Of course. But did you love her at one time?" Almost afraid of the answer, she kept her voice to whisper.

"No, I did not. Not in a romantic way, as you mean it. And as I said, any silly flirtations between us are now firmly affixed in the past. Daisy, unlike my family, understood that no binding promises were ever made. At least, that is my impression. Our families—our fathers got in on the act once they learned of our mothers' enthusiasm—were the ones who jumped to the conclusions, painting the picture they wanted to see.

"So you must understand that it's not Daisy who concerns me, but my family. I simply feel that I must go to her and be absolutely sure that all parties are freed from any expectations whatsoever of our future together. This is not something I feel I should do by letter. This type of errand is better performed in person, even though the urge to take the coward's way out and resolve the matter by missive has crossed my mind more than once."

Sympathy for Byron filled her. "I am glad you are no longer a coward."

His returning smile looked wry. "You are certainly refreshing, Miss Vera Howard."

"Really? What did you expect me to say?"

"I don't know. I suppose some women would have screamed. Some would have cried. Others would have refused to see me again. One or two might have thrown a glass of lemonade in my face."

"My, but you do sound as though you've been through more than one incident involving women." She kept her voice teasing, but the question underneath was serious.

"Being the coward that I was, I kept unpleasant confrontations to a minimum. That is why I face this situation now." He smiled. "And I do thank you for not throwing lemonade at me."

"I prefer to drink it. Besides, I do especially like that suit you're wearing."

They laughed. Their shared humor only heightened their increasing bond.

Chapter 10

oments later, Vera managed to reenter the house without disturbing Alice. Examination of the waiting dough proved it was ready to be formed into rolls. She punched it down, then pulled the elastic ball from the bowl and, after flouring a space on the kitchen counter, began her task. Absorbed in her work, Vera hardly noticed when Alice emerged from her nap.

"Did I hear voices earlier, or was I dreaming?" Alice asked as she passed the threshold from the hall to the kitchen.

Vera hesitated but kept working the dough. "Byron dropped by."

"Byron?" Alice went for the teakettle. "I thought he was in Baltimore."

"Not yet. He soon will be. I served him a glass of lemonade in the backyard. I assure you: All was proper."

Vera waited for Alice to pry, but she seemed satisfied with the news that Byron would be gone for some length of time.

"Would you like some help?" Alice nodded toward the batch of dough.

"Certainly."

The two women sat at the kitchen table, breaking off pieces of dough, shaping them into round forms, and folding them in half to form what they liked to call "pocketbook" rolls since the resulting shape looked much like a lady's purse.

Since they saw each other every day and had no fresh news, the sisters worked in silence. The stillness gave Vera time to meditate on the afternoon. She and Byron had parted with easy banter, but her heart suffered from weightiness now that he had left. Her worst nightmares had come true. Byron had admitted that both sets of parents were expecting a marriage. What if they pressured Byron and Daisy to change their minds once Byron got to Baltimore? Even worse, what if Byron was mistaken and Daisy really did expect them to wed? Then she would be convinced, and the two families could make Byron feel obligated to wed Daisy. But since Byron had recently renewed his commitment to Christ, would he be more malleable and feel he must go along with their wishes for marriage?

A terrible thought visited her. If something went awry, and Byron and Daisy were convinced to change their minds, Vera could lose Byron forever!

Lord, I pray for Thy will, whether it be for Byron to remain in Baltimore and abide by his family's wishes or to return here. Thou knowest best. In Jesus' precious name, I pray. Amen.

The prayer brought Vera a realization. She had not prayed either for her own happiness or for Byron to be convinced to follow the path that she would have him follow. Her feelings were true.

Without a doubt, she had fallen in love with Byron Gates.

Wednesday afternoon, Byron and Clarence arrived in the city via an eastbound B&O Railroad passenger car.

"Look alive, old man." Though he prodded Byron, Clarence looked out the hired carriage window and observed the streets of Baltimore. "Ah, the hustle and bustle of people going places and doing important things. Not like that backwater place we came from." He leaned forward and rubbed his palms together, bringing to Byron's mind how a starving man might anticipate a Thanksgiving Day feast. "We're finally in the city where we both belong."

"Yes," Byron answered despite wishing he were still in the country.

"You seem sullen, old man. Aren't you looking forward to our night on the town?"

Byron wasn't sure how he wanted to answer.

"Now look here," Clarence persisted. "You promised me an evening of merriment, and there's nothing you can do to squirm your way out of it. I'm surprised you'd even try." He patted Byron on the shoulder. "You'll liven up when you get to the gaming tables. I'm sure of it."

"You're assuming I plan to take a few turns, but I don't."

Clarence's expression fell. "Certainly you don't plan to spoil my fun."

"No. I simply don't have any intention of playing any games myself, that's all. But don't despair. You're sure to find many new friends to share in your idea of fun."

At that moment, the carriage passed the Estes residence, a fine brick town home with four windows across the second-story front. "I know why you're in such a dejected mood. You don't want to see Daisy."

Byron looked at the house, glad that no one stood outside to note his arrival in town. He would see Daisy in his own time and not a moment sooner. "Actually, I do. I need to put this ridiculous matter of a marriage to rest, once and for all. It's my mother I hate to disappoint."

For once, Clarence turned serious. "I don't blame you for feeling that way. No man, not even a scoundrel such as myself, wants to disappoint his mother. But your dear mama will recover. Mothers have a way of forgiving their sons no matter what the cost."

Byron chuckled. "You should know," he said in jest.

They turned into the gateway of Byron's childhood home, which, with its well-tended yard and abbreviated porch, looked much like the Estes family's house in style and bearing.

The butler had barely greeted them before Mrs. Gates, who bore the same blue eyes as Byron, rushed to embrace him. "Oh, my darling son, I've missed you so."

"And I missed you, Mother."

She took him by both forearms and gazed into his face. "Let me look at you."

"Mother, I've only been away a few weeks, not ten years." He chuckled.

"Oh, but it feels like ten years. Maybe longer." She inspected him from head to toe. "Well. Strikingly handsome as always." She nodded to Clarence. "I see you've been taking good care of him out there in the country."

Clarence nodded. "I've been trying."

Mother motioned for them to follow her into the parlor. "I've already told Mattie to bring in tea. Now tell me all about the country, Byron. How many hearts have you broken?"

"At least one," Clarence said.

Byron's mother kept her attention on her son. "Only one? You must indeed be settling in to the idea of the wedding. When are you and Daisy going to set a date? Oh, please say you're finally ready. Her mother and I want to start planning the bridal dinner and reception."

"Don't schedule the caterer yet, Mother."

"Oh, why not, Byron?" Clarence teased.

Byron shot him a dirty look, and Clarence snickered. Byron's mother looked at them both indulgently, as though the two grown men were nothing more than mischievous, albeit charming, little boys.

Byron couldn't remember an afternoon when he had looked forward to teatime less.

Chapter 11

The following day, the Esteses' butler took some time to respond to Byron's knock, even though Daisy always kept Thursday afternoons open to greet callers. Byron could only hope she hadn't become indisposed, given how much he didn't want to have to gather up the courage to make the approach to her house a second time.

He was about to rap on the door once more when it finally opened. The butler greeted him as warmly as a proper butler permitted himself, and Daisy, thankfully, didn't keep him waiting long.

She entered the formal parlor on a cloud of pink, her usual color and her dress stylish as always, and greeted him with an embrace. "Why, Byron, I thought you had fled to the country to get away from the city heat." She took a seat on a red velvet divan. Her motion allowed Byron to sit in a matching chair across from her.

"Yes, it's cooler there. I'd forgotten how hot it can get here, even in June."

"Indeed," she concurred. "In fact, you're lucky to catch me today. I just returned from New Hampshire, and I'll be on my way to my cousin's in Rhode Island in three days. Much cooler weather in both locales, I must say. Oh, speaking of cooling off, might I offer you a drink?"

"No, thank you. I just had refreshment at home."

"That's too bad. Cook just baked some tarts, and I know how much you love those. Won't you reconsider?"

"If only I could."

"Have your way, then," Daisy said.

"Might I inquire after your dear mother?"

"She's as usual. All in a dither over what to pack for our visit to Rhode Island. I say, just take everything!" She giggled. "Ah, I'll be glad to have the packing behind us so we can escape. So how are things in the country?"

"Quite pleasant."

"And Clarence?"

"He is in fine form."

"No doubt. Well then," she said, "what brings you back so soon?"

"You do, in fact."

"I do? Oh dear." She put on a blush Byron was sure she must have practiced in the mirror. "Am I as memorable as all that?"

"Of course you are memorable." He bit his tongue. He hadn't been with Daisy for any amount of time, and already he had slipped down the slope of flirtation. Fallen right into the abyss, rather.

"You are the flatterer as always," she said, confirming just how deeply he had sunk.

He put on a serious expression. "I am here to set the record straight. About us."

"Us?" She flicked her hand. "Is there an us?"

"I think you know the answer to that. My mother greeted me upon my arrival with probing questions regarding our impending wedding date."

To his surprise, Daisy's cheeks turned white.

"What's the matter, Daisy?"

"I know our mothers have been conniving and scheming, but I've been doing my best to discourage them. Well, I've been trying to discourage my mother, anyway." She sent him a fearful look. "You. . .you didn't think. . ."

"No. No, I didn't." Then, realizing he sounded as though he were rejecting her, he rushed to add, "Not that any man wouldn't be honored to marry you."

Daisy let out a laugh. "This is the reason why you stay in trouble, Byron. You don't know how to keep your lips from spilling words as smooth as glass. No wonder all the women in Baltimore wish they could be by your side. All except Elizabeth Reynolds. And maybe a few others whose hearts you've broken over the years." She shot him a wry look.

He groaned. "Must everyone in Baltimore know about my follies?"

"The summer drags on, and people do talk." She leaned closer. "I wouldn't waste time worrying about those silly debutantes if I were in your position. Elizabeth in particular really isn't up to your standards. She's much too thin and such an awful nose! Why you even flirted with her, I'll never know."

Her comments took him back to the time when Clarence insisted that Vera wasn't his type. What was it about him that invited such speculation? He decided to pursue another, more interesting angle. "Since everyone is gossiping about me, am I to presume that they believe you to be nursing your wounds?"

She only missed a beat. "Oh, you mean, does everyone think you cheated on poor little me?"

A pang of chagrin visited Byron. "Is that how you feel? That I cheated?"

She laughed. "Indeed not! I've known you since we were children, Byron. And I know our mothers and their plans. We are both pawns in their dreams, even though no doubt they want what's best for us."

"And our families."

"Yes, that, too." She swallowed. "And now it's my turn to say that any woman would be fortunate to land you. You have it all: charm, good looks, a fine family name, and wealth."

"Then why aren't you chomping at the bit to take your place in line?" he jested in spite of himself.

"You know as well as I do. Because we're more like brother and sister than romantic mates. We'll always be the best of friends. But lovers? I know you too well for that." She crossed her arms and sent him a mischievous smile that reminded him of the time when they were but six and eight and had taken penny candy from Mr. Ashe's corner store.

"Should I be relieved or insulted?" The rhetorical question parted from his lips before he remembered to practice discretion.

She laughed. "Whatever you feel, you feel. But resist any urge to think I have insulted you. I wouldn't dream of it. I'm much too fond of you."

"And I, you."

"Good. Now that we have that all settled, which one of us will break the news to our mothers and clear the air once and for all?"

Byron didn't bother to conceal his distress. "I suppose you'll have to set your mother straight, and I'll have to talk to mine. Not a prospect I relish."

"Perhaps you can console her with the news that you have found an enchanting companion out in the country. No doubt her cheeks are as ruddy as fall apples and her skin is as creamy and white as the milk she gathers from the cows each morning."

Byron shook his head. "Why do I sense that your tongue lies firmly in your cheek?"

"Because it does. Really, Byron, will you be happy forever and ever with a naive little thing from the country?"

"She's not naive. And how do you know about Vera, anyway?" Byron asked.

Daisy crossed her legs. "So that's her name. A blond, I hear?"

"You hear correctly. But from whom?"

She smiled. "Clarence wrote to James, and he told Edna, and she told yours truly."

"The gossip mill is always grinding, I see."

"Of course. You are ever so interesting, and everyone wants to know all about your doings." She sat back on the divan as though she were about ready to take in a show.

"So you say. Why anyone would be interested in someone they think to be a cheater, I'll never know."

"It's because you dare to do the things that no one else does. That's part of your charm."

"It won't be for much longer. Since visiting the country, I have become more spiritual."

She covered her lips with both hands to suppress a hearty laugh. "You? Spiritual? The only spirits I know of associated with you are port wine and cognac."

The truth stung. Viewing himself through the loving though unflinching lens of an old friend—a compassionate female rather than his reckless friend Clarence—showed him all the more why he had to change and make that change permanent. "Not anymore."

"Really?" She shrugged. "Well then, we broke our make-believe engagement just in time. I wish you luck in your journey."

"And your journey? What do you believe the future holds for you?"

"It is quite promising, thanks partly to you."

"To me?" he asked.

"Yes. The rumor that you were unfaithful sent me quite a few new prospects. I must remember to thank you. So thank you." Her face flashed naughtiness.

"Why would you care about new prospects? You told me yourself that Horace Moore was your intended beau."

She waved her hand. "Oh, he's yesterday's news." Her face turned serious. "I'll have you to know that Silas Jenkins was among those new prospects."

An image of a short man who was attractive enough but full of bluster entered his head. "Silas Jenkins? Surely you jest."

"You mean because he's not yet in our social set? He will be, I assure you. He certainly has the money to socialize with us."

"Money doesn't buy respectability."

"Maybe not, but having more than enough makes life a lot more fun, doesn't it?"

"Money aside, Jenkins has displayed quite a bit of nerve to make a play for a woman as far out of his league as you."

Both of her eyebrows rose. "Jealous words coming from a man who just broke off our so-called betrothal."

"Not jealous, Daisy," he said. "I will always care about you. I would like to see you make a good marriage. And so will your father. You jested about my country companion, but I doubt the prospect of you making a match with Jenkins will give your family much consolation."

She pouted. "I know. Daddy has already told me he doesn't approve. But my heart has spoken to me, Byron. And now and forevermore, Silas's name is etched upon it."

Byron studied her eyes. All sauciness had vanished, replaced by raw emotion. "He is blessed to have garnered your favor. I mean that."

"So you wish me well?" Her wide eyes and voice drained of teasing told him that his approval was important to her.

"Of course I do, although I don't envy you for having to face your father."

"Silas will be by my side, and together we can face anything."

"Spoken like a true romantic."

"A true romantic who's afraid," she admitted.

"I can understand that. Disappointing one's parents is never desirable, but we must be free to make our own decisions." He thought for a moment. "Shall we pray about the situation?"

Her palm dropped on the arm of the chair with such force that it banged on impact. "Pray? What good will that do?"

"I don't know. But maybe God will listen and will speak to your father's heart."

Her expression softened. "You really do mean what you said about this spiritual quest, don't you?"

He nodded.

"I'm sorry, then, that I made fun of you."

"Based on what you know about me, I deserved it. So will you pray with me?"

She paused. "I don't suppose it can hurt."

Byron bowed his head and spoke. "Father in heaven, please guide Daisy in Thy will for her life. We don't know what the future holds. Only Thou knowest. Whatever Thy plans are, let her and her future husband walk by Thy side. Keep them under Thy guidance and protection all of their days. In the name of Jesus, I pray. Amen."

She looked up and studied him. "That was the oddest prayer I ever heard. Why didn't you ask God to make my parents understand us and accept Silas?"

"Because that may not be what is best for you."

"I thought you were on my side."

"I am. That's why I prayed for God's best. I hope in my heart that His plan coincides with what you want. But sometimes what we think we want can be the worst possible outcome for us."

Daisy shook her head as though she had just heard an incomprehensible university lecture. "I don't know, Byron. Maybe you shouldn't pray for me anymore." Her tone displayed more uncertainty than judgment.

"I won't pray for you if you prefer that I not. But I hope you really don't feel that way. I pray this way now because I am putting my trust in God as my heavenly Father, not as my errand boy."

She took a moment to digest what he said. "I can see what you mean. So who has been influencing the way you look at God now?"

Byron didn't hesitate. "The person you think to be a little ruddy-cheeked milkmaid. Miss Vera Howard."

Chapter 12

Moments later, a free man, Byron whistled as he made his way across the generous foyer of the Estes home. He crossed the threshold, his waiting horse in sight.

Rolling his glance to the sidewalk, he slowed his pace when he realized that someone else awaited, too.

Daisy's father.

The large fellow, dressed in the suit he had worn during his day of toil in the office, lumbered toward him, a smile covering his countenance.

"Byron!" he boomed when he caught up to him on the porch steps. "There you are, my boy. I was wondering how long it would take for you to show your handsome mug around here."

Byron tipped his hat. "Good afternoon, Mr. Estes."

Mr. Estes drew closer. "Have you seen Daisy?"

"Yes, sir. She's looking lovely as usual."

"Of course she is! Now do my eyes deceive me, or does it look like you're trying to make a beeline for the street?" the older man queried.

"I'm due home for dinner soon."

"Nonsense! You're having dinner with us."

"Thank you, sir, but not this evening—"

"What's the matter? A big slab of roast beef isn't good enough for you anymore?" He let out a laugh as hearty as the portion of meat he suggested.

"Oh no, roast beef sounds delicious."

"Well then, there's no reason for you not to stay—if you can stand all the talk that's bound to be happening about the wedding. My womenfolk do like to chatter."

"About that—"

He slapped Byron on the back. "I know, I know. But women get excited about these things. After dinner, we can sneak into the library for a nice glass of port, eh?"

"Really, I can't." Byron looked toward the street.

Daisy's father tugged Byron's sleeve, leading him into the house. "If you're worried about your mother, I'll have Lester send word." He called out Lester's name.

"Please. Don't. I really, really can't stay."

Mr. Estes' face took on an expression of regret. "So you honestly do have plans for this evening? Tomorrow night, then."

"No, not tomorrow night, either."

Daisy joined them. "Daddy. I thought I heard you."

He hugged Daisy with one arm. "My little muffin. How was your day? Wonderful, I'm sure, now that your intended is back from the country."

Byron sent Daisy a look. She shot one back. In spite of his reluctance, he knew the time had come to set things straight once and for all with the Estes family. Surely Daisy's father would take disappointment better with Byron present rather than Silas.

"What's this?" Mr. Estes asked. "Do I sense a little tension in the air? A lovers' spat? Well, you have all evening to make amends. This, too, shall pass."

"No, Daddy, we didn't have a spat. Byron and I are still the best of friends."

"More than friends, I hope."

"Daddy, please come with us and sit in the parlor." Daisy's mouth was set in a firm line.

Her father looked at them both quizzically but complied. Byron sent Daisy an approving, if worried, look. The idea of being sure her father was seated when he heard the news seemed like a good one.

"So what is this about?" Mr. Estes inquired from the comfort of the settee. "Is there some detail about the big day that's distressing you? You know I said you can have anything you want."

"No matter what man she marries?" Byron asked.

Mr. Estes snapped his head toward Byron. "I beg your pardon?"

Daisy cleared her throat. "That's right, Daddy. Will you give me a nice wedding no matter whom I marry?"

He returned his attention to his daughter. "Don't be ridiculous. That's not even an issue. You're marrying Byron. Our two families have been planning this day for years."

"Did you hear yourself?" Daisy asked. "You said our two families have been planning. But you didn't mention the bride and groom."

"What are you saying?" All color left his face, soon to be replaced by a brilliant shade of red.

Byron braced himself. "Daisy is a beautiful woman. A remarkable woman. I suppose that's why I was always reluctant to speak up in opposition to our marriage."

He stood. "You. . .you are opposed to wedding my daughter?" Rage covered his face.

"And I am opposed to marrying Byron," Daisy jumped in, much to Byron's relief.

"Why?" Mr. Estes snapped. "I picked Byron for you."

"That's right, Daddy. You did. And he's a wonderful—friend."

"Good marriages begin with friendship."

Daisy set a comforting hand on his forearm. "If the friendship sparks into romantic feelings. And though, to please you, we have tried for years, all Byron and I have come up with are wet matches."

"A colorful but true analogy," Byron agreed, standing. "I love Daisy like a sister. As much as I don't want to disappoint you—and I know she doesn't want to disappoint you either—we simply cannot go through with the marriage you and my parents have planned for us. I'm sorry, Mr. Estes. I respect you almost as much as my own father, and I regret that I can't deliver the news you desire."

"Me, too, Daddy."

Mr. Estes thought for a moment, but his anger seemed only to increase. "I think I know what this is about. It's about that little country tart, isn't it? I know all about her."

"Country tart?" Byron fought two emotions: the urge to slug the man for referring to his godly Vera in such a derogatory manner and the impulse to laugh out loud at the preposterous designation, which revealed that Mr. Estes didn't know the first thing about Vera.

"No, Daddy, this woman is not what you call a tart," Daisy insisted. "I've been talking with Byron, and I can see that she has changed him. Why, he even prayed with me."

Mr. Estes narrowed his eyes at Byron. "What? You've decided to become a monk now to get out of your obligation to Daisy?"

"No, sir—"

"Daddy, it's not that way at all!"

Though he tried to maintain a brave facade, Byron shook inside. Daisy's father put on a good show, but Byron always knew that Mr. Estes desired him as a son-in-law not because of his person but because of his family's position and wealth. The man who planned to be his father-in-law looked upon the marriage as a union of two families.

Daisy tried to calm her father. "Don't blame him. I have found someone else, too."

His expression tightened, and a vein in his forehead developed sudden prominence. "Who? And why didn't I know about this?"

"Would you have listened?"

Mr. Estes stiffened his jaw. "Who is it?"

Daisy opened her mouth, but Byron didn't hear any words. He could only help Daisy by spitting it out himself. "Silas Jenkins."

Mr. Estes' eyes widened. "Silas Jenkins? Why, he is a nothing!" Rage returned to his face.

Byron cringed upon hearing any human being called a nothing. His regard for the man diminished by the second.

Mr. Estes pointed his finger at them. "I will not stand for this. Do you hear me? I will not stand for it! Byron, you will not divorce yourself of this obligation. You will not be a party to disappointing my wife, who has wanted this for both of you ever since I can remember. You and Daisy will be married by this time next year."

Daisy intervened. "Please, don't force us."

"You are my daughter, and you'll do as I say."

"But you can't make Byron—"

"Oh, can't I?" His gaze bored into Byron. "You will do as I say. Your family is powerful, but so is mine. I have overlooked the rumors, the gossip, the shenanigans. You thought I never was the wiser, didn't you? Well, I know all about you. I'm not surprised you tried to pull such a stunt. But you won't get away with it. You will keep your word, or I will ruin your reputation even more than it already is and undercut your family's business. Don't think I won't make good on my promise."

Byron could see that Mr. Estes was serious, and he could also see there was no way out. He looked at Daisy, who sent him a helpless look before she ran out of the room in tears.

"See what you've done?" Mr. Estes said.

"See what I've done? Don't you care about your own daughter's happiness?"

"Her mother and I weren't in love on the day we wed, yet our marriage is very successful. You and Daisy will grow to love one another just as Mrs. Estes and I have."

"I beg your pardon, but the twentieth century has arrived and, with it, new attitudes about love. Attitudes that I believe will make for even stronger unions."

Mr. Estes huffed. "I beg your pardon!"

Seeing nothing to be gained by incensing the older man further, Byron acquiesced. "I beg your forgiveness for any disruption I have caused here today, sir. I never meant for this to happen."

Mr. Estes nodded curtly. "Then prove it. You have two weeks to get your affairs in order, Mr. Gates. After that time, I expect you to return here, hat in hand, prepared to set a date with my daughter."

Chapter 13

That evening, Byron managed to put on a good front during dinner at his house. After all, Mother had instructed Cook to prepare his favorite chicken dinner, and Byron wanted Clarence to enjoy his stay. He intended to relish the treat unhindered by thoughts about how he was going to make Vera his bride while maintaining the friendship—or at least avoiding adversarial relationships—between the Estes and Gates families.

"Cook has outdone herself," he told his mother.

"I would agree, my boy," Father said.

"I would hope this might be a celebratory dinner," Mother said. "I understand you went to Daisy's today."

Her observation caught him with a piece of meat in his mouth. He choked slightly.

Father rose and deposited several hits to his back. "There, there, my boy. Marriage is a frightening prospect, but your mother and I did just fine."

Byron's choking spasm passed. "I know, Father. You two did more than fine. But you were blessed to find a woman as remarkable as Mother."

"Agreed," Clarence offered.

"You are too kind." Mother smiled sweetly and patted her lips with her napkin. "So, have you and Daisy finally set that date?"

Byron knew the confusion he felt showed on his face. He turned to Father. "You. . .you didn't show her the letter?"

"What letter?" Mother wanted to know.

Father rushed to answer. "He wrote me some foolishness about meeting someone in the country and wanted to know what I thought. I reminded him about Daisy. I thought that settled it." He stared down his nose at Byron. "You failed to understand me?"

"No, sir, but Daisy is not interested in me, nor am I in her," Byron admitted. "I wish I could give you the news you want to hear, but I couldn't even if I had never laid eyes on Vera Howard."

"Oh, surely she's just getting a case of bridal jitters," Mother said. "That will change in the excitement of the parties and prenuptial events."

"No, it won't," Byron told her, though he kept his tone respectful. "Daisy told me today she is intrigued by Silas Jenkins."

"Silas Jenkins?" Father spat out his name. "You shouldn't let him scare you into taking a woman out in the country. You should be able to overcome any competition from him in the blink of an eye. Are you game?"

"No, sir."

"What's that you say?" Father set down his fork, and his voice donned an uncomfortable edge.

Byron strengthened his voice but continued to make a point of not taking on a disrespectful tone. "No, sir."

Mother's china coffee cup rattled as she set it down with too much force against the saucer. "Oh, Jack, I knew we shouldn't have let Byron wander away from home by himself." A tear rolled down her cheek.

Byron pursed his lips to keep from reminding his mother that he had celebrated his fifth birthday two decades in the past.

"So you have given up on Daisy?" Father asked.

"Yes, sir. But as I said, Daisy's heart is not broken. Neither is mine."

Clarence piped up, "Why, I wouldn't be surprised if Jenkins doesn't ask Byron here to be his best man."

Sobbing, Mother rose from the table and fled the room without excusing herself.

"Not again," Byron moaned under his breath.

An embarrassed grimace covered Clarence's countenance as he addressed Byron's father. "I'm so sorry, sir. I was only trying to lighten the atmosphere."

Father threw his napkin over his food. "I just lost my appetite."

"Please, Father. Understand. Vera Howard is a lovely girl. You would proud to have her as a daughter-in-law." He looked at Clarence from the corner of his eye and noticed that his friend was putting on a good show of composing his features into an unreadable expression.

Apparently Father must have caught Byron's furtive glance. "Clarence, what do you think of this girl?"

"Uh—um—"

"Spit it out, Clarence."

"I've known her since we were both children. She is a petite blond with not a whiff of scandal to her name, and her family is highly respected."

"If you don't believe Clarence, ask Raleigh Alden," Byron added. "Miss Howard was Mrs. Alden's companion for a time. She was like one of the family."

"A paid companion? Never let it be said that I look down on working people, but I had thought you would wed someone of breeding. Someone of our class."

"I know, but though Miss Howard isn't in our social set, she is far above many who are. Her character is beyond reproach. She has helped me to become a better man. I believe that if she does consent to let me court her that you and mother will be charmed by her refined manners and reserve once you meet her. Did I mention she's presently helping her sister with her new baby? Mother should like the prospect of a good mother for her future grandchildren."

Mr. Gates looked at his son's friend. "And you confirm this assessment, Clarence? Don't give me any coy answer. I am serious."

"Yes, sir. Everything Byron says is true. Miss Howard does not come from great wealth, but as I have never heard her speak an unkind word, neither have I heard or seen her dishonor herself or her family in any way."

"A woman of honor." Father's expression softened. "And grandchildren. Yes." He drained his wine glass. "I suppose I might be able to convince your mother that the world as she knows it has not ended in light of this development. I don't envy Frank Estes, though. His wife will not be pleased."

"We already broke the news to him, Father," Byron said. "I won't lie. He is very upset, not only with me but also with you. He says he is going to force me to marry Daisy, or he'll ruin us all."

Father's eyes narrowed. "Is that what he said, did he? If he dares to challenge me, he will find he has made the biggest mistake of his life. I'll show him a thing or two about ruination. Now if this Vera girl is the one you want, you take hold of her, Byron."

Clarence chuckled. "That Gates charm wins them over every time."

"Do you boys have plans for this evening?"

"Yes, sir," Byron answered. "We'll be going out."

"Well, that's fine. Don't get in trouble."

———

Later, the men found themselves at one of Clarence's favorite gaming haunts. Clarence motioned for Byron to join him. "Come on, old man. Let's get started."

"Uh, I think I'll sit this one out."

"What's the matter? Did Estes rob you, too?"

"You know I no longer indulge in gaming. I'll get a vicarious thrill from watching you play."

Clarence shrugged. "Whatever you say."

As Clarence played, Byron declined intoxicating beverages and studied his surroundings. Why hadn't he seen how tawdry the activities were on previous visits? Joy didn't exude from anyone, and if it did, the emotion seemed to be a poor imitation of the type of bliss Vera emanated just from the sheer delight of being alive. Why did these people suddenly seem so unlike him? Lives enslaved by Lady Luck. He shook such morose thoughts from his head. No need to take away from his friend's entertainment.

After a modest win, Clarence took a breather. "I'm ahead, old man. Are you ready to join me now? I'll even get you started." To prove his sincerity, he peeled a few bills from a wad of money he carried.

"Thanks, but no thanks."

"Really? You're not any fun to be around anymore."

"I'm a changed man. I told you so. Do you believe me now?"

"Sadly enough, I do." He sighed. "I admit I'm both disappointed and envious. But enough of that. I'm off to win more money!"

The rest of the night, Byron resisted Clarence's efforts to drag him to the tables, as well as the attempts of several women to garner his attention. He had a feeling he disappointed everyone. Everyone except himself. And the Lord.

Clarence gambled until the establishment was ready to close for the night.

"I can't believe I found you right where I left you," he remarked to Byron. "Have you even moved at all this evening?"

"Not much."

"You really are turning into an old man."

"You've called me that all your life. I might as well live up to it."

Clarence laughed. "I didn't mean it literally, old man."

"Perhaps not. So how did you do at the tables?"

Clarence lifted his palms in surrender. "I lost every penny. But I enjoyed myself. Especially since the money was all yours." Clarence laughed like a hyena, and Byron noticed that his friend's voice was slurred from drink. He watched Clarence wink at a nearby woman of plump frame, her lips and cheeks painted red.

"Come on," Byron said in Clarence's ear.

Had he looked like this in the past when he exited the gaming establishments after an evening of frolicking? And to think, he'd been afraid of this evening, afraid he'd be tempted back into his former lifestyle. Yet going to the gambling parlor with Clarence only proved to Byron that he wanted to change and to make the change a permanent one. With clarity he hadn't previously felt, he realized the evening had been a test of sorts. A test he felt he had passed.

I thank Thee, Lord!

With some effort, Byron managed to escort Clarence outside. Almost before they crossed the threshold, Clarence eyed a new man he called a "friend" and summoned him in a drunken slur. Byron tried to wave off the man, but Clarence insisted on speaking with him.

"Some other time, Clarence," Byron suggested. "If he's really your friend, he'll be available to see you another day."

"But I want to speak to him tonight."

"What's so urgent?"

"I have to know his secret. He won big, and I want to win big, too. At least when the money I'm risking is my own."

"Another time."

"No!" With the enhanced strength of a determined drunk, Clarence wrestled himself from Byron's grasp and stumbled toward the man.

"Come back!" Byron called.

"In a minute!" Clarence followed the stranger around the corner.

Worried, Byron decided to follow his friend. He hadn't taken two steps when he felt a hand clap over his mouth.

"Don't say a word, or I'll kill you." The growled threat was reinforced by a stab of what felt like the barrel of a gun in Byron's ribs. Before he could think of how to fight back, the large man shoved Byron into a waiting carriage.

Chapter 14

Byron's anger and indignation overcame his fear. "What is the meaning of this?" he demanded as the carriage jerked to a start.

"You know what this is about."

"I assure you I do not." Ideas flew through his mind. Had Estes set a plan into motion to kidnap him, forcing him to wed Daisy before he could leave town? The thought left just as quickly. Despite the older man's power, arranging such a scheme would consume more than a few hours. Not only that, but Estes would never have him taken by force to be a pawn in a hasty wedding. Appearances were much too important to him. Daisy's wedding would be planned for months, a show to be covered in the *Baltimore Sun*.

Then who?

Byron thought about other enemies he might have made. Was this the work of a jealous beau? If so, Byron wanted to be sure to bring the man who held him in his grip up-to-date. The only woman he had eyes for was Vera, and from all accounts, she had no other beau. Or did she? The thought filled him with envious ire.

They stopped, and the man blindfolded Byron. He could smell the stench of the cloth, a combination of sweat and dirt. He tried not to gag. With rough ceremony, he was escorted into a building and thrown onto a wooden chair. No one spoke until Byron summoned the courage to break the silence.

"If you would kindly remove this blindfold, I would be grateful."

Rude guffaws greeted his request. "What, so you can see us? You must think we're stupid."

Byron debated whether or not to point out that his loss of vision enabled him to observe their voices more closely. He could easily identify them thanks to one's thick Boston accent and the other's scratchy timbre, surely the result of too many years spent in the clogged city air. He decided not to press his luck, opting instead to concentrate on something other than the smell of the cloth covering his eyes.

"You deserve no consideration," the Bostonian growled.

"Listen, if you or the man you're working for, believe I stole his sweetheart—"

The man let out an ugly laugh. "A ladies' man, eh? No, I am not a man led by jealousy. If I was, you'd be dead by now."

Dead. Byron tried not to show his fear by a nervous twitch or swallowing.

His captor continued. "And if you don't do as I say, you may well end up in a ditch. I have no mercy on deadbeats."

The term came as a shock. "Deadbeats? Why, I owe no one any money."

He felt a fist hit his gut. A loud grunt of pain left his lips. Now that they were playing roughly, he steeled himself for blows he couldn't predict. He had to weigh his words carefully to keep from angering them further.

"You owe me money. Lots of it," said Scratchy Throat. "And you are going to pay me or else."

"I would be glad to pay you, if I knew who you were."

"You don't know me by sight, and you never will. I work for the owner of the establishment you tried to rob, and though his card dealers might be softhearted, you will not find me so."

In his mind, Byron ticked off each gaming hall he had entered in the past two years. Recalling no unresolved debt, he stalled. "I admit I was a gambler, but no more."

The fist made contact a second time. The pain left Byron out of breath.

"That's what I think of liars! You wouldn't have been in a gaming hall tonight if you weren't a gambler."

Byron resisted the impulse to explain all. Yet to bring Clarence into the situation would only put his friend in danger, as well. He could only hope that Clarence wasn't experiencing similar terror elsewhere. "You run a fine hall indeed."

"It's not my gaming hall!" The fist hit him a third time. "And if you think it is, then you'll be getting more of the same, only worse. I have spies everywhere, I can track your every move if I choose."

Byron didn't believe the man on the first claim, but he had a feeling he could follow up on the second. He remained silent.

"Now see here. You owe my employer the sum total of one thousand dollars, and I intend to collect. You are to meet me in front of Jay's Haberdashery in one fortnight to the hour with the money."

"And if I refuse?" Byron hardened his abdominal muscles and took the blow that followed.

"You like a fist in yer belly? Then you'll be gettin' more of the same."

"The police have a hard bed and a diet of bread and water for extortionists," Byron spat.

"If you call the police or try to get out of your obligation, Miss Daisy Estes will be the one sitting in this chair the next time."

He froze. "You wouldn't dare."

"Oh, wouldn't I? I have no respect for women who keep company with men like you." The man paused. "Now do you understand, or do you need another blow to the gut?"

His abdomen throbbing, Byron fought the urge to wince. "No. No. I understand. I'll get the money."

"See to it that you do."

They took Byron back to the carriage, where everyone remained silent. Byron's thoughts went back and forth between deciding how to procure such a sum quickly and figuring out how he would conceal his plight from his parents, who had cautioned him against gaming. And of course he wanted to keep Clarence out of the whole mess—and Vera. What would she think if she could see him now, helpless and threatened? He shuddered.

The vehicle stopped. They removed the blindfold and threw Byron on the street in front of the gaming hall where they had plucked him. He would have landed on his knees had he not caught himself in time, landing on both feet with athletic agility.

Stunned, he rubbed his gut where he had been battered. He brushed off his clothes, righted his stance, and went inside the gaming hall. Surely Clarence had gone back in once he saw that Byron had disappeared.

He was thankful to discover that he was right; his friend awaited. He wished Clarence hadn't used the extra time to consume another drink or two, making his posture slack. However, he wasn't about to complain.

"Where were you, old boy?" Clarence asked, his voice even more slurred. "I looked around and couldn't find you."

"I thank you for not leaving me stranded in this part of town without transportation," Byron noted. "But as for explanations, you'll have to wait until later. When you're sober."

"But I wanna know now!" Clarence hiccuped.

Byron hissed in his ear, "Don't make a scene. I'll explain all later."

"You bet your life you will."

Byron didn't even want to joke about the truth given Clarence's drunken state.

The next half hour was spent getting Clarence home and up to his guest chamber without Byron's parents seeing. Though he and Clarence were grown men, Byron didn't like the idea of bringing an inebriated friend into his parents' home, but the situation couldn't be avoided. He said a silent prayer asking forgiveness for not honoring his parents as they deserved.

Byron's faithful valet met them in the hall just as he led his wayward friend into the bedroom. "May I be of assistance, sir?"

"Yes, Philemon. Please undress him. I can take care of myself this evening."

"Very good, sir. I have already laid your nightclothes on your bed."

"Very good. And will you get Mr. Stanley some coffee? Make it strong."

"The spoon will stand up in the cup, sir."

Seeing his clothes awaiting him on the overstuffed mattress reminded Byron just how tired he was. His hours had become earlier on both ends of the day during his stay in the country, and he was no longer accustomed to staying out late. The fact that he only ran into trouble in the dead of night didn't escape his notice. Was God trying to tell him something? For the moment, he brushed aside the idea.

Byron hadn't begun undressing when the valet stepped back in. "Mr. Stanley is asking for you, sir."

Byron yawned. "Tell him I'll talk to him tomorrow."

"Due to the late hour, I made that suggestion, but I'm afraid he's quite insistent. He says he won't sleep until he's seen you. I tried to quiet him, but the more I tried to speak to him logically—but with utmost respect, I assure you—the louder his voice became. I know you don't wish to awaken your parents, sir."

Byron sighed. "Right you are. Tell him I will see him."

"Yes. So sorry I could not be of more assistance, sir."

"That is quite all right. I know how Clarence gets when he's, shall we say, under the weather."

Philemon chuckled. "Yes, sir."

Byron opted to stay in his evening clothes long enough to see Clarence. He stepped into the next room.

Clarence was lying on the bed. He seemed small in the oversized guest bed with its heavy canopy and thick blue coverlet.

"Are you asleep?"

Clarence groaned.

"We can talk tomorrow," Byron suggested.

"No. No. I want to know what happened." His bloodshot eyes narrowed, and he studied Byron with a crooked neck. "Is it me, or do you seem a little bit cagey? You know, I'm used to hiding things, so I can tell when a man's not forthcoming with the truth. Don't deny that something happened. So tell me, what was it?" Clarence burped and looked at the canopy. "If only I could stop the bed from spinning. . ."

Byron shook his head, glad that he hadn't partaken of strong drink. "Are you sure you want to talk tonight?"

"Yes."

"All right, then. While you were socializing with your new friend, I was kidnapped."

"Kidnapped?" Still in a horizontal position, Clarence turned his head to look at Byron. "Where was I?"

"Making a new friend."

"Oh." A chagrined look covered Clarence's face before he recovered. "Then you must be drunker than I am, old man. If you were kidnapped, you wouldn't be standing here. Unless you're an apparition."

Byron knew better than to believe Clarence thought he was a ghost even in his most intoxicated condition. He tried not to allow irritation to slip into his voice. "I was kidnapped but, obviously, returned to the gaming hall."

"Oh. Someone wanted to talk to you, then." His eyes sharpened. "Who? A jealous lover, no doubt."

Byron leaned against the bedpost. "A jealous lover I could handle, especially since I am seeing no one but Vera at present, and I am sure she has no other suitor waiting in the wings. No, this was much more serious. And much more mysterious. The men who talked to me said I owe them money. Lots of it."

"Oh. That's strange. Who were they?"

"If only I could tell you, but I was blindfolded."

"Blindfolded?"

"Yes. They let on that they are men hired to collect debts. I think I could recognize them by voice."

"I wouldn't try to memorize their voices too closely if I were you," Clarence advised. "You have the means. Just pay off the debt you owe and forget them. Forget you ever heard them."

"Good advice. Advice I would take if only I did owe money."

Clarence rubbed his temple. "You don't? Doesn't every gambling man owe someone?"

"I gambled in the past but not anymore. And you know how meticulous I am about paying my debts to everyone from the ragman to the gaming halls. Especially the gaming halls, because they have no compunction about playing nasty games with people who owe them money. Like the one they played with me tonight."

Clarence managed to lift his shoulders up and back, even though he remained in bed. His nightshirt rubbed against the sheets, making a scratching sound. "Like I said, you'd better pay and forget it."

"No. A true debt, I'll pay. But not something trumped up. One must never give in to the demands of an extortionist, Clarence. A man such as that is never satisfied. He'll ask for more and more money until there is no more. If I agree to his terms, I'll die a broken man."

Clarence managed a shrug despite his prone position. "Then don't pay. It's your life."

"If only my life were the sole consideration. What disturbs me is that they threatened Daisy."

"Daisy? What does she have to do with your gambling debts, real or fictional?"

"Nothing, except that I have a past connection with her—"

"A very, very recent past connection," Clarence reminded him.

"Yes. And their willingness to threaten her means they know me."

"Or at least know quite a bit about you."

"Yes." Byron paused. "So what can you do to enlighten me?"

"What makes you think I know anything?"

"You're a gambler, well-known at the local gaming parlors. They said they worked for the owner of the gaming parlor, but I don't believe it. I think they are opportunists or worse," Byron told him. "I was hoping you might have learned about any local thugs causing trouble."

"You're the one who lives here, old man. Funny you should think I know more than you do. Nevertheless, I do not. And if I did, I'd certainly help you." Clarence placed his hand on his forehead. "But I have a feeling that my head will be throbbing too much tomorrow for me to be of much help to anyone."

"Perhaps, but can you remember gossip tonight? You are saying you've heard nothing about a gang of kidnapping thieves?"

Clarence shook his head.

"And you saw nothing this evening that could help us identify the men who took me?"

"No."

Byron's raised pitch showed his desperation. "No carriage? No figures in the shadows? Nothing?"

Clarence shook his head no each time. He groaned. "Uh, I'm not feeling so well. I think you'd better go."

Chapter 15

Moments later, Byron shut the door of his own room behind him. Exhausted, he wanted nothing more than to ask the valet for assistance in dressing but resisted the urge, knowing that Clarence was in worse condition than he and therefore was in greater need of Philemon's assistance.

Undressing, Byron sighed. Though he and Daisy were no longer connected, she was mired in his past mistakes. The past. If only he could erase it, go back, and live a more Christian life. But he couldn't. Though the Lord had saved him from eternal damnation, Byron would have to face the consequences of the poor choices he had made. The time to face them was now.

Would the men really harm Daisy if he didn't pay the money? The thought sent a chill down his back.

Maybe Clarence was right. Maybe he should just pay the money and consider it a gambling loss. But at the same time, to pay criminals would not be rightful retribution for past wrongs; he would simply be buying off dishonest men. He couldn't bring himself to be at peace with such a notion.

Heavenly Father, Thou hast heard more from me these past few weeks than Thou hast heard over the rest of my lifetime. Still, I beseech Thee to forgive me for my past and to protect Daisy and any other person—Byron swallowed—*especially Vera—who may be affected today by my past mistakes. I pray for knowledge regarding my next course of action and the courage to carry forth Thy answer, whatever that might be. I ask Thee, since I am of weak spirit and flesh, to be clear in Thy communication with me, lest I falter so soon on my new journey with Thee. In the name of Thy Son Jesus, I pray. Amen.*

As Byron slipped into bed, he could think only of one person. Vera. He expected a flush of romantic feelings and yearnings to accompany her presence in his mind, but to his surprise, they did not. Instead, he felt a more benevolent emotion, one that seemed to say that Vera could somehow offer him help and protection. But how? He knew without a doubt that Vera had never stepped foot within a hundred yards of any gaming hall. Had he still been a betting man, he would have wagered his very life on that premise. So why did he feel the urge to confide in Vera?

Without warning, the answer presented itself. She was praying for him.

He had to come out of this situation a better man, a man more worthy of the one he loved. This was a test, a difficult one.

He prayed he wouldn't fail.

Alone in her bedroom, Vera tried to concentrate on the blanket she was crocheting in anticipation of Alice's new baby. She wanted to keep the gift a secret until after the birth, so she had made a habit of retiring early and stitching a row or two before nightly devotions. Not knowing whether the new arrival would be a boy or girl, Vera had selected a soft white yarn.

She let out a moan when she realized the last few stitches were too tight. Did they betray how tense she felt? Pulling them out, she decided nervousness had shown itself all day. A vase had nearly met its doom earlier as she nipped it with the feather duster, and a batch of rolls had to make an appearance at the dinner table too brown on the edges and top.

Lord, please console me. You know I will not rest until Byron returns safely. I pray that my constant petitions on his behalf have kept him safe. Bring him back to me soon and in one piece, I beg of Thee. In Jesus' name, I pray. Amen.

The next day, Byron's train headed west into rural Maryland. He had parted Baltimore amid his mother's remonstrances that he should return soon. Clarence had been quiet at breakfast, but if Byron's parents noticed his unusual condition, they refrained from commenting. Clarence rubbed his temple and groaned. "I wish I had stopped before I put down that last pint of ale."

"You say that today, but will you feel the same way the next time someone offers you libations?"

"I can't answer that, old man." Clarence sighed and leaned back in his seat. "I wish I could be more like you in being good."

"More like me? I never thought I'd hear you say that. At least, not now that I have changed."

Clarence's grin was wry. "I didn't either. But I do admire your strength and fortitude in keeping your resolution."

Byron studied his friend. "Why do I have a feeling there's something more?"

"You really do want to shame me, don't you?" As Byron shook his head, Clarence continued. "I know I made fun of Vera in the past, but I can see by the way you look at each other and how you seem to think of nothing but her health and happiness that the two of you have grown to love each other."

"My feelings toward Vera are quite different than past flirtations. I find them much more rewarding. I hope she does, as well," Byron offered.

"I think she does. I admit I used to envy you and the number of comely women you attracted, but now that I witness you involved in something deeper, I must say your position is more enviable now," Clarence admitted. "You are on your way to seeing a woman who truly loves you. But I? I have only gambling losses and no woman to grow fond of me for more than a brief interlude of games of chance."

"Might I suggest that you school yourself in a lesson I had to learn for myself? If you regarded your dealings with women as more than sport, the women might return your affections."

"That is a thought I'm willing to consider."

"I have a feeling that my kidnapping has something to do with your contemplations."

Clarence regarded Byron through bloodshot eyes. "You would be right."

Byron wanted to remind Clarence that the Lord was the true reason for the positive changes, but as Clarence sat back and shut his eyes in repose, Byron decided the time wasn't right. Other opportunities would present themselves.

Instead, he looked at passing scenery and concentrated on Vera. Images of her entered his mind. Welcome portraits of her flawless face framed by lovely blond locks danced as lively as her eyes.

Not bothering to stop for dinner, as soon as he arrived at Clarence's, Byron jumped right on his horse and rode to the Sharpe farm. As he passed through the leafy Maryland countryside, his troubles melted away. All he could think of was his beloved Vera.

Finally, he arrived and then knocked on the back door of the Sharpes' farmhouse. Vera answered.

"Byron! You're home already?" Her face looked even more beautiful than he remembered. Her complexion seemed creamier despite harsh sunlight, her image more ethereal than she had appeared in his wildest imaginings while he was in Baltimore. Perhaps her heightened appearance resulted from a glow of happiness.

"Yes." His voice caught. "I missed you so."

"And I, you."

Unable to resist the urge, he took her hands in his and gave them a light squeeze. She looked down at their hands gripping one another and returned the gesture. How was it that a woman's hands could feel so soft yet exude such gentle strength?

To his regret, she let go of his grasp. "Come in," she whispered. "Alice and the baby are asleep."

"That's right. Their afternoon nap. Alice is going to think I do this on purpose."

Vera let out a musical laugh. "I like that idea just fine. It gives us time to talk."

"Indeed it does." Despite his nonchalant response, Byron didn't remember a time when he had felt more anxiety. It occurred to him that his pride was at stake, an emotion in which he had invested an inordinate amount of time. Was God telling him it was time to let go of his pride?

"Are you hungry? I can look and see if Elmer didn't make off with the last slice of pie."

"No, thank you. I couldn't eat anything now if I tried."

"Something to drink, then?" she offered. "Tea or lemonade?"

He shook his head and noted that the temperature in the kitchen felt pleasant.

Vera glanced past him toward the nursery door. "Maybe we should go outside, lest we wake them."

"That might not be a bad idea. I was just thinking that we won't have pleasant weather much longer."

"Yes. All the more reason to enjoy warm sunshine now."

The couple crossed the back porch and headed toward the familiar wicker chairs. As soon as he sat facing Vera, Byron noticed that the sun shone in one direction, but behind Vera, a huge row of black clouds threatened rain from the southwest.

"Don't keep me waiting," Vera pleaded. "Tell me everything that happened. I want you to know first, though, that I prayed for your safe return the entire time you were gone."

Byron remembered how the gaming hall held no appeal for him that night. Surely Vera had been praying for him at that moment. "Believe me, at times I felt your prayers."

With an attitude of humility, Byron revealed to her what happened. First he told her how Daisy agreed that they shouldn't wed, and about Mr. Estes' emotional response to the news that the Gates and Estes families would not be joined together in marriage.

"Oh, I'm so sorry, Byron. How awful for you to feel you disappointed them. But surely they didn't think they could force the two of you to marry."

"They grew up in another era with different expectations, but even now in our social set, family alliances sometimes override individual consideration when it comes to marriage."

"You make it sound like dynasties based on royal bloodlines."

Byron chuckled. "Some of the people in my set fancy themselves to be royalty."

Vera didn't chuckle along with him. Her increased rate of breathing told him that he was upsetting her and making his family and friends sound intimidating. He thought about Daisy and her flippant attitude toward life and spirituality. He wished he could tell Vera that the two of them would be the best of friends. Yet he couldn't. Daisy didn't possess the depth of character to appreciate someone like Vera.

He cleared his throat. "The ones who are my real friends aren't like that at all. If I valued matching powerful families through marriage so much, don't you think I'd have married Daisy long ago?" A raindrop touched upon his shoulder.

She exhaled. "You have a point. And I must admit, I feel better knowing that

Miss Estes didn't seem in the least upset. I hope that fact didn't bruise your pride too much."

"Not so much. Miss Estes will never lose her place in my heart as a cherished childhood friend." More raindrops followed.

"What a relief that's all settled. Now you can relax."

He noticed droplets wetting her hair. "If only that were so."

Her eyes widened. "There's something more?"

"Regrettably." He peered at the dark sky. "Look, Vera, do you think your sister is still sleeping?"

She nodded. "She usually doesn't awaken until at least four."

"Then let's at least go to the porch to get out of this rain. I'd hate to see you catch a cold."

"Me, too." She grimaced as more droplets hit her face. "It doesn't look like this rain will stop anytime soon."

They hurried onto the porch and watched the shower for a few moments. All was pleasant until a crack of lightning roared through the sky, striking a tune with a clap of thunder that seemed too close for comfort. Wind blew raindrops into their faces.

"Maybe we'd better go in," Vera suggested.

Byron nodded.

They crossed the threshold as the downpour approached from the western pasture.

Chapter 16

Byron knew that had Vera not been so eager to hear about his trip, she would have observed the formality of escorting him into the parlor. He took the oak chair beside hers. "I hope Mrs. Sharpe won't mind my presence in her kitchen too much."

"My sister will warm up to you once she sees that she can do without me around here and that you really have changed." Vera paused. "Alice can't help the fact that she still worries. She thinks it is terribly hard to change, and I suppose she's right."

"It is, but you can believe me when I say I have. Why, I was even able to resist gambling when I went into a gaming hall."

Her eyes widened. "I beg your pardon?"

"Remember how I told you I planned to take Clarence out for a night on the town?"

"Yes, but I suppose I thought you'd be seeing a play or having dinner at a hotel. I feel so stupid. I should have known that gambling would be involved."

"No, no. You should never feel stupid. In fact, I wish we had confined ourselves to the activities you suggest. I would have enjoyed our outing much more. But Clarence insisted on the gaming hall."

"I have no doubt you speak the truth." She swallowed. "So you—you gave in to temptation?"

"What do you mean?"

"You gambled?" she asked.

"No. No, I didn't. I only watched Clarence."

"You weren't the least bit tempted?"

He shrugged. "Maybe for an instant, but any allure the tables once held for me soon passed."

She sighed. "So my prayers were answered in the way we had hoped."

"I'm more than willing to come to that conclusion." He reached for her hands once more. She allowed him to take them in his. Their warmth consoled him. "I want to thank you, Vera."

"For my prayers?"

"Unequivocally. For the first time in my life, I could see how the people there, though seeking fun, were the most miserable lot one could ever hope to see. I do not exaggerate when I say they looked like the walking dead. At least they did in my eyes. Vera, please know that I have no desire ever to go into another gaming hall."

"Really?"

"Really. Perhaps I shouldn't have revealed to you that I went. The fact that Clarence insisted is no excuse, and I won't let him cajole me next time."

"But you admit your folly. And that shows how much you have changed from the man you were rumored to be."

"Good." Her words fortified him, and he pressed onward to assure her. "I am determined not to be anything but straightforward. I can only throw myself on your mercy and hope you will understand. I think, somewhere in my heart, that I needed to go back so God could show me the extent of my former folly." He took in a breath. "And if that weren't enough, He made sure to give me the message loudly and clearly by the next event that happened."

She clasped at her throat. "I'm not sure how much more news I can take in a day."

"I don't have to tell you, then."

"Oh, do tell me. I'd rather know than wonder."

Byron relayed his account about the kidnapping and threats. She listened intently, not interrupting. "So you see, though I am a changed man today, my association with elements from my past life have come back to haunt me."

This time, she was the one who clutched his hands as though she never wanted to let go. Byron thought this not an unpleasant development.

He studied her. "Vera, you're trembling."

"I–I'm sorry." She let go of his grip.

He wanted to take her in his arms and console her, but she made no move to come closer to him. He decided it was best to remain at bay.

She composed herself, her body stiffening with self-assurance, either feigned or real. "I am glad you have developed enough trust in me to take me into your confidence. Yet I almost wish you had not. I am afraid for your safety now, but I fear there is nothing I can do to help you. Nothing practical, in any event. I can only advise you."

"What is your advice, my dear Vera? For surely I must take it, as God has led me to you."

She nodded. "Please. Pay the debt. It will keep you out of further danger."

He felt surprised that Vera had just shared the same advice Clarence had imparted. "But these men are extortionists, and I believe their greed for money will prove insatiable. They will continue to ask for money until there is no more, and I will be left an impoverished man."

"Is that really the way extortion works?"

"I'm afraid so. And where is the justice in paying this debt that I did not incur?"

"I will keep praying."

"Please do so, my sweet Vera. You will be the first person in Washington County to know what transpires." He tried not to allow his gaze to linger upon her pink mouth lest he take a liberty to which he was not entitled. Vera, so innocent yet so wise, deserved their first kiss to take place in the most special of circumstances, not as an impromptu gesture of farewell. He sensed that similar thoughts swam in her head. He gripped her hands and brought them to his lips, allowing them to brush the back of her knuckles. Their indescribable softness made him wish he could linger, but he let go before he changed his mind.

After Byron departed, Vera could hardly concentrate on dinner preparations. She washed by rote the tomatoes she had picked that morning and then peeled them with little attention. Her thoughts returned again and again to Byron. The mere touch of his lips upon her hand burned in her memory, superseding anything he could have said about gaming. She could have forgiven his error but was grateful his efforts to cultivate a relationship with Christ were proving sincere.

She mulled over the details of their visit. As always when she was near Byron, time didn't matter. She lost herself in studying his face. If he had been born in another circumstance, he surely could have been a model for shaving implements or other manly products, using his exceptional appearance to inspire men everywhere. But even such a countenance and form would not have been enough for her to long for him had he not taken the journey to live a life closer to the Lord. How could she not love a man who was her dream inside and out?

Oh Lord, I pray, now that it is finally my turn for love, that Thou wilt keep Byron safe!

Alice interrupted her thoughts. "Mr. Gates always has a way of visiting when I'm napping, doesn't he?"

Vera startled. "Oh, you scared me."

"Sorry."

"So we woke you? We didn't mean to."

"I woke up for a moment, but I turned back over." Alice rubbed her expanding belly. "What did he say?"

"He told me how he resisted temptation."

"I'm glad to hear that. How?" Alice retrieved an extra knife from the drawer and helped Vera with the peeling chore.

Vera debated about how much to tell Alice. "He realized the folly of gambling when he took Clarence, at his insistence, into a gaming hall. He told me the people there were like the walking dead."

Alice shook her head and blinked her eyes. "Byron can pack more action in one day than I can muster in a month of Sundays."

Vera laughed, enjoying the emotional outlet.

318

In contrast, Alice looked worried. "And you forgave him for going into such a place?"

"Of course. I am not his judge."

"I would never forgive Elmer if he did any such thing," Alice said.

"Elmer is not Byron. Your husband has never been tempted to gamble and has no need to overcome the urge by facing—and defeating—his temptation."

Alice clucked. "You have set your heart afire for Byron Gates. I hope it doesn't burn to the point of destruction."

"It only burns with happy emotion. You may not see the circumstances as I do, but I appreciate his willingness to be honest. Most men would have never confided such detail."

"True."

Vera relished the victory of Alice's approval and then ventured a query. "Alice?"

"Yes?"

Vera swallowed. "Would you pray for Byron?"

Alice stopped slicing her tomato. "I know the scriptures. You're just trying to get me to soften my heart to him, aren't you?"

Vera chuckled. "I wouldn't mind that. But he could use our prayers. Please believe me when I tell you this."

Alice sent her a reluctant sigh. "Oh, all right. I'll pray for him."

"Thank you."

"But still, why do I think there's something you're not telling me?"

"He did confide in me, and his willingness to be so forthright with me proved that our relationship is grounded in trust and is honest."

"He confided in you? How unusual it is for a man to confide anything important to a woman," Alice noted. "What, pray tell, is this confidence?"

"I cannot reveal it to you or anyone else. That is why it is called a confidence," Vera said quietly. "Perhaps you have misjudged Byron, Alice. Perhaps all of us did."

"For your sake, I hope I have."

Vera didn't answer. How could she tell her sister that Byron's admission only made her love him more?

"You've fallen in love with him, haven't you?" Alice's question sounded more like a statement.

"I—I have. And I think he may feel the same way about me."

"I was afraid he'd take you away from me. If you do marry, I shall miss you terribly. For your helping hands, certainly, but for your company, too. There's a reason why you were paid to be a companion to Mrs. Alden, you know."

Vera twisted her mouth into a wry grin. "I think my ability to listen helped me more than my attempts at conversation."

"You are well read and keep up with the times. I'm sure she enjoyed talking to you very much," Alice said. "I know she must miss you, judging from the frequency of her correspondence to you. And even though Elmer would hire a nurse and a maid to help me should you leave, no other person in your capacity could ever give little Paul the love that you do."

"True. But I would never move so far away that I couldn't see you often. I would never, ever leave my Maryland."

Chapter 17

After a fortnight had passed and at the appointed wee hour, Byron stood on the poorly lighted corner in front of Jay's Haberdashery. The store's pretentious name befitted its location in the business district. But to its left was a pitch-black street that led to Baltimore's northern docks.

Byron's palms sweated as he waited to meet his kidnappers. He hadn't summoned the police, a fact he regretted. Cover of night would hide the identities of the criminals, but Byron was determined to observe as much as possible about them.

Lord, put Thy hand upon me, and grant me Thy protection.

Byron also remembered that someone more worthy than he was praying for him right at that moment as they had agreed. Surely the Lord would listen to the plea of Vera Howard.

From the dark street behind him, the Bostonian's voice interrupted his pleading. "Good. You showed up. Smart fellow. You better not have any police waitin' for us. If you do, you'll be sorry."

Scratchy Throat whispered, "Step back to us, and don't be turnin' around."

Byron could tell that the man meant what he said. They had both seemed large the night they kidnapped him; tonight they sounded even larger. He swallowed and complied. "I still maintain that I am a man of honor, in my way, and I don't owe anyone this sum of money. But for the sake of Miss Estes—"

"We don't got time for speechifyin'. We just want our money," said Scratchy Throat.

Unaccustomed to being interrupted in midsentence, Byron bit back the urge to reprimand the criminal for his rudeness. Instead, he handed over the sack of bills.

The Bostonian grabbed the loot and then tilted his head toward his companion. "You watch him while I count. I don't take kindly to any man who tries to rob us."

Byron wanted to blurt that he, not Byron, was the robber but decided his life could depend on his ability to hold his tongue.

As the Bostonian leaned forward into the edge of light so he could see the bills, Scratchy Throat kept what felt like a gun barrel against Byron's ribs.

Please, Lord, I have learned my lesson. I never want to return to my past ways. And I never will. Let them just take their money so this can be the end of this ordeal and

I can get on with the rest of my life.

The Bostonian looked up and growled. "What's the meaning of this?"

"I beg your pardon?" Byron said.

"It's not all here."

"Surely you're mistaken," Byron responded with a stammer. He felt the gun barrel poke more deeply into his side. "I watched the bank clerk count out the bills myself. Then I counted the money again just before I left my room. I'm not holding back any of it. It's all there. I promise."

"It's only one thousand dollars."

Genuine confusion visited Byron. "Only? But that was the amount we agreed upon."

"No, we need fifteen hundred."

Byron tried to swallow but couldn't. His worst fears had materialized. These evil men were not out to collect an honest, if mistaken, debt. They truly were extortionists, planning to keep him dangling with their threat to harm Daisy if he didn't give them more money. How long would they keep him mired in their scheme? Where would it end? How much money would it take to satisfy them? And how would he be able to obtain additional funds? He didn't like the feeling of desperation such musings brought to his mind.

He decided to appeal to whatever humanity the criminals might possess. "See here now, I apparently misunderstood. It was an honest mistake."

Scratchy Throat snorted. "He says his so-called mistake was honest. Like we think he's an honest man. Ha."

Byron ignored the insult. "Look here, you made one thousand dollars with a small amount of effort and no resistance on my part. Why can't we all be gentlemen here and call our business an even exchange?"

"But you owe us a third again of what you gave us," the Bostonian said. "I think that is too much for our boss to overlook."

Byron resisted the urge to point out that the alleged debt was half again what he had already given them, not a third.

"Yeah," said his companion. The gun dug deeper.

Byron saw no other alternative than to agree. "All right, then. I'll get you the extra money. When shall we meet?"

"Tomorrow."

"Tomorrow?" Byron shuddered. "I'm sorry, but even under the most ideal circumstances, I cannot come up with that kind of money so soon. I need at least a week."

"I don't think so. Tomorrow."

"Father in heaven, I've been such a fool." Byron hadn't meant to utter the words, but they flew into the night air with intensity.

The Bostonian guffawed. "What's that, you say? A prayer? What makes a gambling man like you think he can get the Man Upstairs to answer his plea?"

"I'll bet you this here gambler's gettin' religion," Scratchy Throat said. "Whaddya say, boss? Ya wanna take that bet?" An ugly laugh filled the air.

The Bostonian shushed him. "Do you want to call attention to us, you fool?"

A well-dressed man crossed the lighted thoroughfare at that moment. "See now, gentlemen, is there some kind of trouble here?"

Byron looked into the man's face, which shone clearly from his approaching position relative to the streetlight in front of the haberdashery. Afraid for his would-be rescuer, Byron sent the man a slight shake of his head to warn that trouble could ensue, and he braced himself to feel the tip of the weapon jab his rib. But the renewed threat never occurred.

"Is there some way I may be of assistance, Mr. Ames?" The fair-haired man addressed the Bostonian and stepped onto the corner, with Byron on his left.

"How did you know—" He took in a breath and started over. "I mean, I–I'm not Ames. You don't know me." For the first time since Byron encountered him, the Bostonian trembled. His speech became more rushed and his accent more pronounced. "And we are simply concluding a very successful meeting. I was just telling this gentleman—who we're doing business with—that I look forward to sharing a pint of ale with him next week. Isn't that right?"

He looked at Byron. At last Byron could discern the Bostonian's features. He was older than Byron had imagined, with bushy gray eyebrows and an irregularly shaped dark mole on his left cheek.

Byron repeated, "We'll be meeting here again. . .in one week's time."

"This man here doesn't need to know the boring details." The Bostonian's voice revealed more than a hint of danger.

"Right you are. By your leave, I'll be on my way. Good night, Mr. Gates." The blond set his blue-eyed stare upon Byron's waiting horse, a sure sign that Byron should make a quick exit.

"Good night." Byron took advantage of his chance to flee before the terms of the forced agreement could change. He broke away from the men and, with a practiced swagger, approached his horse, mounted, and trotted into the night.

He looked back just long enough to be sure the two criminals hadn't decided to chase him. To his relief, they had not. The men stood by the streetlight. From a distance, they looked like statues. The blond man was nowhere to be seen.

Byron wondered how that could be but had no inclination to contemplate the puzzle. He only wanted to escape.

After Byron had traversed a few blocks uphill toward his house, he relaxed his muscles just a bit. He allowed his horse to slow his gait, and he realized his breathing had grown ragged. Clutching at his throat, he noticed it still felt constricted. He loosened his shirt collar.

Determined to concentrate on something—anything—other than what had just happened, he tried to take notice of his surroundings. The closer he drew to his home, the more the character of the streets and houses improved. Seeing the houses of childhood playmates and friends left him feeling more secure.

Since there was the probability of being spotted by someone of his acquaintance in spite of the lateness of the hour, Byron tried to appear casual. He said a silent prayer that his presence would not be noticed, possibly bringing up questions that could embarrass his family. Realizing how selfish he would be to leave the prayer with just a petition, he added a praise for the stranger who had saved him from trouble. Afterward, he contemplated what had transpired. Had the appearance of the stranger been an answer to prayer?

Chapter 18

After he had encountered the criminals, Byron couldn't get on the train heading back to the country fast enough. Despite his mother's protests at breakfast that he needed to stay in the city longer, Byron wanted to return to Vera. As they had agreed on their last meeting, he traveled by the noon train to Hagerstown and made his way directly to the Sharpe family's farm.

As soon as he saw Vera, he felt as though he had come home. Vera normally greeted him in a plain housedress, but on that day, she wore her flattering green Sunday dress. The scent of rose water emanated from her, making him want to draw nearer.

To his relief, she hurried him into the semiprivate parlor.

"What happened?" Vera wanted to know. "Oh, I was so worried about you. I've been praying my heart out."

"Thank you." He remembered the fair-haired man who had appeared just at the right time. "I have no doubt you have."

"So you made the payment, then? I was right, and you'll never see those men again?" Vera shook her head up and down rapidly, reminding Byron of a little girl trying to get her parents to agree to buy her a new doll. He smiled.

Unfortunately for Byron, Vera misinterpreted his gesture, which only made things worse. "Oh, I'm so glad!"

Byron turned his expression serious. "No, Vera. It's not like that, I'm sorry to say. The problem is still not solved. They want more money, and I'm supposed to meet them again next week."

"More money? How can that be?" A stricken look crossed her features. "You have just started being honest with me, Byron. There isn't some secret they are agreeing to keep in return for payoff, is there?"

"No. It's not blackmail but extortion. They are still threatening to hurt Daisy. And while we are not a couple, she is a friend, and I don't want to see her get hurt."

"Of course not!"

"Who's getting hurt?" Alice's voice interrupted. Holding the baby, she stood in the doorway. Her mouth had pressed itself into a fine line.

When both Byron and Vera hesitated, Alice looked at the clock. "Dinner will be ready in an hour. I suggest you stay, Mr. Gates."

"Stay for dinner?" Vera asked.

"Why, of course." Byron looked surprised but hastened to agree. He looked at Vera, hoping to see an expression of encouragement on her face. Why did she seem worried?

⸻

After a meal of fried chicken, mashed potatoes, and vegetables, Alice brought up the subject Vera feared most: what had really happened in Baltimore.

"You must be losing track of what is told to you, my dear," Elmer jested. "Byron has already given us an account of his trip."

"He has, has he? Not all of it. Vera herself told me he confided something important to her, and as her sister and guardian, I intend to find out what it is."

"Byron owes you no explanation," Vera objected.

"I disagree," Byron said.

"You what?" Vera asked.

"I'm sorry, Vera, but your sister is right. True, I took you into my confidence, and I'm glad I did. Once again, you have demonstrated a tremendous ability to forgive. In my view, that capacity should be emulated by all Christians."

"That doesn't mean you must tell all," Vera pointed out.

"I think it does. That is, if I am to remain a part of your life. And I do hope that will happen. I've kept secrets long enough. As the Bible says, 'The truth shall make you free.'" Without further ado, Byron explained to Alice and Elmer how he had been kidnapped and was being extorted.

"None of this is Byron's fault," Vera hastened to defend him as her sister and brother-in-law paused to digest the information. "He is a changed man."

"A changed man with a past that is still unresolved." Elmer's tone betrayed disappointment and distress rather than rage. He stared at his empty dinner plate.

"I wish I could go back and make things right," Byron told them. "I wish I could change the man I once was. Admittedly, I am facing the consequences of my past. I deserve such. But though this experience is frightening and painful, I believe I am learning more about why a life that glorifies God is better spent than one wasted in idle pursuits. Of course I would be more comfortable if my past actions didn't affect my present life, but then, what would I learn?"

"Your degree of insight is commendable," Elmer noted.

Alice crossed her arms and stared Byron in the eye. "I'm glad you have learned your lesson, but I am reluctant to say that your confession entitles you to keep company with our Vera. She did not help you create this mess, Mr. Gates, and our good family name need not be sullied by any rumor that Vera is socializing with a betrothed man. Not when there are plenty of godly men your age right here in this community who would eagerly court her."

Vera pursed her lips. She hadn't encouraged any man. At least, not until Byron's visit. True, she had been busy tending to Alice and her new son. Even if

Vera hadn't been so occupied, her reputation as a wallflower attracted no suitors. Vera was unsure of what her sister hoped to gain by attacking Byron's character.

"Luckily for me, none of those many men made their intentions known," Byron interjected.

Vera sent him a grateful look.

"So you are saying you would like to court Vera in earnest?" Elmer asked.

Byron, obviously emboldened by the suddenness of the query, blurted out, "Yes. As a matter of fact, I would. With Vera's consent, of course." He smiled at Vera.

A joyous bolt of lightning made her body quicken. "Y—yes."

"Elmer!" Alice pleaded.

Elmer shook his head at Alice and then directed his attention to Byron. "If only you had asked me in private. While I might have been open to the suggestion before today, this new development of the events in Baltimore darkens my view. You have too many loose ends—dangerous loose ends—hanging there to be free with your affections here."

"Byron will straighten out everything," Vera assured. "I know it."

"That is all well and good, and I wish you all the best," Elmer told Byron. "But until you can rise out of the mire, I cannot agree for you to pursue a courtship with my sister-in-law."

"Thank you," Alice breathed a sigh.

"Wait! Don't I have anything to say about this?" Vera asked.

"Since our parents are with the Lord in heaven, you know the answer to that. My husband is your closest male relative, and so you are to take his advice," Alice proclaimed. "I have full faith and confidence that he is saying exactly what Father would have said had he been here for you."

"Alice is right," Elmer concurred. "I am doing my best to guide you as I believe Mr. Howard would have if he were here."

"I appreciate and respect that, but—"

"No buts," Elmer said. "Byron, you can see the disruption you have caused this family. I don't believe that was your intent, but that has been the result of your involvement with Vera. I hope you will respect my wishes regarding your relationship with her."

Byron's dessert remained untouched, but he laid his napkin over it and rose from his seat. Though distress showed itself on his face, he kept his tone civil. "I understand, and I believe this should mark the conclusion of our dinner." He nodded to Alice. "Mrs. Sharpe, thank you for a lovely dinner. Mr. Sharpe, I bid you a good evening."

Before Byron could say his farewell to her, Vera spoke. "I'll see you to the door, Byron."

"That won't be necessary," Alice said.

Disgusted by Alice's constant meddling, Vera rose from her seat. "He is my guest, and I will see him to the door."

Vera rarely disobeyed a direct order from her sister, and Alice was too stunned to object. Vera noticed that Elmer tightened his lips into a thin line and shook his head ever so slightly at his wife. Though he had given in to Alice, he hadn't deserted Vera. At least he was willing to give her a moment to tell Byron good-bye.

Once they reached the front door, Vera peered back, hoping her sister wouldn't try to overhear them. She had a feeling Elmer was doing all he could to restrain his wife.

But she quickly returned her attention to Byron. She looked into his eyes. If only he didn't have to leave.

"Are you going back to Baltimore forever?" Vera tried not to let emotion color her voice.

"I haven't decided. I must confess that your brother-in-law has given me much to contemplate. I do need to straighten out the mess in the city before I can even begin to think of courting you. Perhaps then I can be on better terms with your sister. Her approval is important to me, because I know she loves you."

"And I love her, but she can be judgmental at times."

Byron sent her a wry smile. "Yet what she said about my past affecting my present is all too true. I am not worthy of you at this time."

Eager to stop his departure, Vera touched his forearm. "I said it before, and I'll say it again: I don't care about your past sins. If God can forgive you, so can I."

"So you will see me once I release myself from the Estes family's expectations and from the extortionists?"

Vera nodded. "I shall keep you in my thoughts and prayers until the hour you return."

Byron clasped her hands and gave them a gentle squeeze. "Your prayers shall give me the strength I will need to face tomorrow."

Chapter 19

Since Daisy was still in Rhode Island when he returned to Baltimore, Byron prepared himself to meet with Mr. Estes alone. The butler greeted him at the door and escorted him to Mr. Estes' library.

"Well," Mr. Estes noted from his position in an overstuffed wing-backed chair, "here you are. I was wondering how long it would take you to come back from the country." He motioned to a waiting chair. "Sit down, sit down."

Byron obeyed.

Mr. Estes took a deep draw of his cigar. The older man blew a smoke ring and let it dissipate before looking Byron squarely in the eye. "I hope you are here to tell me that you are ready to start making serious plans with my Daisy for your upcoming nuptials."

Before meeting with the man who wanted to be his future father-in-law, Byron had contemplated how he would answer the expected query. In the past, he might have flattered Mr. Estes or even charmed his way out of the situation. Now he wanted to keep from debating while still being forthright in his communication. "I am sorry, but no. We still do not wish to marry. I don't know what else to say."

"You can simply say that you will go forward and fulfill your commitment to this family. I know you're scared, but that will wear off soon enough. Trust me."

"I don't find marriage to Daisy nearly as scary as what happened to me the other night."

"Oh?"

"It is a grave matter. I hate even to discuss it, but I feel that I should be forthright," Byron explained. "It has something to do with my past."

"Oh, that." Mr. Estes leaned over and patted Byron on the knee. "Now, now, we men all have our little skeletons in the closet—things we want to keep confidential. Not that everything about your life is a secret. But I can tell you, Mrs. Estes doesn't know every folly I committed as a bachelor. As the saying goes, boys will be boys. A few little misadventures are all part of growing up, readying you for the responsibilities of manhood. I did see your father at the club the other day, and he tells me you're just about ready to take the mantle of the business from him."

Not so long ago, that idea had struck fear into Byron's heart. But when Mr. Estes introduced the prospect at the moment, a surge of awe filled him instead.

Mr. Estes continued. "His willingness to retire and leave his life's work in your hands tells me you are ready to take on the duties and burdens of manhood."

"I do believe I am, Mr. Estes."

"Good. Then I expect you to leave your childish things behind, as the Good Book says. And when you do, I may decide to retire myself." He paused. "You do realize what that means for you as Daisy's husband, don't you?"

"I–I'm not sure."

"That means you can combine my business with yours. The result would be a formidable enterprise. Unbeatable, really."

"Why am I not surprised by your idea," Byron mused. "Yes, that would be quite a legacy." Yet to him, the prospect of such a life didn't seem as valuable as it did to Mr. Estes.

"You are a lucky man, Byron Gates. My daughter will make an excellent society matron, and you two will be a powerful couple here in Baltimore."

"True." The prospect of such a bright future should have been balm to Byron's ears. Yet pursuing it would mean giving up Vera. He wasn't prepared to take that step.

Daisy's father sat back and savored his cigar. "Now about that wedding date. . ."

"Thank you, but I doubt if we should discuss that yet."

"I'm getting impatient, my boy." As if to illustrate, Mr. Estes drummed his fingertips against the arm of his chair.

Byron braced himself. What he was about to say would change his life forever. "I know, but I have something too important not to tell you. You see, I was kidnapped, and money has been extorted from me, even though I was innocent and did not owe the debt the kidnappers claimed."

He stopped drumming. "What?"

Byron elaborated.

Mr. Estes listened to the story but didn't respond right away. Instead, he looked at Byron as if seeing him for the first time, taking methodical puffs of his cigar all along.

"There are so many things I wish I could change, but I can't go back," Byron noted to break the tension. "I hope you can forgive me."

"Forgiveness is not the issue. I am not your confessor." The elder man tapped his cigar and let the ashes fall in a silver tray designed for that purpose. "This is a disappointment. I knew you were loose with money, but I had no idea you had run up such outrageous debts that unsavory types would come looking for you."

"But that's just it. I didn't. I owe no gaming establishment any money. Did I gamble in the past? Yes," he admitted. "But I always paid my debts."

"Yet these people say you didn't."

"They are wrong. And they are greedy."

"Greedy, you say." Mr. Estes shook his head. "You expect me to believe that these men picked you up on the street for no rhyme or reason? I would argue that they knew you were a gambler, or else they wouldn't have chosen you."

"Yes, they did seem to know who I am. And I understand they had no way of knowing I have given up gambling."

"You say you have given it up, but I have a feeling you have no idea how difficult it can be to rid oneself of a bad habit. And this is not just any bad habit, like taking an extra dessert every night. You say you have no debts, yet these men are after you. This life you have been leading is more than just idleness. It now poses danger to your business and to your personal health, apparently." His gaze focused on Byron. "Does your father know about this?"

"No. I am hoping you will not see fit to tell him. I don't want him involved, lest the criminals believe they should go after my father's fortune, as well as my own."

Mr. Estes let out a *harrumph*. "At least you are man enough not to drag everyone else down with you—for now. You know this won't end here, don't you? Before you know it, these men will bleed you—and your family coffers—dry."

"I am hoping to avoid that." Dreading the next news he had to share, Byron felt his palms sweat. "Speaking of involving others, there is something more."

"More? What else can there be?"

"I am distressed by the fact they mentioned Daisy's name."

"Mentioned her name?" In a split second, he put two and two together. "You mean, they threatened my daughter?"

"Please, do not worry. I will be paying them in full so her safety is assured."

Mr. Estes' face turned bright red, and he stubbed out his cigar. "I beg your pardon, but her safety is never assured as long as you are involved in this dilemma. A dilemma of your own making."

"I suppose you're right. I asked before, and I beg of you again—please, forgive me."

"Apologies and recriminations are not good enough. Not for me, nor for my daughter. Even Silas Jenkins, as repulsive as he is, manages to keep his nose clean."

Byron tried not to flinch. "If only I could say something that would make all of this go away. You can take my word that I am more upset by this entire situation than you could ever be."

"Is that so? Your foolishness threatened the life of my daughter. I'm willing to overlook a lot of character flaws, but this is too much!" He rose to his feet.

Byron followed suit. "What can I do to make amends?"

"I'll tell you what you can do. You can simply exit my house." Mr. Estes wagged his finger in Byron's face. "And I'll tell you one thing. If anything, anything at all happens to Daisy—if a hair on her head is touched, even a fingernail chipped—I shall hold you responsible!"

Byron realized that Mr. Estes's speech was motivated by a father's concern and anxiety. He tried to remain calm. "I understand, Mr. Estes. But I do plan to have the matter resolved by the time Daisy returns from Rhode Island. By then, the culprits should be in jail and she will be safe from harm."

"She certainly will, because I never expect you to see her again. The engagement is officially off." A sad look crossed his face. "You and Daisy would have made an excellent match, one that would have been the talk of society for ages. Your indiscretions have shattered that dream."

"I feel badly for you, sir."

"I feel even worse for whatever woman you take as a wife—if you can find such a creature."

His words made Byron all the more aware that he wasn't worthy of a fine woman such as Vera.

"Good day," Mr. Estes prodded.

"Yes, sir. But before I leave, would you do me one kind favor?"

"What is it?" Mr. Estes snapped.

"Please let Daisy know that I wish the best for her and that I pray for her happiness."

"You? Praying?" Mr. Estes scoffed. "I thought Daisy was joking the other day when she said you prayed with her."

Remorse filled Byron. "I know the idea must sound ludicrous to your ears, and I can't say I blame you. But you'll tell her, won't you?"

"All right. I will." Mr. Estes strode to the library door and opened it. "You may see your way out."

"Yes, sir. Good day."

As he exited the Estes house, Byron knew someone he wanted to inform about his progress. Without ado, he made his way to the telegraph office.

The next day, Byron's carriage made its way to the wharves. He had taken a great risk after he visited the Estes house, a risk that he hoped would pay off in ridding himself of the criminals once and for all. Ever since he had sent a courier to the police station, he had been watching his back, hoping no one unsavory had discovered the deed that defied his instructions. So far, no threats had made themselves evident. At this moment, he was on his way to meet the detective who had responded, one Jonathan Pierce.

Too nervous to think of what might happen if the extortionists found out about his correspondence with the police, Byron pondered his sudden and unexpected freedom. Living through Mr. Estes' wrath had been no picnic, but he sensed that the man who would have been his father-in-law was no longer bent on punishing him or his family. Keeping his promise to Daisy, he prayed for her and Silas.

His thoughts focused on Vera. If only his freedom meant that he could return to Washington County and claim her as his bride. But he could not. He could not offer to court any woman. None could associate with him in safety until he rid himself of the extortionists.

I know I brought this on myself, Lord. Though I do not owe this debt, had I not been at the gaming house, I doubt I would have been singled out by these men. If I had not been disobedient to Thee in the past, then I would not be suffering the consequences of my sins today. I pray that Thou wilt will keep the innocent—Daisy and Vera—from suffering along with me.

"This is it, sir," the driver announced. "Pier Five."

"Thank you." Byron disembarked and examined the spot where he and Jonathan Pierce had agreed to meet. In light of the men's threats, Byron didn't dare venture near a police station. Thankfully the lean figure of the police detective, aided by the cover of darkness on a starless night, made his identity difficult to discern to the unaware. "Wait here," he instructed the driver. "This won't take long."

"Yes, sir."

Byron didn't mince words after he and the detective exchanged greetings. "So what can you tell me about the men who kidnapped me?"

"We at the department are very aware of those men. That man you know as Ames is the leader. They are a ring of extortionists who prey on men with reputations for gaming."

"The sins of my past," Byron muttered.

"What was that?"

He shook his head. "Nothing. Tell me more."

"First, can you tell me how you have responded to their demands thus far?" the detective asked.

"I've been cooperative. In fact, I plan to meet them again tonight to give them what is to be the last installment of the debt."

"The last installment, you say? You must have qualms about that since you contacted me."

"I don't want others to fall prey to their schemes, Detective. I know full well that I owe not a penny to any gaming hall, yet because they threatened the safety of the woman to whom I was engaged—"

"Was?"

"Yes. Our betrothal is no more," Byron said.

"I offer my condolences."

"Yes, the situation is regrettable. But that is neither here nor there. What concerns me now is keeping my other friends and acquaintances safe and retaining my own sense of well-being."

"And you think you can accomplish that by paying them the money they demand?"

Byron let out a breath. "I hope so."

"You are playing a dangerous game, Mr. Gates. If the way this ring of thieves has operated in the past is any indication, you will not win. As long as you continue to pay, the stakes will grow higher and higher until finally you are bankrupted.

These men have already ruined two gamblers in town because their targets were too embarrassed to report them so they could be stopped. I'm glad you had the courage to come to me and tell the truth."

"I have a confession to make. I might not have been so courageous if I had still been a gambler."

The detective chuckled. "Did the men scare you into quitting?"

"No. I had sworn off gambling before then. I was only in the area to accompany a friend. The Lord has given me the strength to shed my old ways."

"The Lord, so you say?" Detective Pierce looked off into the twilight. "Too bad He wasn't there when you were being kidnapped."

Byron thought about the stranger who had intimidated the men into giving him extra time to pay. "Oh, I think He was there. He was there all along."

The detective gave him a half nod and extracted a pouch of tobacco from his vest pocket. "Will you join me in a smoke?"

"No, thank you."

He shrugged and rolled the tobacco into a crisp white paper. "I think I can help you."

"Good. What is your plan?"

The detective lit the tobacco. The resulting smoke carried with it a pungent scent tinged with sweetness. "I will accompany you to the meeting place from a distance, along with two other plainclothes detectives."

"Then what?"

"We'll watch the exchange to be sure we have enough evidence to nab them. We'll close in and apprehend them and get them off the street forever."

Byron tipped his hat in farewell. "Let's hope you're right."

Chapter 20

Byron's hands shook ever so slightly as he got ready to make the drop of money in front of the haberdashery. Night had made its full appearance, lending a sinister element to his errand. The extortionists were already standing close to the store's corner entrance when he arrived. They stood in the shadow of the doorway, revealed partially by a streetlight.

Father in heaven, protect me!

The Bostonian advanced from the shadow and reached for the satchel as Byron tied his horse. "Hand it over."

Byron complied without debate. He surveyed the nearest alleys and flinched as his gaze covered the spot where he knew the detectives to be. They weren't visible to him, so the criminals would never suspect they were being observed. For the first time since he had appeared on the appointed corner, he felt grateful for night's cape of black.

A pleased light entered the Bostonian's eyes. "It don't look like you brought anyone, just like I said. It's good that you can follow instructions. If you hadn't, you'd be dead now."

Byron swallowed, though he remembered he was safe with the police watching.

"The money had better all be there," the criminal said.

"It is, I assure you."

He riffled through the bills and then nodded. "It looks like it's all here. That was a very wise decision on your part. Very wise."

"Good." Byron wished the detectives would make their appearance. "This should conclude our business."

The leader closed the satchel. "Not so fast. I found out you owe us more than I was originally told."

Remembering that the extortionists were about to be captured, Byron maintained his composure, resisting the urge to protest in strong terms. "I don't understand."

"It seems you're in arrears to the tune of five thousand more dollars."

"Five thousand dollars?" A suddenly dry throat caused the words to sound like a croak.

"That's right. But since you've been so good about paying us what we demanded promptly and without incident, we're willing to show you some consideration.

We are willing to accept installments of five hundred dollars a month, due the first day of each month. We'll continue to meet here unless I say otherwise."

Byron darted his gaze to the alley and back. "And if I object?"

"We'll be keeping an eye on Miss Daisy Estes."

He winced. "Miss Estes and I are no longer engaged."

"Is that so?"

Though he didn't allow himself a sigh of relief, Byron thought for the briefest of moments that he had won a victory.

The extortionist didn't allow him to celebrate long. "Well then, the rumors about your sweet girl in the country must be true."

Byron shivered. He couldn't let Vera be endangered. "You know how rumors are. It's hard to separate truth from fiction."

"You'd like that, wouldn't you? As if we couldn't find out anything we wanted to know about you." The Bostonian let the words hang in the night air. "Maybe you're tryin' to take us for fools. I promise you that won't happen. We'll make it our business to find out what woman in your life means the most to you. Maybe your mother."

"You leave my mother out of this." Byron's voice sounded so threatening that he barely recognized it as his own.

The men let out ugly laughs. Byron would have sent blows to both their faces except for what he saw. Detective Pierce and the two other men approached in silence but with haste from behind the men. The officers had drawn their pistols.

"Hold it right there. You're under arrest." Detective Pierce's voice sounded menacing.

Before either man could react, the plainclothes officers grabbed each of them. The first officer wrestled the Bostonian to the ground, locking him into position with his knees. Scratchy Throat struggled until the officer dealing with him seemed to have no choice but to shove him against the side of the haberdashery. As two more officers joined in the shakedown, the criminals realized they were outnumbered and offered no more resistance. Detective Pierce snatched Byron's money from the Bostonian, who relinquished it with a disappointed grunt. Then, searching the extortionists, the officers confiscated two pistols.

"See here, what's the meaning of this?" the leader demanded.

Pierce didn't back down. "I repeat, you're under arrest."

"On what charges? Don't three friends have every right to greet one another on the street?" the Bostonian asked.

"You won't get out of this that easily," Detective Pierce growled. "We heard everything."

"It's not what you think. He. . .he was merely paying a bill. A debt he owed us," the criminal tried to explain. "Why, he's nothin' but a rake and a gambler. See here, officer, why don't you let us take care of our own? You have no need to deal with the likes of such a lowlife."

Byron kept his face unreadable, yet the man's words hurt. He had never denied he was once a gambler and rake, but he had no idea that even criminals looked down their noses at him. The bold statement made him realize how wise he had been to turn his life over to God—not for the sake of his reputation or the opinions of others, but for the health of his soul.

"I doubt that Mr. Gates is concerned about your opinion of him," Detective Pierce observed. "But we have plenty of people planted in every gaming hall in town, and we know that he owed no gaming establishment, including the one you said you represent, any money. According to our sources, except for the night you abducted him, Mr. Gates has not darkened the door of a gaming hall in months."

"But—"

"I'll not hear any more arguments." He nodded to the others. "Load them in the wagon, boys."

As he watched his tormenters being carted off by burly officers, Byron allowed himself a relieved sigh. "For a minute there, I was wondering if you'd show up at all."

"Oh, we never let your safety become threatened. But since the leader was so talkative, we held back until we were able to get the full case against them and prove your claim of extortion. You can rest assured that they won't be bothering you or anyone else for a long time."

Byron noticed that his palms had ceased to sweat. "Thank you."

"Be sure we have your current address," Pierce advised. "We'll be needing your testimony in court when their trial comes up."

"I'll be there."

The detective handed Byron the bag, which Byron accepted. "I'm sorry," the officer said, "but I doubt we can get the rest of the money back for you."

"The first installment?" Byron confirmed. "As much as I would like to claim that money as my own, I realize now that such a sum is a small price to pay for a valuable lesson. I hate to contemplate the fortune I wasted on such pointless amusement."

"Perhaps all amusement could be considered pointless if one takes that viewpoint."

Byron pondered the idea. "I suppose some forms of entertainment are more pointless than others. In any event, I will be spending my idle moments in activities that will prove more uplifting to both body and soul. I am grateful that God has shown me mercy by sparing me much greater consequences for my sins."

"Yes, that's commendable. Save the preaching for the choir, Mr. Gates. I'd better bid you a good night. The wagon awaits, and I've got work to do. In the meantime, the city of Baltimore thanks you for possessing the courage to help us catch these extortionists."

As Byron made his way back to his childhood home, he felt relieved and gratified until he realized that he might suffer the greatest battle of all—convincing Vera's family that he was worthy of her. A wry thought crossed his mind: He couldn't convince them because indeed he wasn't good enough and he never would be. All he could do was to show them that he really did want to stay committed to Christ and that, with Vera's help, he would stay on the path. He had to fight for her, and he would. He couldn't lose Vera.

Vera tried to concentrate on her stack of mending but to no avail. All she could think about lately was how Byron had fared in Baltimore. What man could be safe meeting with known criminals? Worry visited her too often.

She knew one fact: He had been successful in breaking his engagement with Daisy. His message contained no further news. She had been praying for the Lord's protection for Byron ever since.

Clarence sent word that Byron planned to return. The closer his scheduled return date approached, the more jittery she felt.

"My, but you seem slow today, Vera," Alice noted from the rocking chair near Vera's. "I do believe I'm several socks ahead of you in darning."

"You haven't changed since we were girls. You always did like to challenge me by how fast you could complete your chores."

"And I always won," Alice pointed out.

"Might I remind you that I have no incentive to speed now. These socks belong to your husband, not to mine," Vera teased.

"Yes, and though we don't compete with one another as we once did, I might remind you that you have grown plodding in your work lately. You don't seem to be able to concentrate on your chores." Alice sighed and shook her head at her sister. "You can't stop thinking about Byron Gates, can you?"

"No," she admitted. "He's due back from Baltimore soon, and I keep praying all will be resolved upon his return."

"Mr. Gates seems to be a determined man." Alice set the sock she was darning in her lap. "Still, I have my reservations. Nothing I can say to you will change your mind about him, will it?"

"I'm afraid not."

"I suppose there is no arguing with passion. Too bad you couldn't have fallen in love with a man as fine as my Elmer instead of a cad like Byron Gates."

"I understand you want what's best for me, and I suppose if the situation were reversed, I would share your feelings. But Byron is no longer a cad. I just know it."

"I only hope that your idea is not just wishful thinking."

"Even you must admit that you haven't seen or heard of Byron engaging in any untoward behavior since you first met him."

Alice contemplated the idea. Her furrowed brow and pursed lips told Vera she was thinking a little too hard to find something unfavorable to say. "No, I must say I can't think of anything. I haven't heard a whisper of impropriety."

"And Elmer seems to like him well enough."

"Elmer always had a soft spot in his heart for you." Without warning, Alice sniffled and kept her eyes focused on the sock.

"Alice!" Vera exclaimed. "Are you crying?"

"No. No." Alice shook her head with too much vigor. Ever since she was a child, Alice had always acted this way whenever she was trying to keep tears from falling.

Vera set down her mending and moved toward her sister. "Alice, don't worry. I'll never leave you."

"Of course you will, you ninny! You'll leave the minute you marry." Alice gathered her handkerchief to her eyes.

"But I'll visit."

"Not from Baltimore, you won't. At least, not all that often." Alice sniffled.

"Oh, I'm sure you'll find someone else who'll be glad to take care of little Paul and the new baby once it arrives."

"It's more than that, and you know it. I won't be losing a nursemaid. I'll be losing my sister and best friend."

Vera rubbed her shoulder. "You won't ever lose me."

"Is that so? I hardly saw you when you were Mrs. Alden's companion in Baltimore, and now you've fallen in love with a man who promises to take you back there. Tell me, is city living all that special?"

Vera didn't have to think long before she answered. "It wasn't so special when I was a companion. Mind you, the Aldens made my life pleasant enough. You know, I hadn't thought much about this before you mentioned it, but now that I think of it, the idea of running my own house in the city—well, that would be tremendous indeed."

Alice's sniffles turned to sobs. "I wish I hadn't said anything. Now your ideas have grown larger than ever."

"Oh, Alice, can't you be happy for me?"

"I'd be happier if Byron Gates were a local farmer. Or a merchant in town."

"I know. And in some ways, that would make me happier, too. If I do end up moving back to the city, I'll miss you. And little Paul." Vera brought her own lace handkerchief to her misty eyes. "Oh, I don't want to think about that. Aren't we both as silly as can be, daydreaming and planning a future that might not even happen?"

"Oh, it will happen if that's the Lord's will," Alice said. "And if Byron is the man who will make you happy and as long as he's a Christian, then I hope that marriage to him is what the Lord has in mind for you."

339

Byron couldn't decide which made him more nervous—his experiences the night he dropped off the money or the prospect of seeing Vera again. Just because he had gotten rid of the criminals didn't mean he was any more worthy of her now than he had been before, but at least he no longer had to fear for her safety since the extortionists were in police custody. Was that good enough?

Lord, I don't deserve Vera, but I pray she will accept me all the same. I pray Thy will is to soften the hearts of her family, as well. In the name of Thy Son, I pray. Amen.

Clarence had agreed to put him up during his stay and expected him to arrive at his home soon. But Byron was in no mood to face his friend—not until he had seen Vera. He couldn't wait to be near her again, to regard her lovely face, to inhale a breath of the light scent she wore, to be in the presence of her sweet warmth.

Chapter 21

As Byron pulled up to Vera's drive, he took in a breath. Vera stood on the stoop, her posture relaxed. She was dressed in a lovely cream-colored frock. A pink ribbon accentuated her tiny waist. He watched her as the carriage approached. Suddenly her posture became charged with anticipation. Did she look forward to seeing him as much as he did her?

With the dignity of a lady, she stood in place and allowed him to greet her as he stepped onto the stoop.

"Byron, you're back earlier than I expected." Her eyes were wide with eagerness. "Do tell me what transpired in the city!"

"I have all the time in the world to tell you my story. At this moment, I only want to bask in the knowledge that we are together once more. If I may be so bold, I couldn't wait to return to you." In a sudden impulse, he took her petite hand in his and brushed his lips against the back of her knuckles.

She looked at him through softened eyes. "I see your charm has only increased since your stay in the city."

"As has your own." He made a show of observing her and smiled in approval. "Surely you didn't dress for me. You must be on your way to an engagement?"

"An ice cream social at Lily's. Why, didn't Clarence tell you? I'm certain he was invited."

"I didn't stop by Clarence's yet. I wanted to see you first."

She averted her eyes. "I am honored."

"Clarence is a social fellow. No doubt if he's been invited to eat a bit of ice cream with friends, he didn't linger for me. I'll just be on my way so you can go to the social. By your leave, we can meet tomorrow, perhaps?"

"Never mind the social. They can all wait. Or better yet, you and I can stay here and feast on the peach ice cream I churned today for the event. They'll never miss me."

"Anyone in his right mind would miss you. I did while I was in Baltimore."

Her shy smile was his reward. "I have an idea. Why don't we both go to the ice cream social; then you can come back here with me, and we can sit for a spell."

"Are you sure Lily won't mind? And what about Alice? I don't want to do anything to antagonize her."

"Surely you jest. Everyone would be quite upset with me if I didn't bring you

341

along to the social now that you're back. And as for Alice, well, I think maybe she has warmed up to you."

Byron couldn't imagine such a scenario, but he wanted to believe Vera. And the idea of seeing his friends in the country again appealed to him. Sharing good times at the social would prolong his time with Vera. All were good reasons to comply with her suggestion.

Alice stepped out onto the stoop.

"Good evening, Mrs. Sharpe."

"Good evening, Mr. Gates. I didn't expect you to be back so soon." Though she didn't look at him as though she were greeting a long-lost friend, Byron did sense a little less frigidity in her face and tone.

"My business in Baltimore is complete, Mrs. Sharpe. I hope you don't mind that I stopped by to see your sister."

"No, but she was just on her way out. Mr. Sharpe had planned to take her to see a friend." Alice turned toward the door and called, "Elmer! Did you get the ice cream?"

"Getting it now!" His voice sounded muffled.

Vera placed a hand on her sister's arm. "You don't mind if Byron takes me instead, do you? I know Elmer really doesn't want to go, and everyone will be ever so happy to see Byron again."

Alice didn't answer right away. Keeping her expression even, she answered, "I'm sure."

"I would be honored to escort Miss Vera to the social, with your permission, Mrs. Sharpe."

"Oh, please, Alice?"

Alice twisted her lips. "Vera! You needn't beg."

"Then it's quite all right. Good!" Vera smiled and kissed her sister on the cheek. "Thank you, Alice."

Byron sent Alice a grateful look. Her eyes were soft, her lips not set in a stern line. For once, he felt she might even like him. One day.

⸻

Despite being in Byron's company during the ice cream social, Vera thought the event would never end. She was eager to learn everything that had transpired in Baltimore. At least she knew by his presence that he remained in one piece, and a lack of bruises on his face told her he hadn't engaged in fisticuffs. Those two facts kept her spirit fueled throughout the gathering.

As soon as they could excuse themselves from Lily's without seeming impolite, Vera nudged Byron in an unspoken plea for them to leave the party. He didn't hesitate to comply, and they soon found themselves back in the carriage.

"Here we are," Byron said with too much gusto when they pulled into the Sharpe farm drive.

"Yes." Vera trembled with anticipation. "Will you visit with me for a spell in the parlor? It's really not so late."

"I would be honored."

Under Alice's watchful and begrudging eye, Vera prepared tea as Byron passed the time in easy conversation with Elmer, who didn't voice any objection when she took Byron into the parlor. Vera knew full well that Alice would be keeping an open ear. The thought didn't worry her as she escorted Byron into the parlor.

"I've been waiting to hear your news from Baltimore, Byron. Please, tell me what happened," Vera implored.

"You don't take any time for pleasantries before getting right to the point, do you?" Though his tone suggested playfulness, he shifted on his side of the mahogany divan.

"We've spoken in pleasantries all evening. Pleasantries I have hoped it was my right to enjoy. After all, you did wire me that the engagement with Miss Estes is officially broken. Is that still true?"

He nodded.

"I'm so sorry."

"Don't be. Daisy and I were childhood friends, and the match was one between our families rather than between us. Mr. Estes especially wanted the match because he envisioned our family businesses combining into a powerful enterprise."

"Romantic, isn't he?"

Byron chuckled. "In his own way, he wants what's best for his daughter."

"He reminds me of someone else I could mention." Vera looked pointedly toward the kitchen so Byron would know she referred to her sister.

"Yes. We are both blessed with families who love us, even if their visions for us are not always what we would have for ourselves."

An unhappy thought crossed her mind. "I hope all is well with the Estes family now."

"Yes. I think they all shall recover. Why, I even expect to see Daisy's engagement announcement in the paper soon."

"Good." A relieved sigh escaped Vera's lips. "Then there is a happy ending for all concerned."

"Except for me. But that may change."

Chapter 22

S uddenly the parlor seemed silent. Vera watched Byron shift in his seat. She clasped her hands, tensing.

"You. . .you think your life may change soon? How?" Vera suspected, but she wanted to hear the words.

"My happiness depends on your reaction to our conversation here tonight."

"You are placing quite a bit of responsibility on my shoulders."

"I ask you to take no responsibility that you find too burdensome. All I ask is that you be honest with me."

"I always have been, and I always will be."

"I'll start by reiterating that no one expects me to marry Daisy. No one."

"That's a blessing. I hope settling that matter wasn't too painful."

"It wasn't pleasant. I'll spare you the details about that. Now for the extortionists." Byron took in a breath. "I notified the police, and they offered their help. Apparently these men have been making sport—and a great deal of money—with false claims of debts owed by known gamblers. They assumed that men such as these would be unwilling to go to the police. And for a long time, they were proven right."

"But they didn't count on choosing an uncooperative target in you."

Byron smiled. "Indeed. True, I was a known gambler who wasted time and money—time and money I wish I could get back now, only that is impossible."

"I must confess, if I may be so bold, I don't understand the attraction of easy money, especially for a man such as yourself who is heir to a considerable fortune."

"That's a good question." Byron peered at the corner of the room for a moment, apparently immersed in thought. "One I haven't contemplated."

"You don't have to answer, then."

"No, I think I should, especially since you are a friendly audience. No doubt I will be asked that question repeatedly when I share my testimony, and I need to have a good answer." He pondered the idea only a few more seconds before responding. "I suppose any man, whether rich or poor, likes to feel that he has outwitted a worthy opponent. A gaming house, with the odds stacked in its favor, is a worthy opponent indeed. I remember the few times I did leave the halls with a good sum of money. I felt quite witty and that luck was on my side. Of course, now I know neither of these ideas held truth. When one plays games of chance often enough, one is bound to win sooner or later. And you can trust me, it is most often later."

"You mentioned that Clarence was gambling that night. Where were you?" Vera asked.

"I was watching him. He would return to me from time to time for more money."

"No doubt. But I must ask, weren't you tempted in the least to join him? I know Clarence well enough to surmise that he practically begged you to take part."

"As the saying goes, misery loves company." Byron chuckled. "I confess, I was a little apprehensive about going back to my old haunt. I thought I might be tempted. You don't think me too weak for that, I hope."

"No. I think it took courage for you to admit it to me. I am tempted, too."

"You? Why, I can't imagine a pure soul such as you would find yourself in situations often where temptations abound."

"I do try to avoid occasions for sin." Vera didn't want to admit her weakness, but since Byron had taken such a bold stand and had spoken well about honesty, she knew she had to return the favor. "But of course, I'm far from perfect. I'll confess that I have been coveting a few yards of the most delicious cloth at the general store lately. It's a beautiful shade of red. Can you imagine? Red! And yet I'm so drawn to it that I find I cannot venture into the store without taking a peek at it. I often touch it, even. It's so soft I can't imagine I could sew anything practical out of it. And it costs much more than any decent person should spend on fabric. But my, it is beautiful." To her embarrassment, a sigh escaped her lips before she could stop it.

"That does sound beautiful. And I can understand why a woman as lovely as yourself would enjoy pretty fabric."

"True. Sadly, that does prove we all experience temptation in one form or another. How easily you seem to have overcome yours!"

"Only with God's aid. He helped me to see things I was unwilling to admit in the past: the desperation in some of the gamers' eyes and the look of the people who believed themselves to be having a good time but were, in fact, doing anything but."

"Funny how you can see things differently once you're looking at things from God's perspective. Of course, I have never set foot in a gaming hall, but I have seen people mired in sin. It's not a pretty sight. I rejoice that you have thrown off that yoke. Though in all probability you will face temptation again throughout your life, you have shown that you are able to resist it."

"And I am determined to resist temptation wherever it meets me from now on."

"But that doesn't answer the question as to what happened with the men."

"Oh yes. The police knew about these men and were more than happy to assist me in arresting them. I went to deliver the extortionists' money, knowing the police weren't far behind. As soon as Detective Pierce and his men gained enough evidence to assure conviction, they made themselves known to the criminals, and now I have no doubt they will be serving a good amount of time in prison."

"You'll be testifying in court?"

"I'm sure I will be called upon, yes."

"How exciting!"

"Living through such excitement is not as glamorous as one might think, although I suppose such adventure sounds enticing to a person who has never encountered the criminal element. The experience made me all the more grateful for what our police do for us every day. In this case, not only did they assure my safety, but with the capture of the criminals, they have ensured your safety and Daisy's, as well."

"My safety?"

He winced. "Yes. Once I assured them I was no longer associated with Daisy, they threatened you."

Vera gasped. "They had heard rumors about our relationship."

"Yes. That they would stop at nothing to find out anything they could about me and that they threatened people close to me made them especially dangerous."

"So you were right," Vera realized out loud. "They did plan to keep bleeding you for who knows how long."

"Until I was too poor to be of further interest to them," Byron said.

"This time, I will beg your forgiveness and you can't stop me. I truly regret giving you such terrible advice about how to handle the situation."

"Please, you were only sharing your opinion. I respect you more than any other woman I know except my own mother, but I would not look to you first and foremost as an expert on the average extortionist."

"I suppose not." She couldn't help but smile. "I'm glad you didn't listen to me and that you summoned the police. I was afraid the men would make good on their threats of violence upon you if you told the police."

"That's understandable. And I admit, I was nervous at first, too. But hindsight is always superior vision, and I'm glad I got the police involved. Your concern for my well-being gratifies me. I must say it was tough going for me during my conversation with the men. But that's over now, and all is resolved. Except for what that means for you and me."

She took in a breath. "What do you mean?"

"I'm saying that if I hadn't learned my lesson about returning to my past way of life when I took Clarence to the gaming hall I certainly did after my encounter with the extortionists."

"This is all Clarence's fault. If he hadn't insisted on that bet, you never would have been in Baltimore that night and they would have chosen some other man to bilk."

"And they would still be doing their vile business, ruining many men in the process. I believe God used this to work to the good. Not only did He show me again and again not to be tempted by gaming, but He used me to bring evil men to justice."

Vera pondered his words. "You have something there. I am always amazed by how the Lord works."

"I am becoming more amazed by Him myself, every day."

"Now if the Lord can only reform Clarence."

Byron chuckled. "Clarence's heart never has been as hard as mine was. If God can change me, He can change Clarence. I have a feeling He will." He paused. "So what about you, Vera? Do you think you could sustain interest in a man with a checkered past?"

Her heart beat faster. This was the moment for which she had been waiting, yet the idea of committing boldly left her feeling shy. "I hope you don't mean Clarence."

"No I don't." His eyes held a hopeful light. "I mean, now that I have discarded my past and have no interest in returning to it and now that your safety is assured, I hope you will allow me to ask Elmer if I might court you in earnest."

"Yes. Yes, I would like that." Her voice sounded much smaller than she desired. "Why don't you ask him now?" As soon as she made the suggestion, she regretted sounding so forward.

"That is the most splendid idea I've heard all evening. I'd like to talk to him now." He rose from his seat.

Moments later, Vera wasted no time in running to Alice in the kitchen while the men retreated into Elmer's study.

Alice sat at the table, relaxing after putting Paul to bed. "Is Byron asking Elmer what I think he's asking?"

"Yes, and you are not going to do a thing to stop it. I've never been happier."

"I know. I can see it in your eyes. And no, I won't object if Elmer agrees. I've been selfish long enough. It's time for me to let you go so you can find your own happiness. You have served others long, well, and sweetly, Vera. You deserve love with Byron if that is where you have found it."

"I have."

"Then I see no reason why Elmer won't give his consent."

Moments later, both men emerged from the library. Vera could see from Byron's relieved and happy expression that all had gone well.

"Come, let us enjoy the stars," Vera said.

Alice raised her eyebrows, but Vera chose to ignore her. Her turn had finally arrived, and she was not planning to let any admonishment mar the moment.

She didn't wait long after the door shut behind them to speak. "Well, what happened?"

Byron broke into a smile. "He gave me his permission. Now my only hopes are that you don't mind the prospect of moving back to Baltimore and that you don't want an exceedingly long courtship."

"No, I don't mind the prospect of moving back to Baltimore, even though I'll miss everyone here terribly. And no, I don't want an exceedingly long courtship."

"Good. That's what I was hoping you would say."

She looked deeply into his eyes. Studying them with such intensity, she almost didn't realize that his lips approached hers until they met her mouth. They felt softer than she expected and even warmer than she had imagined. The tenderness yet strength of his embrace assured her that she would always be loved.

Epilogue

October 1904

Byron clasped Vera's hand in his and led Vera to an alcove outside the little white church. The leaves on the trees nearby had begun to turn, providing a glorious backdrop for the day.

"Byron, what are you doing, making me leave our own wedding reception? Don't you know they'll miss us?"

Looking even more dashing than usual in his finely tailored wedding suit, he held her hands in his. "True. You are conspicuously lovely today. Not that today is any different from any other in that regard. You are so beautiful I must kiss you right this moment."

Byron made good on his promise. His warm embrace made the brisk autumn day seem as though a lovely summer sun shone. Her heart increased its beating as their lips met, emotions taking Vera to a world where she didn't care about the reception or even the prospect of a honeymoon in Europe. All she cared about was that she was finally Mrs. Byron Gates.

A cheerful female voice, now familiar to Vera, interrupted. "There you are, you two lovebirds."

Reluctantly they broke their kiss.

"Mother," Byron greeted her. "You're not asking us to go back to the reception yet, are you?"

"Clearly you have forgotten your manners, leaving your guests to their own devices," the elder Mrs. Gates, looking attractive herself in blue, said. "Although I must say there is no lack of food and good music. Your sister outdid herself in planning your wedding, Vera."

"Yes she did." Vera thought perhaps she was the only person in the world who appreciated just how much her sister's efforts meant. She looked to Byron for confirmation and noticed that he was peering off in another direction. "What do you see that's so fascinating, Byron?"

Byron didn't miss a beat. "That blond man. I—I've seen him before. The night. . ."

"The night?" Mrs. Gates prodded.

Byron cleared his throat. "The night I made the payment to my kidnappers. He interrupted us, and they panicked. Because of him, I got a reprieve."

"What?" Vera asked. "Mr. Ginson was there? What was he doing in Baltimore?"

"You know him?" Surprise was evident in Byron's voice.

"Yes, he's a friend of Elmer's." Immediately seeing what must have happened, Vera exclaimed, "Byron! Do you suppose Elmer sent Mr. Ginson to Baltimore to help you?"

"I—I don't know. Would he do that for me?" Byron nearly choked with emotion.

"Yes," Mrs. Gates said. "I recall you mentioning a blond man. If you know him, Vera, then your brother-in-law must have interceded to help you both."

"I–I'll have to thank Elmer," Byron said. "And his friend. Although there's nothing I can do to repay them."

"You can repay them with your happiness," Mrs. Gates advised.

"That will be easy enough," Byron agreed and gazed into Vera's eyes. Unabashed now that they were married, Vera returned his look of love.

"Well," said Mrs. Gates, "I did have a reason for chasing you two out here. I wanted to see you alone before you left for the honeymoon. I have something for you, Vera."

"For me?" Vera felt a catch in her throat. She knew that Mrs. Gates had once wanted Byron to marry Daisy Estes. But during Vera's courtship with Byron, she and the older woman had discovered a mutual love of books, leading to intriguing discussions. Soon Vera had developed a genuine fondness for her future mother-in-law, a fact Vera knew pleased Byron. "You didn't need to give me a special gift, Mrs. Gates."

"Oh, but I want to. Very much." Her face looked soft, her eyes so much like Byron's. "You have made my son very happy. I want to thank you for that." She handed Vera a black velvet box. "Look inside."

Vera opened the gift and gasped. "Pearls!"

"Yes. Those pearls were given to me by Byron's mother the day we married. I wore them on my honeymoon." Her voice sounded dreamy. "I had them restrung for you, and I hope you will enjoy them for many years."

Vera took in a breath. "They're beautiful. I would be honored to wear them. Your gesture means more than I can express. Thank you!"

The women embraced, with Byron observing.

"I think those pearls will look especially nice with that beautiful red dress Byron ordered for you," Mrs. Gates opined.

"Mother!" Byron chastised her.

Her eyes widened. "I'm sorry. Did I say something wrong?"

Byron sent his mother an indulgent look. "That's all right. I was going to surprise Vera, but the secret's out now."

"What?" Vera pressed.

"Remember telling me about the red fabric you coveted in the store? I bought it, and Alice made me a lovely gown for you, using a pattern from the latest Paris fashion."

Vera couldn't speak for a moment. "I don't know what makes me happier— that you did such a wonderful thing for me or that Alice and you worked together on such a sweet gift." She felt her eyes mist. "You truly have made this the most exquisite day of my life."

"That's what I wanted to hear," Byron said. "And you, too, Mother." Byron then hugged his mother. "Thank you for giving Vera the pearls. I think Grandmother would be thrilled."

"As do I." Mrs. Gates latched the strand around Vera's neck.

"How do they look?" Vera modeled the pearls.

"Lovely," Byron and Mrs. Gates agreed.

Mrs. Gates clasped Vera's hand and let it go. "I'll see you two back at the reception. Don't tarry too long. This day is brief, and you have your whole honeymoon ahead of you."

"Indeed," Byron told Vera as his mother disappeared, "our future is before us."

"Yes. And we shall live happily ever after," Vera murmured as she and her new husband melted into another kiss.

A Letter to Our Readers

Dear Readers:

In order that we might better contribute to your reading enjoyment, we would appreciate your taking a few minutes to respond to the following questions. When completed, please return to the following: Fiction Editor, Barbour Publishing, Inc., P.O. Box 719, Uhrichsville, OH 44683.

1. Did you enjoy reading *Maryland Brides* by Tamela Hancock Murray?
   ❑ Very much—I would like to see more books like this.
   ❑ Moderately—I would have enjoyed it more if _____

   _____

   _____

2. What influenced your decision to purchase this book?
   (Check those that apply.)
   ❑ Cover   ❑ Back cover copy   ❑ Title   ❑ Price
   ❑ Friends   ❑ Publicity   ❑ Other

3. Which story was your favorite?
   ❑ *Love's Denial*   ❑ *Vera's Turn for Love*
   ❑ *The Ruse*

4. Please check your age range:
   ❑ Under 18   ❑ 18–24   ❑ 25–34
   ❑ 35–45   ❑ 46–55   ❑ Over 55

5. How many hours per week do you read? _____

Name _____

Occupation _____

Address _____

City _____ State _____ Zip _____

E-mail _____